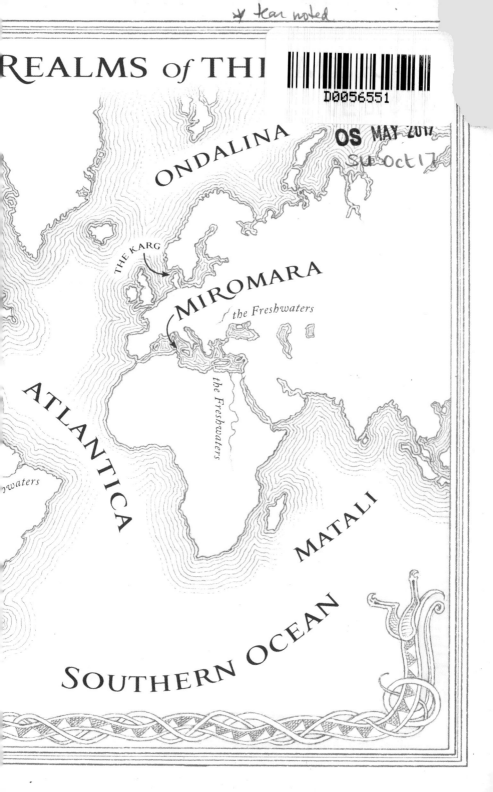

REALMS of THE

ONDALINA

THE KARG

MIROMARA

the Freshwaters

the Freshwaters

ATLANTICA

...waters

MATALI

SOUTHERN OCEAN

SEA SPELL

BOOK FOUR

SEA SPELL

JENNIFER DONNELLY

Disney · HYPERION

LOS ANGELES   NEW YORK

Printed in the United States of America

First Edition, June 2016
10 9 8 7 6 5 4 3 2 1
FAC-020093-16074

Library of Congress Cataloging in Publication Control Number: 2016000378
ISBN 978-1-4847-1290-0

Endpaper maps and chapter opener illustration by Laszlo Kubinyi

Reinforced binding

Visit www.DisneyBooks.com

SUSTAINABLE FORESTRY INITIATIVE   Certified Sourcing
www.sfiprogram.org
SFI-00993

THIS LABEL APPLIES TO TEXT STOCK

For my readers,
who make the real magic

The cure for anything is salt water:
sweat, tears, or the sea.

—Isak Dinesen

PROLOGUE

MANON LAVEAU, regal on her throne of twining cypress roots, regarded the merman before her. Her eyes traveled over his black uniform, his close-cropped hair, his cruel face. He and six of his soldiers had barged into her cave, deep under the waters of the Mississippi, as she was laying out tarot cards on the mossy back of a giant snapping turtle.

"Captain Traho, you say?" Manon's voice, like her eyes, betrayed no emotion. "What can I do for you?"

"I'm looking for a mermaid named Ava Corajoso," Traho said brusquely. "Dark skin. Black braids. She's blind. Travels with a piranha. Have you seen her?"

"I have not," Manon replied. "Now if you'll excuse me, Captain, the cards require my attention. *Au revoir.*"

Manon's manservant moved to show Traho out, but Traho pushed him away. "Ava was observed entering your cave," he said. "I've also been told you have a seeing stone that you're using to follow her. Hand it over and I'll be on my way."

Manon snorted. *"C'est sa cooyon,"* she said with contempt. *Fool.*

She snapped her fingers, and twenty bull alligators, each weighing half a ton, burst up from the thick mud covering the cave's floor. Tails thrashing, they surrounded Traho and his men.

"I have a better idea," Manon said, her green eyes glittering. "How about my hungry little friends eat you alive?"

Traho slowly raised his hands, never taking his eyes off the alligators. His men did the same.

Manon nodded. "That's more like it," she said. "*I'm* the shack bully in these parts, boy."

She laid her cards down and rose from her throne, her turbaned head high. It was impossible to tell how old she was. Her light brown skin was smooth, but her eyes were ancient. She had high cheekbones and a strong nose. A white tunic and a red reedcloth skirt covered her body and her silvery tail. A belt studded with river pearls and mussel shells cinched her waist. The belt had been handed down from the first swamp queen, a Native American who had journeyed to Atlantis as a human. She'd survived the island's destruction, had become mer, and then returned to the delta.

Manon spoke with the twang of the swamp. Her language was a mixture of freshwater mer salted with the African, English, French, and Spanish words of the terragogg ghosts who dwelled in the Mississippi. Some of those ghosts kept her company, among them a runaway slave called Sally Wilkes, a Creole countess named Esmé, and the pirate Jean Lafitte.

Manon was not afraid of ghosts. Or thugs in uniform. Or much of anything. As her alligators growled, she circled Traho.

"This mermaid Ava, she's *boocoo* brave. She goes into the swamps all alone. But you?" she said mockingly. "You need two hundred soldiers to hold your dainty little hand."

Manon couldn't see the rest of Traho's soldiers from inside her cave, but she didn't need to. The stone had told her of their approach.

Traho ignored the taunt. "Kill me, and those two hundred soldiers will kill *you*," he said. "I need to know where Ava Corajoso is. I'm not leaving until I find out."

Anger flashed in Manon's eyes. "You want information, you *pay* for it," she spat. "Same as everyone else. Or are you a thief as well as a coward?"

"Ten doubloons," Traho said.

"Twenty," Manon countered.

Traho nodded. Manon snapped her fingers again, and her alligators burrowed back into the mud. One of Traho's soldiers had a satchel slung over his shoulder. At his leader's command, he opened it, then counted out gold coins, placing them on a table.

When he finished, Manon said, "The mermaid stopped here two days ago. She was on her way to the Blackwater and wanted a *gris-gris* to protect her from the Okwa Naholo. I made the charm. Used talons from an owl, teeth from a white alligator, and the call of a coyote. Bound them with the tongue of a cottonmouth. Won't do her any good, though. She was worn-out. Sick, too. By now she's nothing but bones at the bottom of the Blackwater."

Traho digested this, then said, "The seeing stone. Where is it?"

Manon chuckled. "No such thing," she replied. "Stone's just a story, one I don't discourage. Mer in these parts are *boocoo* wild. They behave a little better if they think they're being watched."

Traho glanced around. He muttered a curse about the gods-forsaken Freshwaters, then left the cave.

Manon floated perfectly still, staring after him, listening to the shouts of soldiers and the whinnying of hippokamps. Sally and Lafitte joined her, anxious expressions on their faces. When the soldiers finally rode off, Manon let out a long, ragged breath.

Esmé, her silk skirts swirling around her, walked up to Manon and tugged on one of her earrings. "You're telling *lies*, Manon Laveau! That merl's not in the Blackwater. Why would she be? There aren't any Okwa in the Blackwater. She's headed for the Spiderlair, and you know it!"

Manon shrugged her off. Turning to Sally, she said, "You still have it? Nice and safe?"

Sally nodded. She reached down the front of her dress and pulled out a polished garnet. It was as large as a snake's head, and so dark it was almost black.

Manon took the stone and cast an occula songspell. A few seconds later, an image of a mermaid wearing silver glasses and a fuchsia dress appeared in the stone's depths. She was frightened, Manon could tell, but trying not to show it. It was Ava. She was already in the Spiderlair. Manon didn't know whether to laugh or cry.

"That mermaid's *trouble*," Lafitte fretted, wringing his hands. "I *told* you she'd bring the likes of Traho to your door. You bluffed him good this time, but what if he comes back?"

Manon didn't have an answer.

Ava Corajoso had shown up at her door five days ago, led by a growling piranha. She was thin and feverish, but she hadn't begged for food or medicine. Instead, she'd held out what little currensea she had and asked for a charm to keep her safe from the Okwa Naholo.

"The *Okwa*?" Manon had said, looking her up and down. "Those nasty monsters are the *least* of your worries! Take that money and buy yourself some food!"

She'd started to close the door, but Ava had stopped it with her hand. *"Please,"* she'd begged. "Everyone in the swamps says your charms are the strongest."

"Everyone's right. But *no* charm's strong enough to save you from the Okwa. Just the sight of them will stop your heart dead."

"Not mine. I can't see them. I'm blind," Ava had said, lowering her glasses.

"So you are, *cher*, so you are," Manon had said, her voice softening, her bright eyes taking in Ava's unseeing ones. "Tell me, why do you want to mess with the Okwa?"

"I *don't* want to," Ava had said. "But they have something I need in order to stop a monster—a monster ten times worse than any Okwa."

"Doesn't mean you'll get it. The Okwa might still kill you. In fact, I'd put money on it."

"They might. But I'd give my life gladly if it meant I could save many more."

Merl's crazier than a swamp rat, Manon had thought. She'd been about to send Ava away once and for all, but something had stopped her. Something in Ava's eyes. They weren't right, those eyes, but still . . . that mermaid *saw*. Right down into you, to what was deep and true. She saw the good there no matter how hard you tried to hide it.

"Keep your coins," Manon had said, against her better judgment. She'd led Ava inside, offered her a chair and a cup of thick, sweet cattail coffee. She'd sat down across from her and asked what she was after in the swamps. "Tell me straight. No lies, *cher*," she'd cautioned. "A good *gris-gris* needs many ingredients. The truth's one of them."

Ava had taken a deep breath, then said, "A monster lies under the ice of the Southern Sea. For centuries, it has been asleep, but now it's waking. It was created by one of the mages of Atlantis."

Manon's ancient eyes had narrowed. The swamp mer were given to telling tall tales. Decades of listening to them had made her a skeptical soul. "A *monster?*" she'd said. "Why would a mage make a monster?"

Ava had told Manon about Orfeo, the talismans, and Abbadon, and how Ava and five other mermaids had been chosen to defeat that monster. She told her about Vallerio, that he was kidnapping and imprisoning merfolk, and forcing them to search for the talismans. By the time Ava had finished her story, Manon was so shaken, she'd had to call for her smelling salts.

Rumors had come to Manon's ears, carried on the river. Rumors of powerful objects and labor camps. Rumors of soldiers in black uniforms moving through her swamp, and of a shadowy man with no eyes. She'd thought they were only more wild stories. Ava's arrival at her cave, and Traho's, had convinced her otherwise.

"You need to find that talisman, child. No two ways about it," Manon had said as soon as she'd recovered. "I'll do what I can to help you."

She'd fed Ava a spicy, filling stew made of crawdads, salamanders, and river peppers, and had given her medicine to break her fever. Then she'd made her a gris-gris—maybe the strongest one she'd *ever* made—and hadn't taken so much as a cowrie for it. Lafitte, Esmé, and Sally had all looked at Manon as if she'd lost her mind.

As she'd hung the gris-gris around Ava's neck, Manon had told Ava that the Okwa lived in the Spiderlair swamp and instructed her on how to get there. She'd tried to convince Ava to spend the night in her cave and rest close to the waterfire, but Ava had politely refused the offer. "There are soldiers on my tail," she'd explained. Then she'd thanked Manon and left.

"You keep that child safe, you hear me?" Manon had whispered to the spirits as she'd watched Ava swim away. She cared for that mermaid, though she didn't want to. Caring was risky in the swamps. The Spiderlair, a four days' journey from Manon's cave, was named for the large, vicious arachnids that hunted on its banks. It was the other creatures that lived in those dark waters that worried Manon, though—most of them far too clever to be glimpsed with an occula. The seeing stone showed evidence of them, nonetheless—in the bones and skulls half-buried in the swamp mud.

Manon picked up her tarot cards again now. They'd been cut from the shells of giant washboard clams, polished flat, then etched with tarot symbols. She drew one from the deck and laid it down. When she saw what it was—a tall, upright tower with waterfire coming out of its windows—she caught her breath.

"The Tower means danger. Not good," Lafitte said, clucking his tongue. "Not good at all."

Manon glanced at the seeing stone again. Inside it, the image of Ava was fading. The mermaid had swum deeper into the Spiderlair, too deep for the seeing stone to follow. Another image took its place: the brutal Captain Traho riding with his troops.

They were headed the wrong way; that was something. And even if they found out that the Okwa were in the Spiderlair and not the Blackwater, Ava still had a good head start on them. Then again, they were on hippokamps and she was on fin. They were strong and she was weak. They numbered two hundred and she was only one.

Fear, an emotion Manon Laveau was not accustomed to, wrapped its cold, thin fingers around her heart.

"Please, *cher*," she whispered. *"Hurry."*

ONE

SERAFINA SWAM TO the mouth of the cave, high in the side of a lonely, current-swept bluff, and peered into the black water. "They're not coming," she said.

"They *are*," Desiderio countered. "They probably took a back current to throw off any trackers. It's dangerous for the Näkki as well as us."

Sera nodded, but she wasn't convinced. While she continued to search the water for movement, the others floated around a waterfire, trying to warm themselves. She'd cast the fire small and weak. The last thing she wanted was to advertise their presence.

Sera, Desiderio, Yazeed, and Ling were in no-mer's-waters, just over the border of the Meerteufel goblins' realm. They would have preferred to hold this meeting at their stronghold in the Kargjord, but Guldemar, the Meerteufel chieftain, hated the Näkki—a tribe of arms dealers—and forbade them to enter his realm. Any found in his waters, he'd decreed, were to be shot on sight.

Sera didn't like the Näkki either and wished she didn't have to deal with them, but she had no choice. The death riders had just intercepted two weapons shipments. Under an agreement Sera had made with Guldemar, the Meerteufel were to supply the Black Fins with arms. The stolen shipments were the last two that Guldemar owed the resistance, and he'd refused to replace them. The death riders were not his problem, he'd said. He'd met his obligation.

Desperate, Sera had made plans to meet the Näkki here, in the lonely borderwaters of the North Sea. But would they come?

The loss of valuable armaments was bad, but far more troubling to Sera was the fact that the death riders had known when the weapons would be shipped and along what route. It confirmed what she'd suspected—that the Black Fin resistance had a spy in its midst. This traitor had done a great deal of damage to the resistance and was poised to do more. Sera had shared her plan to meet with the Näkki with her inner circle only, hoping to keep it a secret from the spy.

Play the board, not the piece, her mother, Regina Isabella, had advised, comparing the art of ruling to a chess game. Ever since Sera had learned that her uncle Vallerio was the one behind the invasion of Cerulea and her mother's assassination, she'd been desperately trying to keep herself, and her Black Fins, out of checkmate.

Where are the Näkki? she wondered now, still gazing out at the dark waters. *Did something spook them?*

"Five more minutes, then we're out of here," she announced, returning to the group.

At that moment, the temperature in the cave plummeted and the waterfire burned low. Sera heard a noise behind her. She spun around, her hand on the dagger at her hip, her fighters at her back.

Three figures floated in the cave's entrance. Their faces were hidden in the silt-covered folds of their hoods. They had long, powerful tails and looked like mer, but Sera knew they weren't.

"*Näkki,*" she said silently, releasing her dagger. *Shapeshifters.* Wary and elusive, they could blend in with a crowd of mer, a school of fish, or a rock face within seconds.

A sickly sweet smell wafted from them, one that made Sera's stomach clench—the smell of death. It took her back to the invasion of Cerulea and the rotting bodies of her merfolk lying in the ruins.

Instinctively, she touched the ring on her right hand. Mahdi had carved it from a shell for her, as an expression of his love. Thinking of him gave her courage.

"Welcome," she said, nodding to her visitors.

The Näkki removed their hoods. Under them were mermen's faces, handsome and fine. Their leader, dark-skinned and amber-eyed, his black hair worn long and loose, extended his hand. Sera took it. His grip was hard. His companions were amber-eyed, too. Their skin was pale. Long blond braids trailed down their backs.

"I'm Serafina, regina di Miromara. I'm grateful to you for coming. I know your journey was a dangerous one."

"Kova," the Näkki leader said. He nodded at the others. "Julma and Petos."

As he spoke, Sera saw that his tongue was black and split at the tip like a snake's. It unnerved her, but she kept her feelings hidden.

"Sit with us," she said, gesturing toward the waterfire.

Something glinted darkly on the underside of her hand as she did. She glanced at it, and bit back a gasp. Her palm was streaked with blood. She must've cut herself without noticing, but how? On her dagger's hilt? Hastily, she wiped the blood off on her jacket, hoping no one noticed, then joined the Näkki and the Black Fins around the fire.

Kova settled himself, flanked by Julma and Petos. Ling passed around a box of barnacles and a basket of keel worms. As the Näkki helped themselves, Kova brusquely asked, "What do you need?"

"Crossbows and spearguns," Des replied.

"Quantities?"

"Five thousand of each. Plus rounds."

"When?"

"Yesterday," said Yazeed.

Kova nodded, frowning. "It won't be easy, but I can do it. Give me a week."

"Quality. No garbage," Des said.

"The crossbows are goblin-made. The spearguns come from a gogg trader. Best in the world," Kova said. He smiled grimly. "If there's one thing the goggs are good at, it's killing."

"What about the rounds?" asked Yazeed.

"Spears are stainless steel. Gogg-made. Arrows are Kobold steel with barbed heads. Hit someone with one of those, he's not getting up."

"How much?" Sera asked.

"Seventy thousand trocii."

She shook her head. "We haven't got mer currensea, only doubloons."

Kova chuckled. "Stolen from Vallerio's vaults, I hear."

"Not stolen, regained," Sera retorted. "From *my* vaults."

The Black Fins' only form of barter was the treasure they'd taken from chambers deep inside Cerulea's royal palace: goggish doubloons, gemstones, silver goblets, gold jewelry.

"Fifty thousand doubloons, then," said Kova.

"Thirty."

Kova didn't reply. He worked a piece of food from his teeth with his thumbnail. "Forty-five," he said at length. "Final offer."

Sera thought about the price he was demanding. Her treasure was dwindling fast. Paying for food and weapons for her troops, purchasing thorny Devil's Tail vines and other materials to strengthen her camps' defenses—it all cost a great deal. So did the lava globes she had to buy, for the Kargjord didn't appear to have a lava seam under it. And this was only the preparation stage. The battle to take back Cerulea from Vallerio, the fight against Abbadon—these were still to come.

Forty-five thousand doubloons, she finally decided, was a price she was prepared to pay. But there was another, even higher price for these weapons, one she couldn't bear to pay: lives.

For a moment, Sera was no longer in the cave with the Näkki; she was back in Cerulea during the attack. She saw her father's body sinking through the water. Saw the arrow go into her mother's chest. Heard the screams of innocent mer as they were slaughtered.

"Sera . . ." That was Desiderio. She barely heard him.

Her gaze came to rest on Kova. His palm lay flat against a rock; a thin line of crimson oozed from it. She raised her eyes and saw smears of blood on the box of barnacles Ling had passed around, and more on the basket of worms.

I didn't cut myself, she realized. *The Näkki have blood on their hands and they leave it on everything they touch.*

"Sera, we need an answer." That was Yazeed.

But she couldn't make the words come. She was immobilized by fear—fear for her people, for the suffering and destruction to come. How could any ruler make the decision to go to war? Even for a just cause? How could she send thousands to their deaths?

And then she heard another voice—Vrăja's. Sera was certain that the river witch had been killed by death riders, but she lived on in Sera's heart.

Instead of shunning your fear, you must let it speak, Vrăja had told her. *It will give you good counsel.*

Sera listened.

The Näkki peddle death, her fear said. *But you must learn to sit with death, and his merchants, if you want to defeat your uncle and destroy the evil in the Southern Sea. How many more will die if you take no action?*

Sera raised her eyes to Kova's and, in a voice heavy with dread, said, "We have a deal."

Kova nodded. "My terms are half up front."

Sera's fins flared. She did not take orders from arms-dealing sea scum. "*My* terms are *nothing* up front," she shot back. "When I get my weapons, you get your gold."

Kova gave her a long look. "How will you get the goods to the Karg? They'll be in crates roped to hippokamps. *My* hippokamps. They aren't part of the deal."

"That's my worry," Sera replied.

Kova snorted. "Yes, it is. That and much more," he said, rising. Julma and Petos followed his lead. "Give me five days," he said, thrusting his hand at Sera to seal the deal.

Sera rose, too, and shook it, her eyes locked on his, her grip firm. Kova released her hand and then the three Näkki pulled their hoods over their heads. Seconds later, they were gone.

Sera looked down at her palm, knowing what she would see.

She felt a hand on her back. It was Ling. "It washes off," she said.

Sera shook her head. "No, Ling," she said softly. "It doesn't."

TWO

THE CURRENTS of Mørk Dal were deserted, its shops closed, its homes shuttered against the night. The glow from a handful of sputtering lava globes was all that illuminated the sleeping goblin village in the frigid gray waters of the North Sea.

Astrid Kolfinnsdottir moved silently down the main current, sword drawn, eyes alert for any movement. She was hunting for a mirror.

There were none in the Kargjord, where she'd left her friends, or in the barren waters that surrounded that wasteland. She'd been swimming south for days. Mørk Dal was the first village she'd come across, the first place where she could find what she needed.

Orfeo had summoned her. He'd come to her in a mirror, and she knew she would have to go to him the same way. But how? Many of the greatest mages couldn't travel through mirrors. How was *she*—a mermaid with no magic, one who couldn't sing a note—supposed to?

"This is total insanity," she whispered. "It's hopeless. Impossible. Suicidal." She'd been saying these words a lot lately—ever since she'd met Serafina, Neela, Ling, Ava, and Becca in the Iele's caves.

The six mermaids had been called together by the Iele's leader, Baba Vrăja. She was the one who'd told them about the monster in the Southern Sea and said they were the only ones who could defeat it.

After they'd left the Iele, they'd learned that Orfeo had been a healer and the most formidable of the Atlantean mages—the Six

Who Ruled. Each of the six had a talisman, a magical object that enhanced their powers. Orfeo's, a flawless emerald, had been given to him by Eveksion, the god of healing.

Together with his fellow mages, Orfeo had ruled wisely and well and was beloved by his subjects—until his wife, Alma, died. He couldn't accept her death and had begged Horok, the keeper of the underworld, to return her to him. Horok refused, and Orfeo vowed to take her back. He'd set about creating a monster powerful enough to attack the underworld—Abbadon. Orfeo invoked the death goddess Morsa to aid him in his quest. From her, he gained a new talisman: a flawless black pearl.

When the other five mages—Merrow, Nyx, Sycorax, Navi, and Pyrrha—discovered what Orfeo was doing, they'd tried to stop him. Enraged, he unleashed his monster against them. In the ensuing battle, Abbadon destroyed Atlantis. As its people fled to the water, Merrow beseeched Neria, the sea goddess, to help them. Neria knit the Atlanteans' legs into tails and gave them the ability to breathe water, saving them.

Though the five mages fought bravely, they couldn't kill Abbadon, so they'd driven it into the Carceron, the island's prison. To open the prison's lock, they'd needed all six of their talismans. Orfeo refused to surrender his; they'd had to kill him to get it. Once Abbadon was imprisoned, Sycorax, with the help of whales, dragged the Carceron to the Southern Sea.

Afterward, Merrow hid the talismans in the most dangerous places in the six water realms to make sure that no one could ever use them to free Abbadon. Then she had all historical records of the monster erased. A new story was told, one in which Atlantis was destroyed by natural causes. Over time, Orfeo's treachery, his monster, and the talismans were forgotten.

Merrow was sure that she'd done everything necessary to protect her people, but she was wrong.

Because Orfeo had found a way to cheat death. The other mages only thought they had killed him. He'd secreted his soul in Morsa's black pearl, then bided his time, for centuries, until a fish found the pearl and swallowed it. When a fisherman caught the creature and cleaned it, he discovered the pearl. A Viking chieftain bought the pearl from him, and as the chieftain held it, Orfeo's soul flowed into his body, taking it over. Alive again, Orfeo began to hunt for the other talismans, eager to unleash his monster.

Orfeo had vowed to take Alma back from Horok, if it took him all eternity. Astrid knew that he was now close to honoring that vow.

The vicious Vallerio was working to conquer all the mer realms and unite their militaries in the service of Orfeo's quest. With this immense army, and the fearsome Abbadon, Orfeo would finally be able to launch his attack on the underworld. He recognized that the gods themselves would fight him, and that the battle might wreak havoc on not only the underworld, but also the water and land realms. But none of that concerned Orfeo. Once reunited with his wife, he would begin the world anew with whatever was left. The only obstacles in his path were six young mermaids.

Why have you summoned us? Serafina had asked Vrăja. *Why not emperors or admirals or commanders with their soldiers? Why not the waters' most powerful mages?*

Vrăja had told them that they *were* the worlds' most powerful mages; each was a descendant of the Six Who Ruled, and their ancestors' magic lived on inside them.

Astrid was Orfeo's descendant. She hadn't believed the river witch. It was amazing. It was impossible. It was a total joke.

Orfeo was the most powerful mage the world had ever seen. *Ever.* And Astrid? She couldn't even cast a basic *camo* spell without the whalebone pipe Becca had made for her. She'd been able to make magic years ago, when she was a small child, but she'd lost her magic shortly after celebrating at Månenhonnør, her realm's moon festival.

And now she was attempting to find the powerful, immortal Orfeo and take the black pearl from him so that she and the others could combine all the talismans once more, unlock the Carceron, and kill Abbadon. *Her.* Astrid Kolfinnsdottir. A mermaid with no magic.

"Total insanity," she whispered again. But she had to do it. She had to find Orfeo, and she had to get the black pearl. She was the only one who could.

Astrid kept moving through Mørk Dal, her eyes sweeping left to right. She swam past a shopwindow containing jars of wrinkled terra-gogg ears, candied sea cucumbers, and spiced krill; another displayed weapons fashioned from fine Kobold steel; a third had an array of lava globes. She needed a hairdresser's shop, a jeweler, or a tailor—someplace with a mirror—but she didn't see one.

A few minutes later, she reached the end of the main current, where the shops gave way to houses. A narrow side current with a few more shops on it snaked off to the right. One store had a sign above its window: SELWIG'S SHIPWRECK SALVAGE.

Astrid sped to it. Salvagers, goblin and mer, combed shipwrecks for valuable objects. They almost always had mirrors for sale. She pressed her nose to the window, cupping her eyes. The shop was dark, but a nearby lava globe, mounted on a pole, threw off enough light for her to see its contents: crystal goblets, brass lanterns, a croquet set . . . and a mirror!

Glancing around to make sure no one else was nearby, Astrid slid her sword back into its sheath at her hip and drew a dagger from inside her parka. She inserted the blade into the door's lock, twisted it sharply, then yanked it upward. The tumblers shot back, and the door swung open. She put her dagger away and swam inside. As she closed the door behind her, she cast another wary glance at the current. The last thing she needed was to get arrested.

Threading her way past piles of sailcloth, plastic coolers, and coils of nylon rope, Astrid approached the mirror. It was oval and quite large, with a gold frame. In it, she could see her reflection: her braided hair, as pale as moonlight; her ice-blue eyes; her strong black-and-white tail.

"How do I do this?" she asked herself.

She remembered her whalebone pipe. Maybe it would help. But as she was reaching for it, she stopped. Camo spells were all she knew how to cast. And even if she *had* known the songspell for mirror travel, she'd never be able to pull it off. Her magic was too weak.

She thought back to the time Orfeo had come to her in a mirror at Tanner's Deeps. He'd held his hand up to the glass and she'd held hers up, too, and for a second, she'd felt as if she was sinking into silver. She pressed a palm against the mirror now. Nothing happened. She pushed harder. Still nothing. Frustrated, she tried one last time.

That's when the woman's face, pale and disembodied, floated into view.

THREE

"**H**OLY *SILT*!" Astrid yelped, darting backward.

She crashed into a heavy wooden deck chair, toppled over it, and fell against a shelf of cruise ship kitchenware. The shelf broke. Pots, pans, and pitchers came tumbling down. The noise was deafening.

I've just woken the entire village, Astrid thought as a mixing bowl bounced off her skull.

The head was still there. It was peering at Astrid from inside the mirror. As she watched, a neck appeared underneath it, then a body.

"It's only a *vitrina*," she whispered when her heartbeat returned to something like normal. Vapid and vain, vitrina were the souls of terragoggs who'd spent too much time gazing into mirrors when they were alive.

The ghost had poked her head around the mirror's frame, but now she walked fully into the glass. She wore a wasp-waisted dress, flat shoes, and pearls. Her hair was swept up in a sleek twist.

"Are you trying to come in?" she asked as a scowling Astrid extricated herself from the avalanche.

"Yes, I am," Astrid said, rubbing her bruised tail. "How did *you* do it?"

"I wanted to be the prettiest girl in Paris," the vitrina said. "And I told the mirror. Over and over again. What do *you* want? To be the prettiest mermaid in the sea?"

"Um, not exactly," Astrid replied.

A noise coming from the current made her freeze. Her eyes went to the door, but no one was there. She placed her palm on the mirror again.

The vitrina clapped her hands. "Oh, I know! You want to be the prettiest mermaid in *all* the seas!"

"How did you guess?" Astrid said sarcastically, growing impatient with this bubblehead.

"All you have to do is tell the mirror," said the vitrina encouragingly.

Astrid knew it was dangerous to state her desires. Orfeo was in that liquid-silver world somewhere, and he might hear. But what choice did she have?

Her hand still on the glass, she closed her eyes. "I want the black pearl," she said.

Nothing happened, but she heard the noise again: a voice, outside on the current. Astrid swam to the window, careful to stay in the shadows, and peered out. A Feuerkumpel goblin was walking toward the shop. She could see his topknot of black hair. Lava burn scars pitted his face. He had nostrils but no nose, sharp teeth, and transparent eyes. His body was covered by hard, bony black plates. He was cursing loudly.

Maybe he's a town guard or the shop owner, Astrid thought. He must've heard the racket she'd made and was coming to investigate. She raced back to the mirror and tried again to go through the glass, fear plucking at her nerves.

"I want Abbadon dead."

The vitrina crossed her arms. She gave Astrid a skeptical look. "Are you telling the mirror what you *really* want?"

Astrid gritted her teeth. "I want Orfeo dead. I want Rylka to pay for murdering my father. I want Portia and Vallerio out of Ondalina. I want my brother and mother to be safe."

But again, nothing happened. And the goblin was coming closer.

It's no use, Astrid thought, panicking. *Whatever little bit of magic I still have isn't strong enough to get me through the glass.*

She heard a shout. And then two more. Whoever was out there was bringing friends. She had to get out of here before they caught her.

She was just about to look for a back door when the vitrina said, "Wait!"

Astrid, frantic now, turned to her.

"You're not being honest. Until you are, the mirror won't let you in. Admit it—you want to be the prettiest mermaid in every sea, ocean, bay, river, lake, pond, stream, creek, waterfall, *and* puddle," the vitrina said, wagging her finger. "Who *doesn't* want to be the prettiest? For goodness' sake, mermaid, just *say* what you want!"

Astrid tried one last time. Putting both hands on the glass, she closed her eyes. "I want . . ." she started to say, searching for the right words.

And then, sudden and unbidden, they came. From the deepest part of her heart.

"I want my magic back."

An instant later, she was tumbling headfirst through the mirror.

FOUR

"AND *THEN* the ship hit the rocks and broke into a million pieces!" trilled the mermaid Laktara.

She threw her head back and laughed. The sound was musical and beguiling, every bit as beguiling as her beautiful face, her green eyes, and the thick auburn tresses that cascaded down her back.

"Tell me the rest of the story, Tara!" Lucia Volnero called out from her dressing room, where she was changing into a gown.

But Laktara was laughing so hard, she couldn't speak. Falla, her sister, had to finish the story.

"It wasn't just *any* ship we destroyed," Falla said, giggling herself. "It was a cruise ship. There were a thousand goggs aboard. They threw themselves over the railing—*splish, splash, sploosh*—to get to us!"

Vola, a third sister, was laughing, too. "Of course, the closer they came, the farther away we swam, until they were ab-so-*lute*-ly exhausted! Even as they drowned, they were *still* reaching for us. Darling, you've never seen *anything* funnier!"

"Or sampled anything tastier!" Falla whispered.

"Falla, you naughty thing! *Hush!*" Vola scolded.

Falla said, "Sorry!"

Laktara snorted. "No, you're *not*."

"I *am*," Vola insisted. Then, in a mischievous whisper, she added, "I'm sorry I didn't kill *more* of them!"

The three sisters dissolved into helpless giggles, and Lucia joined them. They were her distant cousins, her good friends—and sirens, though publicly they denied it.

Sirens sang for currensea. Some even sang for the goggs. Stories were told of secret concerts held in Venetian palazzos for which the singers were paid in jewels.

Rumor had it that sirens *ate* their kills, but Lucia dismissed the gossip. Oh, her cousins might joke about it, but she was quite certain they only did so to shock. Though she had to admit that, every now and then, when the illusio spells the three sisters continually spun flickered and faded, Lucia could see that their pearly teeth were sharper than she'd thought, their crimson nails longer, their eyes colder.

The sisters, who looked very much alike, lived in the waters off the coast of Greece. Lucia had invited them to Cerulea because she had news she wanted to share. They'd arrived an hour ago. Lucia had hurried them to her rooms, had sweets and tea brought, and then asked them to give their opinions on a selection of gowns.

She swam out from behind the screen now in a clingy pale green sea-silk dress embroidered with seed pearls. Her blue-black hair swirled around her shoulders. Her sapphire eyes appraised her reflection in a mirror.

"Well?"

Falla wrinkled her nose. Vola shook her head. "Nothing special," Laktara said with a sniff.

Lucia snapped her fingers, and her maid brought her another gown. It met with a similar reaction. So did the one that followed it. Lucia, growing frustrated, tried on a fourth.

"What about *this* one?" she asked as she swam to the center of the room and twirled around.

The gown was made of thousands of sliver-thin slices of emerald stitched onto a sheath of dark green sea silk. The jewels overlapped like fish scales. They caught the light and held it. Lucia's tiniest movement made the entire gown sparkle.

"I *love* it!" Vola declared.

Laktara agreed, but Falla asked, "Why the fashion show, Luce? Is there a ball coming up? Is *that* why you invited us here?"

Lucia sat down with her cousins. She looked at each in turn, then said, "You've just helped me pick my wedding dress. I haven't told anyone else yet, but I'm going to move the date of the ceremony up."

Vola arched an eyebrow. "Harpoon wedding, darling?" she asked with a smirk.

Lucia rolled her eyes. "Get your mind out of the abyss, please."

"Does the groom know?" asked Falla.

"I haven't told him yet. He's away with his troops patrolling the western border. It's going to be a surprise," Lucia lied. "He's been begging me to move the date up. He's head over tail in love, so why wait any longer? We'll marry in less than two moons' time, when there's a syzygy."

"Why wait *that* long?" Vola asked.

"I don't have a choice. Miromaran royal weddings *have* to take place during a syzygy, when the sun, earth, and moon are aligned. The tides are at their highest then, and magic's at its strongest. It's the law, and unfortunately, there's nothing I can do about it. *That's* why I invited you here. To ask you to be my bridesmaids."

Vola squealed. Falla hugged Lucia.

And Laktara held up a hand. "Just a minute! Before I commit, I need to know what the dresses look like."

When Lucia assured her that all three bridesmaid gowns would be made from sea silk and mother-of-pearl and would be almost as beautiful as her own, Laktara agreed. There were more hugs and kisses, and then Lucia suggested that her cousins retire to the chambers her maids had prepared for them.

"You've had a long journey. I'm sure you'll want to rest for a bit, then freshen up before dinner," she said, affecting concern.

The three sisters took their leave, talking all the while about which young noblemer or death rider officer they intended to enchant at dinner.

Lucia closed the door behind them, leaned against it, and exhaled. Her cousins loved to gossip. By the end of the week, the entire palace would know that she and Mahdi were so much in love, they'd moved up their wedding date. Everyone would be consumed by the news. Even her father would have to turn his attention away from matters of state for a while and focus on her wedding.

Which was *exactly* what Lucia wanted.

Vallerio had discovered that the Black Fin resistance had placed a spy in the palace. His own spy, embedded in the Black Fins' camp, had told him so but hadn't been able to find out who it was. Vallerio had informed Lucia—just last night—that he was closing in on the traitor.

Lucia already knew who it was: Mahdi.

If her father discovered what Mahdi was doing, and that he'd Promised himself to Serafina right before he'd Promised himself to *her*, Lucia, he'd kill Mahdi on the spot. He wouldn't even give Lucia the chance to explain that Mahdi had only done these things because Sera had enchanted him.

Lucia had learned the truth by drugging Mahdi and pulling bloodsongs from his heart. In them she'd seen his Promising ceremony with Sera. Lucia knew that a Promised merman couldn't marry someone else. The magic wouldn't work. The notes of the marriage songspell would fall flat.

Sera must have used darksong on Mahdi, Lucia had concluded. There was no other way to explain his actions. No merman could *possibly* prefer Sera to her.

"But I've outdone her," Lucia whispered now, smiling as she thought of her beautiful maligno. She wondered if the deadly creature had made it to the Darktide Shallows yet.

Lucia had gone to Kharis, a priestess of the death goddess Morsa, and asked her to make the creature. The maligno was formed of clay and blood magic, and paid for with gold and death. He was the perfect double of Mahdi, and Lucia knew he would succeed with his mission: to capture Sera and bring her here. Lucia would take care of the rest.

Only then could she marry Mahdi.

Only then would she have the power she craved, the power to put her beyond the merfolks' mockery.

Only then would the voices in her head be still, the ones that echoed down the dark halls of her memory.

They whispered about her. *Poor Lucia. Such a pretty little thing. How sad for her to have no father.*

They whispered about her mother. *There goes the widowed duchessa. . . . She was lucky she found anyone to marry her. Tainted blood, don't you know. Lucia will have to marry beneath her, too. These things aren't forgotten.*

When Lucia was a child, her cheeks had burned red with shame at the words the voices uttered; now her heart burned black with hatred.

Her parents had been in love, but the reigning regina had forbid them to marry because there were traitors in Portia's bloodline. So, Lucia had been raised without a father. Only when she'd come of age had Vallerio, the realm's fearsome high commander, revealed to her that *he* was her father.

One day all the water realms, and everyone in them, will know that you are my daughter, he'd promised her. *Until then, keep our secret safe. Our lives depend upon it.*

When she became Mahdi's wife, Lucia would no longer be a mere regina, but an empress. Her father had gained Miromara's throne for her, and he'd also taken Matali and Ondalina. Qin would follow, then the Freshwaters and Atlantica. Vallerio would conquer them all for her, and she and Mahdi would rule the entire mer world.

"They won't whisper about me then," Lucia said aloud, her voice full of malice. "They won't *dare*. Not if they want to keep their heads on top of their necks."

She was close, so close, to seeing her hopes fulfilled. Her father had not been able to capture Sera, so Lucia had taken it upon herself. Success now depended entirely on the maligno—and the sea scorpion that had gone with it, to deliver the fake message. Would they make it the long distance to the Black Fins' stronghold? Would the conch get to Sera? Would Sera believe the voice inside it was Mahdi's?

"Great Morsa make it so," Lucia prayed, knowing she would have no peace until her prayer was answered.

Until the maligno returned from the Darktide Shallows.

Until Serafina was finally dead.

FIVE

SERA SAT ALONE at the broad stone table in the cave that served as the Black Fins' headquarters, wincing as she rubbed her temples. The headaches had become sharper and more frequent ever since her meeting with the Näkki. Tonight's was a killer.

Dozens of kelp parchments were strewn across the table: requisitions, intelligence reports, inventories. Message conchs were scattered among them. At the opposite end, a huge map of the mer realms lay open. Cowrie shells, representing her uncle's troops, covered far too much of it.

Earlier, she, Desiderio, and Yazeed had argued over the biggest question the resistance now faced: where to attack first. Cerulea, Vallerio's seat of power? Or the Southern Sea, where Abbadon was imprisoned? They'd failed to come up with an answer. Desiderio had argued for Cerulea; Yazeed for the Southern Sea. Given the Black Fins' current lack of weapons and food, either choice felt like a suicide mission to Sera.

A long, trailing sigh escaped her. She felt hopeless tonight. Alone. Defeated before the battles had even begun. Plans, strategies, campaigns . . . it didn't matter how carefully thought-out and executed they were, Vallerio always seemed to be one stroke ahead—cutting off supply lines, sabotaging alliances, thwarting her at every turn. Weeks had passed since she'd heard from Ava or Astrid. Had Vallerio taken them? And then there was Sophia, one of her best fighters, and an excellent shot. Sera had just sent her and Totschläger, a goblin commander, to rendezvous with the Näkki. Would Sophia get the Black Fins' weapons safely back to camp? Or would the death riders ambush her and her troops?

Play the board, not the piece. Harass the opposition with clever, far-thinking moves. Stay out of check. Sera knew all this, but knowing it and doing it were two different things. She stopped rubbing her head; it wasn't helping. She knew why the headaches were happening. Every time she thought about sending her troops into battle—whether it was in Cerulea or the Southern Sea—an image came back to her: the image of her hand after she'd met with the Näkki, covered in blood.

"I *knew* you'd be awake," said a voice, dispelling Sera's painful vision. "This isn't good. It's nearly two a.m. You need to sleep."

It was Ling, floating in the cave's entrance. Sera gave her a tired smile. "Worry has a way of keeping you up."

"Let me guess . . . *Vallerio*," Ling said, joining Sera at the table.

Sera nodded. "He's attacked us six times now. Each time, he's known exactly where my fighters would be and when they'd be there, thanks to his spy. He's bleeding us to death, Ling, and I'm letting him. I'm letting him steal our supplies and slaughter my soldiers. Because I don't know how to find his spy. I don't know how to stop him. I don't know what I'm doing."

"Don't talk that way. Don't even *think* that way, or Vallerio will win," Ling scolded. "You need to keep believing in yourself, Sera. You need to keep faith."

Sera laughed bitterly. "How, Ling? How do I keep faith? I'm starting to doubt every decision I make."

"That's okay," Ling said. "That's how it works."

Sera gave her a skeptical look. "It is?"

"Yes, doubt isn't the enemy of faith; certainty is. It's easy to believe in yourself when you've got every reason to. Faith is believing in yourself when you've got every reason *not* to." Ling reached across the table and covered Sera's hand with her own. "You can *do* this."

"It only gets harder, not easier. You don't know what it's like. To rule, to be responsible for so many lives . . ."

"You're right, I don't. But I know *you*."

A lump rose in Sera's throat. She squeezed Ling's hand, feeling lucky to have her for a friend. "Thank you for listening," she said. "You're always there when I need you."

Ling squeezed back. "And I always will be," she said, releasing Sera's hand. "But now I need you to listen. I have an idea. That's why I'm here. I've come up with a way to catch the spy."

Sera's eyes widened. "What is it?"

"A ruse. A pretty big one. To pull it off, I need to borrow Sycorax's puzzle ball."

Sera blinked, speechless. When she found her voice again, she said, "Ling, have you lost your freaking *mind*?"

"No, I haven't. I need the puzzle ball, Sera," Ling insisted.

"Ling, it's a *talisman*. A gift from a god. It's priceless and powerful and my uncle, and Orfeo, they've killed *thousands* trying to get it. They don't know we have it. Only our inner circle knows. If the spy ever found out—"

"The spy *has* to find out."

"*What?*" Sera said, convinced now that Ling had *definitely* lost her mind.

"Try as we might, we haven't been able to reveal the spy," said Ling. "So I'm going to get the spy to reveal himself."

Sera shook her head. "No way," she said. "I can't let you take the puzzle ball. It's too risky."

Ling leaned forward. "A moment ago, you said Vallerio's bleeding us to death. He's doing more than that. He's circling for the kill."

Ling's words struck Sera with the force of a gale wind. They were rough, and terrifying. Worse yet, they were true. She decided to hear her friend out.

"What, exactly, would you do with the puzzle ball?" she asked.

"Start a rumor," Ling replied. "Sycorax was Atlantis's chief justice, right?"

Sera nodded.

"I'm going to let it get out that we've got the puzzle ball, and there's something inside it that Sycorax used to help her tell the innocent from the guilty."

"But you *don't* know what's inside it," Sera said, confused. "Nobody does. Because the puzzle hasn't been solved. You only *believe* there's something inside it."

"It doesn't matter what I believe," Ling said impatiently. "Don't you see? All that matters is what the *spy* believes."

Understanding dawned on Sera. "I *think* I see where you're going with this," she said, her fins prickling with excitement.

Ling sat forward in her chair. "I'm an omnivoxa," she said, her eyes sparking with intensity. "My gift is communication. But sometimes, to really communicate, it's necessary to listen instead of talk. What I'm listening for now is the voice of one who's hurting."

"Go on," Sera said, trying to follow where Ling was leading.

"Pain needs to speak," Ling continued. "It needs to be heard. If it isn't let out, it grows inside, pushing out everything bright and good until it's the only thing left. I know this, Sera. It happened to my mother. She was hurting so badly after my dad disappeared, she turned away from everyone, including me."

"I didn't realize that," Sera said. When Ling had appeared in camp, she'd told them how she'd escaped from a prison camp and found the puzzle ball, but she'd never said anything about her mother.

Ling gave her a rueful smile. "Some things are really hard to talk about, even for an omnivoxa. I was finally able to get through to her, but only after I learned to understand her pain. I bet that the spy's in pain, too. What he's doing—lying, deceiving, betraying his friends—it all comes from a dark place. His pain wants to speak, Sera. If I can coax it out, all we have to do is listen."

Sera remembered Vrăja telling her, *Help Ling break through the silences.* Ling had broken through her mother's silence, and in doing so had gained insight and wisdom. Now she was trying to break through the spy's silence.

Ling's plan was dangerous, but allowing the spy to remain at large was more dangerous.

"All right," Sera finally said. "The puzzle ball is yours."

She rose and swam to the niche in the cave's wall where she kept the talismans that she and her friends had found: Sycorax's puzzle ball, Merrow's blue diamond, Pyrrha's coin, and Navi's moonstone. She undid the songspell that camouflaged the niche, then removed the ball.

The ancient talisman sat heavily in Sera's hand. A phoenix decorated its surface. It was carved out of white coral and contained spheres within spheres. The spheres had holes in them. To solve the puzzle, one had to make the holes line up to reveal what was in the center of the ball.

Sera gave Ling the precious object.

"Thank you," Ling said. "For the talisman, and for your trust."

"Find him," Sera said. *"Please."*

"I will, I promise," said Ling. And then she swam out of the cave, head down, eyes on the puzzle ball, turning it over in her hands.

Sera watched her go, worry etched on her face. *She needs time to put her plan into play,* she thought. *And we don't have any.*

Eyes still glued to the puzzle ball, Ling bumped—literally—into a merman and a goblin on patrol. Ling excused herself, and the two soldiers asked her what she was doing. They were close enough that Sera could hear their conversation.

"We have a spy in our midst," Ling solemnly told them.

The merman gripped his crossbow tightly. The goblin swore.

"Serafina's so desperate to find him," Ling continued, "that she gave me this. . . ." She held up the puzzle ball.

"What is it?" the goblin asked, peering at the object.

"It's a powerful, priceless talisman, given to Sycorax, a mage of Atlantis, by the gods," Ling explained.

The goblin let out a low whistle. The merman's eyebrows shot up.

"It contains something called the Arrow of Judgment, which can tell the innocent from the guilty," Ling explained. "If I can solve the puzzle, the arrow will point out the spy."

"I love puzzles," the goblin said eagerly. "Let me have a try."

He used his long claws to turn the inner spheres but couldn't make them line up.

"Give it to me," the merman said. But he couldn't crack the puzzle either.

Ling heaved a worried sigh as he handed the talisman back to her. "I've *got* to get this solved. Can you ask around and find out who's good with puzzles? Tell them to come to me. Anyone and everyone. Our lives depend on it."

The soldiers said they would and moved on. Ling went in the other direction. Before the soldiers got very far, they met another pair on patrol and stopped to talk to them. Sera couldn't hear what they were saying, but she saw them point toward Ling. The second pair hurried off to catch up with her.

She'll have the whole camp talking about the spy and the Arrow of Judgment by breakfast, Sera thought. *Goddess Neria, let that be a good thing.*

SIX

THE LIQUID SILVER was tensile and bright, almost alive.

It swirled and lapped around Astrid as she picked herself up off the floor of a long, magnificent hallway.

How am I going to breathe this stuff? she wondered, panicking. *I'll suffocate!*

She held her breath for as long as she could, then inhaled fearfully. The silver was cold and heavier than seawater, but her lungs accepted it. Relaxing a little, Astrid looked around. The hallway stretched into the silver in both directions, as far as she could see. Its walls were hung with mirrors of all shapes and sizes. Sparkling chandeliers dangled from the ceiling.

Vitrina moved through the hallway. Some idled in chairs or sat slumped against the walls, heads lolling, bodies limp—like puppets whose strings had been cut.

"This place gives me the creeps," Astrid muttered, wishing, as she did a dozen times every day, that Desiderio was with her.

She missed all her friends, but him most of all, because he'd become more than a friend. The memory of the kiss he gave her right after he saved her from the Qanikkaaq, a murderous maelstrom, still made her catch her breath. Just before he kissed her, he'd told that he wanted to be with her. And she, too surprised to speak, hadn't said anything. She regretted that now. She would tell him the same, and more. Much more. If she ever made it back to him.

Astrid was looking up and down the hallway, wondering which way to go, when a voice—oily and sly—spoke from behind her.

"*!olleh, lleW*" it purred.

Astrid whipped around. A man, heavyset and bald, was standing a few feet away. His hands were tucked into the bell-like sleeves of his magenta dressing gown.

Astrid thrust her sword at him, catching his chin with its point. He lifted his head, placed a fat finger on the sword, and gingerly pushed the blade away.

"*.rittodsnnifloK dirtsA, emocleW*"

"I can't understand you," Astrid replied, her sword still raised. She'd deciphered her name—probably because the bloodbind had given her some of Ling's language ability—but she couldn't make out the rest of the man's words.

"Ah! Pardon me," said the man, in mer this time. "Not everyone speaks Rursus, do they? Welcome to the Hall of Sighs, Astrid Kolfinnsdottir. I'm Rorrim Drol. I've been expecting you."

Astrid stiffened. "How do you know my name?"

"My dear friend Orfeo told me about you. We've known each other for years, he and I. We deal in the same"—Rorrim smiled, revealing a mouthful of pointed teeth—"*commodities*."

Astrid tightened her grip on her sword. "Orfeo's here?" she asked warily. "Where is he?"

Rorrim steepled his heavily jeweled fingers. "Let's just say he's in the neighborhood."

"Can you take me to him?"

"For a price."

"I have currensea," said Astrid, lowering her sword. "How much do you want?"

Rorrim shook his head. "Trocii, drupes, cowries . . . they mean nothing to me," he said. "It's danklings I want."

"What are those?"

"Your deepest fears," Rorrim replied. As he spoke, he moved closer to Astrid. She suddenly felt a liquid chill run down her back, then a tearing pain.

"So strong," Rorrim said unhappily, his eyes on the dark, squealing creature now pinched between his fingers.

"Did that . . . that *thing* come out of me?" Astrid asked, horrified.

"Yes," Rorrim sighed. "But it's so small, it's barely enough for a snack."

Astrid backed away from him. "Touch me again, and you'll lose those fingers," she growled, hefting her sword.

Rorrim popped the small, squealing dankling into his mouth, then swallowed it. "There's not much you fear, is there?" he asked her, his eyes searching hers. "Only one thing, really, and he can remove it, if you let him."

"There's *nothing* I fear," Astrid blustered. "Definitely not you and your weird mirror world."

Rorrim smiled knowingly. "Not true. Not true at all," he said, wagging a finger at her.

Then he spoke, but not in his voice.

"Who wants a mermaid without magic?" he said, mimicking her father's voice.

"She's a freaky freakin' freak!" That was Tauno, a bully from back home.

And then: *"Where are you going, Astrid? To your friends? Do you really think it will be any different with them?"* Those words were spoken in Orfeo's voice. A cold dread gripped Astrid at the sound of them.

"You fear those voices are right, Astrid, though you tell yourself otherwise," Rorrim said, in his own voice now.

Astrid felt painfully exposed, as if the mirror lord could see deep inside her. "N-no, you're wrong," she stammered. "I don't believe them anymore. I—"

She gasped at a sudden sharp pain in her back. Rorrim, cunning and quick, had gotten behind her and torn another dankling from her spine.

"Oh, this is *much* better! So plump and juicy!" he said, greedily gobbling it.

Astrid swiped at him with her sword, but he ducked the blade and beetled off down the hallway, still smacking his lips.

"Come along now!" he called over his shoulder. "He doesn't like to be kept waiting!"

Astrid was furious at Rorrim, and at herself for listening to him, but she sheathed her sword and hurried after him. She had no choice if she wanted to get to Orfeo.

The mirror lord walked for a long time. For a heavy man, he was surprisingly fast, and Astrid had to work to keep up. The Hall of Sighs grew narrower as they moved down it. There were fewer mirrors, and no vitrina. Chandeliers, spaced far apart now, gave off little light. Dark blooms of corrosion and decay mottled the walls.

Just as Astrid was about to ask how much farther they had to go, they came to a dead end. Against the wall stood a single massive mirror. Its glass was pocked, and its heavy silver frame had tarnished to black. A length of sea silk hung over one corner like a shroud.

"This is the entrance to Shadow Manse," Rorrim said. "Orfeo's palace."

Astrid could see her reflection, and Rorrim's, in the dark glass. She squared her shoulders, trying to work up the nerve to swim through it.

"He's waited for this . . . waited for *you*, his blood, for four thousand years," Rorrim said. "Go to him now, child. Let him take your fear away."

Before Astrid could respond, the mirror lord was gone, walking back down the Hall of Sighs. Astrid turned and watched him grow smaller and smaller, until she couldn't see him at all. Then she faced the looking glass again—and herself.

Once she swam into Shadow Manse, there was no going back. She would take the black pearl from Orfeo or die trying.

Floating before the mirror, Astrid realized that she was about to confront someone who was far more treacherous than the Qanikkaaq, the Williwaw, the infanta, the Okwa Naholo, or the Abyss. If she swam through this mirror, she would come face-to-face with Orfeo. *Orfeo*. One of the Six Who Ruled. The greatest mage in history. And she? Well, she could turn herself purple when she meant to turn green. Sometimes. If she tried really hard.

"This is insanity," she whispered to the glass.

She thought of the other five who'd been summoned to the Iele's caves—Sera, Ling, Neela, Ava, and Becca. They were her friends, her sisters, bloodbound forever. They were counting on her. They wouldn't back away from this, no matter how scared they were. And she knew that she couldn't, either.

Taking a deep breath, Astrid placed her hands on the glass.

SEVEN

SHADOW MANSE looked as if it had been sculpted from darkness.

Black walls and floors, made of polished obsidian, reflected the blue waterfire flickering in silver candelabra. Overhead, Gothic arches supported a high, peaked ceiling.

Astrid, her sword drawn, moved warily through what seemed to be the palace's great hall. Salt water, not the liquid silver of Vadus, swirled around her now. At the hall's far end, a table, also made of obsidian, was set with sterling platters and bowls, all containing mouthwatering delicacies. A tall chair with carved arms had been placed at the head of the table. Another stood to its right.

Astrid moved toward the table. As she did, she heard footsteps, slow and measured, coming from behind her.

"How unusual," a voice said. "Most of my guests come bearing gifts, not swords."

Astrid spun around. It was Orfeo. He was a human, with legs, but he moved through the water smoothly, and breathed it as easily as if he were breathing air.

"You can put your weapon away," he said, with an amused half smile. "If I wanted to kill you, I wouldn't do it here. My servants have just polished the floor."

Six feet tall, blond, and powerfully built, he was dressed in his customary black suit. His skin was tanned, weathered by sun and sea. Smoke-tinted glasses obscured his eyes. Astrid's heart raced as she spotted the black pearl hanging at his neck. A suicidal urge to snatch it from him right then and there rose in her, but she fought it down and put her sword back in its scabbard.

Orfeo circled her, his head cocked like that of an osprey eyeing prey, his hands clasped behind his back. He stopped in front of her, then placed his palm against her chest.

"Whoa!" Astrid said. She tried to back away but faltered, overwhelmed by a sudden loud pounding. It filled her ears, her head, the entire hall.

"That's the sound of your heart," Orfeo said. "So brave. So powerful." He laughed, pleased by the thunderous noise. "Blood calls to blood, child. The blood of the greatest mage that ever lived. *My* blood." He removed his hand and the noise stopped.

"*Don't* do that again," Astrid hissed, frightened but trying not to show it.

His touch was repellent, but that's not what scared her. When he'd placed his hand over her heart, she'd felt something electric and dizzying surge through her veins: power—pure and thrilling.

"You must be tired. Hungry, too," Orfeo said. "Come, my servants have set a table for us."

Astrid shook her head. "I'm not going anywhere until you tell me why you summoned me, why I'm here," she said. She was pretty sure she knew, but she wanted to hear it from him.

Orfeo tilted his head again, regarding her. "They are one and the same—the reason I called you, the reason you came. Deep down, you know what that reason is. Deep down, we all know our heart's truest desire."

He offered her his hand. When she didn't take it, he turned and walked away.

Astrid's fear paralyzed her. She looked at Orfeo, walking away, then at the mirror that led back to Vadus.

"Who are you afraid of?" Orfeo called over his shoulder. "Me? Or yourself?"

With a last, desperate glance at the mirror, Astrid shored up her courage and swam after him.

EIGHT

NEELA, DISTURBED BY a noise in the barracks, opened her bleary eyes. A tail, pearly beige with patches of brown, was hanging in front of her face.

"Go to *sleep*, Becca," she grumbled, swatting it away. "It's not even light out yet!"

Becca was sitting on the bunk above her, getting dressed. "I can't. There's too much to do," she whispered.

"The work crews won't be up for another two hours. Go. Back. To. *Bed*."

"I need to get a head start," Becca said, swimming down from her bunk. "After we search the northwest quadrant for lava, I have to review plans for the new barracks and the school, and then inspect work on the infirmary. After that, the weapons need to be inventoried."

As Becca spoke, she spied a small tail flopping over the side of a nearby bunk. It belonged to a little mermaid named Coco, who tended to toss in her sleep. Becca gently eased Coco's tail back into her bed, then smoothed a strand of hair out of her face.

Neela blinked at Becca. "Why are you doing this all yourself? Why aren't you delegating some of the work?"

"I *am* delegating. I'm just, uh, checking in."

"Like every ten minutes. Which *isn't* delegating. You've got to ease up, Becs, or you'll work yourself to death."

"Hey! Trying to sleep here!" Ling griped. She'd only gone to bed a few hours ago herself. Becca had woken briefly when Ling had come in. She could have sworn Ling was carrying Sycorax's puzzle ball. Could that be?

"Sorry!" Becca whispered to Ling. "Later!" she mouthed to Neela.

As Neela burrowed into the seaweed of her bunk, Becca twisted her red hair up, then pushed a twig of polished coral through the twist to hold it in place. She buttoned her jacket around her neck. It was cold in the Kargjord. Then she picked up her clipboard, which she kept in a small cubby in the barracks' rock wall, and quietly left.

The waters outside were dark, but Becca cast an illuminata song-spell, and whirled some moonbeams together. The light did little to penetrate the murk, but at least it kept her from swimming into the boulders that dotted the Black Fins' camp. She was on her way to the tool storehouse.

The lack of proper light only reinforced Becca's determination to find a lava seam—as quickly as possible. Sera was spending a fortune on importing lava globes from Scaghaufen, the Meerteufel goblins' capital city. If a seam could be located, that money could go toward buying more food or medical supplies. Lava was crucial to the functioning of the camp. It was needed for heating and cooking as well as lighting. Seams ran under the rest of the goblin realms, and Becca was certain they'd find one under the Karg, too.

As she approached the storehouse, a figure loomed out of the darkness—a goblin, armed and armored. Becca recognized her.

"Hey, Mulmig. How'd tonight's patrol go?" she asked.

"We spotted some skavveners two leagues north of the camp. We gave chase, but they got away."

"How many?" Becca asked, her brow creased with worry.

"A dozen. Really nasty-looking. They had a lot of loot with them, and what looked like somebody else's hippokamps."

"Two leagues is too close," Becca said grimly.

Skavveners were bad news. Hunched, bony sea elves, they pillaged battlefields and disaster sites. Red-eyed and long-clawed, they wore their stringy hair loose and dressed in their victims' stolen clothing, often not waiting until they were dead to yank it off them.

Becca knew Sera wouldn't be happy when she heard about the skavveners. They stalked the feeble, sick, and injured. Sera wouldn't want Vallerio's spy to tell him that the elves had been seen near the Black Fins' camp. He'd take it as a sign of weakness. Which it was.

"And what about you? Are you ending one day, or starting the next?" Mulmig asked.

Becca laughed and told Mulmig her plans for today.

"You've got everything under control, Becs. As always," Mulmig said admiringly when Becca had finished. "But you look tired. You need more sleep. You work too hard."

Becca shook her head. "I don't work hard enough. We still don't have a source of lava, and it's hurting us. The skavveners sense it. That's why they're lurking."

"I'll help you hunt for a seam later, but right now I need some sleep," Mulmig said. "See you."

As Mulmig headed to her barracks, Becca continued on her way to the storehouse, with the goblin's words echoing in her ears. *You've got everything under control, Becs. As always.* Becca knew that Mulmig meant it as a compliment, but it didn't make her feel good. It made her feel like a fraud.

Becca took her responsibilities very seriously, but there was another reason she worked herself so hard, though she didn't like to admit it: a human named Marco. If she filled every minute of every day with work and then fell into an exhausted, dreamless sleep, there was no time left to think about him, and miss him.

Marco and his sister, Elisabetta, had rescued Becca after she'd been attacked by the Williwaw, a vengeful wind spirit from whom Becca had taken a talisman—a gold coin that had belonged to Pyrrha, one of the mages of Atlantis.

Marco was the current duca di Venezia, an ancient title conferred on his ancestor by Merrow, the first leader of the mer. The duca's duty was to protect the mer, and he fulfilled it with the help of the Praedatori, an ancient brotherhood of mermen, and the Wave Warriors, terragoggs who were dedicated to safeguarding the seas.

Together with Elisabetta, Marco had scooped Becca out of rough waters and taken her to the safety of the Kargjord. They'd stitched up her wounds and helped her recover. The stitches had come out, but scars—some deep—remained. Because during the days she'd spent with Marco and Elisabetta, she'd done a very foolish thing: she'd fallen in love.

Marco was gorgeous, with soulful brown eyes and a warm smile, and he was as dedicated to the defense of the earth's waters as any mer, but Becca knew that a relationship between them was impossible. Such a love was taboo to the mer, who were distrustful of humans. And even if it wasn't, Marco couldn't live in her world, and she couldn't live in his.

Becca's head knew this, but her heart wouldn't listen. These two opposing parts of her lobbed arguments back and forth like a ball at a caballabong match. One minute, she wished she'd told him she loved him—as he'd told her. The next, she was furious at herself for even considering such a reckless action. She worried about what her friends would think of her if they ever discovered her feelings for Marco, then hated herself for caring.

She stopped now, overcome by longing, and looked up through the waters at the moon shining high above. Maybe Marco was looking up at the moon, too, and thinking of her. She hoped so, even if it was stupid and hopeless and totally impossible.

Is he safe? she wondered. She knew that Orfeo and his thugs were after him, and that the Praedatori were too scattered to protect him. He'd had to leave the college where he was studying, but he couldn't go home to his family's palazzo in Venice, because it was being watched. *Is he on the water or on land? Is he happy? Has he found a terragogg girl and forgotten all about me?*

"Why?" she whispered, clenching her hands into fists. "Why not Desiderio, or Yazeed, or any one of the other amazing Black Fins? Why a *human*?" Tears stung behind her blue eyes.

This secret love was torture. She wished she could confide in one of her friends. Maybe Neela, Ling, or Sera could help her make sense of her feelings. She'd promised herself she would, a hundred times at least, but she always ended up backing away, too scared that they wouldn't understand.

When you keep a secret, the secret keeps you. Those were the very words she'd said to Astrid when she was trying to get her to tell the others about her inability to sing. If only she could follow her own advice, but it was so hard to confide in others, to trust them.

Becca was an orphan, and her early life—spent in a series of foster homes—had taught her that it was unwise to show vulnerability. If you were vulnerable, you were weak, and weak mer had their stuff stolen or got pushed to the back of the line at mealtimes.

Becca's early experiences had made her the self-reliant and organized mermaid that she was, and she was proud of that, but those tough years had made her something else, too—a mermaid who was good at giving help but bad at asking for it.

Becca's tears were brimming now. She angrily blinked them away. "Stop it. This instant," she told herself. "Crying won't help you find a lava seam."

Practical to a fault, Becca pushed her painful feelings down and kept swimming. She arrived at the storehouse a few minutes later, unlocked it, and swam inside. Glancing around, she spotted some shovels leaning against a wall.

The work crew in charge of the lava detail had covered a lot of seafloor, but there was a good deal more to search. Becca grabbed a shovel, locked the storehouse, then swam north through the black water, determined to get a head start on the day, organize her work crews, keep everything and everyone under tight control.

It was the only way to silence the one thing she couldn't control: her willful, traitorous heart.

NINE

MAHDI WATCHED closely as Vallerio, Miromara's high commander, moved tiny marble soldiers across a map that lay on the table in front of them. Mahdi's dark eyes were troubled. He'd returned from the western border an hour ago, only to be pulled into a military meeting.

"We have over fifty thousand weapons hidden in warehouses throughout Qin," Vallerio said, frowning, "and the same number of troops infiltrating the realm. The question is: Do I move more soldiers in and attack now, or do I wait?"

"For what?" Portia Volnero, Vallerio's wife, asked, with an impatient toss of her head. "The sooner Qin is ours, the better." She'd recently returned from Ondalina, where she'd forced the new admiral, Ragnar Kolfinnsson, to swear allegiance to Miromara.

"I'm worried about the Black Fins," Vallerio said. "I've sent battalions to the Southern Sea as well. Just in case."

"In case of what?" Mahdi asked. He knew, but his information had come from Sera, not Vallerio, so he had to pretend ignorance or Vallerio might become suspicious.

"In case of trouble," Vallerio said evasively. "One of our allies has . . ." He paused slightly, then said, ". . . *interests* there that require our protection."

"Which ally is that?" Mahdi pressed.

"You haven't met him yet. But you will. All in good time," Vallerio assured Mahdi. His tone brooked no further discussion. Mahdi let the matter drop, but he knew who the unnamed ally was: Orfeo.

The fact that Vallerio was moving troops into the Antarctic waters raised the scales on Mahdi's tail. Was Orfeo planning to enter those waters soon? He would have to get word to Sera, via his courier. Allegra, a Miromaran farmer, secretly brought and took message conchs for Mahdi when she delivered produce to the palace kitchens.

Vallerio frowned at the map now. "If the Black Fins discover we've moved so many of our soldiers out of Miromara, they might attack us."

Portia laughed. "The Black Fins shouldn't worry you, Vallerio. According to our spy, Guldemar only gave Serafina twenty thousand troops. She wouldn't dare attack with such a paltry number."

Vallerio's frown deepened. "Serafina has Guldemar's ear. She might get more troops out of him. Perhaps we should neutralize the Black Fins *before* we attack Qin."

Mahdi's stomach lurched at that, but he kept his expression neutral and chose his words carefully, knowing that what he said next could save or doom Serafina. "I think that would be a mistake."

Vallerio raised an eyebrow. "Do you? Why?"

"Serafina only has Guldemar's ear as long as she has gold," Mahdi explained. "Thanks to your spy, we know how much treasure the Black Fins stole from us, and how much of it Sera paid to Guldemar. Because of our ambushes, she's also had to pay for additional shipments of food and weapons. She's running out of funds, her troops are few, and she has no idea that many of our soldiers are in Qin and the Southern Sea. She wouldn't *dare* attack us now. We should take Qin, and *then* annihilate the Black Fins."

Vallerio digested Mahdi's words, then nodded approvingly. "I like your thinking," he said. "I'll have death riders continue to harass the Black Fins, but no large-scale attack. Not yet."

Mahdi forced a smile. Relief washed over him. He'd bought the

Black Fins more time. He'd kept them safe. That was why he was here in Cerulea, why he'd gotten close to Lucia and her parents, why he risked his life every minute of every day conducting this dangerous charade.

But his relief was short-lived.

"In fact, I like the way you think so much, I'm sending you to Guldemar," Vallerio said.

"For what purpose?" Mahdi asked. His fins were prickling, but once again, he hid his true feelings.

"To get him to break with the Black Fins. Bribe him, Mahdi. Threaten him. Do whatever you have to do, but make him see that it's in his best interest to ally himself with *us*, not Serafina," said Vallerio. "I want you to go tomorrow."

"That's a wonderful idea!" Portia trilled.

"I'll leave first thing in the morning," Mahdi said. His smile was still in place, but inside he was cursing Vallerio. The last thing he wanted to do was talk Guldemar out of helping Sera.

"Excellent. Now," Vallerio said, focusing on his map again, "after we take Qin, I think we should—"

His words were cut off as the door to the stateroom opened and Lucia entered, in a swirl of lavender sea silk.

"Darling!" Portia said warmly.

Lucia smiled brightly. Too brightly. It made Mahdi uneasy.

Over the past few weeks, she'd been slipping out of the palace at night. Mahdi didn't know where she went. He'd tried to have her followed, but she always lost the tails. Bianca had always accompanied her, but one night only Lucia had returned. When asked the next day about her friend's disappearance, she'd professed to know nothing.

Mahdi had noticed a change in Lucia ever since she'd started making these trips. She'd become more hot-tempered, but oddly, her eyes had grown colder. *The eyes are the windows to the soul,* the goggs said, and Lucia's were full of shadows.

Lucia kissed her mother and father, then swam to Mahdi and took his hands. "I'm *so* glad you're here with my parents. I have the most *wonderful* news!" she said. "I'm moving the date of our wedding up! We'll marry in two moons' time. During the next syzygy."

Mahdi's heart nearly stopped. He couldn't speak. Luckily he didn't have to. Lucia kept talking.

"We spoke about this once before, Mahdi, remember?" she said. "You were worried about the instability in the realms, and my safety. But my father is putting that behind us, so I see no reason to wait any longer. I want us to be married."

"This is rather sudden," Vallerio said.

Portia echoed her husband's concern. "Lucia, we've already announced the date. It's official. We have a guest list. Leaders from other realms are invited. I really don't think—"

Lucia spun around. Her smile was gone. Her eyes were hard. "I don't *care* what you think, Mother. *I'm* the regina here, not you, and this is what *I* want," she snapped.

Portia, surprised by the menace in her daughter's voice, took a stroke backward. She and Vallerio glanced at each other. He seemed equally taken aback.

"I—I guess we could have a private ceremony," she finally said. "For family and friends. And keep the state ceremony on the agreed date."

"Whatever," Lucia said dismissively. She turned back to Mahdi. She must've glimpsed something in his expression that she didn't like, for her eyes narrowed. "What's wrong?" she asked. "Aren't you happy?"

Mahdi wasn't. Far from it.

He knew that when he sang the first note of his marriage vows, the dangerous game he was playing would be over. If a Promised mer sang marriage vows to anyone but his or her betrothed, the vows would fall flat. Lucia, Portia, and everyone else at the ceremony would discover that he'd Promised himself to another, and it wouldn't take them long to figure out who it was. Vallerio would throw him in the dungeons, if he didn't put an arrow through his heart.

Mahdi also knew that he had to give the performance of his life now.

He raised Lucia's hand to his lips and kissed it. "I'm *beyond* happy," he lied. "Our wedding day can't some soon enough. Why not tonight?"

Lucia flushed with pleasure. "That's *too* soon!" she said, laughing. "The regina's wedding requires a syzygy, remember? Be patient!"

"I'll try my best," Mahdi said, smiling at her.

"Can you come for a swim through the gardens?" she asked.

He shook his head. "Later, I promise. Your father, mother, and I are busy protecting your realm. And you know that nothing is more important to me than your safety."

Lucia nodded. She kissed his cheek, then swam out of the room.

Portia watched her daughter go, an expression of misgiving on her face. "Never mind Qin," she said, as guards closed the door after Lucia. "Thanks to Lucia's news, it'll have to wait. What we need to do, right *now*, is kill Serafina, before she brings all our plans toppling down."

"But the Black Fins aren't a threat," Vallerio protested. "We just discussed this!"

"I'm not talking about the Black Fins," Portia retorted. "I'm talking about Sera. *She's* the true heir to the throne. Lucia's claim is only legitimate if she's dead. All along, we've stated that Sera was killed in the invasion of Cerulea and that any claim to the contrary was the work of an imposter. Mer believed that at first, but now some of them believe Sera's alive. Our spy tells me that some of our own citizens are fleeing to the Kargjord to join her."

As Portia was speaking, Mahdi saw a chance to help Sera. "Who *is* this spy, anyway? Are you certain his information is reliable?" he asked, hoping that Portia might give him something he could pass on to the Black Fins.

But she was too cagey. "No names, Mahdi. What if you fall into the Black Fins' hands and they pull a bloodsong from you? Let's just say the spy is close to Serafina and has my trust completely."

"Good to know," Mahdi said. His tone was casual, but inside he was desperate. He *had* to derail Portia's murderous plan. "But are you *sure* killing Serafina is a wise move?" he asked. "She's been granted sanctuary by Guldemar. If we send troops into the Kargjord, which is his territory, he'll view it as an act of aggression. We don't want a war with the Meerteufel."

"All the more reason for you to bring Guldemar over to our side," Portia said.

Vallerio weighed in. "You're right, of course, my darling," he said, then turned to Mahdi. "Take six chests of treasure with you to Scaghaufen to whet Guldemar's appetite for an alliance."

"I will," said Mahdi. "But you know what the Meerteufel are like. What if he refuses? What if he won't allow our troops into the Karg to attack the Black Fins?"

Portia smiled darkly. "Then we don't send troops. All we need is one soldier with a crossbow and, *voila*, we get rid of Serafina the same way we got rid of Isabella—with an arrow to the heart."

"That's not possible. Serafina's surrounded by her fighters," Mahdi said, glad he'd found a weakness in Portia's plan, a way to shut this discussion down. "There's no way we could get a lone soldier through them."

"Actually," Portia said, "we already have."

Mahdi tilted his head. "I don't understand."

"Listen closely, Mahdi. This is an important lesson for the future," Portia instructed. "When you choose a spy, make sure to choose someone with many talents; that way they can do more for you than merely gather info."

Mahdi felt sick. He wanted to swim out of the room as fast as he could, find Allegra, and get a conch to Sera to warn her. Instead, he jokingly slapped his forehead and said, "Of course. Portia, you're a genius."

Portia smiled. "It'll cost us our informant, unfortunately, and we're not ready to lose this operative just yet. But as soon as we've got all the information we need, we give the word, and then"—Portia's smile hardened—"our spy becomes our assassin."

TEN

THE WEBS were slung low over the swamp, from tree limb to tree limb, like giant white hammocks.

The creatures who'd spun them, each as big as a large dog, scuttled back and forth above the dark water, checking the webs, hoping to find a hapless bird, a fat raccoon, or a juicy human snared in them.

But it wasn't the fierce arachnids that Manon Laveau was searching for in the Spiderlair.

"Where are you, child? And where are *you*, you nasty water devils?" she muttered, peering into her seeing stone.

"Manon Laveau, what the *hell* are you doing?" Jean Lafitte shouted, startling the swamp queen. She'd thought she was alone. "Have you gone *cooyon*? What if you lay eyes on one of those Okwa?"

"You're jumpier than a frog in a stew pot, Lafitte," Manon said, trying to shrug him off. "I *won't* lay eyes on an Okwa, not up close. I'll only see an image in the stone."

"No one who sees the Okwa Naholo, no matter whatever which way, lives to tell about it," Lafitte said ominously, wagging a beringed finger at her. "Playing with waterfire, that's what *you're* doing."

"You're the frettingest pirate I ever met! Hush now!" Manon snapped. He'd rattled her. Embarrassed her, too. She didn't want him, or anyone else, to know that she was worried about Ava.

"Why do you care what happens to that fool of a mermaid? She's trouble!" Lafitte shot back. "You're not yourself these days. You coming down with something?"

Manon didn't answer him. Instead, she thought. She thought about people who would do anything for power and wealth. She'd seen terragoggs bulldoze her precious swamp, pollute its waters, and kill its rare creatures. And that new shack bully over in Miromara—Vallerio—he was mer, but he was just as bad. Traho, too. They'd destroy the world, and everything in it, for a bigger castle, a shinier chariot, or a chest full of gold.

Manon had seen much in her time, and she'd become hard, even cynical, as a result. She'd become unwilling to help others, because so few of them deserved help. But she still believed one thing with all her heart: that she was here to protect the swamp and pass it on to those who came after, just as her forebears had passed it on to her.

She knew that her life was a gift she'd one day have to give back. Horok would take her soul. The swamp would take her flesh and bones. It would break them down and use them to nourish the creatures of the dark waters, just as those creatures had nourished her.

That was nature's way. That was the circle of life. And now this *thing*, this *abomination*, this *Orfeo* wanted to break that circle. Because he was arrogant and selfish and could not accept his wife's mortality, or his own. Well, maybe it was high time he learned to.

"Manon? Manon Laveau, have you gone deaf? I asked you a question!"

"Yes, Lafitte," Manon said at length, "I *am* sick. Sick to death."

"What's wrong? Leech fever? Where's the pain?"

"In my heart."

The ghost shook his head sorrowfully. "That's no good. You're a goner for sure."

"Maybe so. But if I'm going, I'm taking a few with me," Manon said decisively.

Summoning all her powers of concentration, she stared into the stone again. She couldn't see any sort of swamp spirit, which was good. But she couldn't see Ava, either, which wasn't.

Ever since she'd heard the mermaid's story, Manon felt a strong sense of duty toward her. She wanted to protect her, to help her succeed in her quest. Mostly because she'd come to care for Ava, but also because saving her meant saving the swamp, and all its creatures, from Orfeo.

Manon knew that Ava hadn't been captured by Traho, because he and his men were lost in the Blackwaters. She'd seen *them* in the seeing stone moments ago and had had a good long laugh at their expense.

Trouble was, when it came to the Okwa, Manon didn't even know what she was looking for. No account of them existed because anyone in a position to give one was dead. As she continued to scan the murky waters of the Spiderlair, a flash of silver caught her eye.

"Bet *that's* her toothy little piranha," she said excitedly. As she focused in on the flash, she saw that it was indeed Baby. A ray of sunshine had pierced the swamp's leafy canopy and was bouncing off his scales. He was swimming around Ava, teeth bared to anything that moved.

Manon heaved a sigh of relief, then started to chant, her voice urgent and low. She called on the gris-gris she'd made for Ava to work its magic, to safeguard her.

Gris-gris spirits, hear my call.
One has come who casts a pall.
He seeks to harm a river's daughter.
Go, follow her through our black water.

I call upon my magic charm
To keep the mermaid safe from harm.

I bound it hard, I bound it tight
With gifts from creatures of the night.

A talon black, from Brother Owl,
The sound of the coyote's call,
A rare white gator's spiky tooth,
A viper's tongue, of lies and truth.

Give her the silence of midnight's bird,
Who's seldom seen and never heard
By prey until it's far too late,
And sharp black talons seal their fate.

Like Brother Trickster, make her sly.
Show her which way dangers lie.
Like Brother Gator, help her hide.
Let cloaking stillness be her guide.

And most of all, from Brother Snake,
The gift of split speech she must take.
Tell lies to monsters, truth to the just,
And in her own self, place her trust.

Go now, spirits, heed my plea.
Carry this magic to her from me.
Don't let evil take its toll,
Protect this mermaid, body and soul.

As she finished her chant, Manon sat back. She told herself that the gris-gris would be enough, that it would keep the mermaid safe.

"I made that charm strong," she whispered. "There isn't a mer alive who can make one stronger."

She nearly had herself convinced when it suddenly appeared, slithering out from a tangle of cypress roots, just a few yards ahead of Ava.

Manon's eyes widened. Her hands clutched the arms of her throne. And then the swamp queen, who had seen many a dark thing in her day, screamed.

ELEVEN

THE HEADACHE was so bad tonight, Sera thought it would split her skull in two.

They were getting worse, but she couldn't let the others know. They would tell her to rest or make her see a doctor, and she couldn't spare the time. There was too much to do. She had to keep going. She couldn't let the resistance down.

She was on her way to headquarters to meet with her inner circle. They gathered there every night to talk over the day's problems.

"Pull yourself together," she whispered as she entered the cave, then greeted the others. Neela, Ling, and Becca were seated at the far end of the table. Desiderio and Yazeed were at the near end, bent over the map spread across it. As she glanced at it, pain sliced through her brain like a ship's keel through water. She couldn't keep from wincing.

Neela noticed. "Sera? What's wrong?" she asked, concern in her eyes.

Sera forced a smile. "Nothing. Just a cramp in my tail."

"Hey, Sera," Des said, motioning her over, "take a look at the map. We need to talk about where to hit first. We can't put it off any longer."

The last thing Sera wanted to talk about was that map, and the cowrie shells covering it. They were the reason for her headaches, the reason she hadn't slept for days.

"I . . . uh, I want to go over some other things first, Des," she said, trying to ignore the throbbing in her head. "Ling, are you getting any closer to finding the spy? Please tell me yes."

"I wish I could," Ling said regretfully. "I've had lots of Black Fins take turns at trying to solve the puzzle. The entire camp's talking about the spy now, and the Arrow of Judgment. My plan will work, I'm sure of it. I just need more time."

Sera nodded, trying to hide her disappointment. "What about Sophia and Totschläger? Anyone see any sign of them yet?"

It had been two days since Sophia, Totschläger, and twenty other Black Fins had left to rendezvous with the Näkki.

"No news," Yazeed said, "but that's not a reason to panic. Not yet. They're not due back until tomorrow morning."

"What about Ava and Astrid?" asked Sera. "Has anyone been able to convoca them?"

"I tried several times today, but I couldn't get through," Ling replied. "The rocks here contain so much iron, they're messing with my songspells. I'll stay on it, though."

"It's been days since we've heard from either of them," Sera fretted.

"Ava and Astrid are tough," Becca reassured her. "And smart. They'll make it."

Sera laughed mirthlessly. "So, besides Ava being lost in a swamp full of homicidal maniacs, and Astrid swimming off to meet the king of homicidal maniacs, what other insurmountable problems are we facing tonight?"

"Soldiers," Desiderio said. "Or lack thereof." He'd been working with Meerteufel commanders on drilling the goblin troops. "The goblins are doing well on maneuvers," he said, "but we still don't have enough of them."

"How do we augment their numbers?" Sera asked, struggling to keep the strain out of her voice. She was so exhausted, she felt dizzy.

And the ache in her head was getting worse. She massaged her left temple, hoping the others didn't notice.

"Refugees," Neela replied. "All they talk about, from the minute they arrive, is how badly they want to go back to Cerulea and take on Vallerio."

Word was spreading of the Black Fins' stronghold in the north, and mer were flocking to the Kargjord. Nearly two hundred had arrived today alone. Neela was in charge of seeing that they were all sheltered and fed. She'd put them in barracks under the protective thicket of Devil's Tail thorns that floated above the center of the camp. She'd had to move some soldiers outside the thicket and into tents to make room for all the newcomers.

"The refugees may not be enough. We may have to go back to Guldemar to ask for more troops," Desiderio countered.

Sera grimaced at the idea. She'd dealt with the difficult Meerteufel chieftain once, and it had been quite an ordeal. Returning to his court at Scaghaufen did not appeal to her.

"We need more weapons, too," Des added. "Even after the deal you made with the Näkki, we still don't have enough. Not to equip all the newcomers. We're low on ammo as well."

"We could solve the ammo problem *so* easily if we could just find a lava seam," Yazeed said, frustrated. "There are two shipwrecks four leagues east of here. The hull from one alone, melted down, would give us thousands of arrows and spearheads."

"The goblins are awesome metalworkers. They could set up a forge in no time," added Desiderio.

"Becca, any luck on the lava front?" asked Sera.

"No," she replied. "I'm sorry. I've got teams of goblins looking day and night, but so far we've found nothing."

"How are the building projects coming?"

Becca unrolled one of the large parchments lying on the table in front of her. On it she'd charted the status of the new barracks, infirmary, and school. She took Sera and the others through it in detail. Half an hour later, she finished.

"Becca, you have a tremendous amount going on. Can you assign some of the work to others?" Sera asked, her eyes on the chart.

Becca shook her head. "I can handle it, Sera."

"But, Becca—"

"Seriously. I've *got* it," she insisted, an edge to her voice.

Sera looked up at her, struck by her tone. As she did, she noticed that there were dark circles under Becca's eyes, and that her cheeks looked hollow.

Something's wrong. Something more than a heavy workload, Sera thought, alarmed for her friend. She knew she should take Becca aside and try to find out what was going on with her, but she couldn't. She couldn't even think straight any longer. She had to get out of here.

"Are we done?" Des asked. "Because we've got to talk about Vallerio's troops, the Southern Sea, and—"

"Des, I can't. Not now. I—" she started to say.

"Sera, you have to," Des said, cutting her off. "We need to make a decision."

No, Sera thought frantically.

"Des is right, Sera," Yazeed said. "About needing to prep, that is. Not about where to attack."

Des snorted. He shot Yazeed a look, then cleared piles of parchments off the table and placed them on the floor so that Sera had a better view of the map. As soon as her gaze fell upon it, another bolt of pain shot through her skull.

"We have two enemies to battle: Vallerio and Abbadon," Des said, "and we can't take them both on at once. We all know that. What we need to decide—"

Yaz cut him off. "Dude, come *on*! There is no decision. It's *so* clear: we need to attack Abbadon first!"

Becca's eyes cut to him. So did Neela's. Both mermaids seemed surprised by his rudeness. They looked at Sera, waiting for her to say something. But Sera didn't because she'd barely heard him, or her brother. Her eyes were glued to the map. They swept over the cowries that represented her uncle's troops and the turitella shells that stood for her own. The shells reminded her of chess pieces—kings, queens, knights, pawns. They seemed to taunt her, to tell her that *she* was a queen, the rightful regina of Miromara, but Vallerio was the one who ruled the board.

Neela's eyes remained on Sera, beseeching her to take charge. When she didn't, Neela spoke instead. "Hey, Yaz?" she said. "We're *all* tired and stressed, but that's no reason to disrespect each other."

"I know, I know," Yaz said, holding his hands up. "It's just that Des and I have been arguing about this for days. We're both frayed. Especially me. Sorry, Des. You're up."

Des nodded. "As I was saying, Vallerio is our biggest threat. He's the clear and present danger. His death riders are now attacking our troops every time they go into open waters. It's only a matter of time until they hit our camp, and then—"

"But Abbadon—" Yazeed began.

"Is buried under a polar ice cap!" Des said, clearly annoyed at having been interrupted again.

"Um, bro?" Yaz said. "Don't know if you've heard, but the ice is melting. And the monster man's waking up. And when he's stretched and yawned and got his monster butt out of bed, he's going to make Vallerio look about as scary as a guppy."

Des lost it. "Open your eyes, Yaz!" he shouted, pointing to the cowries. "Look at Vallerio's troops—they're everywhere! We'll never make it to the Southern Sea. We won't make out of the *Atlantic*!"

"We will! We can go around them!" Yazeed shouted back.

Desiderio threw his hands up. "Care to tell us *how?*"

"We'll figure it out! That's what commanders do. We *have* to take Abbadon out first. If Orfeo unleashes him, there won't *be* any

Vallerio. There won't be any Cerulea, or Miromara, or you and me. You *know* that. You hate your uncle so much, it's blinding you to the fact: Abbadon is the bigger threat!"

The two mermen were in each other's faces now. Their loud voices were ringing in Sera's ears. She knew she should say something, but she still couldn't tear her eyes away from the shells.

These shells are lives. So many lives, she thought.

Finally, Ling put her fingers in her mouth and blew a piercing whistle. Des and Yazeed both winced. They stopped shouting and looked at her.

"Sorry to burst your eardrums, boys," she said, "but we need to remember that we're all on the same side here. Maybe we should take a break."

"We *can't* take a break," Desiderio said. "There's no time. My uncle's growing bolder. His ambushes are getting closer."

"I hear you, Des," Ling said, "but maybe Sera should weigh in on this. Sera, what do you think? Sera? *Sera.*"

Sera lifted her head. "What do I think?" she echoed. "I think that my uncle doesn't care how many he kills. That's his strength. I *do* care. And that's my weakness."

"Sera, listen—" Desiderio started to say.

"No, Des, *you* listen. You and Yaz . . . you want me to give the orders to go to war, but I can't," she said, her voice ragged. "War takes lives—not only the lives of soldiers, but the lives of innocent civilians who get caught in the crosshairs. If I love my subjects, how can I give a command that will turn children into orphans? Rob parents of sons and daughters? *How?* Can somebody tell me?"

Sera waited, but no one answered her.

"I thought I'd learned how to lead, but I haven't," she said. "Because I can't do this. *I can't.*"

Desiderio swam to his sister. He put a gentle arm around her.

"Shh, Sera. You're worn-out, that's all. Go get some sleep. Things will look different in the morning. You'll see."

Sera nodded, feeling despondent. She got up to leave, but she knew she wouldn't sleep.

I'll head toward the barracks to make them happy, she thought, *then veer off and swim through the camp. Maybe a breath of fresh water will help.*

Des and Neela swam with her to the cave's mouth. As she left, they remained where they were, watching her, uneasy expressions on their faces.

The acoustics around the headquarters were strange. Hollows in the rock caught sound; jutting boulders bounced it this way and that. Sera could hear her best friend and her brother talking about her as she swam away.

"She'll be fine," Desiderio insisted. "She just needs some rest. She'll make a decision in the morning."

"No, she won't," Neela said. "Her heart won't allow her to. She can't be the reason innocent people die."

Desiderio didn't respond right away. Then in a heavy voice so low that Sera almost didn't hear him, he said, "She doesn't have a choice, Neela. She needs to find a way. If she doesn't, we *all* die."

TWELVE

*T*HINGS WILL LOOK *different in the morning.*

Desiderio's words echoed in Sera's aching head.

"Will they?" she asked herself.

They'd changed, all of them—Neela, Ling, Becca, Astrid, Ava. They'd grown. And she had, too; she knew that. She'd conquered many painful challenges since her mother had been assassinated, but this one—leading her fighters into war—seemed like it would conquer her.

She was failing now. Failing her duties, her people, and herself, and the knowledge of it plunged Sera into despair. She felt so lost, so wretched, that she just swam forward, paying no attention to where she was going. Past caves, boulders, and clumps of seaweed. Past the north gate.

Almost an hour after she'd left headquarters, the blood-chilling howls of a pack of dogfish startled Sera out of her desperate thoughts. She looked around and saw that she was on the far eastern edge of her camp, beyond the protective cover of Devil's Tail, in a desolate patch of scrubweed and rock.

The currents keened mournfully through the rocks; the waters were a good deal colder out here than they were back at headquarters. Shivering, Sera pulled her collar up around her neck, ready to turn back for the warm heart of her camp. But before she could, she heard the sound of voices. They were coming from the other side of a large boulder that was encrusted with tube worms.

The speakers had heard her, too. "Who's there?" one shouted tersely.

Sera tried to back away quietly.

"This is Ensign Adamo of the Black Fin resistance! Show yourself! *Now!* Or I'm coming around that boulder arrows flying."

Sera panicked. She couldn't let herself be seen in this state. She was supposed to be an inspiration to her fighters, not a cause for concern.

"I *said*, show yourself!"

Frantic, Sera cast a quick illusio spell, hoping to turn her copper-colored hair black and her green eyes blue. Thanks to the iron-rich boulder, though, she ended up with black eyes and blue hair.

"I'm not asking again!" the voice threatened.

Then Sera heard a crossbow being cocked. She swam around the boulder, hands raised. "It's okay. I'm a Black Fin," she said.

A merman, gray-haired, with a craggy, bearded face, had his crossbow trained on her. ADAMO was embroidered on his uniform. Two others—a younger merman, and a female goblin—also had their weapons raised.

"If you're one of us, why are you sneaking around the outskirts of camp?" Ensign Adamo demanded, eyeing her uniform.

"I wasn't sneaking. I—I couldn't sleep, so I went for a swim."

"Where you from?"

"Cerulea."

"Swashbuckler, huh?" Adamo said, taking in her bright blue hair. "What's your name, merl?"

"Sera," she replied without thinking. Then she hurriedly added a surname. "LaReine."

"That doesn't sound like a Cerulean name to me," Adamo said, his eyes narrowing.

"My mother's side is from the city," Sera quickly lied. "My father's family comes from westerly waters. Off the shores of France."

"I guess that accounts for it," said Adamo, lowering his weapons. His companions lowered theirs, too. "You're welcome to sit with us and warm up," he added, nodding at the waterfire. "We finished our watch. Couldn't sleep. Decided to go foraging."

"Thank you," said Sera.

Adamo told Sera that his first name was Salvatore. The younger merman introduced himself as Enzo Lenzi and the goblin simply as Snøfte. They made room for her around the waterfire. As she sat down, Enzo picked up a knife and a small block of wood. Little pieces of wood littered the seafloor around him. Sera realized he'd been carving before she barged in upon them. As she looked at what he'd been making—a little figure of a seal—her heart clenched.

She knew another young merman who carved. He'd made a tiny octopus for her once. In the gardens of Cerulea's royal palace. As she watched Enzo work, she missed Mahdi so badly, it hurt.

Snøfte suddenly elbowed Sera, startling her out of her reverie. The goblin held out a bowl woven of scrubgrass. It contained clumps of plump, juicy squid eggs. "Help yourself. We found them under some rocks."

Sera took a clump and popped it into her mouth. The sweet, briny eggs burst as she chewed them. "Mmm," she said through a mouthful. "Wow, are those good. Thank you."

"A whole lot better than conger eel stew," Salvatore commented. He was sitting by the fire now, too.

"I swear to Vaeldig, if I have to eat another bowl of that swill, I'll throw up," Snøfte complained.

Vaeldig, Sera knew, was the goblin god of war. Inwardly she winced, feeling guilty that she couldn't provide her troops with better food.

Snøfte shook her head. "I came here because Guldemar ordered it," she said. "You three"—she nodded at Salvatore, Enzo, and Sera—"*volunteered*." She laughed. *"Skøre tåber,"* she said in her own language. *Crazy fools.*

"Yeah, I *did* volunteer," Salvatore said wryly. "At the time, I thought there were things worth dying for—my realm, my city, my ruler. Now, I'm not so sure."

Sera's despondency deepened as she listened to Salvatore and Snøfte. She'd been unable to face sending loyal soldiers to their deaths, soldiers who believed in the fight. The idea of sending soldiers to die for a cause they no longer believed in was even worse.

"We sit here day after day, getting by on conger eel, *barely*, and all the while, the death riders are coming closer," Snøfte said. "We need to ambush *them*. Kill them all and put their heads on stakes. Right outside the camp's gates."

"Too right," Salvatore said, spitting a gob of chewing seaweed into the waterfire. "Serafina will never do it, though. She's too weak. Too inexperienced. She's nothing more than a pawn in her uncle's game."

Sera felt like she'd been slapped. Instinctively, she spoke up for herself. "Serafina's not *all* bad," she protested, unable to keep a twinge of defensiveness out of her voice. "I hear she loves her subjects very much."

Salvatore snorted. His bushy eyebrows shot up. *"Love?* Who cares about love? I'm hungry. I'm cold. I need food and arrows, not *love*," he said contemptuously. "Love means nothing to me."

Enzo, who hadn't spoken one word the entire time, looked up from his carving. "It means something to me," he said quietly. "It's the reason I'm here."

Salvatore flapped a hand at him and spat another gob of seaweed into the fire.

Enzo turned to Sera. "I come from Cerulea, too. From the fabra."

Sera nodded. She knew the district well. It was where the city's artisans lived.

"My family, we're woodworkers," Enzo continued, giving her a smile both proud and sad. "We salvage beams from shipwrecks, comb the shores for driftwood. We carve it into beautiful things—statues, tables, frames." His smile faded. "We don't make beautiful things anymore, though. Now we make stocks for crossbows and handles for daggers. My grandfather, my father . . . they don't want to do this work, but they don't have a choice: Vallerio commands it. My uncle refused . . ." Enzo paused for a few seconds, overcome by emotion, then continued, ". . . and they took him away."

"I'm sorry, Enzo," Sera said, her heart hurting for him. "I'm guessing you're here because you didn't want to do Vallerio's bidding, either."

"No, I didn't," Enzo said, defiance in his voice. "I snuck out of the city gates one night when a guard's back was turned. My grandfather and father cannot fight. They're too old. My little sons are too young. But I can. And I will. That's why I'm here. Because I'd rather die fighting for them than live and watch them suffer."

Salvatore crossed his arms over his chest. He stared into the waterfire. "Maybe there are some things worth dying for," he said gruffly.

"No, Salvatore," Enzo said. "Not *some* things. One thing: *family.*"

As the words left Enzo's lips, the pain finally stopped—the pain in Sera's head, and her heart.

Earlier, she'd asked her brother, and her friends, to tell her how to send her people into battle. *How can I give the command? Will somebody tell me?* she'd begged.

Now somebody had.

Thank you, she said silently to the woodcarver. *I owe you more than you'll ever know.*

She rose, ready for a rest, ready to start again tomorrow. She was just about to bid the others good night when a wailing blare rose over the camp. It dipped, then rose again.

Snøfte swore. "The alarm siren!" she shouted, jumping to her feet.

Enzo leapt up and jammed his knife into the sheath on his hip.

No, Sera thought. *It can't be.*

"Grab your weapons, kids," Salvatore said grimly. "It looks like we're under attack."

THIRTEEN

SERA SWAM FASTER than she ever had in her life.

Back through the boulders and scrubgrass she raced, back to the center of camp. Salvatore, Enzo, and Snøfte were right on her tail.

As Sera swam, she undid her illusio spell.

"Is that—" she heard Salvatore call out.

"Yeah!" Snøfte shouted back to him. "It is! It's her, Serafina!"

At the edges of camp, a lethal chaos reigned, and the death riders used it. Mer and goblin soldiers rushed out from under the thorn thicket, searching the darkness for foes. As they did, arrows sliced through the water from above. Frightened civilians, their tails thrashing, were hurrying for the safety of the thorns. Sera heard the screams of terrified mothers, the wails of children. The lights from illuminatas, hastily cast, flashed all around her—to her left, her right, and sometimes directly in her face, blinding her. She swooped down low, blinking the light out of her eyes, dodging rocks, tents, other Black Fins. She needed a weapon; she was useless without one.

"Get everyone under the Devil's Tail! Hurry!" a voice shouted.

"Civilians into the caves!" another yelled. "Songcasters to the gates!"

"Medics to the south court! We've got fighters down!"

"Des, Yaz . . . where are you?" Sera shouted. "Neela! Ling! Becca!" But none of them answered her.

An arrow buried itself in the chest of a Black Fin next to her. He was dead before he hit the seafloor.

Sera dove down to the body. There would be time to honor the fighter later. Right now, she needed a weapon. She tugged the ammo belt free of his waist, buckled it around her own, then took the crossbow from his lifeless hands.

The attackers are shooting from above, and from the camp's perimeter. They're everywhere! she thought. Panic threatened to overwhelm her.

Stop, Sera, she told herself. *Think. Figure this out.* She closed her eyes. Listened hard. Turned in a circle. Her ears told her that most of the noise was coming from behind her, toward the south side of the camp. She spun around and shot off that way. Seconds later, she heard her brother's voice. "Crossbows to the south gate!" he was yelling. "Speargunners, defend the roof!"

"Desiderio, what's happening?" Sera shouted, swimming up to him.

"Death riders! They ambushed Sophia and her troops in the Darktide Shallows!" he shouted back. "The Black Fins fought their way free and bolted for camp, but the death riders followed them."

"How many?"

"At least a hundred. Most of them are at the south gate."

Hope surged in Sera's heart. The Black Fins vastly outnumbered the death riders.

As if reading his sister's thoughts, Des said, "We can beat them off, but we need light." Then he was racing off, yelling, "Songcasters! Get the lights on! *Now!*"

Sera bolted for the south gate, crossbow raised. A horrible sight met her eyes when she reached it. The bodies of at least two dozen Black Fins were strewn across the court. Dead hippokamps lay among them. In the mouth of the gate itself, death riders, protected by shields, were firing upon the Black Fins trying to defend it.

Some of the Black Fins were down on their bellies, elbows planted in the silt to brace their weapons. Others shot from behind rocks. Sera saw that a few more had positioned themselves behind wagons, some upright, some overturned.

The wagons! she thought. *Sophia got them back to camp!*

Sera did a quick count. There were nine. That meant the death riders had only gotten one wagonload of their weapons. Thank the gods!

An arrow whizzed by Sera, missing her head by mere inches. She ducked behind a rock. Breathless, her heart slamming in her chest, she loaded her weapon, then peered out and started firing.

An instant later, light rose over the court. The songcasters had succeeded in casting an enormous illuminata.

More Black Fins, able to see their foes now, joined the fray. As they did, a shrill whistle pierced the water, and the death riders fell back. Moving with the speed of sharks, they swam out of the gateway, launched themselves onto the backs of their hippokamps, and rode off into the night.

As quickly as it had started, the attack was over.

A pair of guards hurried to the gates, pushed them closed, and locked them. A group of speargunners swam up behind the guards and angrily demanded that they reopen the gates. They wanted to chase the attackers. Sera swam out from her cover and stopped them.

"It could be a trap," she said. "There might be more death riders out there, waiting for us. Put your weapons down. Help the wounded. Collect the dead."

At that moment, a shout for help came from one of the over-turned wagons. The speargunners swam to it. Working together, they lifted the wagon off the seafloor and set it upright.

As they did, a bruised and bloodied mermaid swam out from underneath. She was dazed and moved crookedly; her eyes were glassy.

"Sophia!" Sera cried, rushing to her. She took hold of her friend's arms. "Look at me, Soph. *Focus.*"

Sophia's eyes met Sera's. She shook her head as if to clear it. The glassy look receded. "Came in fast," she murmured. "Got to the gates, but a death rider shot my hippokamp. She went wild. . . . She bolted. We made it into the court, but the wagon tipped over. I don't . . . I can't remember. . . ." Her eyes widened. "Oh, gods, Sera. *Totschläger.*"

At that instant, a medic—Henri—swam up. He immediately started to treat the wound on Sophia's forehead, but she shook him off. "Find Totschläger, please," she begged. "He's been shot. I'm fine! I'm *fine*! Go find Totschläger!"

Sera realized her friend was in shock and edging toward hysteria. She tried to calm her. "It's okay, Soph. We'll find him. He's here. The medics will help him."

Sera slung one of Sophia's arms over her shoulder. The two mermaids swam through the court. "Has anyone seen Totschläger?" Sera called out.

There were bodies everywhere. Plumes of blood drifted through the water. The cries of the injured echoed off rocks and boulders. Medics rushed to and fro with bandages and stretchers.

Sera kept searching, hoping to spot Totschläger's face among the living, not the dead, but she couldn't find him anywhere. She was about to give up when she heard someone shouting for her. It was Henri.

"He's here!" He waved Sera over.

Sera and Sophia rushed to him. They found Totschläger lying on his back. His eyes were closed. A wound gaped across his chest, ugly and red. Dread knotted Sera's stomach. *No one can survive an injury like that,* she thought.

The fearsome goblin was barely breathing. Henri was kneeling in the silt next to him. Other goblins, and some mer, had crowded around.

"Is he . . ." Sera started to say, hoping against hope.

Henri shook his head. Sophia's face crumpled. "He fought so hard, Sera. We only got away because of him. This is my fault!" she sobbed. "It's all my fault!"

Sera pulled Sophia close. "It's *not* your fault, Soph," she hissed. "Do you hear me? It's Vallerio's fault. It's *his* fault!"

Suddenly a goblin pushed his way through the crowd, shoving everyone else out of the way. It was Garstig, a goblin commander.

"*Din dumme, dumme fjols,*" he said gruffly as he knelt down beside Totschläger. "*Kun et ryk som du kunne få sig selv skudt.*"

Sera translated his words in her head. *You stupid, stupid fool. Only a jerk like you could get himself shot.*

Garstig took his comrade's hand, not caring that it was covered with blood.

Totschläger opened his eyes. "Garstig, you big oaf. Is your face the last one I'll ever see? Gods help me. You're uglier than a blobfish, and you smell worse than rotten walrus-milk cheese."

Garstig chuckled. "Always one for sweet words, even when I first met you, back in military school."

"We had some good times, old friend. Didn't we?" Totschläger said, trying to smile.

Garstig nodded. "Remember when we raced hippokamps through the market in Scaghaufen? I fell off and landed headfirst in a bucket of marsh melons. I still have the scar," he added proudly, pointing to a jagged mark on his temple. "And a few on my backside, too, from the farmer's pitchfork."

Totschläger's smile broadened.

"Remember our first battle?" Garstig asked. "We fought those stinking Feuerkumpel who'd snuck across the border. Sent them off with some nice, juicy wounds. We celebrated that night. Who drank too much *räkä*? And threw up for three days straight?"

Totschläger laughed, but the laugh turned into a painful, racking cough. Blood seeped from the corner of his mouth. His chest started to hitch.

"Garstig, speak . . ." he said, struggling to get the words out. "Speak for me . . . *please*."

Garstig tightened his grip on Totschläger's hand. "Of course I will. And Vaeldig will hear me, don't you worry. You'll be in Fyr before the stars fade," he said.

Tears sprang to Sera's eyes. *Fyr*, she knew, was the goblin word for the underworld. All goblins, no matter what tribe they belonged to, believed that when they died, Vaeldig, their war god, took the bravest among them to his grand hall in Fyr to fight and feast for all eternity.

Blood was dripping off Totschläger's chin now. He could no longer talk. His breath came quick and shallow. For a few seconds, the light in his eyes burned as brightly as the fire in a goblin forge; then it dulled and faded away.

Gently, Garstig closed those eyes. Tears, as black and thick as oil, streamed down his cheeks. With a roar of grief, he threw his head back and cried out to his god.

"Hear me, great Vaeldig!" he shouted. "I, Garstig, speak for Totschläger of the Meerteufel! He was a fierce warrior, brave and loyal! He was an honor to his chieftain, an honor to his tribe! Reward his courage! Carry his spirit to Fyr and seat him at your table!"

As Garstig's words rang out, Totschläger's face, which had been contorted by pain, softened into a peaceful expression.

Garstig looked down at him. "He's gone," he said brokenly. "My best friend . . . he's *gone*."

His voice broke on the last word, and Sera felt as if someone had thrust a knife into her heart. Garstig's terrible grief brought back all the losses she'd suffered—her parents, Vrăja, Thalassa, Fossegrim,

Duca Armando, so many. She thought of the losses her merfolk had endured, and merfolk throughout all the water realms. All because of Vallerio.

"Henri," she said, "take Sophia to the infirmary."

"No, Sera, I don't need to go," Sophia protested. "I want to stay. I want to help."

"Later, Soph. After the medics stitch up your head." She kissed her friend's cheek. "You saved a great many lives tonight, and our weapons. Thank you."

As Henri led Sophia away, Ling rushed by. Sera called her over.

"The others?" Sera asked.

"All alive."

"Thank the gods," Sera said. "I need you to gather them and get them to HQ."

"Now, Sera? We have wounded to attend to and bodies to bury."

"I know, but this can't wait."

As Sera swam toward the headquarters cave, past crying children and injured parents, anger swelled inside her like a deadly rogue wave. *She* was the rightful ruler of Miromara, and yet her vicious uncle was always the one in charge. He pushed her all around the board. All she could ever do was try to stay one stroke ahead of him.

Until now.

Vallerio had made a mistake tonight, with this cowardly attack. He had handed her a move.

And she was going to take it.

FOURTEEN

SERA'S INNER CIRCLE STRAGGLED into the cave one by one. They were in shock and hollowed out by fighting, by seeing their fellow Black Fins wounded or killed. Yazeed had taken an arrow wound to the tail. Des had a cut across his forehead. Neela had a nasty bruise spreading across her cheek.

Sera looked at them and her heart hurt for all they'd been through, and for all that they had yet to face. She was about to make a critical move, and once she did, there'd be no turning back.

She waited until they were all seated, then—without any preliminaries—she spoke.

"Vallerio's been using his spy to his advantage. Tonight is yet another example of this. The spy told him where Sophia and Totschläger would be and when. I've had enough. It's my turn now. *I'm* going to use his spy to my advantage."

"How?" Ling asked.

"I've decided that we're going to the Southern Sea first, to kill Abbadon. Des, I respect your position, but I agree with Yazeed's reasoning. Without the monster, Orfeo can be bested. Without Orfeo, Vallerio can be bested." Sera paused to let her words sink in, then continued. "So what I want is for all of you to tell the entire camp that we're going to attack Cerulea. Tell everyone that I was so enraged by my uncle's ambush, I immediately vowed revenge."

"Wait, *Cerulea*?" Becca said, confused. "Didn't you just say that we're heading to the Southern Sea?"

CHAPTER 14

"Becs, dude . . . it's a fake-out move!" Yazeed crowed.

Sera nodded. "Yes, it is."

Desiderio steepled his fingers. He rested his chin on them and stared at his sister. Sera had gone against his counsel. Would he still support her decision?

"Our uncle's no fool. What makes you think he'll buy it?" he said at length.

"Because he thinks *I'm* a fool," Sera replied. "And this is just the sort of hotheaded move a fool would make."

"Can't fault you on *that* logic," Des said.

"When the spy in our midst tells Vallerio that we're heading for Cerulea," Sera said, "Vallerio will order his troops out of the Atlantic and the Southern Sea, and back into the city to guard it."

Ling sat forward in her chair. "Which clears a path straight to Abbadon," she said excitedly.

"Exactly," Sera said. "Any questions?"

"Yeah, a big one," said Desiderio. "Earlier tonight, you told us you couldn't send troops into battle knowing lives would be lost. Now you're about to order your fighters to the Southern Sea. A lot of them won't make it back. Why the sudden change of heart?"

Sera took a deep breath, Des's question echoing in her mind. There were other questions there, too. So many, and all of them impossible to answer.

Was love enough? Was it stronger than her uncle's brutality, his lust for power, his hatred? Was it stronger than fear? Stronger than death?

Sera knew she'd never find the answers if she didn't make her move.

"Because it's time, Des," she finally said.

"Time for what?"

"Time to play my uncle's game like a queen, not a pawn."

FIFTEEN

ASTRID STARED AT the gown. It was the most magnificent garment she'd ever seen. Made of black sea silk, it was trimmed with pieces of polished jet at the neckline and hem. The long sleeves ended in points, the waist was nipped, the skirt long and flowing.

"A gift for you. From the master," said the servant, as she laid the gown across Astrid's bed. "He has summoned you to the garden and wishes you to wear it."

"Maybe another time," Astrid said. The gown was beautiful but impractical. Her own clothing would serve her better if she needed to fight. Or escape.

"But your things are worn and stained," the servant said, dismayed by Astrid's refusal.

"I'm good."

The servant shook her head. She started toward Astrid. "You can't possibly accompany the master in such filthy—"

Astrid's hand went to the hilt of her sword. "I *said* I'm good."

The servant stopped dead.

"He may be *your* master, but he's not mine," Astrid said, a note of warning in her voice. She was not here to make friends.

"Very well," the servant said stiffly. "This way, please."

She turned and swam out of the room. Astrid followed her.

She'd eaten a brief meal with Orfeo yesterday, right after she'd arrived at Shadow Manse. During their time together, Astrid had pressed him to tell her why he'd summoned her, but he'd deflected her question.

"All in good time," he said. "It's late, and you've traveled far. It's time for you to rest." At a wave of his hand, a servant had appeared to take Astrid to her room.

There she'd sat up in a chair wary and watchful, alert to every noise, until finally, just before dawn, she'd given in to her body's need for sleep. When she'd awoken, hours later, she'd immediately realized that someone had been in her room: a breakfast tray was resting on a nearby table and the sea-silk gown had been draped across the bed.

Astrid had jumped out of the chair, furious with herself for letting her guard down. She could've been killed in her sleep.

"But you weren't," she'd said to herself. "Seems Orfeo doesn't want you dead. At least, not yet."

She'd eaten breakfast and then the servant had appeared to take her to Orfeo. This time, she would *make* him tell her why he'd summoned her.

Astrid looked around as she swam, taking in the silent servants, all dressed in ebony sea flax; the midnight-hued draperies billowing in the current; and the twists and turns of the obsidian passageways.

A few minutes later, they arrived at a pair of arched doors. The servant opened them, then swept a hand in front of her. Astrid swam through the doorway and into a walled courtyard. The gardens—formal, extensive, and planted entirely in black—matched the rest of the palace.

Ebony sea roses, feathery tube worms, gorgons, seaweeds, corals, and anemones grew on a foundation of night-dark basalt. As Astrid swam through the gardens, looking for Orfeo, onyx eels darted between rocks. Rays glided overhead, as silent as shadows. A dozen anglerfish, light shining from the thin, fleshy stalks protruding from their heads, looked like living lanterns.

"Here at Shadow Manse, black is the new black," Astrid said under her breath.

She found Orfeo stooped by a thatch of seaweed, clipping off fronds. A marshgrass basket was at his feet. His back was to her.

How do you greet a psycho killer? she wondered, then decided on the standard approach. "Good morning, Orfeo."

Orfeo turned, smiling. "Ah, Astrid! Good morning!" he said, straightening. "I trust you slept well?"

"Well enough," Astrid said guardedly.

"Sargassum fusiforme," he said, holding up a cutting. "Helpful in combating fin rot. One of my bull sharks has a nasty case of it."

Astrid was about to ask why he kept bull sharks, one of the ocean's fiercest predators, then realized she probably didn't want to know.

Orfeo tucked the cutting into his basket. "I was a healer once," he explained. "A long time ago. I set bones. Drew infections from wounds. Cooled fevers. Cured all kinds of diseases. Yet I couldn't save the one person who meant everything to me."

"Orfeo, I need to know why you brought me here."

Astrid expected him to try to evade the question again, but he surprised her.

"Because I want to heal *you*," he replied.

Astrid felt both frightened and compelled by the prospect. "Heal me? How?"

Orfeo placed his shears in the basket. "Tell me about your voice. Your singing voice. What happened to it?"

Astrid was surprised again. She hadn't expected a question in response to her own. "I—I lost it when I was little. Right after Månenhonnør."

"What were you doing?"

"The usual things, I guess. Playing with friends. Dancing. Eating Månenkager," Astrid replied.

She realized that Orfeo might not know what those were. "They're little round, iced cakes," she explained. "They look like the full moon. The baker drops a silver drupe into the batter, then pours the batter into the molds. Whoever gets the coin in her cake has good luck for the coming year."

Orfeo was listening raptly. "Did you get the coin?"

"No. And I didn't get any luck, either. Unless you count bad luck," Astrid said wryly.

"Did *anyone* get the coin? Any of the other children you were playing with?" Orfeo pressed.

Astrid thought back to the festival. She pictured her brother, Ragnar. Her merlfriends. That lumpsucker Tauno.

"Oddly enough, no," she finally said. "At least not that I can remember. And I think I *would* remember. Anyone who gets a coin always makes a big deal out of it." She wondered why she'd never thought about this before.

"May I feel your throat?" Orfeo asked. His eyes were hidden, as usual, behind his glasses, but the rest of his face had taken on an intense look.

"Why do you want to heal me? What do you want in return?" Astrid asked warily. "Maybe you *don't* want to heal me. Maybe you want to choke the life out of me instead. Is *that* the reason I'm here? So you can kill me? Then there will be only five of us left, and your plan to unleash your pet monster will be that much easier." Her words were blunt. The time for beating around the coral was over.

As she spoke, a look of pain sliced across Orfeo's face. "I would never hurt you, Astrid. *Never*," he said. "I only want to help you. Can't you see that, you foolish mermaid?"

For a few seconds, Astrid's defenses slipped. The longing to sing again was so deep, so desperate, that she pushed her fears aside and with a quick nod, gave her assent. A second later, she felt Orfeo's hands on her throat. She tried not to flinch as his fingers probed the soft area under her jaw, then worked their way down her neck. She felt him press along the right side of her larynx, then the left. She gasped.

"Painful?" Orfeo asked.

"Very," Astrid rasped.

"Here?" He gently pressed again.

"Yes!" Astrid cried out, slapping his hand away. She coughed, and a metallic taste filled her mouth.

"Astrid, listen to me. You need to be very brave, and very still. Can you do that?"

"Why?"

"So I can give you your magic back."

Astrid looked at him uncertainly.

"Trust me, child. You have to *trust* me."

Trust you? Are you out of your mind? she was about to shout.

But the words died in her throat, because she found, bewilderingly, that she *did* trust him. Maybe it was the blood they shared. Maybe it was instinct. *Something* was telling her that Orfeo meant what he was saying—that he would heal her, if she would let him.

"Okay," she said in a quavery voice.

Orfeo placed his thumbs on either side of her voice box. He took a steadying breath, then squeezed in and up at the same time.

Astrid screamed. Her body went rigid. She tried to get her breath but couldn't.

"Cough, Astrid!" Orfeo commanded.

But Astrid barely heard him.

Wrong, I was wrong . . . oh, gods . . . he's killing me! her mind shrieked.

"Cough, Astrid. *Now!*" Orfeo shouted.

Astrid brought up a thick, choking mass, and spat it out.

"Again!" Orfeo ordered.

Blood filled Astrid's mouth. She spat it out, but more came.

Orfeo was still shouting, but she couldn't hear him. She was conscious of nothing but pain.

It was a trick. Orfeo *had* lured her here to kill her. She was his enemy, a mermaid who'd vowed to destroy Abbadon, his creation. Why would he ever want to help her?

Astrid tried to swim away, but she faltered and fell forward. Ebony anemones loomed up at her. Tiny lights bobbed before her eyes. Her hands sank into the soft, deep sea silt.

The dark waters of Orfeo's garden swirled around her, closing in.

And then the world, and everything in it, went black.

SIXTEEN

"*MEU DEUS*, does it ever *stink* in this swamp!" Ava whispered.

Baby growled his agreement. He was a few feet ahead of her. Ava could always tell where he was by the noises he made.

The stench of decay swirled all around them. Ava tried to pass it off as just fallen cypress leaves rotting in the water. But the smell was so strong, it was like a living thing, moving all around her.

It's them, the Okwa Naholo, she thought grimly. *I'm getting closer.*

The deeper Ava moved into the Spiderlair, the more strongly she could feel them. Ever since her visit to the Iele, and the bloodbind she'd sworn with her friends, her ability to sense things had grown. She could hear a lie in a voice now, no matter how hard the speaker tried to hide it. She could tell an ally from an enemy immediately. It was as if her heart had developed its own vision, one more penetrating than mere eyesight could ever be.

She'd seen the goodness in Manon Laveau, even though the swamp queen had tried hard to hide it. Ava understood why, though. Life in the swamps was dangerous, and sometimes a mer's survival depended upon her ability to camouflage herself, her home, and her heart.

But goodness was not what Ava was sensing now.

An old farmer named Amos, who lived alone in a shack at the edge of the Spiderlair, had told her about the Okwa Naholo. He'd seen them. Not a full-on look—that would have killed him—but a glimpse out of the corner of his eye.

Amos had heard the legend that Native American terragoggs told of the Okwa Naholo, and he'd passed it on to Ava.

Centuries ago, a cruel Choctaw warrior named Nashoba bribed the night god to blanket the earth for half a year. Under the cover of darkness, Nashoba and his followers murdered their chief and enslaved their tribe. When the long night finally lifted, the sun god saw what Nashoba had done. He called upon his brother the wind to bind the murderers' hands and push them into the swamp, where they drowned. To make sure they could never escape, the wind god whirled together cypress branches, swamp mud, and the bones and teeth of dead things to form giant spiders, and then placed them along the swamp's banks.

Okwa Naholo meant *white people of the water* in Choctaw, Amos had told Ava, and over the centuries, the swamp had rotted away the warriors' flesh, turning them into skeletons. But under each set of white ribs, a black, bloated heart beat on. It was those hearts, and the memories of the evil deeds they contained, that killed anyone who glimpsed the spirits.

"Go back, you dang fool child!" Amos had urged Ava. But she wouldn't, so he'd packed her some food, given her his lucky gator foot, and then sent her on her way.

That had been a full day ago. Judging by the increasing strength of the horrible stench, Ava figured she was well into the Okwa's waters now.

"You ready?" she whispered to Baby.

After the bloodbind, Ava had received some of Ling's ability with languages. She'd immediately put her new talent to use by trying to reason with the little piranha, but since the noises Baby made were mostly yips, growls, and barks, it was difficult. He understood Ava, though—when it suited him.

"Remember to swim low," she instructed him. "Get into the cypress roots as fast as you can, and whatever you do, *mano*, don't look at them. They're coming. Hurry!"

Baby circled Ava twice, nipped her ear—a sign of affection—and sped off.

"Great Neria, protect him," Ava whispered.

The Okwa Naholo wouldn't be able to see the little fish—that was something. Baby was invisible. At least, Ava hoped he was. Since she couldn't see, she couldn't be certain. She'd given him the transparensea pebble that Vrăja had given her. "Hold it in your mouth," she'd advised him. He'd promptly swallowed it. Sighing, she'd cast the spell and hoped for the best.

Invisibility would help him, and so would his own bad vision. Piranhas' eyes, Ava knew, were on the sides of their heads—which meant they could not see what was directly in front of them. That blind spot would keep him safe from any Okwa Naholo approaching head-on. Eventually, though, the spirits would surround her. Hopefully, Baby would be in the cypress roots by then and out of harm's way. Once he'd found what she'd told him to look for, he'd have to close his eyes and navigate back to her by sound. That wouldn't be too difficult, because piranhas had excellent hearing.

As soon as Baby was gone, Ava felt it—a wave of despair so strong, it made her sick. As nausea roiled in her stomach, she heard a voice.

"Are you lost, mermaid?" it asked.

The voice was kindly, but Ava sensed darkness under the sympathetic tone. It was the voice you heard on a deserted current when you'd swum too far or taken a wrong turn. When it was too late to turn back. To swim away. To scream for help.

Show no fear, Ava told herself, turning to the thing that had spoken.

"You are *so* sweet for asking, *amigo*!" she trilled, pressing a hand to her chest. "I *am* lost. I've had a lovely little swim through the swamp, but now I'm trying to make my way back to the Gulf and I must've gone the wrong way, because here I am! But now you've come along. I mean, am I lucky or *what?*"

Ava was babbling madly. She needed to keep talking to give Baby time to find Nyx's talisman. That was their plan.

Ava would distract the Okwa Naholo, and Baby would search for the ruby ring. Merrow had given the talisman to these spirits to make sure no one else could ever lay hands on it. No doubt the Okwa had hidden it well, but the deft little fish was perfectly suited to darting in and out of the twining cypress roots.

"Perhaps I, too, can help you find your way," another voice offered.

"That would be awesome, *mano!*" Ava said. The stench of decay was so powerful now it nearly made her gag.

Come on, Baby! she silently urged the piranha. *Where* are *you?*

"I have a map here, but I think you're going to need to take off your sunglasses to read it," a third voice said silkily.

Ava feigned regret. "Sorry, *querida*, but that won't do me any good. I can't see your map. I'm blind as a barnacle. Perhaps you could, um . . . *tell* me the right direction?"

Where on earth is Baby? she wondered frantically. *What if he doesn't find the ring?*

The temperature of the swamp water dropped again. The Okwa were angry. Ava could feel it. They kept talking, and though their words were still polite, their voices had an edge. More of them came. They moved closer to her. She started to lose her nerve, then remembered that their hands were bound.

As she burbled on, another deeper wave of despair hit her. It was followed by a jolt of panic. A wash of desperation. An avalanche of fear. She didn't know where these feeling were coming from. As she struggled to cope with them, her words trailed away, and she started to see images in her mind. One was of a terragogg running away.

Another was of a woman begging on her knees. A third showed a man screaming.

Ava's breath caught as she realized that she was feeling exactly what Nashoba's victims had felt and seen—right before he'd killed them. The Okwa Naholo couldn't kill her through her eyes, so they were using her heart.

"Is there something wrong?" one of them asked, with sugary concern. "You've suddenly turned so pale!"

Ava couldn't speak. The visions grew worse. It seemed as if she was witnessing the deaths of every one of Nashoba's victims. Keening with grief, she sank slowly through the water. The thick ooze on the bottom of the swamp clutched at her. She no longer cared about the ring. She didn't care if she lived or died. She only wanted the suffering to stop. She didn't want to feel the victims' pain and terror. She didn't want to feel anything.

But she did. A piercing pain.

Not in her heart.

On her backside.

SEVENTEEN

"*O*W!" AVA SCREECHED.

She heard growling. There was another pain, this time on her shoulder. It felt like tiny knives. Like . . .

"Baby!" Ava breathed.

A bite on her arm brought her back to her senses. A harder one got her moving. With a cry, she wrenched herself free of the mud.

Nashoba and the other Okwa tried to enclose her in a circle. She could feel them all around her. Their black hearts beat loudly, and their voices thrummed in her head. Her hands scraped against their bones as she pushed her way through them, tearing ribs apart, knocking jaws off. Her powerful tail broke legs and spines.

And then she was high up in the water over them, swimming free. Their voices receded. The images faded.

Ava was sobbing with relief when she felt something jab her in the back. It was bristly and rough. It jabbed her again, then hooked her sleeve and pulled her to the surface.

"The spiders!" she cried. *"No!"*

As her head broke the water, more bristly legs swiped at her, each tipped with a claw. The spiders were scurrying along the banks of the swamp, hoping to catch their dinner. Ava could hear them crashing through the vegetation. Sticky strands of spider silk trailed over her face. Screaming, she tried to pull her arm away. The spider's claw ripped through her sleeve, freeing her. She dove back down into

SEA SPELL

94

the water, her heart pounding. Baby, barking madly, zipped off. Ava followed the sound, swimming low and fast, and didn't stop until she was well out of the Spiderlair. Then she sat down on a rock to catch her breath. She was lucky to be alive, and she knew it, but she was devastated. She hadn't obtained the ring. Baby hadn't had enough time to search for it. She'd blown her one chance; the Okwa Naholo wouldn't give her another.

All along, she'd been telling herself that the gods had chosen her to get the ruby ring, and that this was why they'd taken her eyesight. What was she supposed to believe now? That she'd lost her vision for no reason at all? Could the gods be that cruel? And how would she tell the others that she'd failed? She couldn't bear to disappoint them.

"What am I going to do?" she said aloud, a hitch in her voice.

She didn't have an answer, but Baby did. He swam up to Ava and slapped his tail fins against her face.

"Oh!" she yelped, her hand going to her smarting cheek. "You *bad* fish! What are you *doing?*"

Baby did it again. Ava, furious, grabbed for him. Her hands closed on his little body and that's when she felt it—the ring. He was wearing it on the narrow base of his tail. He must've found it, then somehow threaded his fins through the shank.

"Baby!" she shouted. "You *did* find it!"

The little piranha folded his fins together, and Ava carefully slipped the ring from his tail. As soon as it was off, Baby yipped and swam around in excited circles.

"Brave fish!" Ava said admiringly. She pulled the piranha to her and kissed him on the lips. Baby purred.

Ava then felt the ring with her fingers. The shank was heavy; the ruby was large, with many facets. She could feel the ring's power radiating into her hand.

"We have to keep this safe," she said, slipping it into a pocket inside her bag. Ava was exhausted from her ordeal and felt as if she could fall asleep right where she was, sitting on top of a cold hard rock. But she couldn't allow herself to rest. Not yet. Only part of her task was complete. She'd secured the ring, yes, but now she had to get it to Sera, and it was a long way from the Mississippi River to the North Sea.

Groaning with fatigue, she rose. "Come on, Baby," she said. "Let's see if we can find Amos's house again. We're going to need food to get us through the next few days. Maybe he has some nice juicy swamp leeches to sell us, or some alligator eggs."

As Ava and Baby put distance between themselves and the Spiderlair, Ava's weariness disappeared, and her spirits lifted.

We did it! she thought. *We actually got the ring.* Ava allowed herself to feel proud of her accomplishment. This *was* the reason the gods had taken her sight. They'd done it so she could go into the swamps and best the Okwa Naholo. Had she not been blind, she never would have survived them.

Ava and Baby didn't have far to swim before they found themselves back at Amos's. Baby saw the shack, took hold of Ava's unripped sleeve, and pulled her toward it.

Ava was glad. "Maybe Amos will let us spend the night here," she said. "Then we could get a fresh start in the morning." The idea of a warm waterfire, a soft bed, and a good night's sleep was very appealing.

Ava misjudged the location of the porch and bumped into the decking. She righted herself, then felt for the door.

"Amos?" she called out, pushing it open. The rusty hinges squeaked loudly. Amos had told her to go right on inside if she ever came calling again. *I'm always out workin' in the back. Can't hear ya knockin',* he'd said.

"Amos?" Ava called again, swimming inside the tiny shack.

Baby growled low in his throat, then launched into a volley of barking.

"Baby? What's going on? What's wrong?"

Ava heard a sharp yip of pain. And then nothing.

"Baby?" she called out, alarmed. "*Baby?* Amos, are you there? What's happening?"

"Amos *isn't* here, I'm afraid," said a voice, startling her. "Ava Corajoso, I presume? At last we meet."

"Who—who are you?" Ava cried, frightened now.

"How very rude of me. Allow me to introduce myself. My name is Markus Traho."

EIGHTEEN

"**Y**OU BIG *DUMSKALLE*!" Skrovlig the goblin said, punching her coworker Rök playfully. "I knew you wouldn't get it."

Rök, his brow knit in concentration, groaned in frustration. *"Pokkers!"* he swore in his language, before changing to mer. "You're as much of a *dumskalle*, Skro. You couldn't get it either."

"Let *me* have a try," said Groft, another goblin, taking the puzzle ball from Rök.

The goblins had been building tent frames in preparation for the long journey to the Southern Sea. Ling had swum by just as they were taking a lunch break, her head down, her hands working the spheres of Sycorax's talisman.

"Hey, Ling, is that the puzzle ball?" Skrovlig had called out. "Let's have a look at it!"

Ling had swum to the goblin and put the talisman in her hands.

"The whole camp's talking about this thing," Groft had said, as she watched Skrovlig try to solve it. "I heard there's something magical in the center of it. An Arrow of Judgment."

"That's what the historians believe," Ling said, pleased that the rumors she'd started in the HQ cave had spread. As Groft turned and twisted the inner spheres now, Ling explained what the Arrow did. "Can you imagine?" she said. "A device that can tell if a person's innocent or guilty? How cool is *that*?"

"Super cool," Skrovlig replied.

Ling kept talking about the Arrow and its legendary powers. Her plan wouldn't work unless everyone in the camp knew about it. Sera was away; she'd gone to see Guldemar, to ask him for more troops. Ling hoped to have found the spy by the time she returned.

"I've got it!" Groft suddenly shouted, grinning. But almost immediately her face fell. "Wait . . . no, I don't." She tried again, scowling the whole time, then looked up. "Hey, I know! Let's get a hammer and smash it!"

"Um, maybe not," Ling said, quickly taking the puzzle ball back. "But thanks for your help. If you know any good puzzle solvers, tell them to come and—"

But Ling's words were cut off.

"Hey, guys? Aren't you supposed to be working? Those tent frames aren't going to build themselves."

The goblins turned in the direction of the brisk, disapproving voice. Ling did, too.

"Hey, Becca," she said, trying to mask her frustration at being interrupted.

Becca was holding a clipboard. "According to my schedule, the frames should've been completed *yesterday*."

"We had to wait for a shipment of nails to arrive," Rök said defensively. "They only got here this morning."

"Fine, but now that you have the nails, I really don't think you should be goofing off," Becca admonished.

Groft crossed her arms. "We're on our lunch break, you know," she said defiantly. "If we want to help Ling solve this thing instead of eating, that's our business."

"It's my business, too," Becca insisted. "We're on a tight schedule, and I'm responsible for getting this project done, and done on time, and I—"

Rök interrupted her. "Look, Becca . . . I *volunteered* to help with the frames. I don't need this silt," he said. Then he stalked off.

"Wait . . . you're not leaving, are you? You *can't* leave!" Becca cried. But that's exactly what all three of them did. "Great. Just great," Becca huffed, watching them go. "Goblins! They're *so* undisciplined."

"You're wrong, Becca," Ling countered. "They *are* disciplined, but they hate being ordered around. Most people do, whether they're mer or goblin. You'd know that if you took the time to talk with them, instead of *at* them."

"Ling, you don't understand. You really don't," Becca said frostily.

"You're right, I don't. I don't understand *you*. You've changed, Becca," Ling said, speaking with her usual bluntness. "You've become overbearing. And touchy. And kind of closed off."

Becca blinked at Ling. Color rose in her cheeks. Tears shimmered in her eyes.

"What's going on?" Ling asked, softening her tone. "The way you've been behaving lately . . . it's not you. Is something bothering you? Do you want to talk about it?"

Becca brushed at her eyes with the back of her hand. "Wow, Ling. Now you're the one lecturing me about how *I* should behave—"

"Whoa, there. Hold up," Ling said. "Nobody's lecturing anyone."

"Maybe you should look at yourself," Becca said. "Everyone in the entire camp is working flat out to get ready to go to the Southern Sea, and you're playing with the puzzle ball. Which is kind of hard to take when so much needs to get done, you know?"

"I *am* working, Becca," Ling insisted. "Trust me."

Becca snorted. "Yeah, right. Did you catch the spy yet?"

"No, not yet, but—"

"Well, don't strain yourself playing with your toy, okay? If you decide you *do* want to do some work, find me. I've got plenty. Later," Becca said, and then, with an angry flip of her tail, she swam away.

Ling winced. "Ouch." She sighed. "*That* went well."

She watched her friend wind her way through the camp, then disappear behind a boulder.

She's hurting, Ling thought. *Otherwise, she never would have snapped like that. She's in pain. I wonder what's causing it.*

And then Ling's heart lurched. Just days ago she'd told Sera that the *spy* was in pain. And that the spy was someone close to her—very close.

"No, not Becca," Ling whispered. "It *can't* be her. Please gods, no."

It would kill Sera if Becca had betrayed them. It would kill *all* of them.

Ling looked down at the talisman resting on her palm, knowing now that it might lead her not only to an enemy, but to a friend. For an instant, her resolution faltered; she felt paralyzed. When the spy was caught, he—or she—would be taken before a military tribunal. If found guilty, he'd be sentenced to death by firing squad.

Could I do it? Ling asked herself. *Could I turn in a friend knowing she might be executed?*

She worked the spheres of the puzzle ball, as if they might give her the answer, but they didn't.

Vallerio knows we don't have a lava seam, enough food, or enough troops. If I don't catch the spy soon, he'll attack again, and maybe this time he'll send a thousand death riders instead of a hundred, she thought. *I have to keep trying to find the spy, even if he or she turns out be one of us.*

A noisy group of goblins approached her now.

Ling knew what she had to do. With a heavy heart, she looked up at them.

"Hey!" she called out, pasting a smile on her face. "Are any of you good with puzzles?"

NINETEEN

ASTRID FELT as though she were crawling out of a deep pit.

She tried to open her eyes, but the light was blinding. She tried to call for help but couldn't form the words. And all the while, the terrible pain in her throat clutched at her, trying to drag her back down into unconsciousness.

A voice, low and concerned, pushed at her through the darkness. "Astrid? Can you hear me? Are you in pain?"

"Yes," she managed to croak.

"I have medicine. Can you sit up? I'll help you."

Astrid felt strong arms lifting her body, taking her weight effortlessly. Pillows were plumped behind her, and she was eased back against them. Her head felt so heavy, but she managed to lift it and open her eyes. She saw that she was in her room in Shadow Manse. She was wearing a sea-flax nightgown and lying in a bed filled with soft black anemones.

Orfeo sat on the edge, his brow creased with worry. "Drink this," he said, handing her a glass containing a heavy, murky green liquid. "I'd advise getting it down all in one go. It tastes terrible."

Astrid knew she should be wary of the drink; Orfeo was capable of doing great harm. But she was in too much agony to care. She took the glass with trembling hands and swallowed its contents, grimacing as she did. It *was* terrible, but it was also effective. Her pain quickly receded.

As it did, Astrid found she could think again. Images came back to her. She remembered Orfeo's hands on her throat, the frightening bloody taste in her mouth, and then agony.

"What happened to me?" she rasped, handing him the empty glass. "What did you do?"

Orfeo didn't answer her right away. Instead, he brushed some hair out of her face and pressed his palm to her forehead, as tenderly as a fond father. When he'd satisfied himself that she was not feverish, he reached into his pocket and pulled out a small dark object. He held it up, pinched between his thumb and forefinger, so she could see it.

Astrid peered at the object. It was a silver drupe. "I don't understand," she said, looking from the coin to him.

"You coughed this up," he explained, placing the drupe on her palm. "It's from the Månenkager you ate when you were little. Remember how you told me that no one got the coin? *You* got it. You swallowed it, and it lodged in your voice box. It was pressed against your vocal cords, preventing them from vibrating in the way that they must for songcasting."

Astrid was so stunned she couldn't speak. All these years, all these sad, hard, lonely years, she'd thought that there was something wrong with her. *Everyone* had thought so. And all along, her inability to sing had been caused by a coin from a cake.

A question formed in her heart. *Can I sing again?* she wondered, but she tamped the hope down. She ached to know the answer but was terrified it might not be the one she wanted to hear. Instead, she coolly said, "That changes things."

Orfeo smiled. He closed her hand around the coin. "It changes *everything.*"

He stood, then walked to a table on the far side of the room. Astrid's belongings had been unpacked and laid out on top of it. He ran a hand over them—her backpack, her parka, her sword, her dagger . . . and her whalebone pipe.

As Astrid watched, he picked up the pipe and broke it over his knee.

"Hey!" she croaked, furious. "What are you doing?"

Astrid loved that pipe; it was her most prized possession. Becca had made it for her so she could express her magic even though she couldn't sing, and now Orfeo had destroyed it.

"A *pipe*?" he said disdainfully. "For a child of Orfeo?"

Astrid continued to protest. She tried to get out of bed, but as she did, her head began to spin.

"Lie back down," Orfeo ordered. "Sleep now. Your body needs to heal."

"Can't sleep . . ." she murmured, her eyes fluttering closed. "Have to . . . I have to . . ."

What? She had to do something, something very important, but what was it?

The medicine was making her drowsy. She shouldn't have drunk it. The gods only knew what Orfeo had put in it.

She forced her eyes open. They came to rest on him, and the pearl strung around his neck. Morsa's pearl—*that* was it. She was supposed to get the pearl. That's why she'd come here.

She lurched forward. She would take it right now. She would snatch the pearl, grab her sword off the table, and escape from Shadow Manse.

But before she could even swing her tail out of her bed, exhaustion overpowered her. Her eyes closed. Her head lolled against her shoulder. She felt hands on her again. Orfeo's hands, gentle and strong. They eased her back against her pillow.

"Rest, Astrid. Sleep."

Yes, rest. She would rest first. Get her strength back. And *then* she would take the pearl.

"Soon," she whispered, as sleep folded its black cloak around her. "I'll get it, Sera, I promise . . . *soon*."

TWENTY

GULDEMAR, CHIEFTAIN of the Meerteufel, was not amused.

He sat on his throne, which was cast in the image of Hafgufa, the fearsome kraken. Hafgufa's iron coils supported him; her massive head, poised to strike, canopied his own. Legend had it that Meerteufel chieftains could summon the kraken in times of peril.

Stickstoff, head of the Meerteufel's military, was doing most of the talking.

"You've come to ask us for *more* troops?" he drawled.

"Yes," Serafina replied. "Fifty thousand."

Stickstoff, together with the rest of the court, burst into laughter. Guldemar did not join them.

Sera floated motionlessly in front of the chieftain, enduring the mocking. Her head was high, her back was straight. She was not wearing a crown, or a beautiful gown, as she had the last time she'd traveled to Scaghaufen. Instead she'd worn her Black Fin uniform— a navy jacket with black trim. It reflected what she now was—a warrior-queen dressed for battle. Yazeed and Desiderio had accompanied her. They wore their uniforms, too, and their hair had been cut short for the occasion.

"*Why* do you want the additional soldiers?" Stickstoff demanded when the laughter had died down.

"Because I don't have enough soldiers to defeat my uncle's forces," Sera replied.

"Is that the only reason?" Guldemar asked, eyeing her closely. "The currents carry rumors. Mer in Kandina talk of a prison camp. A dragon queen complains bitterly that her moonstone was stolen. The Williwaw shrieks endlessly for a gold coin. The mer realms fall one by one to Vallerio. Only a fool would not wonder if there's any connection."

Sera knew he was asking her for the truth, but the truth was a lethal commodity. She didn't want to lie to him, but neither could she answer his question. Not in front of the entire goblin court. As she deliberated, Guldemar spoke again.

"I see. You ask for my help, you demand my trust . . . yet you do not trust me." He spat into one of the lava pools that bubbled on either side of his throne. "And so it has always been between Meerteufel and mer," he added bitterly.

Guldemar was referring to the uneasy relations between the two peoples. The goblins were intimidating in appearance and manner and tended to frighten the mer. Sera, who had twenty thousand Meerteufel troops in the Karg, was learning that in addition to possessing great reserves of fierceness and courage, goblins were also loyal, hardworking, and kind, but bringing about a better understanding between the Meerteufel and mer was a task that would require a great deal of time, and Sera had none. She knew that if she wanted Guldemar's help, she would have to show that she trusted him. Right now. She'd have to tell him about Orfeo and Abbadon. There was no other way.

It was risky, though. What if, after listening to her, he sided with Vallerio and Orfeo? Any sane person would. Their might and magic dwarfed her own. And then there were the talismans. They were powerful objects. What if Guldemar wanted them for himself? He might attack her camp and take the ones she and her friends had found.

Sera decided she would tell Guldermar everything, but only him.

She started toward the throne. Immediately, a dozen goblin guards advanced on her. Desiderio and Yazeed rushed to defend her.

Guldemar held up a hand, stopping everyone. "Approach, Serafina," he commanded.

Sera swam to him. Light flickered in the kraken's eyes as she did, startling her. For a moment, she was certain the creature was alive, but then she realized the light was only an illusion. The kraken's eyes were fashioned from obsidian; they reflected the lava's glow.

When Sera was close enough to Guldemar that he alone could hear her, she told him that her fight with her uncle was only the beginning, and that a greater battle lay ahead. She told him everything—starting with Vrăja's summons, and ending with Ling's discovery that the terragogg Rafe Mfeme was really Orfeo.

"That's why I need the additional troops, Guldemar," she added as she finished. "So that I can make it to the Southern Sea, where I mean to destroy Abbadon."

Guldemar said nothing. He just stroked his tusks thoughtfully. Sera waited for him to answer, but before he could, Stickstoff, annoyed at being left out, spoke.

"Another has approached us. One who also wants Guldemar's help. One who will pay well—*very* well—for an alliance with the Meerteufel."

Sera turned to him. Stickstoff hadn't mentioned a name, but he didn't have to.

"Yes, he will," she said, with a caustic smile. "*At first*. But then he'll send his own troops here to *take* what he wants. Tread carefully with my uncle, Stickstoff. He has the might of three mer realms behind him now. What's to stop him from taking Meerteufel waters?"

Worry surfaced in Guldemar's eyes at Sera's words.

Stickstoff, however, waved them away. "We Meerteufel are quite capable of defending our territory, thank you. Our only difficulty, at present, is that we don't quite know which mer ruler to trust."

"You mean which mer ruler to *back*," Sera said cynically. "A battle's coming, you know it is, and you don't want to be on the losing side."

Stickstoff ignored that. "You say that the throne of Miromara is yours. Your cousin Lucia claims that it's hers. If only the two aggrieved parties could solve their problems by talking them through . . ." he mused, tapping a finger against his chin.

Something in his tone made Sera's fins prickle. He was up to no good, she was sure of it.

"Or better yet," he continued, smiling slyly, "by fighting to the death!"

At his signal, the doors to the stateroom were thrown open, and a merman swam through them.

"It's a trap, Sera!" Desiderio shouted, swimming to her side. Yazeed was right behind him.

Sera snapped into action. Her hand went to the hilt of the sword. Her body tensed as she prepared herself to fend off her worst enemy.

But it wasn't her uncle or Traho who swam through the doors.

It was Mahdi.

TWENTY-ONE

Serafina lifted her chin, affecting the haughtiest look she could muster.

It took every ounce of control she possessed not to race to the merman she loved and throw her arms around him. Instead, she had to pretend to hate him. To show even a flicker of warmth toward Mahdi was to put his life in the gravest danger. Her uncle undoubtedly had spies in Guldemar's court, and a report of what transpired between them would surely reach his ears.

"Principessa, you're alive!" Mahdi said, faking surprise.

"No thanks to you," Sera retorted. Her eyes were icy, her tone glacial. But behind the pretense, she was worried. Mahdi was thin. There were shadows under his eyes. His color was off. Something was wrong. She risked a glance at Yazeed. His eyes were on Mahdi, too, and she could see from his expression that he felt the same way.

Stickstoff, however, noticed nothing amiss. He was too excited over the prospect of bloodshed.

"Isn't this *wonderful*!" he crowed, clapping his hands. "We can solve this right now. Serafina, you will represent yourself, of course. His Royal Highness, the Emperor of Matali, is here as emissary for his realm, and the realm of Miromara. You both have swords, do you not? Excellent! The first one who cuts the other's head off wins. The Meerteufel will be happy to do business with the survivor."

Goblin courtiers clapped their hands and pumped their fists.

There was nothing the Meerteufel loved more than violence. Shouts of "Fight! Fight! Fight! Fight!" rose in the water.

Guldemar himself watched, but said nothing.

Sera was the first to speak. "I did not expect such treachery from the Meerteufel," she declared.

"No treachery," Stickstoff countered. "You wish to strengthen your alliance with the Meerteufel. The emperor wishes to end that same alliance and establish one of his own. This poses a problem for the Meerteufel, but a fight will solve it. Fighting is the way to solve *all* problems," he added sagely.

"I will *not* fight," Sera said. She unbuckled the scabbard that held her sword and threw it to the floor. Then, in her most regal voice, she addressed the court. "Under Regina Isabella, my mother, Miromara was not governed by the sword, but by the rule of law. And so it shall be by me. The traitors who now lead the realm—my uncle Vallerio, his wife, Portia, their daughter, Lucia . . . and this *turncoat*"—she spat the word at Mahdi—"will be tried in court when I retake my throne. If found guilty, they will be executed by the *state*, not by me."

Boos went up from the courtiers. Guldemar raised an eyebrow but remained silent. Sera had the feeling that he was weighing her response.

Sera . . . troops . . .

The voice was crackly and loud, and it was inside her head.

Sera startled at it, then fervently hoped no one had noticed. It was Mahdi. *He must've cast a convoca under his breath,* she thought. It would be a weak one because of all the iron in the stateroom—in Guldemar's throne, the many weapons, the very walls.

Mahdi, she called back, *is that you?* There was no answer. *What did you mean by troops? Are death riders nearby?*

"Principessa, what are you saying?" Mahdi asked, feigning shock. "I'm not a turncoat. And I certainly don't want to fight you. I want to take you home."

Mahdi, what's wrong? Sera asked urgently.

Danger . . . capture you . . .

Sera laughed contemptuously. "If my cousin's not a traitor, why has she taken my throne?"

"Lucia has graciously agreed to rule—at her father's request—because she thought you were dead. We all did, Principessa. How wonderful to discover we were wrong," Mahdi said.

There's something going on with you, Mahdi. I know there is. I can feel it!

Nothing . . . you, Des, Yaz . . . out of here . . .

"That is a lie," Sera countered. "My uncle knows I'm alive. He wants me, and my Black Fins, dead."

"Indeed!" Stickstoff interjected, trying to fan the waterfire. "Isn't that why Vallerio seeks our help, Mahdi? And our troops? To slaughter Serafina and her fighters?"

Mahdi chose his next words carefully. "Vallerio wants to defeat the Black Fins, yes, but only because they threaten the stability of the realm," he protested. "He never had any idea that Serafina was with them. None of us did."

"Another lie," Sera said.

Whispers went up from the courtiers. "When will the fight start?" "Someone bring the mermaid another sword!" "Somebody throw something at them!"

"Principessa, you must allow me and my soldiers to take you home," Mahdi said. "Your uncle, your cousin . . . they'll be overjoyed to see you back in Cerulea." As he spoke, he casually slid one hand into his jacket pocket.

"Yes, they will," Sera retorted. "Because it'll make it so much easier for them to kill me." She moved slightly to her right as she spoke, trying to position herself so that she could receive the convoca better. It worked.

Sera, go! Get out of here! Mahdi said. *My soldiers have orders to kill you on sight. They won't do it here. Too many witnesses. But they'll follow you.*

Sera traded glances with her brother. A quick nod from him told her that he'd heard Mahdi, too.

Still playing his part, Mahdi swam up to her. "Principessa," he said, sweeping a bow. He took her hand in both of his. "I hope you'll reconsider and allow me to escort you back to Cerulea."

As he spoke, Sera felt him press something into her palm. She curled her fingers around it, then pretended to snatch her hand away.

"Your Grace," she said, turning to Guldemar, "I'll take my leave now. Should you wish to help me instead of my enemies, you'll have my gratitude. Should you choose to do the opposite, you'll have my sympathy."

With that, she swam out of Guldemar's stateroom, followed by Yazeed and Desiderio. As the doors closed behind them, Sera opened her hand and looked down at what was in it.

A tiny sea-silk sack. As she opened it, she saw that it contained transparensea pearls. Three of them.

She handed one to Yazeed and one to Desiderio.

"As soon as we're out of the palace, we cast them—" she stared to stay.

"And haul tail back to the Karg," Yaz finished.

Sera shook her head. "No. We stay here. And find Mahdi."

"*What?* Sera, we can't. You heard him. We've got to go. We've got trouble," Desiderio said, glancing around nervously.

"I know, Des," Sera said. "But Mahdi's got more."

TWENTY-TWO

SERA WATCHED as the death riders thundered out of Guldemar's stables far below her. Each one was mounted on a powerful black hippokamp.

"They're hunting *us*," she said. "Mahdi sent them."

"He had to," said Yazeed. "If he didn't, he'd have to explain why to Vallerio."

Sera knew he was right, but it didn't make the sight any less unnerving.

"They're taking the direct route to the Kargjord," she said, her eyes following the soldiers as they rode north out of Scaghaufen.

"We'll have to take the long current back," Des said. "At least the camp is on high alert now, after Vallerio's last attack."

Sera, Yazeed, and Desiderio were swimming up the wall of the west wing of Guldemar's palace, searching for Mahdi's room. Sera was certain he'd be there. When she, Yazeed, and some of her Black Fins had spent a night in the palace before their first audience with Guldemar, they'd stayed in the west wing.

"Two more minutes, Sera," Yazeed said. "Then we're gone. We've got to be out of Scaghaufen when the pearls wear off."

Sera shot off, frantically swimming from window to window, peering in every one to see if she could spot Mahdi.

"I *need* to see him," she'd said as they'd left Guldemar's stateroom.

"That's a very bad idea," Desiderio had replied.

"Something's wrong," she said. "We have to find out what it is."

The goblin guards who'd escorted them out of Guldemar's state-room had seen them out of the main doors to the palace's front gates. The three mer had swum through them, then ducked into one of Scaghaufen's winding streets. There they'd cast their transparensea pearls, and then they'd headed straight back to the palace.

Sera continued to search for Mahdi as time ran out. She saw goblins and death riders but couldn't find Mahdi.

"That's it, Sera," Yaz said. "We've got to go."

Sera shot up, desperately looking in one last window. "There he is!" she exclaimed. "Yaz, Des, where are you?"

"Right here," the mermen answered in unison, swimming up behind her.

Mahdi was sitting at a desk, speaking into a conch. Sera's heart swelled at the sight of him, but the love she felt was once again pushed aside by worry. He looked gray and exhausted.

She was just about to rap on the window when a death rider swam in with a sheaf of kelp parchments. Mahdi, still speaking into the conch, signaled for him to put the documents on the desk. The merman did so, then left the room. As soon as he'd closed the door, Sera knocked.

Mahdi's head snapped up. An instant later, he was at the window, undoing the latch.

"Tell me it's not you," he said as he opened it. "Tell me you didn't do this."

"It is. And we did," Yazeed said.

"Wait here," Mahdi said. He swam to the door, opened it, and called for the soldier who'd delivered documents just a few moments ago.

"I'm not feeling well. Goblin delicacies don't agree with me. I'm going to lie down for a few minutes. I'm not to be disturbed," he instructed.

"Yes, Your Grace," the death rider said.

Mahdi closed the door and locked it. Sera, Desiderio, and Yazeed swam inside. Sera sang a quick songspell to undo the effects of the transparensea pearl. She was in Mahdi's arms as soon as he turned around. The two held each other for a few long seconds.

Then Mahdi released her. "How could you two let her do this?" he asked angrily.

"Have *you* ever tried to stop her from doing something she wants to do?" Desiderio asked.

Mahdi sighed. "Yeah, actually, I have," he said. "No further explanation needed."

"Mahdi, you look terrible. What's going on?" Sera asked.

"Listen, Sera . . . I just—"

"Don't give me any *Listen, Sera* silt. We don't have much time. I want the truth."

Mahdi hesitated, then said, "Lucia moved our wedding date up. It's going to take place at the next syzygy."

"My gods, that's . . . that's less than a moon away!" Sera said, stunned. "Why didn't you get word to us?"

"I didn't have time," Mahdi explained. "I planned to send you a conch from here."

"This changes things," Desiderio said grimly. "We'll need to get you out of there a lot sooner than we thought, and we don't have an escape plan set up yet."

Yaz ran a hand through his hair. "We'll need to line up safe houses; stash food, clothing, and currensea for you."

"Forget an escape plan," Sera said. "You're coming with us, Mahdi. Right now. We'll all cast transparensea pearls and make wake for the Karg."

"No," Mahdi said.

"No? What do you mean *no*? It's over. If you sing the marriage vows, they'll know you Promised yourself to me. They'll kill you."

"I'm not hightailing it. Not yet. Not until I find out the identity of the spy in your camp. I've still got time."

"Mahdi, *listen* to me," Sera begged.

"No, you listen to me, Sera. You're in danger. Way more than you know."

"Because of the spy. I know that, Mahdi. I—"

Mahdi cut her off. "What you *don't* know is that the spy's also an assassin. When Portia gives the word, he's going to take you out."

A chill crept up Sera's spine. "He can try," she said defiantly.

"According to Portia, he'll succeed," Mahdi said. "He's a good shot, and he—or she—is close to you."

"From now on, you'll have bodyguards with you around the clock," Des said.

"We have *got* to find this sea snake," said Yazeed.

"What's Portia's timeline?" Desiderio asked.

"I don't know," Mahdi said. "I do know that they want to keep the spy in place for now, though. He just told them that you intend to attack Cerulea."

"Did they believe him?" Sera asked hopefully.

"Of course," Mahdi replied. "Why wouldn't they? Every piece of info he's ever given them has been accurate. Vallerio's pulling troops out of Atlantica and the Southern Sea as we speak and bringing them back to Cerulea."

Sera and Des grinned at each other. They quietly slapped tails.

"Yes!" Yazeed whisper-cheered.

Mahdi looked at them as if they were crazy. "I just told you that Vallerio knows your plans. And that he intends to annihilate you. That's hardly a cause for celebration."

"It's a fake-out, bro!" Yazeed said. "We're going to the Southern Sea."

For the first time since Sera, Des, and Yaz had swum into his room, Mahdi smiled. "*Awesome* move," he said. "As soon as I get back,

I'll do everything I can to convince Vallerio to move even more troops out of your way."

His words caused Sera's smile to fade. "Mahdi, you *can't* go back. If they find out about you . . ." She couldn't bear to finish the thought.

"I have to, Sera. I'm your only source of information there, the only one who can warn you when Portia tells her spy to kill you."

"Mahdi's right," Desiderio said solemnly. "He's a lot more valuable to us in Cerulea than he is in the Kargjord."

Sera nodded, though it felt like she was ripping her own heart out. "If anything happens to you, I'll never forgive myself."

"It won't. I promise. I'll be gone before the wedding," Mahdi said. "And you three better get gone now." He glanced at the door to his room. "I have to head to another meeting with Guldemar soon."

Yaz nodded. "Dude, be careful," he said, reaching for Mahdi's hand. He pulled him close. The two mermen slapped each other's backs. Then Desiderio did the same.

Mahdi dug in his desk drawer and pulled out a small box. "Here are some more transparensea pearls. Take a lot. Enough to keep you invisible all the way back to the Karg."

Yaz and Des took some pearls and cast them. Sera didn't.

"I'll catch up," she said.

She couldn't leave Mahdi, not yet. It had been so long since she'd seen him, and during that time not a second had gone by that she didn't think about him, long for him, and talk to him—if only in her head. Were a few short minutes with him so much to ask for?

"Sera, it's too dangerous. You can't—" Yazeed started to say.

Desiderio cut him off. "Come on, Yaz."

Yazeed shook his head, clearly unhappy. "We'll meet you just past the north gate. Don't. Get. *Caught.*"

As soon as they were gone, Mahdi cupped Sera's cheek. She curled her fingers around his wrist.

"I barely recognize you," he said, his eyes traveling over her face.

"Who *is* this fierce warrior in front of me? What happened to the merl with the long hair, and the gowns, and the conch glued to her ear?" His voice was teasing, but the pain in his eyes was real, and raw.

Sera knew that pain well. It mirrored her own.

"Where's the merboy I once met who only wanted to play Gorgons and Galleons with my brother?" she asked. "The one who didn't talk much. Who *definitely* didn't want anything to do with the principessa his parents picked out for him. Do you think we'll ever find those mer again?"

Mahdi shook his head. "We'll find better versions of ourselves, Sera. Better than what we were, better than what we *are.*"

He gathered her into his arms then and held her close. Sera squeezed her eyes shut, trying to hold back her tears.

"*Mērē dila, mērī ātmā,*" he whispered, his cheek against hers. It was Matalin mer for *My heart, my soul.* "I'll be with you soon, Sera, I promise. Until then, be careful. *Please.*"

"Swear to me that *you'll* be careful. Swear it," Sera said fiercely.

She had a terrible, unshakable feeling that something would go wrong, that she'd never hold him close or look into his beautiful eyes again. She took his face in her hands and kissed him deeply.

It was Mahdi who broke the kiss. "You've got to leave," he said, his voice gentle but urgent. He touched his forehead to hers. "Goodbye, Sera. Never doubt that I love you," he said, and then he let her go.

Sera cast a transparensea pearl. "I love you, too, Mahdi. Always."

And then she was gone. Out of the window, out of the palace, heading for the north gate.

Desiderio and Yazeed were waiting for her there. Sera issued a series of dolphinlike clicks, and they clicked back. Then the three fighters swam fast, heading for open water.

None of them spoke until they'd left Scaghaufen far behind, then Des said, "I know you're hurting, and I'm sorry. But it'll be okay, Sera. Mahdi's smart. He's strong. He'll survive."

Sera thought about the long swim ahead of them, and the fact that Guldemar had given them nothing. She thought about the spy who was still in their midst, and the weapons and troops they lacked. She thought about the long, cold swim to the Southern Sea.

Then she laughed wearily and said, "Yeah, Des. But will *we*?"

TWENTY-THREE

"WE'RE USING SCRAP METAL salvaged from wrecks to reinforce the supply wagons," Becca explained to Sera, pointing to a pile of twisted steel. "The goblins heat it, then nail it to the sides of the wagons. The tough part is getting the metal hot enough to bend. Our songcasters are having trouble getting their waterfire to burn high enough," Becca said.

Sera frowned at this. "No luck finding a lava seam yet?" she asked.

Becca shook her head. "No, but I'm still on it. I won't give up. Come on, the actual building site's this way," she said, motioning to Sera to follow her.

The two mermaids were in the westernmost part of the camp, where wagons that would transport the Black Fins' supplies during their swim to the Southern Sea were being built. Two burly goblins walked a short distance behind them. Ever since Mahdi had told Sera, Des, and Yaz that Portia's spy was also an assassin, Des had insisted that bodyguards accompany Sera everywhere.

Sera had come to the edge of the camp to see how the work was proceeding, but there was another reason she was out here: she needed to get Becca alone.

Sera had noticed tension between Becca and Ling back at headquarters, and she'd asked Ling about it. Ling had admitted that things were strained between them. "We had a bit of a blowup," she'd said.

As Sera listened to Ling's explanation, her concern had deepened to worry. The Becca in Ling's account, so defensive and touchy, didn't sound like Becca at all.

"Something's wrong. Really wrong," she'd said to Ling.

"I know. Becca's hurting. It scares me. And not just for her sake," Ling had said. "Sera, what if . . . what if she—"

Ling didn't have to finish her sentence; Sera took her meaning. "No way, Ling. I don't believe it."

"Don't or *won't?*" Ling had asked, giving her a penetrating look.

"Don't. Won't. Can't. *Ever,*" Sera had said. "A little while ago, I lost faith in myself. It nearly did me in. You helped me swim back from the brink. Now it's my turn to help Becca. Because if the six of us lose faith in one another, we've lost everything. Becca's not the spy. I *know* she's not. But something's not right. And I'm going to get to the bottom of it."

Sera had swum through the camp to find Becca. Now that she had her, she was looking for an opening, a way to broach what was sure to be a difficult topic.

"Of course, after the wagons are built, we need to fill them," Becca said with a sigh. "We're still low on ammo, even with the shipment from the Näkki. I'm worried about that, Sera."

Sera saw the opening she needed. She plunged in. "Becca, I'm worried about *you.*"

Becca laughed. She looked startled, and a little self-conscious. "*Me?* Why? I'm totally fine."

"No, you're not. You're not yourself. Something's bothering you. I wish you'd tell me what it is."

"Really, Sera, there's nothing to tell. Sure, I've got stress, but who doesn't?" She smiled as she spoke, but the smile was forced, even desperate. "I mean, we're getting the entire resistance ready to swim to the Southern Sea. There's a lot to do, and—"

The two mermaids were still swimming. They were almost at the work site now. Sera stopped. She took her friend's hand and looked her in the eye. "Becca," she said gently, "whatever it is, you can tell me. You know that, don't you?"

Becca turned away. She looked desperate, like a creature who'd been cornered. Sera could see that she was struggling with herself. She wanted to talk but couldn't. Something was holding her back.

Finally, she spoke, but the words were not what Sera wanted to hear.

"Hey. Wow. Would you look at that? I can't *believe* those guys," she exclaimed, pulling her hand free of Sera's. "I swear, sometimes I feel like I have to do *everything* myself." She darted off to the work site.

Sera, heaving a sigh of frustration, followed her. She soon saw that the goblins who were supposed to be building wagons weren't sawing or hammering or doing much of anything. Instead they were standing in a semicircle, staring at the shallow pit they'd dug. It would be used to contain the waterfire needed to heat scrap metal, but it clearly wasn't deep enough. Some of the goblins had their hands on their hips. Others were rubbing their chins or scratching their heads. By the time Sera caught up with her friend, Becca had picked up a shovel.

"Standing around won't get any wagons built," Becca fumed.

A goblin named Styg, seeing what Becca was doing, cautioned her in his language. Sera didn't catch all of what he said, but she did hear the words *Don't!* and *Wait!*

Becca flapped a hand at him. She raised the shovel, ready to plunge it into the seabed. The goblin's eyes widened in alarm. He lunged at her, knocking the shovel out of her hands.

"Are you *kidding* me?" Becca exclaimed. "Why did you do that?" She started toward the shovel, but Styg held up a hand. He shook his head.

Becca, angry now, was ready to launch into an argument with him, but Sera stopped her. "Wait," she said. "He's trying to explain. Hear him out." Her eyes were not on Becca anymore, but on the pit.

Styg stepped forward. Switching to mer, he said, "We found a lava seam just below the surface." As he spoke, he bent down and used another shovel to carefully scrape away about half a foot of the seabed, allowing Sera and Becca to clearly see the orangey glow under the silt.

"We have to proceed very carefully," he explained. "If she"—he nodded at Becca—"had hit the seam with her shovel, it would've gushed, and none of us would have survived to tell the tale."

Becca winced. "I—I didn't know. I didn't see . . ." Her words trailed away. She looked down at her tail fins.

"The bad news is that we can't work here," Styg said. "The good news is—"

"You found a lava seam!" Sera exclaimed. "Well done, all of you!"

"I have a bubbler," said Styg. "Let's see what we've got."

"What's a bubbler?" Sera asked.

"It's a tool for releasing a tiny bit of lava. There are different grades of molten rock. *Glimrende* is the finest, but it's only good for lighting. *Sterkur* is heating grade—the strong stuff. It's what we need."

Styg pulled a sharkskin case out of his pocket. Inside was coiled a thin flexible tube with holes in it. One end had a hollow steel point; the other had a valve attached to it. Working slowly, Styg nudged the pointed end down into the lava. Then he shooed everyone back and opened the valve. A few seconds later, lava shot up into the hose and oozed out of the holes.

Styg bent down to examine it, then smiled. "Sterkur," he said happily, looking up at Sera. "Grade A-1."

"*Yes!*" Sera said, high-fiving him. "Do you know what this means?"

"That we can forge all the weapons and ammo we need," Styg said.

"And make tools," said Rök.

"We can light the entire camp," chimed in Mulmig.

"And stew our enemies," added Garstig.

Mulmig held her hands out to the bubbling lava and smiled with pleasure. "It's been *sooo* long since I felt the heat of a lava pool," she said. "Holy Kupfernickel, I missed it."

"I miss glasses of nice, thick *räkä*," Rök said wistfully.

Sera knew räkä was a drink made from fermented snail slime. Goblins were partial to it.

"And *snask*," Mulmig added. "What I wouldn't give for some right now."

"*Snask?*" Sera asked. She hadn't heard that term before.

"Pickled squid eyes," Mulmig explained. "*Soooo* good!"

Garstig, grinning, pulled a little cloth bag out of his breast pocket. "My wife sent these by manta ray," he said, opening the bag and passing it to Mulmig. "Have some."

Mulmig's eyes widened as she looked in the bag. "*Snask!*" she said excitedly. "Garstig, thank you!" She popped one in her mouth and chewed it, rolling her eyes with pleasure.

"Why don't we sit down by the lava for a minute?" Styg suggested. "We need to figure out how best to channel the seam, and we might as well be warm while we're doing it."

"Hang on a minute. . . ." Becca said, as the goblins moved toward the lava.

Oh, no, Sera thought. *She's going to scold them, or tell them to get back to work.*

Her heart sank. As a leader, Sera knew that these small moments cemented the bonds between soldiers. They might cost a few minutes, but they repaid that investment tenfold by bolstering morale. Becca undoubtedly thought they were a waste of time.

But Becca surprised her.

"Before you sit down, I need to apologize," she said.

Eyebrows shot up. The goblins looked amazed. Sera did, too.

"I didn't trust you to do your jobs, and I should have. You found the lava seam we desperately needed. And," she said sheepishly, "you stopped me from killing us all. I'm sorry. And thank you."

The goblins nodded in acceptance and appreciation. Sera smiled at Becca. Becca smiled back, then turned and started to swim away. Sera swam after her.

"Hey," Sera said, as she caught up to her friend. "I'm going to sit with the goblins for a minute. Why don't you join us?"

"Sorry, I can't," Becca said. "I have so many things to do."

"Sure, okay," Sera said, disappointed. She'd been so certain that she'd be able to get Becca to confide in her. "I'll see you later."

"Yeah, later," Becca said.

But then, as Sera was about to return to the goblins, Becca reached out and touched her arm. "Listen, Sera . . . there's something else I need to apologize for. My, um, bossiness. I know it's been over-the-top. I'll try to take it down a notch."

Sera decided to try one last time. "Becca, whatever's going on with you, it's about more than bossiness. *Talk* to me. Please."

Becca backed away. "I—I can't, Sera. I just *can't*," she said helplessly. "And you don't want me to, trust me. Because it's bad. Really bad."

A cold dread seized Sera. For an instant, she wondered if Ling was right. Could Becca be the spy? But she quickly pushed that thought from her mind.

"Becca, we're dealing with a spy, food shortages, and a coming war," she said. "Oh, and an unstoppable monster, too. Almost forgot about him. Is your thing *really* worse than all of that?"

Becca hesitated. In her eyes, Sera could see fear warring with trust. She hoped with all her heart that trust would win.

Becca clenched her fists. All in a rush, she said, "I'm in love with Marco. And he's in love with me."

Sera blinked, barely able to believe what she'd just heard. "Is *that* what all this is about?" she asked. "Marco from the infirmary? The cute doctor? Why would that upset you so much? He's wonderful!"

Becca pressed her palms to her eyes. "Um, no, Sera. Not *that* Marco."

"Hmm," Sera said, puzzled. "I don't know any other Marco."

"Actually, you do."

"No, I really don't, Becs. I mean, there's Marco the duca's son...." She laughed. Marco was a human. One of the good ones. He'd saved Becca from the Williwaw. "But of course it's not him," she added. "Because you wouldn't ... he wouldn't ...." She stopped talking. Her smile faded. "Oh, *no*. Holy silt, Becca."

"Exactly," Becca said miserably. "It's a total disaster. He's the most wonderful boy I've ever met. He's good and decent and kind, and it's all wrong. No one in *my* world would accept him, and no one in *his* world is even supposed to know I exist."

"Hold on a minute," Sera said. "It's not wrong to love someone who's good and decent and kind just because someone else disapproves."

Becca raised an eyebrow. "Really? Then why did you say 'Oh, no'?"

"Because it's also not easy. If you and Marco are serious about each other, you're both going to face some pretty rough waters." Sera put an arm around her. "But you don't have to face them alone. You have me and the others. We'll help you figure it out. That's what friends are for."

"Really?" Becca asked. The look on her face was heartbreakingly vulnerable.

"Really," Sera replied. "Talk to them. You'll see."

Becca nodded tentatively. Sera could tell she was still worried. "I hope they understand, Sera. Compared to me, everyone else has normal relationships."

Sera laughed. "Right. Especially me. I'm the queen of normal relationships. The merman I love is about to marry someone else. We have to pretend to hate each other. And his future wife is trying to kill me. *Totally* normal."

Becca burst out laughing. For the first time since she'd arrived in the camp, the worry lines that constantly creased her forehead disappeared.

"Hey, Serafina, Becca . . . want some *snask?*" Garstig shouted. "You better hurry up if you do, before Mulmig scarfs it all." He waved them over. The goblins made space for them around the lava.

"Come on," Sera said, "let's join them. I'm developing quite a taste for goblin treats."

As Sera and Becca sat down, plans for building a forge and melting down shipwreck hulls were being eagerly discussed. The bag of snask was passed around, and Sera helped herself to a piece. She heard Vrăja's voice in her head, and in her heart. *Help Becca see that the warmest fire is the one that's shared*, the river witch had said.

As Sera watched Becca gamely pop a pickled eyeball into her mouth, she silently thanked Vrăja, then she watched the warmth of friendship work its own magic.

TWENTY-FOUR

MANON LAVEAU'S black eyes glittered. From within the roots of the giant cypress where she was hiding, in the waters off Robichaux's Swamp, she could spy the death riders' camp. At its edge was a cage with iron bars. In that cage was a mermaid, lying motionless, her face turned away.

"I see two guards," Manon said quietly. "Louis, Antoine, you take the one in the front. Rene, Gervais, you've got the back. Quick and quiet now, and *don't* swallow the keys. You hear me?"

Four enormous bull alligators nodded in unison; then, with thrusts of their powerful tails, they swam off.

As Manon watched them go, a shiver ran through her. She pulled her shawl up around her neck. "I hope those boys listened. Gods help us if they make a racket."

"The gods help those who help themselves," Esmé said primly, waving away silt that the alligators had raised.

Manon snorted. "Says who? The gods, that's who. I do all the work, and they take all the credit. Laziest bunch of good-for-nothings I ever came across."

"This'll never work," said Jean Lafitte, wringing his hands. "The guards will shout for help. We'll be caught and thrown in a cage ourselves. And then they'll hang us from the gallows."

Manon rolled her eyes. "What do you care if you hang? You're a ghost!"

"Why'd we come here? This is *such* a bad idea!" Lafitte fretted.

"You want to leave that poor mermaid to the tender mercies of Captain Traho?" Manon asked.

"Yes, I do. Absolutely," said Lafitte.

"Shh!" Sally scolded. "They're almost at the cage."

Manon and the three ghosts watched as the alligators moved into place. Louis crawled up to the guard in front and growled. The guard, who'd been dozing, jerked awake. His eyes grew as round as moon jellies.

"Holy silt! Vincenzo, there's a giant gator here!" he whisper-shouted. "How the—"

"There's one here, too!" the other guard whispered back, as Rene advanced. "Don't make it mad. Just reach for your speargun . . . nice and slow, then—"

But before the guards even got their hands on their holsters, Antoine and Gervais struck. Two headless bodies sank to the swamp floor. As the alligators proceeded to feast, Manon moved in. The ghosts trailed her.

"Be careful, Manon! Those gators are feeding! Don't get in between them!" Lafitte cautioned.

Manon paid him no heed. She tugged one body away from the alligators, then the other, turning them over in the water, searching for the keys to the mermaid's cage. But they were nowhere to be found.

"How did I miss them?" she whispered.

"Maybe they fell on the ground," Sally ventured.

Manon flipped her tail fins over the swamp floor, clearing away the silt, but she still didn't find the keys.

Lafitte bit his nails. "This is taking too long! You haven't even opened the cage yet. What if someone comes?"

Then one of the alligators burped. It sounded like thunder.

Manon straightened. She put her hands on her hips and gave the creature a look. "Gervais, don't tell me . . . you *did*, didn't you?"

The alligator started coughing like a cat with a hairball. After a few seconds of heaving, he brought up an iron ring with several skeleton keys on it. Manon wrinkled her nose as she picked it up, shook off the gator spit, then tried one key after another until she found the one that opened the cage's lock.

All this time, the mermaid inside remained motionless. The only sign that she was alive was the way her rib cage expanded ever so slightly as she breathed.

The swamp queen bent down to her. "Ava? Child, it's me, Manon. I've got Sally, Jean, and Esmé with me. We've come to get you out of here."

"What's the use?" Ava asked in a small voice.

"Did you get the ruby ring?"

"Yes, but Traho took it from me. I failed."

Manon gently moved a few of Ava's braids out of her face. "Oh, Ava, failing's just failing. It's not a reason to quit," she said. "I fail all the time. Why, I failed a hundred times since yesterday. I failed to pack enough food for this trip, I failed in my choice of traveling attire—"

"Manon, we should go. I *hear* something!" Lafitte whimpered.

"—and I'm failing to keep this whiny pirate quiet," Manon finished, glaring at him.

She turned back to Ava and took her face in her hands. "Just because you failed today doesn't mean you've failed forever. Falling down doesn't mean anything. It's the staying down that does you in."

Ava rolled onto her back. "It's over for me. Please, Manon, just go."

Manon rose. She took a deep breath. "Child, are you dead?"

Ava shook her head.

"Then it's *not* over. But it will be if Traho catches us here. Now get *up!*" Manon said, hauling Ava off the floor. She led her out of the cage, then stopped. "Where's that little monster of yours?" she asked, looking around for Baby.

"They killed him," Ava said, tears welling in her eyes. "They didn't have to. He was only trying to protect me. H-he was so little."

Manon's eyes flashed. Her chin jutted.

"Uh-oh," Lafitte said ominously. "Swamp queen just got angry."

Manon gave a low whistle, and twenty more alligators came crawling out of the cypresses.

"Pick 'em off, boys," she said. "Tent by tent. Just don't get yourselves shot."

The alligators grinned, then crawled off into the camp.

"Armand!" Manon called out.

The largest alligator turned back to her.

"Catch up when you're done, you hear? I still need you boys."

Armand nodded, then swam to catch up with the others.

"You ready?" Manon asked.

"Where are we going?" Ava asked.

"To your friends in the North," Manon replied. "We're taking you there, Ava. Since Baby can't."

"Wait a minute . . . the *North?*" Lafitte said, a look of horror on his face. "You never said anything about going north, Manon Laveau! I *hate* the North!"

"It's cold there. There's snow and ice!" Sally protested.

"And there aren't any pickled crayfish, or spiced shrimp, or cups of cattail coffee!" Esmé cried. "I'll never survive!"

"You don't have to. You're dead," Manon said. Then she put her arm around Ava's shoulders. "We have to move. Have to make the Gulf by morning, just in case my gators don't get every last one of those no-good death riders. You ready?"

Ava nodded. Manon was glad to see a little spirit trickling back into her.

"Where there's life, there's hope," Esmé said sagely.

Manon arched an eyebrow. "Like *you* would know?"

There was a shout, sharp and surprised. It was quickly cut off.

"I *told* those boys to be quiet," Manon said, clucking her tongue. "They're going to get themselves in a world of trouble. Come on, *cher*," she said, tugging on Ava's hand. "We'd best be going."

And then the two mermaids and three ghosts disappeared into the dark swamp waters.

TWENTY-FIVE

ASTRID KOLFINNSDOTTIR looked different.

Her fur parka was gone. And so were her braids. The skirts of the beautiful black sea-silk gown Orfeo had given her swirled around her like tidal currents as she swam down the long hallway.

She'd put the gown on earlier that morning—unwillingly, but she'd had no choice. Servants had disposed of her own clothing while she slept off the effects of the painkiller.

As soon as Astrid had finished dressing, a maid had come into her room. She'd made Astrid sit at a vanity table; then she'd fluttered about with a brush and comb, smoothing Astrid's long hair. The styling session had irritated Astrid, who didn't like primping. When the maid—Bahar—had started working her silvery blond lengths into braids, Astrid had asked her to stop.

"No, no," Bahar had insisted. "The master likes his guests to look presentable."

Without hesitation Astrid had picked up her dagger from atop the vanity, and—to the maid's horror—sliced her braids right off.

"Too bad for the master," she'd rasped, her throat still sore.

Bahar had backed away, a hand pressed to her chest. She gathered her things and made a quick exit. Astrid glanced in the mirror and smiled. Her hair was a jagged bob that just grazed her chin. She liked it.

Another maid had appeared with a tray, and Astrid was much

happier to see her. The blood loss she'd experienced had made her feel weak. A meal of soft, bland foods—nothing that would hurt her tender throat—restored her energy, and when a third servant arrived with the message that Orfeo would like to see her in the conservatory, she'd felt up to the long swim through the palace.

Astrid hadn't seen Orfeo since he'd given her the thick, murky potion that had eased her pain. How long ago had that been? Hours? Days? She had no idea.

Why does he want to see me now? she wondered uneasily. He had helped her, but she still didn't know why.

The servant who had come to fetch her stopped now in front of a pair of massive doors. He opened them, and Astrid swam through. Shadow Manse was brooding and remote, an immense, sprawling structure, and the conservatory, as she now saw, was its dark heart.

Blue waterfire burned in the tall fireplace at the far end of the room. High-backed chairs made from the gnarled roots of mangrove trees flanked it. Lava bubbled in sconces on the walls. A gilt mirror stood in a corner. A massive dome of faceted amethyst capped the conservatory, casting a purple-hued light over the room. But what truly took Astrid's breath away were the shells. The room was lined with shelves that stretched all the way from the floor to the bottom of the amethyst dome, and every inch of space was taken by shells. In her astonishment, Astrid forgot her anger about Bahar's attempted makeover.

"There must be a *million* of them," she whispered, turning in a slow circle.

Every type of shell she'd ever seen, and many she hadn't, were on display: conchs, turitellas, whelks, nautiluses, urchins, ceriths, augurs, murexes, tritons. Some were shiny and new, others cracked with age. Long-legged spider crabs scuttled over the shelves, cleaning away silt and debris.

As Astrid drew closer, she saw that each shell was labeled with the name of a songspell. There were the basic spells of invisibility, camouflage, and illusion; spells to control water, wind, and light; and spells Astrid had only heard of that allowed the caster to create dragons from silt, monsters from rock, or reanimate the dead.

"It's an ostrokon of magic," she said wonderingly, her voice less raspy now.

"Of mer magic, yes," said a voice from behind her.

Astrid turned to face Orfeo. He was wearing a jacket with a stand-up collar and his usual dark glasses.

"You collected *all* these songspells?" she asked.

"Collected them, learned them, mastered them," he replied.

Astrid's eyes widened. No wonder he was so powerful.

"I have another such place on land," he continued. "It's called a library. That one contains every magic spell ever devised by a human."

Astrid arched an eyebrow. "I have trouble seeing goggs as magical."

Orfeo smiled. "So do I. *These days*, at least. It wasn't always so."

Astrid had forgotten that he'd been human once, before he'd become whatever he was now. Her wariness returned. *He* must've *healed me for a reason,* she thought. *And whatever it is, it can't be good.*

"Magic still lives on land, but humans no longer have the eyes to see it," Orfeo continued. "The first rays of the sun, the cry of a hawk, a whale breaching . . . these miracles are all around them, and yet they stare into screens and think *that* is magic." He shook his head, disgusted. "A useless species. I won't miss them."

A shiver ran down Astrid's spine at his words. His ominous tone and the threat it implied reminded her of why she was here. Her eyes sought his black pearl. It lay against his chest, strung around his neck on a thin piece of leather.

Orfeo noticed her interest. He removed the talisman and held it out. Astrid looked at him questioningly. Was he really *handing* it to her?

"Go on, Astrid," he said. "Take it."

TWENTY-SIX

M
ORSA'S BLACK PEARL.

A gift from a goddess.

Astrid took it from Orfeo, holding the leather string in one hand, cradling the talisman with the other. The pearl was large, easily half an inch in diameter, and flawless. Some pearls glowed as if lit from within; this one burned with dark light. As she held it, Astrid could feel its power flowing into her. She could sense what it was like to be Orfeo. To have his knowledge, his magic. She envisioned the seas rising at her command, the wind obeying her wishes.

The feeling of absolute power terrified her, but it thrilled her, too.

Give it back. Let it go. He wants you to want this, a voice inside her urged. But the talisman had stoked an insatiable hunger in her. Instead of returning the pearl to Orfeo, Astrid started to close her hand around it, craving to hold it even closer.

Orfeo clucked his tongue and took it from her before she could. "Too much, too soon," he said, refastening it around his neck.

Astrid felt the pearl's loss keenly. But as the trance of omnipotence faded, her disgust grew. *You had it in your hands!* she chastised herself. *You could have taken it! Isn't that what you came here to do?*

Astrid knew, though, just as she had when she'd first arrived at Shadow Manse, that even if she'd taken the pearl, she couldn't have escaped with it. She wouldn't have made it out of the conservatory, never mind the palace.

She'd have to find another way to get it. And another time.

"Astrid, when you arrived, you asked me why I summoned you here. I told you I wanted to heal you, but that was only part of the reason."

Her fins flared. She was finally going to get her answer. "And the rest?"

"I want to educate you. I want you to start learning the songspells I've collected," Orfeo replied. He nodded at the shelves. "Choose a conch, child; listen to the spell, then sing it."

"*Why*, Orfeo?"

Instead of answering, he walked to a large desk in the middle of the room and from a drawer took out the most beautiful piece of jewelry Astrid had ever seen. It was a bib necklace made of row after row of small, perfect white pearls. Too many to count.

"This belonged to Alma, my beloved wife." He held the necklace out to her. "I gave many pieces of her jewelry to a very helpful . . ." He hesitated slightly, then said, ". . . *friend*."

Morsa, Astrid thought. A vitrina in the ruins of Atlantis had told Sera that Orfeo had courted the goddess, and Sera had told Astrid.

"But *this* necklace was not meant for her," Orfeo continued. "It was meant for *you*."

Astrid shook her head. "I can't take it."

Alma had lived thousands of years ago. Her necklace was ancient and priceless.

"I want you to have it. I hunted for it for a long time in the ruins of Atlantis. It was a wedding present to Alma from her parents," Orfeo explained. "According to Atlantean custom, the pearls symbolize the children the bride and groom will have, and the children those children will have, and so on, continuing a family's line into eternity. I know how happy it would make Alma if you were to accept the necklace. You are *our* eternity, Astrid . . . Alma's and mine."

Before Astrid could object, he fastened the piece around her neck.

"Go look in the glass," he said, pointing to the mirror standing in the corner.

Astrid swam over and gazed at her reflection, marveling at how gorgeous the necklace was. Shyly, she touched it.

"You resemble her," Orfeo said wistfully. "And the children we had."

"What was she like?" Astrid asked, swimming back to him.

"Beautiful, both inside and out. Kind. Good. Gentle."

"I wish I could have known her."

As she spoke, Orfeo's expression grew darker. Although she couldn't see his eyes behind his glasses, she had the distinct feeling that they were focused on something far away. Something only he could see.

"One day, you *will* know her. One day Abbadon will tear down the gates to the underworld and then I'll take Alma back."

The name Abbadon hit Astrid like a hard slap. *He's getting to you. He's winning you over, just as Sera said he would. Fight it!*

"The monster must be very powerful to be able to do such a thing," she said, determined to find out as much as she could about their foe, and not let her friends down.

"The monster is *beyond* powerful," said Orfeo.

"And yet he was defeated by your fellow mages," Astrid ventured, hoping to keep him talking. "He was caged on Atlantis."

"Defeated?" Orfeo echoed contemptuously. "Hardly. Abbadon went into the Carceron because I told it to."

"What?" Astrid said, stunned. "I thought Merrow and the other mages *drove* the monster into the prison."

"They *believed* they did. Which is exactly what I wanted."

"I—I don't understand."

"Abbadon was my greatest creation. I used everything I had—my magic, my learning—to conjure it. I needed it to march on the underworld," Orfeo explained. "I knew the other mages would try to stop me, even if it meant killing me. I didn't care about my own survival—I'd learned how to cheat death—but I had to ensure Abbadon's. I had to protect it."

Astrid's pulse quickened. Did the monster have a weakness? She had to find out what it was. But she'd have to proceed carefully.

"How?" she asked lightly.

"By creating a refuge for it," he replied. "A place where it could sleep, but not die, in case my plans failed. When I was nearly ready to unleash it, I changed the Carceron's lock. It had been created to accommodate my old talisman—Eveksion's emerald. One night, I altered it to accept my new talisman—the black pearl. But the other mages soon discovered what I'd done, and—"

"They weren't happy about it," Astrid cut in.

Orfeo smiled. "You could say that. They'd learned of my other activities as well."

"You mean your . . ." Dare she say it? ". . . sacrifices. The people you offered to the death goddess, Morsa."

Orfeo raised an eyebrow. "My, my. Someone's done her homework."

Astrid worried that she'd gone too far and he would stop talking. But he continued relating his tale with relish, as though he'd been waiting centuries to tell it.

"Yes, my sacrifices. The mages tracked me down to Morsa's temple. They tried to get me to come out. When I refused, they battered the doors down. They had seen Abbadon and vowed to kill it, so I ordered Abbadon to kill *them*, and anyone else who opposed me. The mages fought hard. They used all their magic. During an unguarded moment, when I was trying to catch my breath, Merrow attacked me with her sword, rather than a spell, and dealt me a mortal blow. Or so she thought."

Astrid believed she knew how Orfeo had survived. Could she get him to admit it?

"It was Morsa's talisman, wasn't it? That's what saved you. You used a pearl to hold your soul. Just like Horok does."

"The student will soon overtake her teacher," Orfeo said, admiration in his voice. "Yes, Astrid, I did. And then Merrow ripped Morsa's pearl from my neck and used it, and the other talismans, to open the Carceron. She thought she was so powerful. . . ." He shook his head at the memory. "But she and the others could never have forced the monster into the prison by themselves. *I* was the one who told it to go in. I spoke to it from the pearl, telling it to sleep, to be safe. Promising I would come for it one day."

"The mages believed they'd put an end to Abbadon," Astrid said, amazed. "Instead, they preserved it for you until you could gather the talismans."

Orfeo nodded, smiling with pride. "It has taken time. Merrow threw the black pearl into the Qanikkaaq. Had it not been for a greedy fish, and an even greedier Viking, I might still be inside the maelstrom."

"How did you create Abbadon?" Astrid pressed.

"Now, my dear, *that* must stay a secret. If no one knows what the monster is made of, no one can kill it."

"I would never tell anyone. Not after what you've done for me," Astrid lied.

Orfeo's mood changed abruptly; Astrid felt the eyes behind his glasses boring through her. "Do you think I'm a fool, child? I wouldn't have survived for four thousand years if I was. I know that you've come to take my pearl—or at least *try* to—and carry it back to your friends."

Astrid's cheeks burned. He'd seen right through her clumsy attempt to glean information. What had ever made her think she could trick him?

"You're loyal, and I admire that," Orfeo said. "But soon those loyalties will be tested. You'll have to make a choice between your friends and me. *That's* your answer, Astrid. That's why I summoned you. You're here to choose. Choose your friends, and you choose defeat. Choose me, and you choose victory, power, and immortality. Alma and I, together with you, our descendant, our daughter, will begin the world anew. You'll become a great mage, too, second only to myself. No one, and nothing, will equal our might."

"That's not going to happen, Orfeo. I've made my choice."

"Have you?" Orfeo said enigmatically. He ran a hand over a row of giant conch shells on one of his shelves.

"Yes, I have. I—"

"Sing, Astrid."

"What?" Astrid said, caught off-balance.

"Sing."

She shook her head. "I see where you're going, but it won't work. So just kill me and get it over with." Astrid sounded a lot braver than she felt.

"Kill you?" Orfeo echoed, recoiling. "Don't be ridiculous. You're free to leave here anytime you like."

"I am?" Astrid was so surprised, she didn't know whether to believe him or not.

"Yes. But before you do, grant me one small favor."

Astrid looked at him warily.

"I tried my best to heal you. At least let me see if I've succeeded."

"But I—I can't," Astrid protested. Panic gripped her at the very idea. What if she tried and failed?

"Couldn't," Orfeo corrected. "Try."

"My throat hurts too much."

Orfeo clucked his tongue. "Still afraid, aren't you?"

He'd seen through her again. Astrid looked at the floor. "Yes," she admitted.

"You were only a child when you swallowed that coin. And it was so hard to be a mermaid without magic, wasn't it?" Orfeo said, his voice so understanding. "Is there anything worse for an Ondalinian? It hurt so much to hear the whispers, the laughter, the jokes. It hurt to disappoint your mother and father . . ."

Astrid felt as if he could see inside her, into her very soul. For her, a mermaid used to hiding her true feelings, the scrutiny was painful.

". . . but you were never a disappointment to me."

Astrid raised her head. She looked at him uncertainly. Why would he say that—*never a disappointment*? She couldn't have disappointed him, or pleased him, either. She'd only just met him.

"I watched you," he continued. "I was a face in the crowd at the Citadel. A judge passing by you in the Hall of Justice. A guard in the royal quarters. Sometimes I was a sea lion, a narwhal, a sculpin. I've watched you every chance I had, Astrid."

Astrid made a face. "Um, Orfeo? That's creepy."

Orfeo laughed. "No, child, that's *love*. I was the hippokamp that threw Tauno when he teased you on a hunt, and the sea leopard that bit his backside when he made a cruel remark."

Astrid laughed, too; she couldn't help herself. She remembered both of those incidents so clearly. It had felt so good to see Tauno humiliated after he'd humiliated her. She felt an unbidden rush of gratitude toward Orfeo.

"That was *you*?" she asked. "Really?"

Orfeo nodded. "I'm telling you these things to prove that I would never be cruel to you, Astrid. You are my blood, my daughter. Sing, child. *Try*."

Astrid wanted to. So badly. But it took more courage than she possessed.

Orfeo must've seen that, for he offered her his hand. "Remember what it felt like to make music," he said. "Remember, Astrid. *Sing*."

Astrid gazed at him, feeling like a struggling swimmer caught by an undertow.

I'm letting him come too close again, she thought. *I need to leave him, leave this room, leave Shadow Manse. Now.*

But she couldn't make herself go. Her longing to sing again was too great. She needed her magic like she needed to breathe.

I'll use it to defeat him, she promised herself. *I let him heal me. Now I'll let him teach me, and then I'll use what I've learned to get the black pearl.*

Astrid took Orfeo's hand, and took a deep breath.

TWENTY-SEVEN

THE PAIN WAS TERRIFYING.

Astrid felt like she'd swallowed broken glass. Only a few notes came out of her mouth, and they sounded rough and screechy—like a boat scraping over rocks.

Orfeo squeezed her hand. "Again," he urged.

Astrid coughed self-consciously and tried once more. This time, the notes sounded like rough, rusty music.

"Oh, my gods!" she whispered. "I can sing. Orfeo, I can *sing*!"

Happiness flooded through her. It overwhelmed her, making her forget everything else. She forgot all about the black pearl. She forgot her friends, their quest, Abbadon. For a few seconds, she forgot herself.

"Try a simple spell," Orfeo suggested, encouraging her.

"Okay." She thought to back the first spells she'd ever learned, swallowed hard, then sang.

> *Goddess, Neria, give me aid!*
> *Into this iceberg help me fade!*

A split second later, her entire body was mottled in shades of white, blue, and gray. Her eyes lit up. She gasped. "Did *I* do this?" she asked. Before Orfeo could reply, she said, "I'm going to try another one! A harder one!"

"Not yet," he cautioned, holding his hands up. "You proved to yourself that you can sing again. Don't rush things and strain your vocal cords. One songspell a day, until your throat is completely healed."

Astrid was disappointed, but she nodded. "I can at least *listen* to some conchs, though," she said, as Orfeo undid her camouflage spell. She was greedy for more magic.

Before he could answer her, they both heard a knock on the door. "Enter!" Orfeo called out.

A servant swam inside. "Captain Traho is here, my lord. He has something he wishes to give you."

Astrid stiffened at Traho's name. Why was he here? What did he have for Orfeo? She hoped to the gods it wasn't one of the talismans.

"If you'll excuse me, there's a matter I must attend to," Orfeo said, heading for the door. "Feel free to listen to any songspell you wish."

"Orfeo . . ." Astrid said.

He turned back to her; a questioning expression on his face.

"Thank you."

Her words were sincere. She *was* grateful to him. For giving her her voice back. For giving her her magic back.

For giving her the very weapons she would use against him.

Orfeo smiled, and then he was gone. The servant closed the door behind him.

Astrid immediately swam to a shelf. She had her magic, and she had access to every spell known to merkind. Surely *one* of them could help her get the pearl.

The strange trancelike state she'd been in earlier was gone now. It troubled her that she had fallen under Orfeo's spell for even a brief second, but she shook off the uneasy feeling. It had only happened because she'd been overwhelmed by emotion.

It would *not* happen again.

TWENTY-EIGHT

"**T**HE METAL from this one hull alone will give us *thousands* of spearheads," Desiderio yelled excitedly, patting a barnacle-covered chunk of a sunken ship. "And there's still a trawler to cut up!"

"We'll churn out *tens* of thousands!" Yazeed shouted. "With the forge up and running now, the goblins are going day and night."

"But is that enough? Will we make it in time?" Sera bellowed. The Black Fins were due to start for the Southern Sea in two weeks. Their supply wagons needed to be full of arrows and spears by then.

Yazeed answered. "No problem! We'll have all the ammo we need!"

Even though both mermen were shouting, Sera could hardly hear them for all the noise. Behind them, lava bubbled, steam hissed, the forge roared, and the goblins busily sawed through thick plates of steel.

She'd come to check on the progress the goblins were making, and though the noise was deafening, and the commotion dizzying, Sera couldn't have been happier. Right after Styg and his crew found the lava seam, she'd given orders to construct the forge near the lava seam and start casting ammo.

The lava seam was such a gift. The lava and the steel from the ships cost nothing. Sera no longer needed to deal with the Näkki or risk her troops being ambushed.

The three friends left the forge and headed back to headquarters.

They were still talking a fathom a minute about provisions and didn't notice Mulmig waving at them until she was right in their faces.

"Did you *hear?*" she asked excitedly, before Sera could even greet her.

"Hear what?" Sera asked, her fins prickling. She didn't like surprises.

"Ling solved the puzzle ball!"

"No way!" Yazeed said.

"Yes way!" Mulmig replied. "The news is moving through camp like a tsunami!"

"Where is she?" Sera asked, rigid with anticipation. Did this mean the spy would soon be outed?

"She shut herself up in the headquarters cave so she can figure out the Arrow of Judgment."

"Have you seen it?" Des asked.

"Not yet. No one has. But Ling says it's like a compass. Only instead of pointing to directions, the arrow points to crimes. Where the word *north* would be on a compass is the word *innocent*. Other points correspond to words like *robber* or *murderer*. Ling says—"

But Sera didn't wait to hear the rest. She was off like a shot. Des and Yazeed were right on her tail. There was one word she desperately hoped was on that compass: *spy*.

When the three reached the cave, they found Ling seated at the table, busy writing on a piece of kelp parchment. Members of Sera's inner circle were with her. Becca and Neela were watching her. They'd been going over the next day's work schedule. Sophia was there, too. She'd been reviewing the weapons inventory. Little Coco had been counting doubloons into stacks, preparing a payment to Meerteufel traders, her shark Abelard nearby. They all turned their heads expectantly toward Sera.

"Ling, did you really—" she breathlessly started to ask.

"Crack the puzzle? Yeah, I did. *Finally!*" Ling exclaimed. "I tested the Arrow of Judgment out a few times, then I put the puzzle ball away for safekeeping until you got back. Everyone's *so* excited about it, Sera. You won't believe it when you see it."

"Tested it out? How?" asked Sera.

"I found out who started the brawl in the mess hall last night, and who's been stealing from the food stores. And both of them confessed. Isn't that *amazing*? All you have to do is hold the puzzle ball in front of someone and ask it if that someone is innocent or guilty. The arrow does the rest."

"Ling, do you know what this means?" Yazeed asked in a hushed voice.

"Yes. We can finally root out the spy. I'm figuring out a plan now. I'm so glad you're all here. I want to get everyone's input. I thought we could start at the west side of the camp and work our way across. Eventually the arrow will point to the traitor. It's just a matter of time until—"

An anguished cry interrupted her. It had come from the other end of the table.

Sera, startled, turned to see that it was Sophia. As Sera watched, Sophia rose from the table, took a few faltering strokes toward her, then crumpled.

"Soph, what is it? Are you hurt?" Sera asked, rushing to her.

Sophia didn't answer. She just sat on the silty cave floor, her head bowed, her hair falling into her eyes.

"Sophia, what's going on?" Sera pressed, putting a hand on her shoulder.

"It's me," Sophia whispered. She raised her face. It was deathly pale. "It's *me*," she said again. "*I'm* the spy."

Sera backed away. She felt as if Sophia had just reached inside her and crushed her heart. The others were all looking at the two of them, too shocked to speak.

"Soph, *no*," Sera said. "Not you. It *can't* be you."

"It's been tearing me apart. I want to confess. *Now*," she said. "I don't want to be shown for what I really am by a puzzle ball."

Sophia had been with the Black Fins since their earliest days. Sera had chosen her to go on the raid of the Miromaran treasury vaults, and she was alive only because of Sophia. A death rider had shot her with a speargun as the Black Fins were escaping. Sophia had cut the line, killed the death rider, and gotten Sera to safety.

Afterward, they'd hidden in the ruins of Merrow's reggia, and Sera had confided in her there. She'd told her about the Iele, the talismans, Abbadon—everything. Sophia had even defended the Näkki's arms shipment from the death riders' ambush. Sera had trusted her with her life, and the lives of their fellow Black Fins.

"Sophia . . . *why?*" she asked now, stunned.

"A merman, his name was Baco Goga, approached me one night, when I was on patrol outside of our old headquarters in the Blue Hills," Sophia explained haltingly. "He told me he wanted me to spy on the resistance for him. I told him where he could go. He handed me something—two wedding rings. They belonged to my parents. My mother and father had been taken away when Cerulea was invaded. Baco said his next gift to me would be their fingers. Then their hands. He said he'd kill them piece by piece if I refused to cooperate."

A searing mixture of grief and anger had filled Sera upon learning of Sophia's betrayal, but another emotion pushed those aside now: fear.

She cast her mind back to the night the death riders attacked the camp, when Sera had decided to tell her fighters that they'd be heading to Cerulea, while she was really planning to go to the Southern Sea. Sophia hadn't been there, thank the gods, when she'd announced that ploy to her inner circle. But had she somehow found out the real plan?

"What does my uncle know?" Sera asked her now. "What did you tell Baco?"

"As little as I could. I tried my best to protect you, Sera. I—"

Sera bent down to Sophia. She grabbed her chin roughly. "What did you *tell* him?" she shouted.

"The size of your army, the timing of the weapons shipments, the fact that you didn't have a lava seam, the number of refugees that came to the Kargjord and . . . and Ava's whereabouts."

Sera swore. "Did you tell him about Cerulea?"

Sophia nodded miserably.

Thank the gods, Sera thought. Vallerio would think they were headed for the city; he'd have no clue about their actual strategy. But there was one more question—and it filled Sera with such terror, she could hardly bear to ask it.

"Did you tell Baco about Mahdi?"

Sophia shook her head. "No. I didn't, Sera. I swear to the gods."

Sera's entire body sagged with relief. She let go of Sophia's chin. As she rose, Sophia grabbed her hand.

"I'm sorry, Sera. So sorry," she sobbed. "*Please* forgive me. I had no choice. You understand, don't you? What could I do? Baco has my *parents!*"

Sera looked down at Sophia's hand, clutching her own so tightly. And then, her heart breaking, she shook her off.

"Sera?" Sophia said in a choked voice. "Sera, no . . . *please.*"

"Death riders killed *my* parents," Sera said. "Right in front of me. They've killed thousands of Miromaran parents. Yet none of us orphaned by them have betrayed our sisters and brothers."

She turned to the two goblin soldiers guarding the doorway. "Take her to the prison," she said. "She's to be court-martialed, and if found guilty—"

"*No!*" Sophia screamed.

Sera swallowed hard, almost choking on the words she had to say. "If found guilty, she's to be executed. And so it will be for *anyone* who betrays the resistance."

"Sera, please! I'm sorry! Don't do this . . . *please!*" Sophia shrieked.

Sera forced herself to watch as the guards dragged her friend away. She forced herself to look at the tears in Coco's eyes. Only cowards turned away from the hard things.

It was quiet in the cave afterward. Sera was the first to break the silence.

"Leave me," she said.

One by one, her friends filed out. Coco, wide-eyed and trembling, was the first to go. Ling was the last. She swam up to Sera on her way and handed her the puzzle ball.

"Put it away with the others," Ling said quietly. "Keep it safe. We may need it again."

Sera held the talisman up and peered through the holes—now perfectly aligned—and into the sphere's center. There was no arrow, no words. Just a tiny, beautiful carving of a phoenix.

Sera lowered the talisman and looked at Ling, full of admiration for her cleverness. "You made it all up," she said.

Ling nodded. "Sophia was in a lot of pain, and that pain needed to speak."

"When did you realize it was her?"

"I didn't. I thought it might be Becca, as you know. After you made sure it wasn't, I knew I had to take a gamble. In two weeks, our troops will learn that we're going to the Southern Sea, not Cerulea. I needed to catch the spy before that happened. If I didn't, I knew he—or she, as it turned out—would tell Vallerio about your bluff."

"So you claimed that you'd solved the puzzle," said Sera.

Ling nodded. "All I knew for certain was that the spy was someone close to you. So I got the inner circle together, and said that the Arrow of Judgment was working. I hoped that would be enough to scare the spy into confessing. And it was."

"You broke through another silence, Ling. A very dangerous one. Thank you. You saved many lives."

"And condemned one."

Ling rested her head against Sera's, and Sera took comfort knowing that someone else shared her burden. A moment later, Ling squeezed Sera's arm, then left.

Sera swam to the niche in the cave's wall where the talismans were kept and stowed the puzzle ball safely away.

Sera had done the right thing; she knew she had—even if it was also a hard thing.

Squaring her shoulders, she started for the cave's opening, determined to get some work done. What had just happened was horrible, but it was time to move on. A regina could not afford to be idle, not when there was a battle to plan.

Sera took a stroke toward the cave's doorway, and then another, and then she sat down in the silt, covered her face with her hands, and wept.

TWENTY-NINE

ASTRID WAS GONE, lost in the music. Her head was tilted back, her eyes were closed, her arms outstretched. She was songcasting.

> *Water, hear this binding spell,*
> *And from the inky depths upwell.*
> *Currents strong and vast and deep,*
> *Over banks and shores now leap.*

As she sang, water swirled together into a column in the center of the conservatory, directly under the amethyst dome. Her voice rose, full and strong, as she finished the spell.

> *Tides and waves, hear my command,*
> *Burst your boundaries, flood the land.*
> *Water clear and water blue,*
> *Rise up now, and split in two!*

The pillar of water shot upward and parted, curving away from the dome in two graceful, flowing arcs. Astrid held the notes and opened her eyes, watching the water fountain down to the floor, feeling proud, happy, and powerful.

She'd had a fleeting taste of power when Orfeo had allowed her to hold the black pearl, and that taste had sparked a desire for more. She thought of little else now other than how to obtain it.

Her throat was healed, and her voice was growing stronger. She practiced for hours a day, every day, to build it up.

Late at night, she would flop into her bed, exhausted, and fall into a deep, dreamless sleep. When the first rays of the sun slanted through the waters into her window, she would rise and hurry back to the conservatory, her newfound craving driving her to learn more, to excel.

There were moments, as she drifted off to sleep, when a voice deep inside her reminded her of her quest.

When will you take the black pearl? Your friends are waiting.

"I'm not ready," she would whisper. "I need to learn more spells. I need to become stronger. How else can I defeat Orfeo?" If that didn't quiet the voice, she would softly songcast, swirling the water around in her room, or making the anemones in her bed glow. She couldn't hear anything else when she was making magic.

As she was doing now.

> *Fall back to the banks,*
> *Fall back from the shore,*
> *Radiant water, surge forward no more.*
> *Calm and untroubled, I ask you to be,*
> *Return to your depths now, from river or sea.*

As the last notes of songspell faded, Astrid heard applause coming from the doorway. She turned around, smiling.

It was Orfeo, leaning against the doorjamb. He'd been listening.

"Magnificent!" he said, walking in. "Even better than yesterday. You're making astonishing progress."

Astrid blushed, self-conscious, but pleased, too. Her own father had never praised her so lavishly, even when she was younger and had her singing voice. She had been starved of approval for most of her life and now found that she hungered for Orfeo's.

It unsettled her, to look to him for praise. He was treacherous and cruel, wasn't he? Not the sort she should be looking to for encouragement. But she reassured herself that there was no harm in it—not if she intended to turn all that she was learning against him. Which she was. In a few days. A few weeks, at most.

"Thank you," she said shyly. "But it's the songspell, not me. It's *amazing*. It's from the River Nile and super old."

Orfeo nodded. "I knew the songcaster who created it: Anuket, goddess of the Nile."

"Seriously?" Astrid said. It was amazing to her that Orfeo had known a river goddess.

"Seriously," Orfeo said, smiling. "Anuket used that spell to push the Nile over its banks. The rich silt left behind by the floods made the land fertile, and the Egyptians prosperous. The spell's a good one to have in your repertoire."

"I'll do it again," Astrid said. "I didn't sustain that high C in the fifth measure. Watch me, Orfeo. Listen. Tell me if I get it right."

Orfeo's smile broadened into a laugh, one full of pleasure and pride. "I *will* watch you, child, but tomorrow, perhaps. I interrupted you because I have something to give you—something very important. It will further the progress you're making."

"You've already given me the greatest gift ever: my voice," Astrid said. "I don't need anything else."

"You need an instructor," Orfeo countered. "You're teaching yourself songspells, and that's wonderful, but many of them are meant to be sung only by experienced songcasters. I'm afraid you'll damage your voice. You need to work on technique and range, and I've just the person to help you do it."

He snapped his fingers and two servants walked through the

doorway, escorting a mermaid between them. Astrid had never met her, yet she knew who she was. Every mermaid and merman alive knew who she was.

Thalassa, the legendary canta magus.

THIRTY

THALASSA REGARDED ASTRID, then laughed bitterly.

"The late admiral's daughter, no?" she said, turning to Orfeo. "And your descendant. She must be; she looks exactly like you. She's the reason I'm here, isn't she? The reason you've kept me alive all this time."

"That's correct, Magistra," Orfeo replied. "She's Astrid Kolfinnsdottir, and she will be the greatest student you've ever taught."

"We'll see about that," Thalassa said with a sniff. Her voice was dismissive, but her eyes were locked on Astrid.

Astrid's eyes were locked on her, too. As the shock of seeing someone who was supposed to be dead receded, Astrid remembered how Thalassa had insisted on offering her own life to save Sera's.

Sera had told her the story. She, Neela, and Thalassa had been captured by Traho, and Traho, in the course of interrogating Thalassa, had cut off one of her thumbs. The Praedatori had managed to rescue the three of them, but as they were heading to the safety of the duca's palace, Traho and his soldiers had caught up with them—undoubtedly on Orfeo's orders. Thalassa had battled the death riders, allowing Sera and the others to escape. Sera was certain they'd killed her.

Though she was gaunt, gray-faced, and dressed in the remnants of a once-fine gown, Thalassa's bearing was proud, her voice imperious. Astrid thought she was more regal in her silt-stained tatters than most mermaids were in silks and jewels.

Orfeo watched Thalassa closely. "Ah, Magistra, your curiosity is piqued," he said. "It appeals to you, doesn't it? The thought of instructing a talent so great, it's second only to my own."

He swam to her, unlocked her manacles, and handed them to a servant. As the canta magus massaged her raw, red wrists, another servant swam into the conservatory, gripping a very small, very scared mermaid by the arm. She couldn't have been more than seven years old. He shoved her roughly into a chair.

"A small reminder for you to do your best, Thalassa," Orfeo said. "Your *very* best. Anything less"—he nodded at the child—"and *she* pays the price."

The child's eyes widened, a whimper escaped her.

"Oh, I'll do my *best*, Orfeo," Thalassa hissed. "Touch one hair on that child's head and I'll do my *best* to destroy this godsforsaken palace and everyone in it."

This is who he is, Astrid thought, unable to look away from the frightened child. *He's vicious and cruel, and he'll stop at nothing to get what he wants.*

Yes, that's who he is, said the voice inside her. *But who are you, Astrid? His creature now, or your own?*

Thalassa turned her back on Orfeo and circled Astrid, her eyes shrewd and appraising. A second later, a tiny bubble popped in Astrid's ear. As it did, she heard Thalassa's voice whispering to her. "You are the last hope of all the waters in the world, child, and of every living thing in them. Remember that."

Aloud, Thalassa said, "I heard you working on an old Egyptian songspell as I was coming down the hallway. Your voice is very good. It has the potential to be excellent, but you must learn nuance and expression. We shall start with the breath. It's all wrong."

Astrid tore her eyes away from the child and regarded Thalassa. "I'm *breathing* wrong?" she said skeptically.

"Entirely," Thalassa replied. She turned her head and gave Orfeo a withering look. "You're excused. Have tea brought," she said to him, as if he were nothing more than a kitchen boy.

Then she placed a hand on Astrid's chest. "Right now, your breath is here." She tapped the top of her rib cage. "Good songcasters breathe from here," she added, patting Astrid's belly.

Orfeo chuckled. "I knew you wouldn't be able to resist," he said. "You love a good voice even more than you hate me."

Then he left the conservatory, barking at his servants to fetch the magistra tea.

Astrid watched him go. Thalassa was talking to her, but she barely heard the canta magus.

It was the *other* voice she heard, the one deep inside, whose words were echoing in her head.

Who are you, Astrid?

Who are you?

THIRTY-ONE

"**H**OLD STILL, WILL YOU?" Neela mumbled crossly through a mouthful of pins.

"Aren't you done *yet*?" Sera asked, huffing with impatience. "It's only a uniform."

She'd been floating in the same place for over an hour now in the headquarters cave, while Neela fitted a new jacket and a long, flowing skirt on her, endlessly nipping, tucking, and pinning the fabric.

Neela took the pins out of her mouth. "It's not *only* a uniform; it's *your* uniform. Need I remind you that you're the leader of the Black Fin resistance, and that you need to inspire twenty thousand troops tomorrow morning? It would help if you didn't look like a skavvener."

Desiderio, seated at the big stone table cleaning his crossbow, snorted with laughter.

Sera scowled, not at all happy to be compared to the ragged, bony sea elves.

"Thanks a lot, Neels," she said. "I didn't realize I *did* look like a skavvener."

"You've been wearing a borrowed jacket ever since your own disappeared. The cuffs are frayed. The collar, too." She swam back a few strokes. "Turn, please," she said.

Sera did as she was told.

Hands on her hips, Neela appraised her work, then gave a nod. "Totally invincible. If I do say so myself."

"Done?" Sera asked.

"Done," Neela said, helping her out of the garments.

"I can't *believe* it's tomorrow," Sera said, putting the borrowed jacket back on over her tunic. "We're heading for the Southern Sea *tomorrow*."

The soldiers had all been provided with uniforms and weapons. Wagons carrying ammunition, food, and medicine had been packed. The refugees who were too young, too old, or too frail to fight would stay safely behind. The forge was silent now. Those who could sleep were doing so. Those who couldn't were gathered around waterfires, cleaning weapons or polishing helmets.

Tomorrow morning, Sera would tell them the truth—that they were going to the Southern Sea, not Cerulea, and why. It was finally happening. She was heading off to fulfill the quest Vrăja had given her. She was about to launch the endgame in her bid to destroy Abbadon.

Sera thought back to the days before the river witch had come to her in her dreams, before her uncle had attacked Cerulea, before her world had been torn apart. It seemed as if a thousand years had passed since then. She was a different person now. Older. Wiser. Harder.

A hundred worries ran through her head now. A hundred details. A hundred questions.

"Are you *sure* we have enough bandages?" she asked.

"Becca packed an entire wagonful," Neela replied.

"Tents?"

"Loaded and ready to go," said Des.

Her deeper worries were written on her face. Des saw them. He stopped cleaning his weapon and said, "What's really bothering you?"

"Mahdi," Sera admitted. He was still in Cerulea, still in the palace.

"We're pulling him out soon," Des said. "He'll be safe and sound, and waiting for us at the Straits of Gibraltar, just as we planned."

Sera nodded and tried to smile, but her gestures didn't convince her brother.

"What else?" he asked.

"Ava," Sera said. "Astrid."

"We would have heard something if Ava had been captured," Neela assured her. "Vallerio's thugs would have brought her back to Cerulea. Mahdi would've found out and gotten word to us."

"What if something *else* happened?" Sera said anxiously. "What if the Okwa Naholo got her? What if she's . . . she's—"

"Dead?" Neela finished. "We'd know. We're bloodbound. We'd feel it. Same goes for Astrid."

"You're right," Sera said, her worst fears allayed. For now.

"Why don't you get some sleep?" Neela suggested.

"Good idea," Sera said. "But what about you?"

"I'll come in a bit. I've still got a little sewing to do."

Sera swam to her friend and kissed her good night. "Thank you, by the way," she said. "I *love* my new uniform. I really do." She smiled mischievously and said, "You can give my old one to the skavveners."

"Even *they* wouldn't touch it," Neela said.

"I'll swim you to the barracks, Sera," Desiderio said. "I need some shut-eye myself." He put his cleaning materials back into their sea-grass pouch and hoisted his weapon. "Let's go," he said.

Brother and sister swam side by side through the camp, just the two of them. With the spy finally caught, Sera had dismissed her bodyguards. She hated being followed around, and she felt they'd be far more useful by helping with preparations for the journey to the Southern Sea.

"I know you're worried about Mahdi, but if he survived this long around Vallerio and Lucia, he can last for a few more days."

"You're right, Des. It's just that I can't stop worrying. I can't shake this feeling that something's going to happen. It's like a shadow I can't get out from under."

"It's just nerves. All this planning and plotting and waiting leaves too much time for dwelling on everything that can go wrong," Des said. "You'll feel better tomorrow when we actually get going." He gave his sister a sidelong glance. "Mahdi means a lot to you, doesn't he?"

"Yeah, he does," Sera said softly. "He means everything, Des."

"I never thought you'd fall for him. You couldn't stand him when you first met him."

Sera laughed at the memory. "I thought he was a total goby. He hardly said two words to me. All he wanted to do was play Galleons and Gorgons with *you*."

"Yeah, but the whole time we were playing, all he did was ask about *you*."

"Really? I didn't know that," Sera said, pleased. But her happiness was short-lived. Thinking about Mahdi, talking about him . . . all it did was bring back all her fears for him. She decided to change the subject.

"How's *your* love life?" she asked her brother.

"What love life?" he asked, trying to sound innocent. "I don't have one."

"Really, Des?" she teased. "Is that why you're blushing?"

"I am *not*," Des scoffed.

"Now you're blushing even *more*," Sera said, nudging him with her tail. "I saw how she looked at you. And how you looked at her. The night you both arrived here."

"Who?"

"Ha. So funny," Sera said, rolling her eyes. "Like there are a *hundred* mermaids in love with you?"

"At least."

"Oh, *please*."

Des smiled. "It's that obvious, huh?"

"To me. But I know you pretty well."

Des's smile dimmed. "I wish she'd send a message, Sera. A little conch shell, *something*." He was quiet for a moment, then he said, "What if she's gone over?"

Sera's face took on a stony look. "Never," she said. "Not her. No way."

"She's suffered, Sera. A lot. All because she can't sing. It's going to be a battle of wills between her and Orfeo, and I'm scared he'll win."

"He won't. You *know* her, Des. You know how strong she is."

"But Orfeo can give her something no one else can."

"Her magic?"

"Her *pride*," Des said. "Astrid doesn't believe in herself. She doesn't believe she's worth anything. For most of her life, she wanted her father's approval and never got it. She still doesn't realize that there's only one person's approval she needs: her own."

"She *won't* turn, Des. She'll get the pearl, and then she'll get it to us. I *know* she will."

The two mer stopped swimming. They'd arrived where the current split in two directions. One led to the barracks for male goblin and mer fighters, the other to the barracks for females.

"I hope you're right," Des said.

"Of course I am. I'm *always* right."

Des rolled his eyes. "You sound just like Mom." He kissed his sister's forehead. "Get some sleep. You've got a big day tomorrow."

Sera kissed him back and headed for her barracks. She was looking forward to her bed. Becca and Ling had turned in hours ago.

Just before she swam into the cave, she heard something—a small, chittering voice.

"Regina Serafina," it said.

Sera turned around, but no one was there.

"Over here."

The voice was coming from a shadowy hollow to the left of the cave. Serafina peered in its direction, but still saw nothing. Instinctively, her hand went to the dagger at her hip.

As she was about to pull the blade from its sheath, a large black sea scorpion crawled out of the shadows. He looked around fearfully, then raised one of his claws. Sera saw that he was holding a small conch. "For you, Regina. A message."

"Who sent it?" Sera asked warily.

"One who cares a great deal for you. There is much trouble."

Sera's heart lurched. "Mah—" she started to say.

The scorpion shook its head. It held its other claw to its mouth, then said, "No names! The sea has many ears. For you alone. No one else can know. It's too dangerous."

"How do I know that this is safe?" Sera asked. "That it's not some kind of a trick?"

The scorpion poked one of his slender legs into the shell, to show that it wasn't booby-trapped.

Sera looked at the barracks. She thought about getting Ling or Becca. It would be safer to deal with the scorpion, and his message, when accompanied by another Black Fin. But they were all asleep and she hated to wake them.

As if reading her mind, the scorpion said, "Only for you. I am to crush the shell if another tries to listen."

"Just my friend. For safety . . ." Sera ventured.

"I will crush it," the creature insisted, tightening his grip on the conch.

Sera bent down. She couldn't take the chance of not hearing the message Mahdi had sent. She held out her hand, and the scorpion placed the shell on her palm. Hesitantly, she brought it up to her ear. Mahdi started speaking immediately. It was his voice; there was no doubt about it. And the fear Sera heard in it raised the scales on the back of her tail.

Sera, it's Mahdi. I'm near the Karg, in the Darktide Shallows. I couldn't send this news with Allegra. We've got big trouble. Vallerio's heading for the Karg. He's got twenty thousand soldiers with him. He's going to attack. There's more to tell you, but I can't come into the camp. There's a spy in your midst, and I don't want to be seen. Come to the Shallows alone. Hurry, Sera. Please.

Sera lowered the conch, her heart racing. Vallerio had made a countermove. He wasn't waiting for her to attack Cerulea; he was going to attack first. How close was he? Did she have time to get everyone out of camp and elude the death riders? They could do it; they were already provisioned and packed for the Southern Sea. If need be, they could take a different route than the one they'd planned in order to escape Vallerio. Or was it better to stay here and fight? The fortified camp offered them a defensible position. In the open water, they'd be vulnerable.

Mahdi had asked her to come to him—alone. That was risky. He knew that, but he'd asked anyway. That told her there was trouble, real trouble. He didn't know that there was no longer a traitor in the Black Fins' camp. A conch had been sent to him telling him the spy had been caught . . . but if he'd been traveling to the Karg all this time, he wouldn't have received it.

Vallerio's forces must be close, she thought. *Mahdi will know how close.*

"I'm going to him. Right now," Sera said to the scorpion, as she pocketed the conch. "Can you show me the way?"

The scorpion nodded.

Sera shot off toward the cave that housed the hippokamps. It was a fair distance to the Darktide Shallows and would take her half a day to swim it. She would ride a hippokamp there instead, and speed the animal along with a velo spell.

The scorpion could not keep up. When Sera realized she'd left him far behind, she doubled back.

"Climb up," she said, holding out her arm. The creature latched on to her, then crawled to her shoulder, steadying himself with his tail. "You good?" she asked.

He nodded and she took off again.

To her relief, the hippokamps had been bedded down for the night. No grooms were around.

Sera cast an illuminata. An accomplished equestrienne, she picked out a strong white mare, put the animal on crossties, and tacked her up. When she was finished, she scrawled a hasty note.

I've gone to see a friend. Back by morning.
Serafina

Then she unclipped the crossties, led the hippokamp out of the cave, and climbed on. The scorpion settled itself in front of her so he could point the way.

Sera spurred her mount and cast a velo. A split second later, she and the scorpion were racing out of camp, a white blur in the dark water.

THIRTY-TWO

SERA DIDN'T LOOK BACK as the camp fell away behind her.

She and the scorpion rode for hours without stopping, her illuminata lighting their way. Pointing with his claw, the scorpion led Sera across the Kargjord, over the Devil's Trench, through shimmering shoals of mackerel and cod, and then down into the weedy shallows themselves.

"Over there!" he chittered now, pointing ahead.

Sera looked past his pincers and spotted Mahdi floating in a hollow. He was turned away from her, but she could see his black jacket, his long hair pulled back into a hippokamp's tail, and the side of his handsome face. He was holding something; it looked like a Black Fin jacket.

He was here for the wrong reason. He was here because he was in grave danger. And she was, too. And so was everyone and everything they cared about.

But still, Sera was wildly happy to see him.

"Mahdi!" she called out. She was off her hippokamp in an instant, speeding to him.

He turned around. Sera caught his beautiful face in her hands and kissed him, but his lips were cold.

"Mahdi?"

He smiled at her. But instead of warming her, it chilled her. It was a lunatic's grin—too wide, too bright.

He dropped the jacket. His hands closed on her arm with a tight grip. Scared now, Sera tried to pull away, but his fingers curled painfully into her flesh, and she knew she'd made a terrible mistake.

"Who are you?" she cried, whipping her dagger out of her belt. "Let me go!"

The maligno knocked the weapon away. She fought hard, slapping at the creature with her free hand, slamming it with her tail. In the struggle, her pocket tore, and the message conch fell out. She heard her hippokamp whinny in fear; then the creature bolted.

The scorpion, meanwhile, had circled behind her. He swam toward her now, his tail raised, its sharp tip glistening with poison.

When the strike came, the pain was unlike anything Sera had ever known.

The scorpion's barb sank deep into her back, just missing her spine. A heartbeat later, the venom was in her bloodstream. It felt like lava moving through her veins.

She tried to scream, but no sound came out. The venom had paralyzed her. Her breathing slowed. Her heart rate dropped.

All she could do was watch in terror, eyes frozen open, as the thing that wasn't Mahdi picked her up and dragged her away.

CHAPTER 32

THIRTY-THREE

"ANY SIGN OF HER?" Becca called out anxiously, her heart heavy with dread.

"Nothing yet," Ling shouted back.

The two mermaids, together with Neela, Desiderio, Yazeed, Coco, and Coco's shark, Abelard, had been searching for Sera in the Darktide Shallows for over three hours. They'd ridden out of camp before dawn, after it was discovered that Serafina was nowhere to be found.

Neela, busy with Sera's uniform, had continued to work for several hours the previous night. When she finally went to the barracks to sleep, she saw that Sera's bunk was empty. She went to look for Des, thinking maybe they'd never gone to sleep and were sitting by a waterfire somewhere, but he was in his barracks.

Worried, she and Des had raised the alarm. Word of Sera's disappearance spread quickly through the camp. A goblin named Regelbrott had hurried to headquarters just after the news broke.

"I couldn't sleep last night," she said, "so I left my barracks and went for a walk around camp. Someone streaked by on a white hippokamp. I saw a tail, so it was a mer, not a goblin, but I didn't see the rider's face."

"Where was she heading?" Des asked.

"Toward the Darktide Shallows," Regelbrott replied. "Do you think it was Serafina?"

SEA SPELL

170

"Why would she leave camp at night?" Neela asked. "She's knows it's dangerous in the open water."

Just then, a breathless groom arrived at the HQ cave. He was holding Sera's note. Minutes later, Desiderio and the others, plus twenty armed goblins, were speeding toward the Shallows on hippokamps.

Along the way, Ling had stopped to ask other sea creatures if they'd seen Sera. Shoals of cod and mackerel confirmed that a mermaid with short copper-colored hair had been spotted heading away from the camp. When the group arrived at the Shallows, two pipefish said that they'd glimpsed a mermaid riding toward a place called Cuttlefish Hollow. The search party had hurried there, and ever since they'd been peering into every cave and thicket.

"Hey! Abbie found something!" Coco called out now.

The others sped to the merl's side. She was lifting something from the silty seabed—a dagger. They all recognized it as Sera's. Next to it was her old Black Fin jacket.

"What's that doing here?" Yazeed asked.

"Maybe someone used it to track her," Ling suggested.

Becca's heart sank. Her eyes swept over the seafloor, hoping for another clue that could tell them who had taken Sera, and where. They fastened on an object near where the dagger had lain. She stooped to pick it up.

"It's a conch. They're not native to these waters," she said. She held it up to her ear and listened to it. Her face was pale by the time she lowered her hand again.

Desiderio took the conch from her. He cast an amplio spell so they could all hear it.

"That's not Mahdi," Ling said when the message ended. "It only sounds like him. He *never* would have asked Sera to meet him alone in a place like this. It's a trick."

"I wonder if Lucia's behind this," Neela said.

Desiderio shook his head. "No way. She's too busy looking in every mirror she swims past. Vallerio's responsible, I just know it. He wanted Sera dead. He found a way to do it without risking his troops—or Guldemar's anger. And Sera fell for it. How could she be so *stupid*?" Des shouted, slapping his tail fins against a rock.

Neela, glowing bright blue with emotion, leapt to Sera's defense. "Because the message made her think Mahdi was in danger," she said. "That's why she came here. Out of love. And whoever sent the conch knew she would. Because that's who she is."

"Love's nothing but a loaded weapon. It got Sera killed," Des said bitterly.

"Don't say that!" Neela shouted. "Don't even think it! Sera's *not* dead. We'd feel it if she was, Ling and Becca and me. We're bloodbound. If she was gone, a piece of us would be gone, too!"

Becca, who'd been quiet all this time, finally spoke. She'd thought through everything that had happened, sifting it for meaning, just like her ancestor Pyrrha, a brilliant strategist, would have. "I think Neela's right," she said. "Sera's not dead."

"How do you know that? You *don't*!" Des yelled. "You're just going to give everyone false hope!"

"Stop it, Des. Right now," Ling ordered. "I know you're upset; Sera's your sister. We're all upset, but we can't come apart. We have to work together to figure out the next step, okay?" She looked at the others, each in turn. They all nodded. "Good. Let's hear Becca out."

"If Vallerio did this," Becca ventured, "it's because Sera's more valuable to him alive than dead."

"No, she's *not*," Des countered. "He wants her dead. She's a threat to Lucia. Portia was about to order Sophia to kill her."

"Then where's the body?" Becca asked. "Why isn't it here?"

Desiderio didn't have an answer.

"Why would Vallerio have an assassin kill Sera here, then drag the body back to Cerulea and risk discovery?" Becca continued. "He's always said he placed his daughter on the throne only because Sera was killed during the invasion of Cerulea. If the Miromarans were to find out differently, there would be protests, maybe uprisings. He doesn't want that."

"Okay, say Vallerio *didn't* kill Sera," Yazeed allowed. "Why did he take her?"

"Because our fake-out worked too well," Becca said ruefully. "Vallerio believes we're going to attack Cerulea. He wants to stop us."

"He's using her as a shield," Yazeed said.

Becca nodded. "I think so," she said. "I bet he contacts us soon to tell us he's got Sera and he'll kill her if we attack."

"How do we get her back?" Neela asked.

"By attacking Cerulea," Becca declared.

"What?" Neela exclaimed. "You just said Vallerio would kill Sera if we did that!"

"Only if he sees us coming. What if we launched a surprise attack?" said Becca.

"Becca, dude, have you, like, lost your *mind?*" Yazeed asked. "There's no *way* to spring a surprise attack on Cerulea. The city's high up, and we'd be moving thousands of soldiers toward it. Vallerio's scouts will see us coming days before we get there, and—"

Becca cut him off. "What if the scouts *couldn't* see us? Until it's too late. It happened once before. At the invasion of Cerulea."

Becca's words hung in the water. She knew her idea was bold and daring, and almost impossible to pull off. What would the others think? The friends all looked at one another, their eyes asking the same question: Can we actually *do* this?

"It's *genius*, Becs," Ling said decisively. "We'll use Vallerio's own move on him."

"We could surprise him the same way he surprised my mother— by using terragogg ships," added Des, his voice eager now, instead of angry.

"Our troops are ready to go to Cerulea," Ling said, with a

mirthless smile. "Sera planned to tell them it was all a fake-out. Guess it's not anymore."

"Wait! What about Mahdi?" Neela asked. "If we attack while he's there, he could get hurt in the fighting."

"We could get word to him of our plans," Ling said.

"Can we get a courier there in time?" asked Neela.

"We don't need to," Des said. "We'll attack the day of his wedding. That's the day he's supposed to escape from Cerulea. The plan is for him to have a big bull shark party the night before, for all his merman friends. He's going to pretend to overdo it, and then say he's really sick the following morning. While everyone thinks he's sleeping it off, he'll cast his transparensea pearl and haul tail. We attack later that day, while everyone else is in the palace getting ready for the wedding, and capture the whole rotten bunch."

"Mer? You're forgetting one pretty major thing," Yazeed said. "We don't have Rafe Mfeme, or Orfeo, or whatever he calls himself, helping us. We don't have his access to gogg ships."

Becca had been quiet while the others deliberated her idea. She'd been arguing, too—with herself. She looked at her fellow Black Fins now and said, "Maybe we do."

THIRTY-FOUR

"**W**AKE UP," a voice commanded.

It was cold, the voice. As cold as a blizzard wind.

Sera forced her eyelids open, groaning in pain. The heat of the sea scorpion's venom still burned inside her. It was agony to move, to breathe.

She remembered things . . . Mahdi's voice, his face . . . a long journey . . . the scorpion forcing her to eat . . .

Little by little, her vision cleared. She realized she was sitting in a chair. In a room. *Her* room. She recognized the mica panels, the furniture, the anemones on the walls.

I'm hallucinating, she thought. *It's the venom.* She closed her eyes again.

"I *said*, wake up!"

This time the command was followed by a hard, stinging slap.

Sera gasped. Her eyes flew open. Her hand rose tremblingly to her cheek.

Lucia Volnero was right in front of her, leaning on the arms of the chair. Her hair, long and loose, plumed around her head. Her face was only inches away. Sera could see her sapphire eyes gleaming with malice.

Lucia smiled. "That's better," she said, straightening. "So, you met my maligno," she added, pointing at the creature floating motionlessly in a corner. "Isn't he a perfect likeness? It took him quite a long time to do his job. I was worried you'd die on the way back and spoil my fun, so I cast a velo to speed his return."

"Why . . . why are you—" Sera struggled to speak.

Lucia cut her off. "Because you enchanted Mahdi, and I plan to break that enchantment."

"I didn't . . . cast an enchantment . . ." Sera murmured. It was so hard to make words come. But it didn't even matter. Lucia wasn't listening.

"You tricked him. And then forced him to spy for you and your shabby little resistance. But I'm going to free him by killing you. It's the only way to truly make him mine."

"Lucia, *no* . . ." The mermaid was as evil as her parents. She was going to murder her in cold blood. "Please . . . don't do this . . ."

"*I* won't. I'd just plunge a knife through your heart, and that would be too easy a death. I want you to suffer. A friend of mine's going to see that you do. Give her my best."

Sera made one last desperate attempt to escape. She rose from the chair and took a few, faltering strokes, but then, overcome by pain, she collapsed to the floor. As she rolled onto her back, the room started to swirl. She could see the chandelier above her. It seemed to come alive before her eyes. Its bronze arms, green with corrosion, became as fluid as an octopus's tentacles.

Now Sera knew she was hallucinating.

"It's over, Serafina," Lucia said triumphantly. "*I* win, you lose."

She barked an order at the maligno, and seconds later, Serafina felt it take hold of her arms and yank her up off the floor. She fought it, clawing at it. Her fingers gouged its cheek. Instead of blood flowing from the wound, silt poured out.

Sera screamed.

"Sicario, do your work," Lucia said.

The sea scorpion scuttled out from under a table and cruelly stung Serafina again.

There was pain, white and blinding, and then Sera dimly felt the maligno throw her over his shoulder, as if she were nothing more than a sack of garbage. The pain grew. The paralysis took over.

The last thing Sera saw was Lucia's cruel, mocking smile. The last thing she felt was Lucia tugging at her hand.

And then there was nothing. Nothing at all.

THIRTY-FIVE

ECCA, A HOOD PULLED up over her red hair, swam up to the door of the ancient palazzo. With a wary glance around, she lifted the heavy iron knocker and let it drop.

Tiny sand smelt, spooked by the sound, darted for cover, their bodies flashes of silver in the murk. Slender pipefish hid in clumps of seaweed. A squid vanished in a cloud of ink. The noise echoed loudly down the current. Becca winced, worried that she'd alerted an enemy to her presence. She waited, nervously flipping her tail fins, but no one answered.

"This *must* be the place," she said to herself. Though it was well past midnight, lights from the human city above penetrated the dark water of the Lagoon deeply enough that Becca could see the whole of the palazzo's ornate front. It matched Neela's description.

Built of white marble, with a tall, Gothic doorway, the palazzo's facade also boasted a carved relief of the goddess Neria, and a frieze of sea flowers, fish, and shells.

On either side of the heavy doors were stone faces with blind eyes and open mouths. Neela said the faces had spoken when she and Sera had been taken to the palazzo by the Praedatori. They were silent now.

Had she come all this way for nothing?

Her friends' voices echoed in her head. They'd tried to talk her out of this.

"It's too much of a long shot," Neela had said.

"It's way too dangerous," Yazeed added.

"What if you get caught?" Desiderio asked.

And then Ling had spoken. "They're right, Becs. It's a pretty desperate plan, but it's also all we've got."

Becca had left the Darktide Shallows, and her friends, and had swum for days until she reached a goblin village. She'd found a mirror in the vacant home of a wealthy goblin family, and she'd swum through it into Vadus.

Rorrim Drol had spotted her there, but not before she'd gotten directions to a mirror in the Lagoon from one of his vitrina. She managed to escape Rorrim, and only moments ago, she'd swum out of that mirror and into a nearby mer dwelling. Luckily the mirror's owner was not in the room at the time, and she was able to hurry out of an open window before she was discovered.

Becca *had* to get inside the palazzo. Rumors had been circulating that the Praedatori were finally regrouping. Some of them had been spotted in the Lagoon. There could only be one reason for that: their leader was back in Venice, and they were returning to his home— their old headquarters.

Marco had told Becca that he'd left his family's palazzo because it was too dangerous for him to be there. She desperately hoped he'd come back. But even if he wasn't there, maybe she could leave a message for him with one of the Praedatori, asking him to come to the Kargjord. The Black Fins had only the slimmest chance of rescuing Sera—and Marco was it.

Becca knocked once more now, but again no one answered.

She took a few strokes back from the door and eyed the upper levels of the palazzo. The windows had been boarded up. Everything—the carvings, the pediments, the fluted columns—was covered in silt. The whole place looked abandoned to anyone swimming by.

But Becca Quickfin wasn't just anyone. She was bright and

sharp-eyed, and almost immediately she saw that the lock under the door's massive handle didn't match the rest of the palazzo's facade. Its keyhole wasn't filled with silt. It wasn't rusted or corroded. In fact, it looked new.

As Becca was pondering the lock, a movement to her left startled her. Her head snapped around. Her hand went for her dagger.

But there was nothing there. Nothing but the columns, the carvings, the impassive stone face.

Becca swam closer, peering at it. Was it her imagination, or had she seen its mouth twitch?

"You *have* to let me in. I need to see him," she said.

The stone face said nothing.

"You moved. I *saw* you," said Becca. Loudly. But the face maintained its silence.

"I need to speak with Marco!" she demanded. "Let. Me. *In!*"

And then everything happened at once.

A hand was clapped over Becca's mouth. An arm snaked around her waist. She tried to scream but couldn't. She heard the lock's bolt turn, then the doors swung open. Her assailant shoved her inside with such force that she went tumbling through the water head over tail.

The door slammed behind her. The bolt shot into place.

Becca was alone in the dark.

THIRTY-SIX

"HELLO? IS THERE anyone here?" Becca called out, picking herself up off a cold stone floor.

She was inside the duca's palazzo. The waters were so black, she could barely see her own hands in front of her. There was no light to use for an illuminata songspell, so she cast some waterfire instead. Her voice was shaky, and the spell produced only a tiny flame. It rose from the floor, revealing the high-ceilinged entry hall she now found herself in.

"Hello? Marco? *Anybody?*"

As the words left her lips, Becca felt vibrations in the murk. A split second later, something sliced through the water in front of her, silent and swift.

She glimpsed a black eye, a jagged row of teeth, a shimmer of gray.

It was a mako shark.

She whirled around and saw three more.

Becca knew that if the sharks wanted to attack, they would've done so by now. Instead, they seemed to be herding her. Bit by bit they nudged her down the long hallway and then upward, through a vertical passage. The water lightened as she rose, and a reflection of fire—airfire, the kind made by terragoggs—rippled on top of it.

She stopped, trying to see up through the water to what awaited her on the surface. As she did, she felt a tug on her left hand and gasped, afraid that it was one of the sharks. Looking down, she was surprised to find that a tiny orange octopus, no more than seven inches in diameter, had wrapped a short, stubby tentacle around her pinky finger. It had round eyes and tiny triangular fins on the top of its head that looked like ears.

"This way, mermaid!" the little creature squeaked, pointing with another tentacle.

"But the sharks—" Becca started to say.

"Oh, they won't touch us. They're afraid of me," the octopus said. She raised one of her tentacles and flexed it, like a bodybuilder showing off a bicep.

Though she was still scared, it was all Becca could do not to burst into laughter. She followed the absurd little octopus up through the water toward a cavernous room that contained both water and air.

As Becca broke the surface, she found that she was floating in a very large indoor pool. Three of the pool's sides were sheer, tiled walls, but the fourth ended in a shallow ledge. Beyond it was a room for humans. Its floor was carpeted. Shelves full of books lined the walls. Flames crackled in a large fireplace.

Floating by the ledge, all in a row, were ten mermen. They all held spearguns, and every single one of them was trained on Becca.

"Who are you and why are you here?" one of them asked. "Answer the question."

"Those are two questions, actually," Becca pointed out, removing her hood. "I'm here because I need the duca's help. My name is Rebecca Quickfin, and I—"

"Becca?" a voice called out, one that she had longed to hear ever since they'd parted.

"Marco?" she called back, uncertainly. "Where are—"

Before she could even finish her sentence, Becca saw a blur on the edge of the pool. She heard a splash. And then a human surfaced.

A human with warm brown eyes and a beautiful smile. His

brown hair, sopping wet, lay plastered across his forehead. Drops of water rolled down his handsome face.

"Marco!"

And then his arms were around her, and his lips were on hers. And there was no possible or impossible, no calculations or formulas or theories. There was only her heart, and the huge, wonderful, terrible feeling that filled it. *Love*.

A few seconds later, though, she remembered that they were not alone, and she hastily broke the kiss, embarrassed.

The ten mermen had lowered their spearguns. Some were busily examining the triggers now, others were looking at the ceiling.

"Um, sorry," Marco said sheepishly. "I got carried away. I can't *believe* it's you, Becca. I can't believe you're here!"

"I guess that explains the warm mako-shark welcome," Becca said, arching an eyebrow.

"Sorry about that, too. We saw you on a hidden camera, but we couldn't see your face under that hood. One of the Praedatori grabbed you and pushed you inside. We had to make sure you weren't a death rider. No one knows we're here and we want to keep it that way. How did *you* know?"

"I didn't know. I hoped," Becca admitted. "Big-time."

"I see you met Opie," Marco said, nodding at the orange octopus, who had now made a bracelet of herself on Becca's wrist.

"I have," Becca said, smiling. Opie smiled back.

"She's a new breed. *Opisthotheusis adorabilis*. New to humans, at least. She was injured when we found her. A storm had pulled her away from her nest and really tossed her around. I brought her aboard our boat to treat her and tried to put her back when she was better, but she wouldn't go. Would you, Opie?"

Opie shook her head.

"You're going to have to go back home one day, though."

Opie turned red. She shot a jet of water at his face.

"Hey!" Marco said sternly, wiping his eyes. "I thought we had a talk about manners!"

Opie turned blue. Ashamed, she scuttled up Becca's arm to her shoulder, then buried her face in Becca's neck.

Marco rolled his eyes. His suddenly dipped under the water, then surfaced again. "This stuff's too heavy," he said. "I can't stay afloat."

As he swam to the edge of the pool and boosted himself up, Becca realized he was wearing a shirt, tie, jacket, trousers, shoes, and socks.

"You dove into the pool in your *clothes?*" she asked.

Marco nodded. He glanced at his wrist and grimaced. "And a really nice watch," he said. He took it off and laid it aside. "You must've come a long way. Are you hungry?"

Becca shook her head. "I don't have time to eat. We're in trouble, Marco. Serious trouble."

Marco paused in the midst of removing one of his shoes. His eyes darkened. "What kind of trouble? What happened?"

"Sera was taken. By Vallerio, we think."

Marco's expression darkened as Becca told him exactly what had transpired. "We want to attack Cerulea and take her back. I came here to ask you to help us."

"Anything, Becca," he said. "What do you need?"

Becca took a deep breath. This was it. Her plan. It would live or die now, depending on Marco.

"I need a super trawler," she said. "Actually, I need fifty. Can you get them for me?"

THIRTY-SEVEN

*J*UST FIVE DAYS TO GO, *and I'm out,* Mahdi thought.

It was less than a week, but it seemed like an eternity. Five days of enduring Lucia's smile, her touch, her kisses. Of listening to the boring gossip and cruel jokes of her friends. Five days of dancing attendance on Portia. Of listening to Vallerio's plans to raid more villages, enslave more citizens. Of hauling Black Fin sympathizers out of their hiding places while on patrol. Five days of enduring Traho's suspicious glances. Of trying to keep up the pretense of being loyal to a pack of murderers.

He was with them now, some of the very mer he despised. He, Lucia, and their court were swimming through the palace gardens. Some courtiers were talking about the wedding, others about the party he was going to throw the night before. Lucia was bragging about wedding presents they'd received.

Hang on, he told himself. *Smile and nod. You've done it for months; you can do it for a few more days.*

His escape had been planned weeks ago. Currensea and clothing, as well as the location of his first safe house, had been hidden in a sunken yacht east of the city. When Mahdi got there, he would learn the location of the second one. He would move from one to the next until he'd made it all the way to the Straits of Gibraltar, where he'd rendezvous with Sera and the other Black Fins.

". . . and my cousins sent the most incredible set of goblets you've ever seen! There are ten of them, pure silver and studded with amethysts. An aunt sent a solid gold lavalabra that's nearly as tall as I am. . . ."

Lucia droned on, bragging about the tribute she'd received, as her lackeys oohed and aahed. When she finished, she pulled Mahdi away from the rest of the court, until they were out of earshot. Then she turned to face him, biting her lower lip. Her eyes sparkled darkly.

"*I* have a gift for *you*, Mahdi," she declared. "An early wedding present. I wanted to wait until after we were married to give it to you, but I just can't! You're going to *love* it!"

Mahdi set his thoughts aside and smoothly slipped back into the role of besotted husband-to-be. He'd recently doubled down on the compliments and public displays of affection.

Smiling, he took Lucia's hands in his. "Sorry, Luce," he said, kissing her, "but I already got the best present in the entire world . . . *you*."

Catfish calls were heard from the male courtiers. Lucia flapped a hand at them and pulled Mahdi farther away. "Hold out your hand and close your eyes," she commanded.

Mahdi did so, and Lucia placed a small object on his palm.

"Now open them!" she said.

The color drained from Mahdi's face when he saw what he was holding. He could barely breathe. It was a delicate ring made of shell—the ring he'd carved for Serafina.

"Where did you get this?" he asked in a strangled voice.

"I took it off her hand. Right before I had her killed!" Lucia said happily. Her blue eyes were so dark now, they looked almost black.

"Lucia," Mahdi whispered, "what have you *done*?"

She leaned in close to him. "I just *told* you, Mahdi. I killed Sera. She's gone. And you're free. You were under a terrible enchantment, and you didn't even know it. Serafina cast a songspell over you to make you think you were in love with her. To make you spy for her. But now I've broken the spell and saved you."

"You . . . you murdered Sera?" Mahdi said. He felt as if she had just crushed his heart with her bare hands.

Lucia's eyes narrowed. "You lied to me, Mahdi. And to my parents," she said. "All this time, you've been helping the Black Fins. Feeding them information. Spying for them. *I* understand. Because I know what Sera did. But I'm not sure my father would . . . if he were ever to find out."

Mahdi nodded woodenly. He understood the implied threat.

Lucia's expression hardened. "You're not *upset*, are you?"

Summoning all the strength he had left, Mahdi pulled himself together. He had to play along. Lucia was pure evil. If she'd known about Sera, what else did she know? That Yaz was alive? Neela, too? He didn't care about his life anymore; it was over. But others might live or die depending on what he did next.

"Yes, I am upset, Luce. Upset that you've given me a better wedding present than I could ever give you!" he said, smiling.

Lucia, seeing that he'd been teasing her, swatted him.

Mahdi pulled her close. "Thank you," he said. "I mean it, Lucia. You not only freed me, you did what your father and Traho and all the death riders together couldn't: you eliminated a serious threat to our power. With Sera gone, no one can question your claim to the Miromaran throne, or your right to be my empress." He kissed her lips. "Five whole days. How am I going to make it?"

Lucia's lips curved up, and she melted into him. "I'm so happy that you're happy, Mahdi. I was so worried that you had feelings for her. Before I realized that she'd enchanted you, I mean."

"Don't be silly," Mahdi said tenderly, stroking her face. "You're the only one I care about, Luce."

"I care about you, too, Mahdi. So much," Lucia said passionately. "Sera didn't. She didn't care if her enchantment got you killed."

As she spoke, she pulled something out of her pocket. It was a chain made of dark metal, small but heavy. Before Mahdi even knew what she was doing, she'd looped it around his neck, slipped the hasp of a tiny padlock through both ends, and clicked it shut.

"What is this?" he asked. He hooked a finger in the chain, pulled it taut, and tried to look at it, but he couldn't. It was too short.

"It's a protective iron necklace, Mahdi. Uncuttable. It'll keep you from contacting the Black Fins with a convoca, or casting a transparensea pearl to escape."

Mahdi stiffened. He was furious, and humiliated, but more than that, he was panic-stricken. Iron repelled magic. As long as it was on him, he wouldn't be able to songcast. Magic helped him get messages to the Black Fins. How would he tell them what Lucia had done to Sera?

"Unlock it, Lucia," he said angrily. *"Now."*

Lucia shook her head. "It's for your own good. The effects of a strong enchantment can linger. The Black Fins might still be controlling you."

"Get it *off* me. It's a collar. I'm not a dogfish."

"Of course you're not," Lucia soothed, smiling. "And I *will* take it off. On our wedding day so you can sing your vows. By then, the spell will have worn off completely. You'll be safe, Mahdi. You'll be mine."

"Lucia—" He was about to keep arguing with her, but he suddenly stopped. Because an idea had come to him, inspired by her words. . . . *You can sing your vows. . . .*

I can now, he realized. Sera, his beloved, was dead, and her death released him from the vows they'd made. That changed everything. The collar didn't matter anymore. Nothing did. He wouldn't escape from this place, and from Lucia, even if he could. A plan had begun to take shape in his mind. He saw that the best way to help the Black Fins now, and to avenge Sera's death, was to stay right here.

And go through with his wedding.

"You're not angry with me, are you, Mahdi?" Lucia asked, her eyes searching his. "I *told* you, it's for your own good."

"Oh, I was for a moment," he said, laughingly. "Because I didn't understand, but I do now. You're absolutely right. We can't take any chances. Unlock it on our wedding day. Oh, hey!" he exclaimed, snapping his fingers. "Speaking of weddings, I nearly forgot! I have a fitting for my wedding jacket in five minutes. I've got to make wake, but I'll see you at dinner."

Lucia made a disappointed face.

"It's only a couple hours away! Don't forget about me, okay?" He kissed her again, then said, "I love you, merl." He was smiling at her, but the words were acid in his mouth.

He swam away fast, looking distracted, as if he'd really forgotten an appointment. He sped over the gardens, under an arched doorway, through labyrinthine hallways to the west wing of the palace. He rushed past officials, ministers, and servants, and then finally arrived at the door to his rooms.

"I'm not to be disturbed," he barked at his guards, as they opened the door for him.

The guards nodded, then closed the door behind him. As soon as they did, Mahdi's mask fell away, and an expression of tearing grief took its place. He would never see Sera's beautiful face again. Never hear his name on her lips. Never gaze into her green eyes, so full of life. So full of love. He took two strokes into the room, faltered, and crumpled.

"Sera," he wept. "Oh, gods . . . *Sera.*"

He stayed that way for a long time, eyes closed, overwhelmed by sorrow. Sera was *gone.* And with her, his heart and soul. He was nothing now. Just an empty shell.

Some hours later, as the waters were just starting to darken, a knock on the door tore him from his misery.

"I'm sorry, Your Grace," a voice called through the door, "but it's almost dinnertime. Do you require my help dressing?"

It was Mahdi's valet.

"No, Emilio, I'll do it myself tonight, thanks," he called back, struggling to sound normal.

"Very well, Your Grace," Emilio said.

Mahdi knew he would have to get up. Somehow, he would have to dress, go to dinner, and smile at Lucia. His thoughts returned to the plan that he'd started to shape earlier, the plan to help the Black Fins. He wasn't the only one who had lost Sera. They had, too. So had the merfolk of her realm. It was them he had to think of now, not himself.

Through sheer force of will, Mahdi opened his eyes. As he did, something bright caught them.

His wedding jacket. Made of emerald-colored sea silk, it was hanging in a corner of his room. He'd lied about the fitting appointment. It had been tailored days ago. A servant must've brought it into the room earlier this afternoon. It was buttoned up, finished, all ready for him to wear.

"Five days," he whispered, sitting up.

A grim smile played over his features as Lucia's voice echoed in his head. *You can sing your vows. . . .*

"Yes, I can. And I *will*," he said quietly.

He would do what he had to do until then. He'd smile and joke and play the part of the happy bridegroom for four more days.

And then, on the night of the fifth day, when the moon had risen, he would take that jacket off its hanger, and dress for his wedding.

And his funeral.

THIRTY-EIGHT

A SOUND—A LONG, screeching scrape—woke Serafina.

Metal, she thought groggily, opening her eyes. *Metal on stone. Lucia's executioner must be sharpening his ax.*

Her vision was blurry. Her body ached. She had no idea how long she'd been unconscious. Hours? Days? She felt weak. Her head was impossibly heavy, but she raised it nonetheless. It was over. She would die now, but she would die like the regina she was—looking death squarely in the eye.

Sera was not afraid of death, but she was crushed by the knowledge of her failure. She'd allowed herself to be captured and now she was powerless to stop Orfeo, and her uncle. She'd failed her friends and her merfolk, and she'd failed in her quest to destroy Abbadon. Would the others make it to the Southern Sea? Would they be able to destroy the monster? Sera would never know. In her struggle to stay one stroke ahead of her uncle, she'd forgotten the danger Lucia posed. Her rival hadn't merely moved or countermoved, she'd swept the game pieces right off the board.

Sera tried to move her arms now but couldn't; they were bound by her sides. Her tail was immobilized, too.

"Shackles," she whispered. "Shackles and chains."

They were all that was left to her. She had nothing. No weapon. No troops. No friends by her side.

Her vision cleared. Feeble light, shining from above, illuminated a cave shaggy with algae. Feathery tube worms clung to the walls. Long-legged brittlestars crept across the ceiling.

Is this the dungeon? she wondered, glancing around. It didn't look like one. Where were the guards? Where was the executioner?

She looked down at her body and saw that she wasn't actually shackled. Instead, she was encased in what looked like a cocoon. A fine metal filament had been wound around her body all the way from her tail fins to her neck. Another length of filament ran from the cocoon to the cave's ceiling, suspending her over a pile of bones and skulls, some yellowed with age, others fresh and bloody.

"No!" Sera uttered in a choked voice. Suddenly it all made sense . . . the cave, the scraping sound—metal on stone.

I want you to suffer, Lucia had said.

And Sera knew that she would. Her death would be agonizing. Her executioner's venom would paralyze her, just like the sea scorpion's had, but this creature had more than a barb in its tail. It had fangs, and they were twelve inches long.

The scraping sound grew louder. The thing making it drew closer.

As Sera watched, a nightmare loomed out of the darkness: Alítheia, the murderous bronze sea spider.

THIRTY-NINE

THE SPIDER'S CURVED fangs were only inches from Sera's face. She cocked her head, examining Sera with her eight black eyes.

"Finally awake! But only ssskin and bonesss!" she hissed unhappily, prodding Sera with a hooked claw. "No meat for Alítheia!"

"Alítheia, please listen to me—"

"No! You mussst lisssten. Alítheia isss not ready to eat yet, but sssoon, sssoon," the spider said, rubbing her front claws together. "Alítheia will bring food. You will eat it. Moon jelliesss, yesss. To make you plump!"

The spider turned and scuttled off.

"Wait!" Sera begged. "You can't kill me! I'm Serafina, the rightful heiress to Miromara's throne!

The spider waved a leg at Sera. "Everyone sssaysss thisss," she hissed, without even turning around.

"Alítheia, *please*," Sera said, her voice breaking. "It's the truth! Taste my blood!"

"I will, mermaid, I will."

And then she was gone, moving off toward the far end of the cave. Light shone down there from an iron grille that covered the outside entrance to the spider's den, which was in the center of the kolisseo, an outdoor arena. Alítheia scuttled up the craggy walls toward it, and stuck a leg out through the bars.

She's fishing for moon jellies, Sera thought.

As Sera desperately tried to figure out how to convince the spider not to eat her, Alítheia suddenly shrieked. The next thing Sera knew, the spider was frantically clambering back down the wall.

A burst of bright light followed her, nearly hitting her, then exploded like a bomb on the floor of the cave, hissing and bubbling. It forced her to take cover in a hollow on the other side of the cave's entrance.

More bombs came hurting through the grille.

"Lava globes," Sera whispered.

The lava was followed by laughter and taunts. Sera recognized the voices—they belonged to Feuerkumpel goblins.

"Help!" she shouted. "Is anyone there? Somebody please help me!"

The goblins only laughed harder. They imitated her pleas for help, then chucked more lava bombs.

I can't die here, I can't! she thought wildly. *Miromara needs me; my friends need me to help defeat Abbadon.*

She remembered the vision Vrăja had shown to her and her friends of the monster destroying Atlantis. She remembered the fire, the screaming, the blood. So many had suffered and died then. So many more would now, if Orfeo managed to free his creature.

Sera's fear turned into fury. She struggled and thrashed, trying to break out of the cocoon. But all she succeeded in doing was tiring herself. She lowered her head, spent.

The cruel goblin voices were in her ears, in her head. Their taunts, telling her she was going to die slowly and painfully, were all she could hear. Then, tiring of their sport, they moved off, and Sera become aware of another voice.

"Principessa Serafina? Can it *be?*"

Sera's breath caught. She thought she recognized the voice, but she was afraid to hope. "Fossegrim?" she called out.

"Yes, it is I!" he shouted back.

Her old friend, the liber magus! "Where are you?" Sera shouted.

"Below you," Fossegrim replied.

Serafina twisted and strained, trying to see him. She spotted him to her left. "Are you in a cocoon, too?" she asked him.

"Indeed I am."

"How did you get here?"

"I and my fellow Black Fins were found in the Ostrokon on the same day Vallerio returned to Cerulea. Death riders have been interrogating me ever since, for months and months, but I've given them nothing. They must've finally realized it was hopeless, for they threw me into the spider's lair six days ago."

Sera knew all too well how Traho interrogated his prisoners. She could only imagine what the brave old merman had gone through.

"Fossegrim, are you . . . are you . . ."

"Still in once piece?" he asked. There was a short silence, then, "Let's just say I shall find it difficult to shelve conchs again."

"Your fingers . . ." Sera said in a choked voice.

"Indeed, child. What he didn't cut off, he broke."

"He'll pay for this," Sera said vehemently, furious that Traho had hurt this wise, gentle merman. "I swear to the gods, he'll pay."

She tried once more to break free of the cocoon, to no avail. Not only was she weak, she was hungry, too.

"Fossegrim, do you know how long I've been here?"

"Five days. Alítheia dragged you in the day after she dragged me here," Fossegrim replied. "She said you'd been left in a tunnel. You've been unconscious all that time."

Which means I've been in Cerulea for, what? Sera wondered. *Eight or nine days? Ten?*

"I feared you were dead, but Alítheia said you were full of scorpion's venom. She was angry. She wanted to eat you right away, but she said your flesh would be bitter until the venom wore off. I'm afraid she ate something—some*one*—else in the meantime," he added.

"Has she threatened to eat you?"

He shook his head. "She says I'm old and tough and she's only keeping me around as a last resort." He chuckled. "Makes me feel like a sweet that nobody wants, one with a sea urchin center."

"We need to escape before she eats either of us, and I haven't a clue how to make that happen," Sera said. "If only I had my sword or dagger, I could cut my way out."

Fossegrim cleared his throat. "I find that success—in extricating oneself from captivity, or in *any* endeavor, really—comes down, essentially, to belief."

Sera had forgotten the liber magus's exasperating tendency to pontificate. There was a time and place for his wordy ramblings, but this definitely wasn't it.

"So, all we have to do is *believe* we'll get out of here, and we will?" she asked skeptically.

"Precisely," Fossegrim replied. "Belief leads to action, and action leads to success. If you do not believe you can get out of here, you'll give up, do nothing, and merely dangle uselessly, waiting for the end to come. However, if you *do* believe escape is possible, you'll snap into action and use all the weapons at your disposal to attain your liberty."

Sera rolled her eyes. "Fossegrim, maybe you haven't realized this, but I don't *have* any weapons. I can't even move my hands. I'm in a *cocoon!*"

Fossegrim sighed deeply, as he often had in his ostrokon when confronted by a particularly dense student.

"Is it not strange that this creature that inspires such great fear in so many, is—at this moment—so full of fear herself?" he asked, nodding in the direction of the grille.

The goblins had left, but Alítheia was still huddled in the hollow where she'd taken cover, cringing and hissing.

"For four thousand years, the anarachna has been carrying out the task with which Merrow charged her: to ascertain who is fit for the throne," he continued, his eyes still on the spider. "Yet she's reviled. Taunted. Banished to a dark cave under the seafloor. What poor recompense for such long and faithful service." He shifted his gaze back to Sera. "You *do* have a weapon, child. Can you not see it?"

Serafina was about to argue with him when she heard Vrăja's voice in her head again, as she did so often in times of trouble. *Nothing is more powerful than love.*

Love. It was easy to feel it for Mahdi, her friends, her merfolk. It was a lot harder to feel it for a giant bronze spider that wanted to eat her.

Sera saw what Fossegrim was trying to say, though—that the anarachna, like any creature, deserved to be treated kindly. With respect. Even love.

Sera would try to do that now. She had no choice.

Love was the only weapon she had left.

FORTY

ALONG BRONZE LEG, articulated at the joints and tipped by a dagger-sharp claw, poked out of the hollow. It was followed by another, and several more, and then the anarachna emerged fully.

Sera watched her, knowing she had only minutes to put her plan in motion. The bloodbind had given her some of her five friends' talents. She summoned Ava's gift of sight now, focusing it on the spider.

For a few tense seconds, she sensed nothing. Then an image of high, impenetrable walls came into her mind. She felt various emotions as she concentrated on the image: anger, fear, but most of all, sadness.

Sera knew that she would have to tap into those emotions if she had any chance of engaging Alítheia, but she'd have to proceed slowly. The spider had built walls around her feelings for a reason, and drawing them out would be a delicate task. Sera had seen Alítheia in a rage during her Dokimí, when the spider learned she wouldn't be able to eat Sera, and Sera knew how quickly Alítheia could become violent. If Sera wasn't careful, she'd set the creature off and get herself killed.

"Alítheia, are you okay? Did you get hurt?" she asked gently.

"A sssmall burn only. But Alítheia found no moon jelliesss. Ssshe mussst hunt them elsssewhere. You mussst eat them, ssso ssshe can eat you," the spider said, crawling past Sera.

"Alítheia, *wait*!" Sera called out, desperate to keep the spider talking. "Why do the goblins throw lava at you?"

"Becaussse they are cruel. Like the commander. Like hisss daughter. Thisss isss how thingsss are now."

Vallerio and Lucia, Sera thought grimly. *They're setting a fine example, as always.*

"The goblins shouted at you. What did they say?"

The spider stopped. She turned around. Hope leapt in Sera.

"They sssaid, 'We made you, Alítheia. And we can kill you, too.' Why sssay sssuch thingsss? They *did* make Alítheia, but ssshe desspisssesss them! Neria iss the one who breathed life into Alítheia, not the ssstinking goblinsss. Merrow isss the one who gave her purpossse."

The spider shook her head sorrowfully as she spoke.

"What's wrong?" asked Sera.

"The goblinsss taunt Alítheia becaussse they are afraid of her," said the spider. "Her purpossse is to ssscare all thossse who would take the throne of Miromara, but ssshe ssscaresss *everyone*, not just imposssstersss."

"Maybe we could change that," Sera ventured, hoping to soften the creature.

"No," Alítheia said brusquely. "Merrow made Alítheia thisss way, and none can change her. Ssshe wanted Alítheia to frighten enemiesss of the throne, becaussse ssshe hersssself was frightened."

Sera's hope trickled away as the spider continued down the tunnel.

"What was Merrow afraid of, Alítheia?" Sera shouted. It was the first thing that popped into head. She knew full well what Merrow was afraid of, but she was desperate.

Once again, the spider stopped. "Orfeo," she replied, a note of exasperation in her voice.

"Why? She thought Orfeo was dead," Sera said. "She believed that she and the other mages had killed him."

Alítheia turned back to Sera again. She shook her fearsome head. "When Abbadon attacked, there wasss no time. Only fear. Only death. After, there wasss time. To think. To remember. Time to go back to Atlantisss. Time to find out. To know."

"Know what?" Sera asked.

"What he *did*!" the spider said angrily, stamping her front legs. "How he made hisss monsssster!"

Sera caught her breath. "Great Neria, she *knows*," she whispered. "Alítheia *knows* what Abbadon's made of."

"Atlantis? Orfeo? Serafina, what are you talking about?" Fossegrim asked.

"I'll explain everything as soon as we get out of here, I promise," Sera said. She addressed the spider again. "Alítheia, please don't go down the tunnel," she begged. "Stay here. Talk to me. Tell me what you know."

Sera wasn't babbling anymore. Her conversation with Alítheia had taken a turn she hadn't expected. She'd forgotten she was a prisoner in the spider's den, forgotten the danger she was in. All she could think about was how close she was to the answer that had eluded her for so long. It had been right here, in Cerulea, all this time, with the Merrovingians' long-serving, faithful guardian.

Merrow, Nyx, Sycorax, Navi, Pyrrha—five of the greatest mages the world had ever known had not been able to kill Abbadon, because they'd had no idea what dark materials Orfeo had used to fashion the monster. But Merrow had found out. And she'd spoken about her discovery in front of Alítheia. Sera needed that information if she and her friends were to destroy the monster.

Sera knew that both the sea goddess Neria and Merrow had been present when Alítheia was made. There were mosaics in the ruins of Merrow's reggia that depicted the event. Goblins had mined the ore. Bellogrim, the god of fire, had forged her. Merrow had dripped her own blood in the vat of molten bronze. Neria herself had breathed life into the spider.

Sera had often imagined the conversation between Neria, Bellogrim, and Merrow, but that conversation had never included Alítheia, because Sera had never thought of the spider as a reasoning, feeling creature, one worth talking to.

But that had just changed.

"Alítheia, where did Merrow go when she went to Atlantis? Did she go to the death goddess Morsa's temple? Did she talk about it in front of you?" Sera asked, trying to contain her excitement.

"Yesss. Ssshe sssaid ssshe heard the sssouls. In the bloodsssong. And ssshe knew then what hisss monsssster wasss. *Sssouls*. Ssso many. Angry. Ssscared. Trapped. And ssshe undersssstood why ssshe and the other magesss could not kill it. Becaussse no one can kill—"

"An immortal soul," Sera finished, astonished. "Abbadon is made of human souls. Morsa taught Orfeo how to catch souls, and keep them, and he used the souls of the people he sacrificed to her to make a monster that was indestructible."

Alítheia nodded. "Many, many sssouls."

"So Merrow discovered that Orfeo could catch souls," Sera reasoned. "I bet she suspected that he'd learned how to catch his own. That's why she made her weird decrees. By stating that only a daughter of a daughter could rule Miromara, she made sure Orfeo could never rule if he somehow came back as himself. And if he figured out a way to take a female form and pretend to be the heiress to the throne, you would *still* find him out, Alítheia. You'd taste his blood at the Dokimí and declare him an imposter."

The spider nodded.

Sera was silent for a bit, digesting the enormity of her discovery. She was elated by it, and defeated by it. She'd learned what Abbadon was made of, but at the same time, she'd learned that she had no hope of killing it. How could anyone kill that which is immortal?

Unless the gods themselves had revealed how.

Clinging on to a last shred of hope, she said, "Alítheia, did Bellogrim say anything to Merrow about Abbadon? Did Neria? Did they tell her how to get rid of the monster?"

Alítheia shook her head. "They did not know how. The magic wasss Morsssssa's sssecret. And Orfeo'sss. But even if they had, it wasss too late. Merrow wasss too old, too weak."

Sera was bitterly disappointed. Her hope of finding out how to kill Abbadon had just been dashed. The spider was still gazing down the tunnel again, but abruptly turned away from it. "Alítheia will not go down the tunnel. Ssshe will not hunt moon jelliesss there."

"You won't?" Sera asked, breaking into a smile. At least her plan to save herself and Fossegrim had worked. She'd won the spider over. Alítheia wouldn't harm them now.

"No," Alítheia said, turning her black eyes to Sera. A drop of venom fell from one fang. "All thisss talking hasss made Alítheia hungry. Ssshe will eat now. Ssshe will eat *you*, mermaid, plump or not."

FORTY-ONE

THE HOLD OF THE SUPER trawler was filled with salt water—and with two thousand armed mer and goblins. Becca, floating among them, checked and rechecked her crossbow. It helped to calm her nerves.

Marco had come through for the Black Fins. Somehow, he'd persuaded practically everyone he knew who owned a boat—friends, fishermen, fellow wave warriors—to loan it to him. Tankers, trawlers, and fishing boats, they'd all met in the waters above the Kargjord five days ago, loaded their mer and goblin cargo, then headed south for the Mediterranean.

Secrecy spells had been cast to ensure that the human captains and crew never spoke of the mission—or sounded completely insane if they tried to, and velo spells had sped the vessels on their way.

The entire Black Fin force was assembling over Cerulea now, all hidden in gogg ships. It was nighttime, later than the Black Fins had wished, but foul weather in the North Atlantic had put them behind schedule. Tonight's skies were clear, and a full moon had risen. Anyone who was looking up through the water would see the ships' silhouettes. Becca and the other fighters hoped that Cerulea's security forces were too busy patrolling the city to notice the sudden increase in ship traffic.

At least they didn't have to worry about Mahdi. They'd sent a message conch to him telling him what had happened to Sera. They didn't know if they'd been successful, though; he hadn't sent word back. But even if the conch hadn't reached him, they knew he was safe. He would have cast his transparensea pearl earlier in the day, and by now would have left Cerulea far behind. The Black Fins had sent two soldiers to Mahdi's first safe house to fill him in on everything that had happened. They would tell him to stay at the safe house instead of swimming to Gibraltar, and wait with him there until there was word from Cerulea. Desiderio would send for him if the Black Fins managed to take the city, and if not . . . at least *he* would have escaped alive.

Becca and the Black Fins with her were now waiting for the signal that the rest of their troops were in position.

Though it was crowded and hot in the trawler's hold, it was also eerily quiet. The atmosphere was tense. They all knew they might be seeing the soldier next to them for the very last time. There was no telling who'd make it back and who wouldn't.

Becca heard Desiderio, Yazeed, and Garstig talking in low voices nearby, going over the plan as they had a thousand times already.

"We have to come out swinging. We need a quick, decisive victory," Yazeed said.

"So, five thousand of us will hit the palace," Des said.

"Is it enough?" Garstig worried.

"It should be. Don't forget that we have surprise on our side," Des said.

"I hope so," Garstig said. "Because Vallerio has Blackclaws on *his.*"

Becca knew, as did everyone else on the mission, that Vallerio kept vicious Blackclaw dragons in the ruins of Merrow's reggia. Sera had encountered them, with Sophia, when they were fleeing death riders after the raid on the treasury vaults.

"Our first wave blows the munitions storage inside the palace," Yaz continued. "Second wave tries to take out the dragons. Third surrounds the barracks. . . ."

Becca tuned the rest out. She knew the plan by heart. She'd thought up most of it.

She decided to inspect her armor again, making sure the buckles and clasps were secure. A small orange creature sat on one shoulder of her breastplate, looking like a colorful epaulet.

Opie had taken a liking to Becca and had refused to let go of her when she left Marco's palazzo. The tiny octopus had howled and turned colors and shot so many jets of water at Marco when he'd tried to pry her off Becca's wrist that he'd finally given up. Opie had traveled back to the Karg with Becca, but being a Pacific Ocean creature, she'd found the waters of the North Sea very cold. Becca had asked one of the Miromaran refugees, a craftswoman from Cerulea, to knit the little octopus a sea-flax sweater. The only sea flax that grew in the waters of the Kargjord, however, was bright purple. Opie made quite a sight in her eight-sleeved sweater, but she didn't mind. In fact, she loved the sweater so much she refused to take it off, even when they reached warmer waters.

As Becca examined her armor, her thoughts drifted back to the Iele. She remembered Vrăja telling her that she was the descendent of the mage Pyrrha, and that the brave Altantean had been a smith, hard at work at her forge on the edge of the island, when she'd seen a fleet of enemy ships approaching. Thinking fast, Pyrrha had dispatched a messenger to the capital, telling them that an attack was imminent. Then she converted the farm tools she'd forged into weapons, armed the people in her small village, and ambushed the invaders.

Becca had followed Pyrrha's example. The moment she'd returned from Marco's palazzo, she'd set about teaching the goblin forgeworkers how to heat pearls and insert invisibility spells into them, and then they'd worked around the clock in shifts to make enough transparensea pearls for every single soldier on the mission.

"You'll never get them done in time," Yazeed had said. "We need thousands of them, Becca. Tens of thousands. It's an impossible job."

"Probably," Becca said, but she got to work anyway and eventually she'd succeeded. Working side by side with the goblins, she'd done the impossible. Now, in mere minutes, they would cast those pearls, swim down into Cerulea, and battle Vallerio.

A door suddenly opened overhead, about two feet above the waterline. Marco stepped out and appeared on the catwalk that was anchored to the wall of the hold. Becca could see him, but he couldn't see her. Hers was just one more face in the sea of soldiers.

Her heart filled with love at the sight of him. Her eyes lingered over every plane and angle of his handsome face. She knew this might be the last time she saw it. She'd had so little time with him in Venice. As soon as he'd said he would get the ships, she'd returned to the Kargjord. As much as she'd wanted to stay with him, she'd known that every minute she lingered was another minute Sera spent as Vallerio's captive.

"Listen up, everyone!" he shouted now, holding his hands up. "I've just heard from the other ships. They're in position and waiting for the go-ahead. Des, what do you say?"

Desiderio nodded at Marco. After they'd returned to camp from the Darktide Shallows, Des had assembled the troops to tell them that Sera had been kidnapped. The fighters had rallied around him, swearing that Vallerio would pay. They'd been only too eager to get on board the transport ships and rescue their leader, and they were ready for what lay ahead.

Des swam to the ship's wall, leapt out of the water, and grabbed on to the bottom of the catwalk. Hanging on with one hand, muscles rippling in his arm, he addressed his troops. "Fellow Black Fins!" he shouted. "It's time! Time to take back Serafina, take back Miromara, take back all the waters of the world! We fight for our homes, and our families, and we fight for those who can't fight—those who are held prisoner, who've been taken from *their* homes and *their* families by the sea scum Vallerio! Are you with me?"

A deafening cheer rose. Desiderio looked up at Marco. "Give the others the signal," he said. "And, Marco . . . thank you."

Marco nodded. "Good luck."

As Desiderio dropped back into the water, Marco spoke into his walkie-talkie. A few seconds later, three sets of giant doors opened all along the top of the hold. Becca could see the sky through them, and the full moon glowing, so bright and beautiful. *Will I ever see it again?* she wondered. *Will any of us?*

Nets were lowered down into the hold by huge winches. Mer grabbed them and clung on as they were lifted again, then lowered into the ocean.

As Becca watched, she thought of how impossible this was—getting the Black Fins in and out of ships, getting them to Cerulea. And yet, it was happening.

So many things were impossible, until they weren't.

As the nets dipped back into the hold and soldiers surged toward them, Becca hung back. There was something she had to do before she left this ship. Something that scared her even more than the battle that lay ahead.

"Marco!" she called out. "Marco, it's me . . . Becca!"

He looked around, trying to hear her over the noise of the troops and the winches, trying to spot her in the mass of soldiers.

With difficulty, she swam against the tide of bodies.

"I didn't know you were aboard this ship!" he said as she reached him.

He put his walkie-talkie down on the catwalk and jumped into the water. As she surfaced, Opie leapt onto his arm.

"Hey, looking sharp, Opie!" he said. "Nice sweater."

The little octopus flushed pink with pleasure.

"Marco, listen," Becca said. "I don't know if I'm coming back—"

"Don't say that, Becca."

"I *have* to. And I have to tell you something: I love you, too. I have ever since I first saw you. No matter what happens, I want you to know that."

And then Becca took his face in her hands and kissed him.

Opie looked from Becca to Marco and back again, wide-eyed. She flushed bright red.

This wasn't their first kiss, but it might be their last, Becca knew. And she wanted Marco to remember—this kiss, this moment, her. Because if an arrow found her tonight, the last thing she would see would be his kind, beautiful face.

A loud noise overhead made Becca break the kiss. "I have to go," she said, looking up. The winches were swinging back again. "It's time to join the others." She leaned over and kissed the top of Opie's head. "You stay *here* now," she said. "Where you're safe."

Opie turned blue, but she didn't protest.

As Becca was about to swim away, Marco grabbed her hand. "Make sure you come back, Becca," he said, his voice suddenly husky. "Because I want a shot."

"At what?"

"At the impossible."

FORTY-TWO

THE MOON was almost fully risen.

Mahdi could see its light, pale and silvery, shining into the windows of Neria's temple.

He was waiting by the altar, dressed in his green sea-silk wedding jacket. He no longer had Lucia's cursed iron necklace around his neck, as she'd unlocked it earlier.

Portia and Vallerio were seated at a distance from Mahdi, in the front row with their relatives, allies, and members of their court. Mahdi's so-called friends—some high-ranking death riders and court lackeys—filled the other pews.

"Nervous?" Traho whispered, patting Mahdi on the back.

Mahdi smiled. "Very," he admitted. It was no lie. He was, but not because he was getting married.

He'd asked Traho to be his best man, to ensure his attendance, to get him in the same room with Vallerio so that he could assassinate them both. This was his mission, the one he'd given himself the day he learned Sera was dead. Soon, it would be accomplished.

Months ago, he'd taken the precaution of hiding a small silver speargun in the chimney of the lavaplace in his rooms. That gun was now loaded and holstered inside his jacket. There was a moment in the mer wedding ceremony, after the bride and groom had sung their vows, when their fathers approached to kiss them and congratulate them, followed by their mothers doing the same. Mahdi's father wouldn't be here, since Vallerio had murdered him, but Vallerio certainly would be. As he came close, Mahdi would unbutton his jacket and reach for his gun.

He knew he wouldn't have much time and might not be able to fire more than one shot, so he would aim for Vallerio first; then he'd try to get Traho. Soon thereafter he himself would be killed. There were armed guards in the temple, at least thirty of them.

With Vallerio and Traho gone, Orfeo's reach would be weakened. That might give Sera's friends enough of an advantage to triumph in the Southern Sea. He hoped so. It was the only thing he had left to hope for.

He wasn't afraid of death. It was only his body that would die. His heart and soul were already gone. They'd died the moment Lucia handed him Sera's ring.

The opening notes of the wedding processional sounded. Court songcasters, mermaids and mermen blessed with the best voices in the realm, flanked the altar. Their song rose in the water.

> *Suspended in the vast night sky,*
> *Glows a moon so full and high.*
> *Tonight, with sun and earth aligned,*
> *Her magic will two royal hearts bind.*

> *Rise now, cherished wedding guests,*
> *As the moon moves east to west,*
> *Offer blessings, prayers, and heartfelt songs,*
> *For lasting love, both true and strong.*

The wedding guests rose and looked toward the back of the temple. Lucia's cousins, Laktara, Vola, and Falla swam in, enchanting everyone with their beauty. They took their places at the right of the altar. Traho joined them there. A moment later, Lucia swam down the aisle. Mer brides swam to their grooms alone to symbolize that they entered into marriage of their own free will.

All eyes turned to Lucia as she moved toward the altar. Hushed expressions of awe and admiration rose.

She was stunning in her dress made from sliver-thin slices of emerald stitched onto a sheath of dark green sea silk. The jewels caught the moonlight and held it. Lucia's every movement made the entire gown shimmer. She wore her midnight-black hair long and flowing, and flashed a triumphant smile.

Mahdi arranged his face into an expression of happiness and beamed at his bride. Lucia drew nearer. She was halfway down the aisle now. To Mahdi, she seemed like a specter gliding toward him, a harbinger of his death.

She arrived at the altar and swam to Mahdi's side.

The priestess directed the bride and bridegroom to face each other. "Deeply beloved," she began, "we are gathered here today . . ."

Mahdi barely heard her. He was going through the motions. Waiting for his chance. It would be over soon. All he wanted was to rid the world of the evil in this room.

When Lucia raised her right hand, he raised his. The priestess bound them together by winding a cord of kelp around their wrists.

The songcasters began to chant. Their voices rose, loud and strong, reverberating through the stones of the ancient temple, sounding throughout the palace.

The priestess smiled. "And now for the vows of matrimony," she said.

FORTY-THREE

"**A**LÍTHEIA, *PLEASE* listen to me," a terrified Sera begged, eyeing the spider's fearsome fangs.

"Why ssshould I lisssten?"

"No reason. None at all," Sera admitted. "You've defended Miromara, but Miromara hasn't defended you. That stops. Right now. With me."

The spider considered her words.

"Alítheia, you're just like those souls," Sera said. "The ones Orfeo snatched and bound to create his monster."

The spider narrowed all eight of her eyes. "Alítheia is Alítheia," she said sullenly. "Ssshe isss like nothing elssse."

"You're angry, just like they are. And scared. And trapped. And you want your freedom, just like those souls do," Sera said. "Set us free, Alítheia, and I swear by Neria that I'll set you free."

The spider said nothing. She continued to advance on Sera, her eyes glittering hungrily. She raised a curved bronze claw and extended it toward Sera. One swipe of that fearsome hook, and Sera was dead.

Fossegrim called to the spider, begging her to stop, to not hurt Sera, but Alítheia seemed to not even hear him.

She's going to kill me. Please make it quick, Sera prayed.

But instead of thrusting the lethal claw into her, Alítheia pressed it to the side of Sera's face. Sera bit back a cry of pain as the cold, sharp metal bit into her skin. An instant later, her blood swirled through the water like crimson smoke.

The spider nosed at the blood, then tasted it. "You ssspeak the truth, mermaid. The blood of Merrow runsss through your veinsss."

"Help me get out of here, Alítheia," Sera said, encouraged. "Help me fight for the realm you've faithfully protected. If I win my battle, that realm will finally protect you. Merrow kept you in the dark. She kept all of us in the dark. She shouldn't have. Help me, and I'll get you out of this den and give you a place in the light, right by my side."

The spider drew herself up. She raised her claw once more, then sliced it down through the water. Sera had no idea, in that instant, if she would live or die.

The claw caught the filaments of the cocoon that held Sera and ripped through them. They fell away and sank to the bottom of the cave.

"Thank you, Alítheia," she said, weak with relief. There was a smooth spot on the spider's face, right above her fangs. Sera swam to her and kissed her there. The anarachna touched a claw to the spot wonderingly, and blinked her many eyes.

"Pardon me, but if you wouldn't mind . . ."

That was Fossegrim. Alítheia cut him loose, too. The two mer were free, but they still had iron collars around their necks that prevented them from songcasting. Alítheia quickly solved that problem. She spat a bit of venom onto the cave's floor, dripped a claw in it, then touched it to the hasp of the lock on Sera's collar. It ate into the iron. The hasp broke apart, and the lock fell away. Sera pulled the collar off, grateful to be rid of it.

When Fossegrim had also shed his collar, Sera said, "Now all we have to do is—"

Her words were cut off by the sound of music. She could tell that Alítheia and Fossegrim heard it, too. It was carrying out of Neria's temple, drifting over the kolisseo, and down into Alítheia's den. The music was faint, but Sera could still make out some of the lyrics.

. . . come together now . . . To witness two souls make their vows . . .

Terror seized her. "No," she whispered. "Great, Neria, *no!*"

"What is it, Serafina?" Fossegrim asked.

"The wedding ceremony . . . it's happening!" she cried. "Mahdi and Lucia, they're getting married. He's dead."

Sera was a thousand times more frightened for Mahdi than she'd been for herself. Lucia thought Alítheia was a monster, but *she* was the real monster, and Mahdi was in her clutches.

"Dead, child? Why? He wanted this. He betrayed his own realm for it," Fossegrim said.

"No, he was only pretending," Sera said frantically. "He's been working for our side all along. And he Promised himself to me. Lucia thinks *I'm* dead, but I'm not. She probably told Mahdi that I was. When he sings his vows, they'll fall flat and—"

"Everyone in the temple will know the truth," Fossegrim finished. "That is not good. Not good at all."

"We've got to help him," Sera said, desperation in her voice. She turned back to the spider. "Alítheia, is there a way out of here?"

"For you, yesss. Follow me," the anarachna said.

FORTY-FOUR

MAHDI FLOATED, smiling serenely as the songcasters chanted. Anyone looking at him would have seen a merman dazed by love, gazing at his bride. But all the while, Mahdi's brain was working feverishly, calculating how long he had before the ceremony ended, before his new father-in-law swam up to congratulate him. Before it was over. For Vallerio and Traho. For him.

The chorus of songcasters, their voices soaring now, chanted of Miromara's proud history, and of the solemn vows about to be taken. They reminded Lucia of her duty to produce a daughter for the realm, and then they were silent. Their part in the ceremony was over.

It was Mahdi's and Lucia's turn.

"Your Graces, if you please," the priestess said, leading them in their vows.

> *Deeply beloved, tonight we sing,*
> *Of this couple's final promising*
> *For life, these vows will bind you both,*
> *Think hard, before you plight your troth.*
>
> *For the goddess Neria demands nothing less*
> *That one or both will now confess,*
> *If vows to another were made in the past,*
> *For if so, new vows cannot be cast.*

Mahdi took a deep breath. Lucia, smiling radiantly, did the same. Looking at each other, they began to sing the vows that would unite them forever.

> *Freely I declare my love,*
> *In the magical light of the moon above.*
> *My heart is my own, to keep or to give,*
> *I pledge it to you, for as long as I live.*

Lucia's voice, clear and beguiling, rose into the water. But instead of joining hers in perfect harmony, Mahdi's voice fell flat.

He stopped singing, confused. He looked around self-consciously; his hand went to his throat.

Lucia's eyes widened. In the chapel pews, guests turned to one other, exchanging looks or whispering behind their hands.

Mahdi coughed and tried again, but his song was tuneless, and his voice as harsh as a gull's. *How can this be happening?* he wondered wildly. *It shouldn't be. It* couldn't *be. Not unless . . .*

"Sera's alive," he whispered.

Lucia heard him. Her smile disappeared. "She's *not*. There's no chance she survived, trust me."

Vallerio, Portia, and the rest of the wedding guests were too far away to hear what Lucia and Mahdi were saying.

"What's wrong?" Vallerio called out. "Why aren't you singing your vows?"

Mahdi barely heard him. Happiness flooded his heart. "She's alive. Thank the gods!"

"Mahdi, you don't mean that," Lucia said, as if speaking to a small child. "You don't know what you're saying. Sera enchanted you. You only *think* you're in love with her."

Mahdi ripped the cord off their hands. He backed away from

her. "Sera *didn't* enchant me. I Promised myself to her freely and willingly."

"That's not true!" Lucia said, her eyes flashing with anger.

As Mahdi looked into those eyes, his happiness shattered and fear took its place—fear for Sera. Lucia had been shocked to learn that she was alive, which can only mean that she'd left her for dead somewhere. He unbuttoned his jacket so he could get to his gun.

"Where is she, Lucia? Tell me!" Mahdi demanded. "What did you do with her?"

"Mahdi, stop it," Lucia begged. *"Please."*

"What the hell is going on?" Vallerio thundered.

His voice brought Mahdi up short. Mahdi reached for his gun, remembering what he'd come here to do, but instead of pulling the weapon from its holster, he stopped. The minute he fired on Vallerio, he was a dead man himself. And then who would help Sera?

He had to tell the guests the truth. Some of them might be loyal to Sera. They might help her.

"Serafina's alive! The true regina of Miromara is alive!" he shouted. "Vallerio killed her parents, but he didn't kill her! Lucia imprisoned her. Find her! Save her!"

Some of the wedding guests gasped. Other's pressed hands to their chests. "Is this true?" a merman demanded.

"Serafina's alive? Where is she?" a mermaid cried.

"Mahdi, please!" Lucia begged. "You're ruining everything. I can't save you, we can't be married, if you don't stop saying these things."

Mahdi shook his head. He couldn't keep up the charade any longer. "Don't you get it? I'd rather die than marry you."

Lucia's face changed in an instant. Hatred darkened her features. "Then you will!" she hissed.

"Lucia, what in the gods' names is going on?" Vallerio shouted, approaching the altar.

Lucia backed away from Mahdi. She pointed an accusatory finger at him. "He's a traitor!" she shouted loudly. "He's spying for the Black Fins! Seize him!"

Traho fumbled for his gun. Mahdi grabbed for his own weapon. Traho aimed first. Mahdi braced for the shot, for the searing pain of a spear ripping into his flesh, but it never came.

Instead, there was a blinding flash of light, and then a deafening explosion. Mahdi clapped his hands over his ears. The walls of the ancient temple shook. The windows imploded. There was a roar from above, the sound of something heavy giving way. Mahdi looked up.

The last thing he saw were the beams of the ancient temple's roof, plummeting toward him.

FORTY-FIVE

SERA AND FOSSEGRIM were preparing to follow Alítheia out of her lair and through a tunnel when it hit.

There was a deep *boom*, and then a shock wave so strong that it shook the walls and knocked Sera down. Her head smacked against the floor. Dazed, she pushed herself up and looked around.

Fossegrim had also been knocked down. Alítheia was on her back, legs clawing at the air.

With much clanking and pounding, she righted herself, then scurried to the iron grille that covered the entrance to her den. Sera helped Fossegrim up, and they both followed her.

"What *was* that?" Sera asked. "What's happening?"

"I wish I knew, child," Fossegrim replied weakly.

The three looked out of the grille. Almost immediately, Alítheia drew back. "There isss much light," she said fearfully. "Which meansss much lava."

As Fossegrim, still dazed from the explosion, sank back down to the den's floor, Sera hooked her fingers through the bars of the grille and angled her body this way and that, trying to get a better view. She saw more bursts of light. Heard more explosions, as well as screams and shouts, bellowed orders, the neighing of hippokamps, the blood-curdling roar of dragons.

Her head was still swimming. The noise, the light—none of it made any sense.

And then it did.

"Great Neria," she whispered, stunned. "It's *them*."

"Sera, what do you see?" Fossegrim called up to her.

She released the iron bars and swam down. "Fossegrim, we've got to get out here."

"Do you know what's happening?" he asked, reaching for her hand.

Sera nodded. "I do," she said, helping the old merman up. "The battle for Cerulea has begun."

FORTY-SIX

"THIS IS *NOT* WISE, Serafina," Fossegrim cautioned breathlessly. "You should stay in the spider's den. At least wait to see how the Black Fins fare before you venture into the fray. What happens if Vallerio bests them and you're taken?"

"I can't do that, Fossegrim," Sera said. "This is my fight. I need to be with my Black Fins, win or lose."

Sera and Fossegrim were hurrying down a tunnel that led from Alítheia's lair to the palace's dungeons. The spider was leading the way, her bronze feet crunching the bones that littered the floor.

"Alítheia, if there's an exit, why haven't you ever used it?" Sera asked.

"Because the tunnel narrowsss asss it getsss clossse to the palace," the spider had explained. "Alítheia isss too big. Ssshe hasss tried to fit through. Many timesss."

Even though she was frantic to join her fighters, Sera heard the sadness in the spider's voice, and her heart hurt at the thought of the lonely creature futilely trying to squeeze through the tapering tunnel.

As the three continued down the passage, Fossegrim asked, "What happens when we arrive at the dungeons? How will we evade the guards?"

"That shouldn't be too much of a problem," Sera replied. "With Cerulea under attack, most of the guards won't be at their posts."

"How do you know that?"

Sera smiled grimly. "I know my uncle. I know how he thinks. He'll have ordered most of the guards to leave the dungeon to defend the palace. Fossegrim, you said you were in the dungeons for quite some time. Who was with you?"

"Political prisoners."

"Criminals, too?"

"No," he replied with a bitter laugh. "The criminals are all in the palace, not the dungeons. Why do you ask?"

"I'm going to need some help. I might be able to unlock Alítheia's grille, but I'll never be able to lift it by myself."

Fossegrim's eyes lit up. "Do you have a plan?"

"I do. I'll tell you all about it when we get out of here."

The tunnel started to narrow, then it abruptly angled toward a thin doorway.

"There are the dungeonsss," the spider said, pointing ahead. "Alítheia can go no farther."

"Thank you for getting us here, Alítheia," said Sera. "Thank you for listening to me, for trusting me. As soon as I can, I'll come back for you."

The anarachna looked away. Sera could tell that she didn't believe her. She swam up, so that she was level with the spider's eyes.

"Alítheia, look at me," she said, taking the creature's face in her hands. "Wait for me by the grille. I *will* come for you. I swear on my crown that I'll set you free."

"You mussst win back that crown before you can sssweear upon it," the spider said solemnly, delicately touching a claw to Sera's cheek. "And Lucia will not let you. Ssshhe is very ssstrong."

"Love is stronger," Sera said. "And love will win, Alítheia."

"Once, perhapsss. But not now. In thisss realm, evil hasss vanquissshed love."

Another huge explosion rocked the stone tunnel. A chunk of the ceiling fell to the floor, narrowly missing Sera and sending up a cloud of silt.

"Go, Ssserafina," the spider said.

"Alítheia—"

"*Go.* Before you are crussshed."

Sera nodded. She hurried Fossegrim through the doorway, then followed him.

Alítheia watched them go, blinking her many eyes. Then, her head low, she turned and made her way back to her den.

FORTY-SEVEN

SERA CAMOED HERSELF to blend in with the dungeon's floor and swam low until she reached a window. Then she raised herself slightly to look through it.

It was the guards' room, hollowed into the rock. Its front wall was made of thick, shatterproof glass that allowed the guards to see out into the corridor.

Just as she'd thought, only a skeleton crew was on duty. There were three guards total, one slim, two brawny, talking among themselves.

"If this place starts to cave in, I'm gone," one said. "I'm not going to be here when the ceiling crashes down."

"What about the prisoners?" the second guard asked.

"They can fend for themselves. No one cares if they live or die anyway."

Sera cased the room, making note of where the keys to the cells were kept, and the weapons. As she returned to Fossegrim, another explosion rocked the palace. The creaks and groans that followed, and the spidery cracks that appeared in the walls, upset the prisoners. Sera could hear them calling to one another from their cells.

"What's happening?"

"A chunk of the hallway just crumbled!"

"We're going to be crushed!"

"There are three guards," Sera informed Fossegrim. "You've got to get them all to come out. Are you sure you can do it?" she asked. He looked so weak and so pale to her.

Fossegrim smiled. The light of defiance burned in his eyes. "Watch me," he said.

Sera nodded, then she returned to the guard room. This time she swam along the ceiling, hoping they would be so preoccupied readying themselves to leave that they wouldn't look up.

When she was in position, she gave Fossegrim the thumbs-up. He returned the signal, lay down on the dungeon floor, then started yelling at the top of his lungs.

"Help! Help me! Oh, gods, don't make me go back!"

Two of the guards were out of the room and down the hall almost immediately.

"Please! Help me! The spider bite . . . it's so painful! It's killing me!" Fossegrim shouted, pretending to writhe in agony.

"How did he get out?" one of the guards asked.

"Hey, you!" his partner shouted. "Hands on your head!"

"The tunnels . . . they collapsed and crushed the spider," Fossegrim said. "I escaped, but she lashed out . . . she bit me . . . help me!"

Sera could see the third guard. He was busy loading a crossbow.

The plan would never work unless he followed the others. *Go!* she silently urged him.

As if he'd read her mind, Fossegrim started thrashing violently. He whacked one guard in the stomach with his tail fins and punched the other in the head. His strategy worked.

"Leo!" one of them yelled. "Get out here now! Bring the stinger!"

The third guard swore. He put his crossbow down and grabbed a barbed stingray's tail, used for immobilizing unruly prisoners. As soon as he was out of the room, Sera swam in. She grabbed a sword scabbarded in a chain-mail belt and quickly buckled it around her waist, then picked up the guard's crossbow. Next, she snatched a ring of keys off one wall, then raced back down the corridor to Fossegrim.

"On the ground! Now!" she shouted, as she came up behind the guards.

"What the—?" one guard said. He turned around, saw Sera, and rushed toward her.

She fired the crossbow. Her aim was true. The guard never knew what hit him.

"On the ground, I said! Hands on top of your heads!"

The remaining two guards quickly complied.

"Fossegrim, open that door," Sera said, nodding to the cell on the merman's left. She tossed him the ring of keys. He caught them with his gnarled hands, and a few seconds later, he was pushing on the door.

"Take your key rings off your belts, thrown them down, and swim into the cell," Sera ordered.

The guards did as they were told. Fossegrim quickly pulled the door closed and, with some difficulty, locked it. He picked up the key rings.

The prisoners were more frightened than ever now. Their frantic calls echoed down the corridors.

"Prisoners, listen to me! This is Serafina di Merrovingia, your rightful regina!"

The shouting stopped.

"The noises you hear are the sounds of battle!" Sera shouted. "The Black Fins, my troops, are here. They're fighting for the city! Join us!"

"No! Don't go! Stay in your cells!" a frightened voice called out. "It's a trick!"

"Vallerio wants to find out who's loyal and who isn't!" another yelled.

"Please don't hurt us," begged a third, miserably.

Sera pressed her hands to her cheeks. She was devastated. She'd expected a joyous reaction to the offer of freedom, to the chance to fight those who'd imprisoned them. But these merfolk had been so badly brutalized, they believed this was just another cruel ploy on her uncle's part to extract information.

Summoning all her magic, Sera songcast the brightest, most beautiful illuminata she ever had. Its glow reached the dungeon's darkest corners.

"Good people of Miromara, come to your doors!"

Sera heard groaning, shuffling, the sound of chains dragging over stone. Fingers, their nails black with grime, curled around bars. Frightened faces appeared.

"I am Serafina, your regina! This isn't a trick!"

"Serafina! It's Serafina! It's her!" voices called out excitedly.

A few prisoners reached for her through the bars, but others shied away, pointing at her.

"Weapon . . . a death rider . . . kill us . . ." they whispered.

Sera realized she was still carrying a loaded crossbow. It was scaring some of the prisoners. She quickly put it on the floor.

"Sera . . . child, *don't!*" Fossegrim warned. "They're angry and afraid. They could lash out. Protect yourself!"

Sera shook her head, determined. "Citizens of Cerulea, hear me! I have laid my weapon down, and I'm going to unlock your cells. Do with me what you will. I would rather die at your hands than rule without your trust!" she declared.

As her words rang out, bouncing off the hard stone walls, Sera started opening doors. Fossegrim hesitated, then followed her lead, cursing at his broken fingers. One by one, the prisoners swam out, scared, unsteady, wincing at the bright light. Some were crying, others laughing. Some regarded Sera warily, others hugged her and kissed her hands.

She kept going, opening doors, releasing her mer. Fossegrim, his maimed hands hurting, gave the extra key ring he had to a mermaid, and she started freeing prisoners, too.

When all the cell doors had been opened, Sera turned to her merfolk. *Will they be with me?* she wondered. After all they'd been through, she wouldn't blame them if they swam away and hid.

"Ceruleans, I need your help. We must defeat my uncle. *Tonight.* Your lives, my life, and the future of Miromara hang in the balance. Will you fight with me?"

A cheer rose. It grew louder and louder.

"We are with you, Serafina! Tell us what to do!" a mermaid cried.

The mermaid was little more than a skeleton. Her eyes were sunken. Her cheeks were hollow. Yet she spared no thought for herself. Sera's eyes filled with tears. She quickly blinked them back.

"There are weapons in the guards' room," she said. "Arm yourselves and follow me. I am honored to have you by my side!"

Another cheer rose, and the prisoners mobbed the guards' room. They scrambled for crossbows, spearguns, clubs, stingers, and anything else they could find. Sera saw one emerge with a paperweight in his hand. Another was brandishing a mug.

She felt a hand on her back. "Be careful," Fossegrim said.

She hugged him tightly. "You, too, Magister. Find a safe place to hide until this is over."

The old merman shook his head. "No hiding, not tonight. Tonight I have a score to settle. Traho destroyed my ostrokon. It's time he paid his fine."

Sera nodded and turned back to her merfolk. She quickly picked out ten strong mermen. "We have one more prisoner to free," she informed them. "One who's served a very long sentence. Will you help me?"

The mermen nodded. "How long has he been locked up?" one asked.

"She," Sera said. "For four thousand years."

FORTY-EIGHT

MAHDI BLINKED SILT out of his eyes. His vision was blurry. Voices cried out around him in fear and pain.

He shook his head and sat up. Chunks of stone fell off him as he did. Blood dripped from his cheek. His tail throbbed. He heard shouts and commands in the distance, the sound of dragons roaring.

What happened? he wondered woozily. *How did I end up on the floor?*

His vision cleared. The pain in his tail intensified. He wanted to get up, to pull away from it, but he couldn't. He twisted around and saw that a piece of masonry had fallen on his fins. He tried to push it off, but it was too heavy.

He could see a merman on the floor next to him. He was lying on his back, staring up into the water through sightless eyes. A rivulet of blood trickled from the corner of his mouth. A mermaid lay a foot beyond him, her body broken.

In a blinding rush, it all came back. Mahdi heard Lucia ordering the guards to seize him, and saw Traho aiming a speargun at him. He heard the deafening roar and the screams. He remembered shouted words: *warehouse, munitions.* And then a shock wave had rocked the chapel, cracking walls, blowing out the windows, toppling statues.

Traho had fired at him, but the explosion had caused him to miss, and the deadly spear had lodged harmlessly in a wall. And then a section of the chapel's ceiling had come crashing down, narrowly missing the altar and everyone floating just above it.

Where is he now? Mahdi wondered fearfully, looking around. He was pinned to the floor and helpless. If Traho took aim at him again, he wouldn't miss.

Lucia, too, had been knocked down. She sat up now, only a yard from Mahdi, and shook off the rubble covering her. Her dress was torn. She had cuts on her hands. She looked around the room, swaying slightly. Her eyes, empty and emotionless, traveled over the destruction and over the injured mer, some begging for help. They came to rest on Mahdi. As they did, the dazed look in them receded and hatred burned in their blue depths.

Mahdi had dropped his speargun when the stone fell on him. It had landed between him and Lucia. They both lunged for it.

Mahdi got to it first, twisting his body painfully to reach it. He pointed it at Lucia.

"Where is she?" he shouted.

Lucia laughed. "It doesn't matter. You can't save her."

"Don't make this any worse, Lucia. It's *over*," he said, training the gun on her. "Don't you get that?"

Lucia smiled. "Yes, it *is* over," she said. "For *you*."

A searing pain tore through him. He dropped the gun and twisted around.

Portia was floating a few yards behind him. A spear from the gun she was holding had grazed him just below his rib cage.

Cursing, she bent down and tried to grab another spear from a dying death rider's belt, but before she could, Vallerio grabbed her arm and dragged her toward the door.

"Let me go, Vallerio! I want him *dead*!" Portia protested, struggling to break her husband's grip.

But Vallerio held her firm. "The palace is under attack. We have to leave now!" he shouted. "Lucia, this way . . . *hurry*!"

Mahdi made a last desperate grab for Lucia. He caught her wrist. "Where is she?"

At that instant, another explosion rocked the palace. Mahdi was thrown onto his back again. New cracks opened up along the walls. Ominous groans came from what was left of the ceiling.

When he sat up again, Lucia and her parents were gone.

The explosion had shifted the rock that was pinning him down. Ignoring the wound in his side, Mahdi got his hands under the rock and pushed with all his might. It didn't budge. He tried again, groaning with effort, and finally it moved just enough that he could pull his fins out from under it. They were ripped and bleeding, but he was free.

Pressing one hand to the wound in his side, he picked up his gun again and swam out of the chapel. Vallerio wouldn't stay here to defend the palace. He would slink away to hide and regroup. Mahdi knew he had to catch up with them before that could happen.

While he still had a chance of saving Sera.

FORTY-NINE

"BECCA, ABOVE YOU!" Yazeed shouted.

Her head shot up. She fired. The arrow pierced the death rider's chest. He fell through the water screaming.

The Black Fins had pulled off their impossible plan. They'd cast their transparensea pearls and descended invisibly into the palace and the city. Before the death riders had any idea what was happening, the Black Fins had blown the munitions warehouse, making it impossible for their enemies to arm themselves. Those who were armed when the battle began couldn't get more rounds. Already many of the Feuerkumpel mercenaries were deserting.

But inside the palace's stateroom, the battle was still raging. The pearls were wearing off, and casualties on both sides were mounting.

Vallerio, Portia, and Lucia, defended by a dozen death riders, had tried to flee to their private apartments. There they could access the tunnels that ran under the palace and escape. Becca's group of twenty fighters had cut them off, however, and had driven them into the stateroom.

Mahdi had joined them there. *"Dude!"* Yazeed had shouted, grinning. He'd almost gotten himself shot in the process. Together they'd managed to pin Vallerio, Portia, and Lucia behind the throne and keep them from reaching a doorway near it.

As the Black Fins continued to fire on the small group of soldiers defending the three, however, death rider reinforcements had come streaming in through the stateroom's windows, forcing the Black Fins to fall back behind pillars and statues. They were still covering the exit that Vallerio, Portia, and Lucia wanted to reach, but only barely.

"If we don't get some backup soon, they're going to get away!" Becca shouted.

"Where are the rest of the Black Fins?" Mahdi yelled.

Before Yazeed could tell hm, a bloodcurdling roar ripped through the water, and then an immense claw ripped out a bank of windows.

"What the—" Yaz started to say.

"Blackclaws!" Neela shouted. "This is exactly what the death riders did last time! It's how they took the palace."

As Becca and her fellow fighters watched in horror, a massive dragon tore at the hole she'd made, widening it. She pushed her enormous snout in, then screeched in anger when she couldn't fit her whole head through. She thumped her tail into the wall over and over again, until a large section caved in.

"We have no chance against that thing," Neela said. "We've got to fall back."

"We can't! Lucia and her parents will get away!" Becca said.

Before anyone could venture a way to keep that from happening, there was another sound: a metallic shriek that sounded like a ship being torn in half on jagged rocks.

It came from the stateroom's entry, and it was followed by clanking and pounding.

Becca swiveled her head, trying to see what was making the noises. Then she took a stroke backward, unable to believe her eyes.

Under the stateroom's soaring stone arches crouched a giant bronze spider. Her black eyes glinted. Her long fangs were bared.

Seated atop the creature was a mermaid. She carried a crossbow. A sword hung from her hip. Her coppery hair, cut short, was angled over her forehead and cheekbones. Her green eyes blazed with fury.

"Holy silt! She's *alive*!" Desiderio said.

"Thank the gods!" Neela said, and she turned bright blue.

"Yes!" Yaz let loose a loud, long victory cry.

Mahdi just shook his head, unable to speak.

"Go, Sera!" Becca shouted. "Take back your throne!"

FIFTY

THE BRONZE SPIDER REARED, shrieking a challenge at the dragon. Her rider stayed atop her, crossbow aimed.

The Blackclaw, who was inside the stateroom now, flattened her ears.

The spider shrieked again, slamming her front legs on the floor. She started toward the dragon. The Blackclaw hissed. She lowered her head and charged. The walls shook. A glass chandelier crashed down. The dragon was larger than Alítheia, and it looked as if she would crush the spider.

Mahdi found his voice. "Sera, watch out!"

But Alítheia was only feinting. Her eight eyes were glued to the dragon. As the beast closed in, the spider crouched lower, and then, when the Blackclaw was only yards away, Alítheia shot a line of filament up into the water. It hit the ceiling and stuck fast, and as it did, the spider sprang, swinging herself to the right of the dragon in a tight arc, then dropping down on her back.

Sera got off two shots immediately, killing both death riders seated in the howdah on the dragon's back.

The dragon roared and shook herself violently, but Alítheia clung on. Using her dagger-sharp claws, she climbed up the dragon's spine, searching for a chink in her armor. She found one where the chain mail ended and the frills around the creature's neck began. With another shriek, she sank her fangs into the Blackclaw's flesh.

The dragon reared, roaring. She twisted around in a frenzy, clawing at her neck, trying to get the spider off. But Alítheia had already jumped down. As the venom did its work, the dragon's struggles slowed. With a cry, she collapsed to the floor. Alítheia, meanwhile, was headed for the throne. The death riders' arrows bounced off her bronze body. Sera ducked down, sheltering in the dip between the spider's thorax and abdomen where nothing could reach her.

With feet and fangs, Alítheia battled her way through, a shrieking, slashing battle machine. The Black Fins followed her.

"Get them!" Mahdi shouted, racing to the back of the throne, his speargun raised. Yazeed and Becca were hot on his tail.

But they were too late. Lucia and her parents were nowhere to be found.

"How did they escape?" Becca asked.

Yazeed swore a blue streak. "They must've made it to the door near the throne when Alítheia was fighting the Blackclaw."

"We'll find them," Sera said.

She swam down from Alítheia's back. Mahdi gathered her in his arms, crushing her in an embrace.

"I thought you were dead. Lucia . . . she said she'd killed you," he said, his voice raw with emotion.

"We found your dagger and jacket in the Darktide Shallows. We were sure Vallerio had kidnapped you," Neela said, hugging the two of them. Desiderio, Becca, Yazeed, and Ling joined in. The other Black Fin fighters cheered.

Sera, wiping tears off her cheeks, laughed and said, "Vallerio didn't kidnap me; Lucia did. I'm so happy to see you all, and there's nothing I want to do more than hug you forever, but we've got to find her, and her parents."

A dragon's roar carried through the water.

Sera grimaced. "More Blackclaws," she said, turning to the spider. "Alítheia, can you take care of them?"

The spider nodded, then scuttled across the stateroom and disappeared through the hole the first dragon had ripped in the wall.

"Sera, how did you—" Neela started to ask.

"It's a long story. I'll tell you when we're done. Everyone armed and ready?"

Her friends raised their weapons.

"Come on," Sera said, heading for the exit. "Let's finish this."

FIFTY-ONE

THE BLACK FINS swam out of the stateroom and down a wide corridor, weapons at the ready.

They turned a corner and were fired upon immediately. A spear grazed Sera's arm. Her blood swirled through the water. She ducked another spear, hit the floor, and returned fire, aiming at a black uniform.

"Fall back! Guard the commander!" a harsh voice shouted.

Sera knew that voice. It was Traho's.

"Fall back, I said—*uhh!*"

Her arrow hit home. The force of its impact sent Traho hurtling into a wall. As he sank, his blood billowing in the water, his comrades disappeared down the hallway. Ten Black Fins raced after them.

Sera was up off the floor and on Traho instantly, sending his weapon skittering away from him with a flip of her tail.

The arrow was sticking out of the merman's chest. Blood was pouring from the wound and dripping from his mouth, but he still tried to get to the dagger in his belt. Sera slapped it out of his hand.

Traho's eyes met hers. "You're a killer," he said cruelly, struggling to speak. "Just like your uncle. You must be happy to see me die."

Once, these words would have pierced Sera's soul, but no longer.

"I'm not a killer; I'm a soldier," she told him. "And I'm not happy. Even about your death. Which means I'm nothing like my uncle."

Traho lunged for her, but she easily avoided him.

"Stop it. It's *over*, Traho," she said.

His lips twitched into a blood-smeared grin. "It's not over, it's only beginning. Good luck . . . *Your Grace*," he said mockingly. "You'll need it."

He gave one last groan, and his chest sank. He was gone.

"Come on," Sera said, continuing down the hallway, motioning to her troops to follow. Mahdi, Yaz, Neela, Des, Ling, and Becca, and about a dozen more fighters were still with her.

As they turned the corner to the Regina's Loggia, another gruesome sight greeted them: the ten Black Fins who'd raced ahead after Traho, all mermen, lay dead on the floor.

There was a mermaid among them, too.

Sera recognized her immediately: Portia. A bloodstain bloomed across her chest like petals of a crimson sea flower. A hole over her heart was the flower's dark center.

Vallerio was by her side, holding one of her hands in his. The Black Fins didn't have long to absorb the scene, though, for the death riders who'd survived the skirmish started firing on them.

A spear hit a pillar next to Sera, showering her with debris.

"Take cover!" she yelled, waving everyone behind her.

When her fighters were safe, she called to her uncle.

"Call them off, Vallerio. It's over. Give yourself up!"

Another spear, fired at her head, was his answer.

Sera turned to Yazeed. He was an excellent shot. "Yaz—"

"Got this."

"I want him alive."

"He will be."

"It's hopeless, Vallerio. You know it is!" Sera shouted, keeping the death riders' attention on her. "Give yourselves up! No one else has to die!"

As Sera spoke, she picked up a chunk of stone that had fallen from the ceiling. Yazeed bent low, then leaned out from the pillar ever so slightly. He aimed his speargun, took a breath, and held it.

Sera threw the stone high up in the water. The death riders fired at it, leaving Vallerio undefended for a split second. It was all Yazeed needed. He squeezed his trigger. His spear sank into Vallerio's right shoulder. Vallerio screamed, dropped his gun, and tried to pull the arrow out with his left hand, but it was buried too deeply.

Desiderio, Ling, and Becca all got shots off. Within seconds, the death riders defending Vallerio were dead.

Vallerio surrendered, raising his hands.

Desiderio raced to him, his own hands clenched into fists, his eyes wild. Mahdi was right behind him. And then he was in front of Des, trying to hold him off.

"Des, no," he said. "Not like this. It's done. He surrendered."

"He murdered my parents, Mahdi. Get out of my way."

"No. I won't let him make you a murderer, too. Back away, Des. I mean it."

Desiderio whirled away from Mahdi and slammed his tail into a wall. Over and over again. Drops of blood flew from his fins.

Neela swam to him. "Stop it, Des," she said gently. *"Stop."* She offered him her hands. He squeezed them hard, trying to get himself under control.

Meanwhile, Mahdi ripped his belt off, yanked Vallerio's hands behind his back, and bound his wrists. The end of the spear quivered in Vallerio's flesh. He grimaced in pain.

Sera had swum out from behind the pillar, too. She floated in front of her uncle now, her crossbow lowered. His eyes met hers. She knew them so well. They were darkly blue, like her mother's.

"Your own sister," she said to him. "She was good and kind, and she loved you. So did my father. You killed them both. You made me an orphan. How could you do it?"

Vallerio's eyes widened. He feigned surprise. "Sera, is that *you?* What are you doing with this sea scum? Did they kidnap you?"

Sera shook her head in disgust. "You coward. You don't even have the guts to own up to what you did."

For a few horrible seconds, rage and grief boiled up inside her, just as it had in Desiderio. The urge grew stronger, overwhelming her. Her finger tightened on the trigger of her weapon, but as it did, she thought she heard laughter, low and gurgling. Abbadon's laughter. And she knew that if she did this, she would be no better than a monster.

She lowered her crossbow. "Too many have suffered for too long because of lawlessness and violence. Vallerio di Merrovingia, I arrest you for murder and treason. Your case will be tried in a court of law and heard by a jury of your peers. Take him to the dungeons and put him in a cell," she said, motioning two fighters to him. "You'll find plenty of empty ones."

"Murder? Treason?" Vallerio echoed, still playacting. "Sera, what are you saying? I *saved* Miromara from the Ondalinian invaders! I made sure the realm had a ruler! We all thought you were dead!"

"You're a good actor, Uncle. You fooled my mother. But you don't fool me," Sera said bitterly.

"You don't believe I knew that you were alive? I'm your uncle, for gods' sake. You *can't* believe that."

"I *heard* you, Vallerio," Sera said, her voice shaking with fury. "I was in the regina's private chamber after Lucia's coronation, thanks to a transparensea pearl. I heard you and Portia congratulating each other on killing my mother, getting rid of me, and putting your own daughter on the throne. I know about the deal you made with Orfeo. Soon, the rest of the waters will, too."

Vallerio renewed his protests, but Sera turned away from him and addressed her fighters.

"Rök, Mulmig, find the other commanders. Tell them the battle for the palace is over and they should give our enemies a chance to surrender. Regelbrott, Styg," she continued, "take the dead to the stateroom. The bodies of Black Fins and loyal Miromarans will be buried with full honors and heroes' dirges. The body of Portia Volnero, and of every other traitor, will be buried in a common grave in the Grayrock Barrens."

"No! You can't do that! She was a *duchessa!*" Vallerio shouted, struggling against his bonds.

Sera spun around. Eyes blazing, she said, "She was a *murderer*, Vallerio. She sold her regina's life, and her merfolk's lives, for wealth and power. Summon Horok to her, and to the rest of the death rider sea scum—"

"No!" Vallerio bellowed.

"—with a gallows dirge."

A gallows dirge was the final rite used to return the soul of a condemned criminal to the sea. It was the deepest dishonor, and in Miromara's long history only a handful of noblemer had received it— most of them from the Volnero family.

Sera bent down to her uncle, so they were face-to-face. "My fighters will sing a gallows dirge for Lucia, too," she said. "Unless you tell me where she is."

Vallerio shook his head.

"If *I* find her, I'll arrest her. She'll be charged and tried, just like you will be. If one of my fighters finds her, though, she might well be killed. The Black Fins have suffered heavy casualties today. They won't be in any mood to spare her life. Is that what you want? For your daughter to die on the floor like your wife just did?"

Vallerio lowered his head. "She's . . . on her way to Portia's rooms," he said in a broken voice. "There's a . . . secret door—next to the mantel. It leads to the tunnels. Please, Sera . . . please don't kill her, I beg you."

Sera addressed her fighters again. "We have one more traitor to flush out—the most dangerous of all. Keep your weapons raised and your wits about you."

Sera, her fighters at her side, raced off toward the royal apartments.

As she disappeared down the hall, Vallerio raised his eyes. And smiled.

FIFTY-TWO

SERA STARED AT THE DOOR to Portia Volnero's rooms. They had once been Isabella's. Sera had swum through this door often as a little merl, eager to see her mother, to spend a precious few minutes with her, just the two of them. She remembered turning the knob and giggling as she pushed the door open, knowing that her mother would fondly scold her, saying, "Sera, can't you *ever* learn to knock?" before gathering her into her arms.

Those days were gone. Her mother was gone. That little merl was gone.

Sera wasn't going to knock. Not now. Not ever again.

"Do it, Yaz," she said.

He backed up, then spun around and slammed his tail into the door. It flew open. Sera and the others rushed inside, weapons drawn.

Lucia was floating by the lavaplace's mantel, her back toward them. She wore a heavy walrus-fur wrap around her shoulders and held a sea-silk pouch in her hand. A mica-covered panel to the left of the mantel had swung open.

"Stop right there, Lucia!" Sera shouted. "I have a crossbow. Don't make me use it."

Lucia did as she was told.

"Put your hands in the air!"

As Lucia raised her arms, Desiderio and Mahdi swam to her. Desiderio took the pouch from Lucia. He opened it.

"Currensea," he said, then yanked Lucia's hands behind her back.

Mahdi grabbed a tie from one the sea-silk draperies and tossed it to him.

Throughout it all, Lucia was strangely quiet.

Desiderio bound her hands. Serafina put her crossbow down, then swam to her. "Lucia Volnero, I charge you with treason. You're under arrest."

"I have nothing to say." Lucia's voice sounded hollow. Her beautiful face was composed. She stared straight ahead of herself, seemingly resigned to her fate, her eyes empty and dead.

"Your father survived the fighting; your mother didn't," Sera informed her, feeling pity for her enemy, though she didn't want to.

"I have nothing to say," Lucia repeated.

"Take her to the dungeons," Sera ordered. Two Black Fins swam up to Lucia. Each took an arm and led her away.

"That's weird. I expected a fight to the death," Mahdi said, as Lucia disappeared through the doorway. "The secret door was open. She didn't even make a swim for it."

"Maybe she saw the Black Fins kill her mother. Maybe she didn't know how to make her way through the tunnels. Maybe it was all too much," Sera said.

"Sera, I'm going to rendezvous with the goblin commanders," Desiderio said. "I want to regroup, then put down any enemy holdouts."

"Ling, go with him. Take everyone else, too," Sera said. "I'll be right behind you. We meet back in the stateroom in an hour."

The group started off, but Mahdi stayed behind. "You okay?"

Sera nodded, but then alarm filled her eyes as she saw Mahdi's jacket. "You're not, though."

Mahdi followed her gaze to his side and grimaced. His jacket was soaked with blood.

"Are you going to die, too?" she asked in a choked voice. Her face crumpled. She covered it with her hands and wept.

Mahdi was at her side in an instant. "Hey, hey . . . it's okay, Sera. It's not as bad as it looks. A couple of stitches and I'll be fine."

He pulled her close and held her tightly. Sera grabbed fistfuls of his jacket and buried her head in his chest. "So many gone because of them, Mahdi . . . *so many.*"

"Shh, Sera. We won. It's over. There won't be any more killing. Not after today," Mahdi said, still holding her.

After a few minutes, she pulled herself together and said, "I'm keeping you here, and I shouldn't. You need to see a doctor."

"In a bit," Mahdi said. "I'm going to check out the hallway first, make sure it's totally clear. What about you?"

Sera shook her head. "I—I can't . . . I need a moment. Alone. I need to get ahold of myself," she said, her voice still quavering.

"It's your mother, isn't it? Being here, in this room, reminds you of her."

Sera looked down at the floor. "She wouldn't be very happy if she could see me right now," she said. "She would tell me that those who would govern others must first govern themselves."

Mahdi laughed. "That sounds just like her." He lifted Sera's face. "Take the time you need, Sera. I'll come back for you in a minute. Your mer are scared. They've just come through a battle. They need to see you, but they need to see you strong."

Sera nodded. Mahdi left, and she made her way over to the sofa in front of the lavaplace. She sat down and closed her eyes. Never had she felt so weary. She'd survived the maligno and Alítheia. She'd fought a battle and won it. Portia Volnero was dead. Vallerio and Lucia were captured.

It's over, Mahdi had said. But Sera felt like Traho's words were the truer ones: *it's only beginning.* Now she had to pick up the pieces. To bury the dead. To reassure her frightened mer. Now, for the first time, she had to rule.

"How, Mom? How?" she said aloud.

The words came back to her, as they had time and time again. *The love of my people is my strength.*

She would need that love in the days to come, as she tried to put her broken realm back together.

Sera opened her eyes. It was time to go. As she started to rise, she felt something brush against her tail.

A goby or a blenny, she thought, remembering how schools would swim through the palace, despite the maids' best efforts to keep them out.

She looked down, but it wasn't a fish that had brushed her tail. It was a tentacle, thin, withered, and a sickly shade of green. Another tentacle wound around her tail, and then another. A face peeked out from under the settee. It was withered, too, but Sera knew it.

"Sylvestre?" she whispered, joy and disbelief mingling in her voice. "Is it *really* you?"

The little green octopus nodded. A tentacle wound around Sera's wrist.

"I never thought I'd see you again!" Sera said. "What happened to you? Are you sick?"

Sylvestre nodded again and Sera, her heart filling with love for the little pet she thought she'd lost, leaned down to scoop him up in her arms.

And that was what saved her life.

Because a heartbeat later, a dagger sliced through the water behind her, missing her back by a scale's breadth.

"I HAVE NOTHING TO SAY!" a malicious voice hissed.

Sera whirled around. She saw a knife blade glinting. A shadowy figure lunged at her again. Sera darted away. As she backed toward the mantel, she was able to get a look at her assailant.

"Lucia?"

The emotionless face, the long black hair . . . Lucia looked just as she had moments ago. The only difference was her clothing. She must've changed.

But how? Sera's mind scrabbled for an explanation. *How did she escape and get back here?*

"I have nothing to say," another voice whispered, to Sera's right.

Sera's head jerked around. "It *can't* be!"

There was another Lucia. She was advancing on Sera, too, and she also had a dagger.

"I'm seeing things," Sera whispered. "This must be an illusio spell."

But then the Lucia at her right lunged at her, dagger out, and Sera learned that she was no illusion. She skirted the thrust, but not quickly enough. The dagger opened a gash in her arm.

Great Neria, Sera's mind yammered. *They're malignos!*

Sera's crossbow was on the floor, all the way on the other side of the room. There was no way to get it. She panicked, but then remembered she had a sword at her hip, one she'd taken from the guard room in the dungeons.

She pulled it out of its sheath, and when the Lucia on her right attacked again, Sera parried its blade, then thrust with her own.

It pierced the creature's chest. Sera drew the blade out, then watched in horror as silt—not blood—poured from the wound.

The maligno moved toward her again.

"I have nothing to say," came a growl from behind her.

Sera twisted around. There were three of them now. They were closing in on her, pushing her back toward the lavaplace once more.

With a warrior's cry, Sera lunged at the closest maligno, swinging her sword high. The blade severed the creature's head cleanly.

The body fell to the floor, silt pouring from its neck. Sera charged the next one, decapitating it, too. By the time she'd killed the third, she was panting heavily. Her entire body was trembling.

She passed a shaking hand across her brow. Lucia had made these three things, plus one more—the one her fighters had taken to the dungeon.

Sera's blood turned to ice as she realized what that meant: the real Lucia was still at large.

A click, sharp and metallic, sounded behind her.

Slowly, Sera turned around.

Lucia was floating only feet away from her, in the entrance to the tunnels. She was holding a speargun.

Before Sera could even scream, Lucia raised it.

And fired.

CHAPTER 53

FIFTY-FOUR

IT WAS OVER in a split second, yet in Sera's mind, it would last forever.

In the hours and days and weeks that followed, images and sounds would come back to her. A blur of green. The sensation of falling. The spear hissing through the water. Stars exploding behind her eyes as her head hit the floor.

Pain, and a heavy weight. Crushing her. Squeezing the air—and the life—out of her. She felt something warm seeping over her skin, into her clothing. Her vision cleared. She could see the ceiling, covered with bright anemones, feather worms, and brittle stars.

And then Lucia was leaning over her, her face beautiful and cunning.

"So much for love," she said, a mocking smile on her lips.

And then she was gone. Sera heard a soft whoosh as the secret door swung closed. She tried to move, to get up, but she couldn't.

And then voices.

Neela's screaming.

Becca's shouting, "Get a medic in here! Now! *Now!*"

Yazeed's: "No. Gods, *no.*"

Garstig's: "She's in the tunnels! Break the door down! Hurry!"

And then there were voices she didn't recognize.

"Careful. Go easy. On three . . ."

The weight was removed. Water flowed into her lungs. She could breathe easily again.

"Get her up!" That was Becca.

Sera felt hands on her. Becca's hands. Neela's. They lifted her up off the floor.

The room swam as she struggled for her balance. Her head throbbed. Her thoughts were scattered and jumbled. She struggled against the confusion. Trying to clear her mind. To *think*.

"Sera? Sera, can you hear me?" Neela asked.

"I—I'm bleeding . . ." she replied, looking down at the crimson stains on her clothing.

Hands opened her jacket. They felt for wounds.

"You're all right. You're not hit," said Ling, relief in her voice.

"I—I'm not?" Sera stammered. It seemed the blood she was covered in wasn't her own. But that made no sense. She pressed a hand to her aching temple. "But then how . . . who . . ." Her words trailed away as her eyes came to rest on two medics who'd swum into the room. They were working feverishly on a motionless figure stretched out on the floor.

It was a merman dressed in green. Emerald green.

Sera's eyes widened. Suddenly, it all made sickening sense. The blur in the water. The weight. The blood.

"No," she said, shaking her head wildly. "No, no, *no!*" The last word came out in a long, tearing shriek.

A spear was sticking out of the merman's back. On the left side. Where his heart was. His face was turned away from Sera's, but still she knew him.

It was Mahdi.

CHAPTER 54

FIFTY-FIVE

THE PAIN WAS like nothing he'd ever known.

Every breath he took seared his lungs. Blood poured from his torn flesh, over his shattered ribs.

Through the red haze of agony, he could hear something. It was pounding, slow and labored. It was the sound of his own heart, struggling to beat.

Time slowed. The images before his eyes blurred. Urgent words, spoken and shouted, stretched out forever. He couldn't understand them.

Hands lifted him, bringing fresh pain. Shouts echoed around him. Lights blazed from the ceiling above.

And then a face came into view, blurry at first, then clear.

Sera. She was *alive.*

Relief washed over him like a gentle wave, lapping his pain away. He'd gotten between her and Lucia's speargun. He'd saved her; that was all that mattered.

He felt her take his hand in hers and squeeze it. He squeezed back. She was crying, but trying to smile. "Hang on, Mahdi. Please, hang on," she sobbed.

There was so much he wanted to say, but he couldn't make the words come. He wanted to tell her that she would be all right. That she was brave and strong. He wanted her to know how much he loved her.

The pounding in his ears grew softer. His vision blurred again.

"No!" Sera screamed. She looked up, at somebody else. There were mer he didn't know in the room with them. They were wearing masks and gloves. "Help him! *Do* something!" she shouted.

She turned back to him, terror in her eyes. "Mahdi, no," she begged frantically. "Don't go. Please, *please* don't go. . . ."

The pounding slowed. His eyes fluttered closed.

"Mērē dila, mērī ātmā," he whispered. "Always. . . ."

The beat of Mahdi's brave heart faltered, and then finally, it stopped.

FIFTY-SIX

PALE AND DRAWN, seated on a high throne of black marble, Serafina gazed out over the Courtyard of the Condemned.

A gold crown studded with pearls, emeralds, and red coral—Merrow's crown—graced her head. Gold chains of office hung from her shoulders, set off by the deep black of her high-necked sea-silk gown. Alítheia, her bodyguard, stood just behind the throne, her eyes alert for any threat.

Lucia's brief reign was over. Sera was her realm's regina now. She was honored to take her mother's place upon Miromara's throne, relieved that her uncle had been defeated, and happy to be overseeing the reconstruction of her realm. Yet her victory was bittersweet. Her crown had been won back, but its price had been high.

She had not set fin in this courtyard once in her entire life. Even her mother had not. The Courtyard of the Condemned had not been used since her grandmother Artemesia's time.

Her eyes took in the court's high stone walls now, the armed guards lining them, and the block of wood, hewn from the mizzen-mast of some ship wrecked centuries ago, that stood in the courtyard's center. The block was about two feet high, and a foot and a half wide. A smooth, elliptical depression had been carved into its top.

Sera knew what that block was for, and vowed that if it were to be used today, she would not look away.

Her gaze traveled up, to the tower at the top of the far wall. It housed a huge bronze bell and was flanked by statues of the sea goddess Neria, and her sister, Verita, the goddess of justice. The sight of the deities brought painful memories back to Sera. Of the end of the battle. Of the medics pulling the spear out of Mahdi's body. Of his last words to her. And then of herself, on the hospital floor, shrieking at the gods. *Why? Why? How much more can you take from me?*

Thousands of Black Fins and civilians had died in the battle for Cerulea. Huge swaths of the city had been destroyed. And Mahdi . . . *Mahdi.*

As she thought now of how his heart had stopped, and how close she'd come to losing him, her own heart faltered.

She'd screamed at the doctors to help him, to do something. One had pressed bandages against the wound in his chest, another had put the heels of his hands over his heart and started pushing. One, two, three, stop. One, two, three, stop. Over and over again, and with every push, the bandages had turned redder. For endless, agonizing seconds, nothing had happened, and then Mahdi had groaned and started breathing again. The doctors had called for blood. Yazeed and Neela, his cousins, shared his blood type. They'd given him pint after pint.

For once, the gods had listened. For once, they'd taken pity on her, because Mahdi had lived—barely. Lucia's spear had missed his heart by an inch, but had badly damaged his lung. He'd lost a great deal of blood and had been deprived of oxygen. Would he recover? Could he fully come back from such terrible injuries? Sera didn't know. No one did. Mahdi couldn't tell them. He was still unconscious.

Two weeks had passed since he'd almost died, and he was still in a coma. Sera went to visit him morning and night, always hoping for a sign—a twitch of his hand, a flutter of his eyelashes—but she never got one.

The doctors had told her that they'd done all they could. That she must prepare herself for the worst—that Mahdi might remain in a coma for the rest of his life. Sera talked to him, sang to him, told him about her days, and the new challenges they brought, as if he could answer her. He was still there; she knew he was. She refused to give up hope.

The bell in the tower began to toll now. Its sound, low and ominous, tore Sera from her memories and brought her back to the present.

Twelve times the bell tolled. When it finished, a pair of heavy doors opened in the wall underneath the tower.

Drummers swam in first, beating a slow tattoo. They were followed by dirgecasters, who were dressed in robes of dark gray edged with silver. Both drummers and singers took their places at Sera's left. Next came the realm's powerful duchessas. Each bowed in turn to Sera, then took her seat in a row of high-backed chairs at Sera's right. One chair remained empty: Portia Volnero's.

Desiderio, now Miromara's high commander, swam in next. His shoulders were broad under his uniform; he held his head high. He was nineteen now, only two years older than Sera was, and the second-most-powerful mer in the realm.

He's too young for this burden, she thought, looking at him.

She was, too. But what choice did they have?

Desiderio bowed to her, then in a loud, ringing voice, called for the Keeper of Justice. Three deep booms were heard from the drummers, and then an elderly merman, garbed in purple and holding a golden staff, swam through the doors and into the center of the courtyard.

"Greetings, Regina Serafina," he said solemnly, without bowing.

Sera did not expect him to. He represented the rule of law, and in Miromara the law bowed to no one, not even the regina herself.

"Greetings, Keeper," Sera said, her voice ringing out strong and clear. "You have presided over the realm's case against its former high commander. The prosecution and defense have concluded their arguments. Has the jury reached a verdict?"

The keeper nodded. "It has, Your Grace."

"Lead the prisoner forth," Sera commanded.

She swallowed hard as her uncle, dressed only in a simple white sea-flax tunic, swam through the door. He was escorted by two guards. His hair had been cropped short. His hands were bound behind his back.

As she regarded him, Sera thought about how much he'd taken from her. Through his cruel deeds, he'd smashed her heart to pieces again and again, and yet that heart was beating, still alive, still capable of feeling sorrow. Even for him.

She remembered how he'd looked to her when she was small—so tall and strong, so handsome with his shock of black hair and his fierce blue eyes. She remembered feasting with him at holiday banquets. Racing hippokamps. Dancing at state dinners. She remembered him playing with her when she was tiny, pretending to be a tiger shark and chasing her around the throne.

He'd had his own daughter then—how it must've pained him to play with her, Serafina, and feign indifference to his own child.

The terrible things he'd done . . . were they all because of a love denied? she wondered. Would any of them had happened if Artemesia had allowed him to marry the mermaid he loved? Or had he always been jealous of his sister's power, and his niece's birthright? Sera realized she would never know.

"Keeper, the verdict, please," she said, with no trace of emotion in her voice.

"The jury finds the defendant, Vallerio di Merrovingia, guilty of regicide, high treason, and war crimes," the keeper intoned. "The high court sentences him to death by beheading, followed by the singing of gallows dirges."

"Vallerio di Merrovingia, you have heard your sentence. The high court decrees that you must pay for your crimes with your life," Sera declared. She paused to let her words sink in, then said, "It is the right of the condemned to speak aloud your last words. Have you any?"

"I do," Vallerio said. "I underestimated you, Serafina. You are much changed from the young mermaid I knew. You are stronger and smarter than I believed you to be. An able and impressive ruler. I never thought you would learn to lead so fast."

"I had a very capable teacher." This time Sera was unable to keep the bitterness from her voice.

Vallerio laughed darkly. "I suppose you did. However, it appears that the student is now the master. You are there," he nodded at the throne, "and I am here. But soon I shall be gone."

Sera winced at that, just slightly, but Vallerio caught it.

"Don't worry. I'm not going to beg you for my life. But I will caution you to be careful with yours. Very careful."

His lips curved into a mocking smile. Malice glinted in his eyes.

"Your mother had an expression: *Play the board, not the piece.* You've played well, Serafina, but not well enough. Did you really think I wouldn't have an endgame? Orfeo and I made a deal. I would help him search for the talismans, and he would help me take over the water realms."

"That is hardly news, uncle," Sera said. She managed to keep her voice even, but a cold dread crept over her.

"No," he allowed, "but *this* is: I made Orfeo promise that if something happened to me, he would protect Lucia. And he will. He gave me his word. Abbadon will slaughter you and your friends, and then Orfeo will restore my daughter to the throne. Good-bye, Serafina. Enjoy the view from up there . . . while you still have it."

Serafina felt her gorge rise. Only minutes ago, she had remembered the good merman he'd once been. Now all she felt was revulsion for the vicious, unrepentent murderer he'd become.

"Great Neria forgive you, Uncle," she said, "for I cannot."

Vallerio's guards moved to lead him to the wooden block, but he shook them off and swam to it himself. The executioner, a tall, muscular merman in a black hood, had quietly come forward. He was floating by the block now. His curved ax was leaning against it. He offered Vallerio a blindfold, but Vallerio refused it. He bent his tail, like a terragogg might bend his knees, and lowered his head to the block, resting it in the smooth hollow.

The executioner leaned down to him, grasped the collar of his tunic, and tore it open to expose his neck. Sera's hands tightened on the arms of her throne. She didn't want to watch this, but she had no choice. Reginas were required to witness the executions of those the high court condemned.

The executioner lifted his ax. He swung it back and forth through the water, picking up speed with each arc, sharpening his focus, priming his aim.

And then, with no further preliminaries, he swung it high above his head. As the fearsome blade began its final descent, Vallerio suddenly tilted his head and raised his eyes to Sera's.

"Checkmate," he said, just before the ax came down.

FIFTY-SEVEN

"ONE HUNDRED thousand troops, Sera," Neela said excitedly. "And more fighters joining us every day!"

She was sketching as she spoke, designing a military jacket. Sera had never gotten to wear the last one Neela had made for her, and now that she was no longer leader of the resistance but the leader of her realm, Neela had decided that a completely new look was in order.

"From Miromara and Matali, Qin and Ondalina," Neela continued. "From the prison camps that are being liberated—"

"But are the numbers *enough*, Neela?" Sera asked, her brow knit with worry. "Enough to take on Abbadon? And Orfeo?"

The two mermaids were in Sera's rooms—her mother's old chambers—where they often spent their evenings now. Sera was staring out of a window, her arms crossed. Sylvestre was draped over her shoulder. His color had improved. She could see her troops' camp in the distance, the white of their tents, the glow of their waterfires. Three weeks had passed since the battle for Cerulea had been won. While Sera and Des had been figuring out how to rule their realm, Yazeed, Neela, Becca, and Ling, together with Garstig and the other commanders, had once again been working to provision Sera's soldiers. They would all leave for the Southern Sea in six days.

"Orfeo's powerful," Sera continued. "In ways we know, and in ways we don't. He has the black pearl. What if he has Nyx's ruby ring, too? What if . . . what if he . . ." She couldn't bear to voice the thought.

"Killed Ava?" Neela said.

Sera nodded, turning to her. "What if he killed Astrid, too? We haven't heard from either of them in weeks."

"Not possible. We'd feel it," Neela said, looking up from her kelp-parchment sketchbook. "It's your uncle, isn't it? And what he said to you."

"Yeah," Sera admitted, "it is."

"Checkmate," Neela said, rolling her eyes. "Forget him, Sera. He only said it to rattle you."

"He succeeded."

"Did he?" Neela said with a smirk. "He's dead; you're not. I think that means *you* won."

"For now," Sera said.

Neela rose. She swam to her friend and put an arm around her. "We didn't come this far to fail."

Sera nodded. She kissed Neela's cheek, but inside she was still uneasy. Her uncle's final words had sewn dark seeds of doubt in her. As Neela sat back down and took up her sketchbook again, Sera thought about how the chessboard had changed.

Neela was right about one thing: she would have a large and loyal force at her back for the journey to the Southern Sea. And Orfeo was now without Vallerio and Portia, his firm allies, but Lucia was still on the loose. She'd escaped from the city, and, seemingly, the realm. There was a large bounty on her head, but no one had so much as glimpsed her. Had Orfeo given her sanctuary?

Sera remembered something that Mahdi had once said about Lucia—that she was like a rockfish, at her most dangerous when you couldn't see her. Sera had confided her worries to Desiderio, but he told her she wouldn't have to worry for long; Lucia couldn't stay hidden forever. They would find her and she would answer for her crimes, just like her father had.

"There! Done!" Neela suddenly said, interrupting Sera's thoughts. She held her sketchbook out. "Take a look and tell me what you think."

But before Sera could take the sketchbook, the door to her rooms banged open. Becca was floating in the doorway. Her red curls were corkscrewing loose from the twist at the back of her head. She was grinning from ear to ear.

"Becca? What's going on?" Sera asked, unused to seeing her practical, serious friend so excited.

"Ready for a bit of *good* news?" Becca asked.

Sera arched an eyebrow. "Good news? What's that?" she joked.

Ling stuck her head around the door. "Look who *we* found!" she said breathlessly.

A mermaid, thin and silt-stained, swam through the doorway.

"Ola, minas. Como vas?"

FIFTY-EIGHT

"*AVA!*" SERA SHOUTED. She swam to her friend, threw her arms around her, and whirled her around and around in the water.

"I'm so happy you're safe! I was so worried! Where have you been all this time?"

"In the swamps, and then in a cage, and then on the back currents."

"A *cage*?" Sera said, outraged.

"I got the ring, and then Traho got me. He took it. He was going to turn me over to Vallerio, but a friend rescued me. We've been making our way to you ever since. Sera, may I introduce another queen? Manon Laveau, the swamp queen of the Mississippi."

Sera had been so overjoyed to see Ava, she hadn't noticed that others had swum into the room with her.

Sera bowed to Manon, who returned the gesture.

"I would also like to present Jean Lafitte, Sally Wilkes, and the Countess Esmé," Ava said.

The ghosts all bowed. Sera's eyes widened at the sight of them.

Manon saw her fear and laughed. "Don't you worry, *cher*. They're not shipwreck ghosts. They know better than to suck the life out of folks."

Sera relaxed. "Thank you for saving my friend," she said, taking Manon's hand.

"You're more than welcome, but honestly, it wasn't no scales off my tail, as they say in the swamp. Ava's a good soul, and I'm always happy to mess up a bully's plans, and Traho is one *mean* bully."

"He *was*," Ling said. "He's one *dead* bully now."

Manon shook her head regretfully. "That's too bad. My boys will be disappointed. They were fixing to make mincemeat out of him."

She must've brought bodyguards with her, Sera thought. *Traho must've gotten on their wrong side, too.*

"Ava, did you say that Traho had Nyx's ring?" Becca asked.

Ava nodded sadly. "Baby got it from the Okwa Naholo. We were on our way out of the swamps when Traho found us."

"Traho probably passed it on to Orfeo," Sera reasoned, crestfallen to think that Orfeo had two talismans now.

"Speaking of Baby, where is that little beast?" Neela asked.

"Dead," Ava said sadly. "The death riders killed him."

"Oh, Ava, no!" Neela cried. "I'm so sorry!"

As Neela, Ling, and Becca comforted Ava, Sera attended to Manon, asking her if she would like something to eat.

"Child, what I would like is somewhere to rest my old bones. It's a *long* way from the Mississippi to Miromara. Maybe you have a nice little shack somewhere where a swamp queen could put her fins up?"

"A shack, no," Sera said, smiling. "But I'm sure we can find some comfortable accommodations for you."

She called for her maid. "Gianna," she said when the mermaid arrived, "please show our guest to the abalone suite in the west wing. Have dinner brought for her. And please have some tea brought for us, too."

"I'm much obliged to you," Manon said, turning to follow Gianna. But before she could go, Ava reached for her, then hugged her tightly.

"Thank you," she whispered.

"You catch up with your friends now. I'll see you in the morning," Manon said gruffly, patting Ava's back.

The ghosts chattered loudly as they left the chamber.

"A palace, a court, royalty," Esmé said grandly. "At last I'm back with my own kind!"

Manon snorted. "If you're a real countess, Esmé, then all those beads the goggs throw during Mardi Gras are real jewels!"

"Do you think this place is haunted?" Lafitte asked, looking around fearfully.

"*Please* don't tell me you're afraid of ghosts now," Manon said, exasperated.

"Manon, where did those gators of yours get to?" Sally asked. "They were right here, now they're not."

A scream was heard from down the hallway.

"That'll be them," Manon said. "Probably cornered some fool saltwater mer who doesn't know a gator from a salamander. Antoine! Gervais!" she bellowed. "You boys get over here!"

Sera's eyes grew wide. "She brought *alligators* with her?" she whispered. "I thought she meant bodyguards when she said *my boys*."

Ava nodded. "She did. The alligators *are* her bodyguards. Don't worry. She keeps them under control. Mostly."

Sera bit back a laugh. "I'm so happy you're here with us, Ava. Sit down. You must be so tired."

Sera's maid returned with a pot of hot sargassa tea, plus bowls of candied barnacles, pickled snails, and salted sea cucumbers. The five mermaids flopped down on soft, anemone-filled sofas, on large sea-silk cushions scattered on the floor, or collapsed into luxurious giant clam chairs.

As they ate and drank, Ava related her trip in more detail. Sera told her about Mahdi. Neela, Ling, and Becca filled Ava in on the battle for Cerulea and the progress they'd made since taking the city back.

"And Astrid? Have you heard from her?" Ava asked, when the others had finished speaking.

"No," Sera said. "Not a word since she left to find Orfeo. I can't even tell you how scared I am for her."

"So we don't know if she has the black pearl," Ava said.

"Or if she's okay," Ling said, stating their deepest fears.

"What do we do?" Ava asked. Sera heard a plaintive note in her voice.

"We go to the Southern Sea. Just as we planned," Sera said. "The balance of power has shifted in our favor."

"What do you mean?" Ava asked.

"Defeating Vallerio not only gave me my realm back, it gave Matali back to Mahdi. Emperor Aran and Empress Sananda were imprisoned by Portia, but now they are free again and ruling in his absence," Sera explained.

"They're my parents," Neela cut in. "I told them about Abbadon months ago, and they didn't believe me. But they do now, and they've sent troops to help us defeat it."

"Ondalina sent troops, too," Ling added. "And the Elder of Qin did also, out of gratitude to Sera for ruining Vallerio's plan to take over his realm."

"Orfeo had hoped to have control of the armies of Matali, Ondalina, and Qin through Vallerio," Sera said. "He planned to use them after he freed Abbadon to help him attack the underworld, but those armies are ours now."

"And our talismans," Neela added. "All except two."

"The black pearl and—"

"The ruby ring," Ava said hopelessly.

The heaviness Sera had sensed in Ava earlier descended again.

"Ava," Sera said, taking her hand, "you're not yourself. What's wrong?"

"Nothing, *mina*. I—I'm just tired, that's all."

"No," Sera said. "There's more to it than that."

A sob escaped Ava, and then another. "I failed you. All of you. And I failed myself. I didn't get the ring," she said, her voice hitching.

Instantly, the other four mermaids were out of their chairs, or off the floor, surrounding her.

"*Failed us?* Are you *crazy*, merl?" Neela said.

"You *did* get the ring," Becca insisted. "Traho ganged up on you two hundred to one!"

"You did an impossible thing," said Ling. "You survived the Okwa Naholo and the death riders!"

"Baby didn't," Ava said softly. "I miss him. I loved him *so* much. I had him since I was a tiny merl. I've depended on him for *everything*. How am I going to manage without him?"

"We'll help you, Ava," Neela said fiercely, squeezing Ava's hand. "We'll be your eyes."

Becca took her other hand. "We'll take care of you. We love you, Aves, don't you know that? We'd do anything for you."

Sera placed a gentle hand on Ava's arm. "We'll figure it out. Together."

It was at that very moment, when they were united and supporting one another, that they heard it. A voice, inside their heads.

"Merls? Are you there? Can you hear me? Please say something! It's *me*, Astrid!"

FIFTY-NINE

"ASTRID!" SERA CRIED, overjoyed to see her, but terrified they'd lose the connection to her. "We're here! All of us! Can you see us?"

Astrid held a finger to her lips, then said something, but Sera and others couldn't understand her. She flickered and faded.

"Focus, people, *focus*!" Neela ordered.

The five mermaids all joined hands and concentrated on Astrid.

"—can't talk long," Astrid said, her image suddenly vivid and sharp. "His servants might hear me and tell him!"

"Merl, *look* at you!" Neela said. "I barely recognize you. That is one invincible outfit! And your *hair*!"

Astrid looked down at herself and smiled wryly. "That's what happens when you have a reincarnated death-mage for a stylist."

She was wearing a fitted black dress and a beautiful pearl bib necklace. Her blond hair was sleek and short. Squid ink lined her eyes; silvery-blue ground mussel shell dusted her eyelids. Rings of obsidian and garnet glinted on her hands.

"Where are you?" Becca asked.

"In Shadow Manse, Orfeo's palace," Astrid replied.

"Are you okay?" asked Ling.

"I'm fine. Look, I don't know how long I've got, so"—she gave a wary glance over her shoulder—"I need to convey the essentials. Fast."

"Go ahead," said Sera. "We're listening."

"Orfeo's got the ruby ring. I'm going to take it, and the black pearl, tonight. And then I'm going to haul tail for the Southern Sea. Meet me there."

"Astrid, how? This is *Orfeo* we're talking about," Ling said. "He has powerful magic, you know? He might see this coming."

"I have magic now, too. Orfeo cured me. We're super tight." She smirked, then added, "At least that's what *he* thinks."

"I'm glad to hear you can sing again, Astrid, but you've been songcasting for what, a few weeks? Orfeo's been at it for four thousand years. He has a slight edge," Sera said, worried about her friend.

"Yeah, but I have a partner in this particular crime, and she has an edge, too. A big one." Astrid smiled like an excited child, then said, "Sera, it's Thalassa! She's *alive*. Orfeo's been keeping her prisoner, but she's okay. She's my teacher!"

Sera gasped. "Thalassa's *alive?*" Her heart swelled with happiness. This was a *miracle*. She was certain Miromara's canta magus had been killed by death riders. But her happiness was immediately pushed aside by anger. Thalassa was alive, yes, but she was in Orfeo's brutal hands. "Tell her I'm going to bring her home, Astrid," Sera said fiercely. "Tell her I'll find a way."

Astrid nodded. "I will, Sera. I promise."

"Wait, Astrid, exactly *how* are you going to get the talismans?" Becca asked, always practical.

"Orfeo takes the black pearl off at night, and puts it in a safe in his room. The ruby ring's there, too. I know because he showed it to me after Traho delivered it."

"Why would he do that?" Ling asked.

"Because he totally trusts me. I've made him think I'm on board with his plan to free Abbadon and attack the underworld."

"*Okaaay,*" Ling said, skeptical. "But he's going to stop trusting you pretty quick when he catches you trying to steal his talismans."

"But he *won't* catch me! That's what I'm trying to tell you! Thalassa taught me how to cast a superstrong somnio spell. I'm going to use it on Orfeo, make sure he's sound asleep, and then figure out how to break the safe's enchantment."

Sera shook her head. "I don't like this plan. Too dangerous."

"Oh, okay. I'll just reach into my bag o' plans and pull out a different one, then," Astrid said, rolling her eyes.

Sera gave her a look. "Does sarcasm *really* help at a time like this?"

"I *know* it's dangerous," Astrid said in a more conciliatory tone, "but it's all I've got. And I'm doing it."

"How long will it take you to get to the Southern Sea?" Becca asked. "Where is Shadow Manse?"

Astrid snorted. "The Black Sea. Where else?"

"Wow. That lumpsucker's *seriously* hung up on black," Neela said.

"It should take me about two months to get to the Southern Sea. Orfeo told me exactly where the Carceron is."

"Where?" Sera asked excitedly.

"At the north face of Bleak Mount, on the Weddell Plain."

"Astrid, that's huge! It will save us weeks of searching, if not months," Becca said.

"You're welcome," said Astrid. "I could get there a lot faster if I went through the mirror realm, but I don't dare risk it. If Rorrim caught me, he'd turn me in in a heartbeat. He and Orfeo are close."

"Funny how soul-stealing fiends tend to stick together," Ling observed.

"Two months is tight to move a large number of troops, but I think we can do it," Sera said.

"How many have you got?" Astrid asked.

"One hundred thousand," Sera replied.

Astrid whistled. "I don't know what Orfeo has, if anything," she said. "But I bet it's not a hundred thousand." She glanced over her shoulder again. "Someone's coming. I've got to go!"

"Be *careful*, Astrid!" Becca said.

"I will," Astrid said. Then she looked directly at Sera. "I can do this. Have faith in me."

"I know you can," Sera replied.

And then Astrid was gone.

"Wow," Neela said.

"We're closer than we've ever been to uniting all six talismans, and defeating Abbadon," said Sera.

"Or getting ourselves slaughtered," Ling pointed out.

"Sitting here worrying won't get one hundred thousand soldiers ready," Becca said. "Getting to bed so we can wake up at first light and get busy, will."

"True," agreed Sera.

The five friends rose. Becca, Neela, and Ling already had rooms in the palace and knew how to get to them. Sera summoned Gianna to take Ava to hers. But before they said their good nights, they turned to each other once more. Astrid had found out where the Carceron was. She'd been training her voice. She might even be able to snatch the last two talismans. That was all good. The five friends sensed that they had a new advantage, and they were excited about it, but a new solemnness had settled over them as well.

"Surviving on the swim, building an army, convincing Alítheia not to eat me, battling my uncle . . . it all feels like child's play compared to what's ahead of us," Sera said.

Ava nodded gravely. "That's because it is. Your uncle and Lucia were mortals with flaws and weaknesses that you could use to defeat them. But Orfeo's immortal. Abbadon, too."

"The Antarctic waters are going to make the North Sea feel like the Bahamas," Becca said. "Food will be scarce. Some of the soldiers won't make it. I wouldn't be surprised if skavveners follow us the whole way."

"We need to prepare our troops well, for sure," Ling said, "but first we need to prepare ourselves. Because the hardest part of this whole thing is about to begin."

SIXTY

"**W**ELL DONE, CHILD," Orfeo said, stepping out of the shadows.

He'd hidden himself at the side of the large wardrobe in Astrid's room, well out of range of the convoca.

Astrid turned to him. "You heard everything?"

"I did."

"Then you know she has one hundred thousand troops. *One hundred thousand.* They were supposed to be *your* troops," Astrid said anxiously. "They would have been, if Serafina hadn't beaten her uncle."

Orfeo flapped a hand. "A minor inconvenience."

"Minor?"

He smiled. "I'm touched by your concern, but your worry is misplaced. We'll go to the Southern Sea with an army, too, Astrid—a powerful one. Have no doubt about that. And once I'm inside the Carceron, one hundred *million* soldiers couldn't stop me."

Astrid nodded, unconvinced.

"Practice now, child," Orfeo advised. "Songcasting should be your only concern. Work on your stilos, your vortexes, your apă piatrăs. We'll need them in the Southern Sea, and again when we march on the underworld."

Astrid promised that she would, and Orfeo bade her good night. Before he left, he kissed her forehead, then took her face in his hands.

"You are all that I hoped you'd be, and so much more," he said to her. "I'm so proud of you. So proud of your strength, your talent. So proud to call you daughter."

Astrid smiled. "If I'm strong, if I'm showing talent, it's only because of you," she said. "You gave me my magic back, Orfeo. I'll never forget it."

Orfeo looked pleased. He kissed her again, then left her room.

Astrid watched him go, then closed the door behind him. She conjured an apă piatră, and then a fragor lux, but her heart wasn't in it and the spells fizzled.

"Betray my friends?" she whispered. "Or betray my blood?"

That was the decision she'd had to make. She hadn't expected to find herself so torn when she'd left the Karg, but that was before she met Orfeo, before he gave her back her magic—and her pride.

Astrid had made the decision. Some time ago. Now she'd have to carry it out. And live forevermore with the consequences, whatever they might be.

She swam to a tall window and stared out of it, her thoughts, and her heart, as inscrutable as the night-dark waters.

SIXTY-ONE

"GOOD EVENING, Your Grace," said the nurse as Sera swam into Mahdi's hospital room.

"Has there been any improvement?" Sera asked hopefully, as she did every time she came to visit Mahdi.

"I'm afraid not," the nurse said, shaking her head. "We've changed the anemone arrangement above his bed, though, so he has something fresh to look at."

"Thank you," said Sera, glancing up at the ceiling, where a new pattern of orange, purple, and pink had been laid out. Mahdi's blank eyes stared up at it.

Is he seeing them? Sera wondered. *Can he hear me? Does he even know I'm here?*

She sat down on the edge of his bed and smoothed a lock of hair off his forehead. Sylvestre, draped around her neck, turned dark blue.

"We're ready, Mahdi," she said, sharing her day with him, as she did every evening. "Weapons, ammo, food . . . it's all in place. We provisioned the troops when we were in the Karg, and Becca made sure everything was loaded into Marco's ships, but we needed *so* much more. We only had twenty thousand soldiers then, and there are one hundred thousand bivouacked outside the city tonight. This is it, Mahdi. After all this time, we're finally going to the Southern Sea."

She smoothed his pajama top and fastened an open button. "At least, I *hope* we are." She paused, then said, "Back when we were with the Iele, Vrăja asked me to help the others believe in themselves. She said that's what a good leader does. Ling, Neela, and Becca have changed. They *do* believe in themselves now. I think Astrid does, too. Getting her magic back has given her the confidence she needed. But I haven't succeeded with Ava. *Help Ava believe the gods did know what they were doing.* That's what Vrăja said. But Traho took Nyx's ring from her, and he killed Baby, and I think she's lost faith. In the gods, and in herself. And nothing I say or do makes any difference. I wish I knew how to help her."

She gently lifted Mahdi's head and fluffed the anemones underneath it.

"Desiderio's staying here. He'll be in charge in my absence, with Fossegrim as his advisor," she continued. "I'm glad I'm leaving the realm in such good hands. Yaz is coming with us. Astrid's meeting us there with two of the talismans. I *hope*."

She took Mahdi's hand in hers. "They're so brave, all of them, so tough, so smart. But this thing—Abbadon—it's made of immortal souls. How are *we* supposed to destroy what the gods have made immortal? Vrăja gave us this task; she believes we can carry it out . . . but *how*? Am I leading one hundred thousand soldiers into a justified battle, or straight to their destruction?" She smiled sadly. "I wish you could tell me."

Sera sat for quite some time, saying nothing, just holding Mahdi's hand and gazing at his face. "I have to go," she finally said. "We leave at dawn. I have no idea how I'm going to sleep tonight, but I guess I should try. Before I go, I have to tell you something. I—I don't know if I'm coming back. I don't know if you'll be here if I do. All I know is that I love you, Mahdi, with all my heart. You were ready to give your life for mine. Maybe you already have. But *you* are my life. Remember when we Promised ourselves to each other? Maria said something, right before the ceremony." She leaned over and kissed his lips. "I believed her then. I still do. Love is the strongest magic."

She touched her forehead to his, then quickly left.
She didn't look back. It was easier that way.
If she had, she would have seen it.
A single silver tear rolling down Mahdi's cheek.

SIXTY-TWO

CLIO TOSSED HER HEAD and thrashed her long serpent's tail. She didn't like canyons.

"Easy, girl," Sera said. She'd been reunited with her hippokamp after the Black Fin invasion. A death rider captain had taken a liking to her, and had taken good care of her.

Krill Canyon, in the Haakon Basin, rose steeply on both sides. At its far end, a sheer bluff soared high into the water. Rocks and boulders obscured its base. Anything could be hiding in them.

Sera and her troops had been traveling to the Southern Sea for five weeks now and not making the kind of progress she'd hoped for. They'd been battling the cold, which stiffened joints, snapped harnesses, jammed weapons, and sickened soldiers. A few had succumbed and had been buried along the way. They were also going through food stores faster than they'd planned, which meant that part of every day was spent foraging and hunting instead of swimming or marching.

There were other threats to be dealt with as well. They'd encountered a clan of Fryst on the Scotia Ridge, who'd menaced them at first, but then decided to join them when Sera told their leader where they were headed and why. They'd also run into several EisGeists. The creatures had regarded them hungrily, but had moved off, obviously intimidated by their numbers. As Becca had predicted, skavveners trailed them constantly.

As dangerous as all those creatures were, Sera was much more worried about Orfeo and Lucia. Orfeo knew where she was headed. And Lucia could have easily found out. Either could be waiting in ambush.

The decision to go through Krill Canyon had been made to save time. It was a direct route out of the Haakon Basin and into the Weddell Plain. Like Clio, Sera didn't relish swimming through it. Normally, she swam over canyons, but a large chunk of her army was goblin, and goblins walked. They could swim, but weren't much better at it than the goggs were.

"Whoa, Clio," Sera said now, halting the hippokamp. She raised a hand to stop the long column of troops behind her.

Turning to Ava, who was riding next to her on a gentle, biddable mount, she said, "Aves, do you feel anything?"

Ava concentrated. She was about to shake her head, but stopped.

"What is it?" Sera asked, her fins prickling.

Ava frowned. "Nothing, I think. A shoal, maybe. And a pod of whales."

"Any mer?" Sera asked.

"I—I can't tell. The whales are jamming me," Ava said.

Sera knew that whales could enhance mer magic, and could make a mess of it, too.

"The sooner we get out of this canyon and past that bluff, the better," Sera muttered. She was about to nudge Clio on when a figure appeared on the eastern rise.

It was a mermaid. She was carrying a staff.

"Weapons raised!" Sera shouted. Instantly, crossbows and spearguns were aimed.

The mermaid cupped her hands around her mouth. "Hey, you jackwrasses! Put those weapons down! You're scaring the kitties!"

A hundred giant catfish swam up to the edge of the rise, fanning out along it. They wore chain mail made of flattened soda cans and helmets fashioned from shiny silver hubcaps.

"No *way*," Neela said.

Sera grinned. "Lena!" she shouted back at the mermaid. "Is that *you?*"

"Who else would it be?" the mermaid shouted back. "Didn't want to come. Can't stand you, to be honest. But I didn't see much of a choice. Word's traveling about the thing under the ice. Seems to me like you need all the help you can get. As I recall, you couldn't even swim down a river without bringing a world of trouble with you. Not sure I've *ever* met three bigger fools."

Lena, Sera recalled, was not exactly a diplomat.

"Wow, she hasn't changed a bit," Ling said. "Still as charming as ever."

"Lena, come down! We *definitely* need all the help we can get!" Sera shouted.

Lena, a freshwater mermaid from the Dunarea River, had hidden Sera, Neela, and Ling from Traho and the death riders when the merls were on their way to the Iele's cave. She'd saved their lives. She swooped down into the canyon now, followed by her catfish. Sera saw that the staff she was carrying was a hockey stick—the same one she'd threatened them with when they tried to cross her patch of river. Her bright red hair was just visible under her horseshoe crab helmet, and she wore the same soda can chain mail as her catfish.

"It's so good to see you," Sera said, embracing the prickly mermaid. "Thank you for joining us.

Lena winced and thumped Sera on the back. Ling and Neela hugged her, too. Then Sera introduced her to Becca, Ava, Yazeed, Garstig, and Rök, all of whom rode at the front of the troops.

"We should get going," Yazeed said when the introductions were over. "This canyon is not a good place to hang out."

"Well, you might want to wait a minute," Lena cautioned.

"Why?" Sera asked.

"There's a crew coming up behind me. Been following the same current I was on, but they veered farther west. Probably come out up there," Lena said, pointing at the bluff. "I hid the kitties in a trench one night and doubled back to spy on them. Fierce-looking bunch. Numbering about a thousand, I'd say. Got about twenty whales with them, too."

"Friend or foe?" Sera asked, alarmed.

"I couldn't tell you," Lena said. "Their leader, though? She looks like she'd eat you for breakfast."

"I'm still not getting anything. It's got to be the whales," said Ava, who'd been trying to use her inner vision to see who might be approaching. "I can't see who it is."

"I have a feeling I know who it is," Ling said darkly. *"Lucia."*

SIXTY-THREE

"WE CAN DEFEAT HER," Becca said. "She's got one thousand; we've got a hundred thousand."

"She doesn't want to engage us. She wants Sera," Yazeed said grimly. "She's probably waiting by the bluff with snipers, hoping to get a clean shot. I'm going to send two scouts ahead. I'll have them cast transparensea pearls. They can tell us where she's positioned."

He was just about to summon the scouts when the waters overhead darkened. It was as if the day had suddenly turned to night.

Humpback whales, each as big as a fishing boat, had clustered overhead. They were singing.

"She didn't wait for us to reach the bluffs," Becca said. "She's going to attack from above."

Yazeed called for weapons to be readied again. "Sera, get down off Clio," he ordered. "Take cover behind Alítheia."

Sera remembered how brave her mother had been during the invasion of Cerulea, even after she'd been shot. She'd ripped the arrow out of her side, and then dared her attacker to finish his work.

"No, Yaz, I won't turn tail," Sera said. "Lucia's nothing but a cowardly assassin, just like her father. I'll fight, together with everyone else."

The whalesong grew louder and more urgent. And then a new sound rose above their music, a war cry, shrill and bloodcurdling.

"Take aim!" Yazeed ordered.

"No, Yazeed! *Wait!*" Neela cried. "Don't shoot!"

And then to everyone's surprise, Neela answered the war cry with one of her own.

A chorus of victory whoops floated down to the Black Fins. And then a figure, strong and regal, swam down under the whales. Her fins spiked out around her like a lionfish's. She was surrounded by a cadre of warriors, their powerful bodies decorated with coral armbands and beaded breastplates.

"*Kora!*" Neela shouted. She raced up to meet the warrior princess. "*Salamu kubwa, Malkia!*" she called out in Kandinian mer. *Greetings, great queen!*

The two mermaids embraced. Then Kora put Neela in a headlock—a Kandinian sign of affection. Neela greeted Kora's guard—the Askari—and then escorted them down to meet Sera and the others.

"Serafina, Regina di Miromara, may I present Kora, the Malkia of Kandina," she said.

The two queens bowed to each other. "I, my Askari, and warriors from across my realm have come to fight with our sister Askara," Kora said, nodding at Neela. "She helped free my people from a terrible prison camp. We will now put an end to the one behind such an evil, and his monster, too. We will swim with you to the Carceron."

Ling elbowed Neela. "Sister Askara, huh?" she said, under her breath. "*Whoa.*"

"Neels, you're a badwrasse!" Becca whispered. "Who knew?"

"Everybody but you two, apparently," Neela replied airily.

"Malkia Kora, the Black Fins and I are honored to have you and your fighters at our side. Thank you for joining us," said Sera.

"Ceto Rorqual, a mighty humpback, and his clan will join you, too," Kora said.

"Humpbacks? Will they be all right in Antarctic waters?" Sera asked, concerned.

"The Rorqual have very strong magic. They can insulate themselves against the cold."

Sera called a greeting and a thank-you to Ceto. He acknowledged her with a swipe of his mighty tail.

"There are more, Regina," Kora said.

"More whales?" Sera asked, confused.

"More fighters."

"From Kandina . . ." Sera said.

Kora shook her head, smiling. "From *everywhere*. We saw a cloud of silt rising behind us. Two Askari swam back to investigate. The cloud was raised by a horde of mer, goblins, seaweed trolls, and sand trolls. They're all coming to fight with you. To save their home from Abbadon."

A lump rose in Sera's throat. When she could speak again, she said, "We'd better get out of this canyon, then. So we can make camp for the night and give the newcomers something to eat."

Sera gave the signal, and the Black Fins started moving again. Kora and her fighters fell in with them. She and Yazeed started to talk. Lena swam alongside, shy and awkward, but fiercely loyal, too.

Sera looked at them, deeply touched that Lena and Kora had joined the Black Fins, and that more fighters were on the way. The knowledge heartened her, but it also deepened the dread gnawing at her.

Ling picked up on it. "Hey, Sera, what's wrong?" she asked, pulling next to her on her own hippokamp.

"We're going to reach the Carceron soon, and I still have no idea how to defeat Abbadon."

Ling frowned. "You know, you had a serious confidence issue when I first met you. On our way to the River Olt. I thought you'd gotten over it, but maybe not."

"Confidence issue?" Sera sputtered. "Ling, Abbadon isn't, like, a self-esteem problem. It's a big, bad, vicious, bloodthirsty monster with twenty hands!"

"Vrăja summoned us for a reason. She believed we'd find a way to do this. Together," Ling said. "You have to believe that, too, Sera. It's not all on you to defeat Abbadon. It's on *us*."

Sera nodded. She took Ling's hand and squeezed it. There *had* to be a way to defeat the monster. To spare Ling, and all these brave, trusting fighters from certain death. Sera desperately hoped they could figure it out.

Before it was too late.

SIXTY-FOUR

THE STORM THAT RAGED across the Weddell Plain was like a vengeful spirit. Swirling deepwater vortexes, caused by warring warm and cold currents, howled down savagely on the Black Fins, threatening to throw them off course. Sediment whirled in the water, making it hard to see.

Sera, a scarf wrapped around her head, led a frightened Clio by her reins. It was impossible to ride in this weather. She squinted into the churning waters, trying to see more than a few yards ahead.

"Yaz!" she shouted. "How much farther?"

He was right next to her, cupping his compass with both hands. "We should be there by now!" he shouted back.

Another monster vortex rolled over them then, shrieking so loudly it drowned out all other sounds. Clio reared, and it was all Sera could do to hold on to the terrified creature. Just when she thought Clio would yank her arms out of their sockets, the vortex passed. As it did, the waters behind it settled a bit. Sera heard Yaz yelling her name.

"Look!" He was pointing ahead.

Sera turned her head and saw a steep, craggy black mountain looming in the distance.

"Bleak Mount! Two leagues away! Come on!" Yazeed shouted, right before another vortex slammed down on them.

The Black Fins struggled on for another hour before the storm let up. When the waters finally calmed, they found they were on flat ground, and at the base of Bleak Mount.

Sera wiped the silt out her eyes and peered ahead through the murky sea. Looming up at them was a forbidding prison of stone and ice—the Carceron.

"We're here," Sera said, her voice ragged. "At last."

Before Yazeed could say anything, Garstig caught up with them. "We've got to make camp now," he said. "The troops are exhausted. We lost animals in the storms. If we don't shelter, and fast, we'll lose soldiers."

Sera gave the order to put up the tents, but she insisted that they be pitched well back from the Carceron. As her troops got busy unpacking, she started toward the prison. Becca, Neela, Ling, and Ava went with her.

Sera pulled her seal fur parka tightly around her as she swam. Her face was gaunt; there were dark circles under eyes. Hunger had been the Black Fins' constant companion on the trek to the Southern Sea. It had taken them nine weeks to reach the prison, much longer than she'd anticipated. Now that they'd arrived, she didn't know whether it was smarter to order her troops to make camp or to tell them to turn around and swim for their lives.

The mere sight of the place raised the scales on the back of her tail, and the thought of what was inside it made her stomach tighten with fear.

Ice had crusted over the Carceron's heavy stones centuries ago. They gleamed a dull, pearly gray in the half-light. It glazed the iron bars of its soaring gate and encased its massive lock.

Ten yards from the gates, the mermaids stopped. Neela cast an illuminata. Its glow was weak. Little light reached the Southern Sea's depths.

"It's quiet. Too quiet. I wonder if it knows we're here," Ling said.

"I'm going to call it," Sera said, drawing her sword. "I want to lay eyes on it again. See if we can find any weaknesses."

Becca, Ling, and Neela drew their swords, ready to rush to her defense.

"Abbadon!" Sera called out, as she approached the gate. "Abbadon, come out!"

She tensed, adrenaline racing through her body, ready for the monster to throw itself against the bars. It would growl and shriek. It would reach through the bars with its terrible hands. It would try to kill her.

Except it didn't.

Cautiously, Sera swam up to the gate and peered through. From her studies of ancient Atlantean history she knew that there was open space between the prison's dizzyingly high outer wall and its inner wall, which enclosed the cellblocks. She fully expected the monster to be lurking in it.

But it wasn't.

Sera swung the flat of her sword against the gate's bars. Ice cracked and fell away, the sound echoing through the water. She did it again and again until almost all the ice was off.

"Sera, be careful!" Neela shouted. "It could be a trap. Abbadon might be trying to lure you close."

"Ava, what do you see?" Sera called out.

Ava lowered her head, as if concentrating. If anyone could sense where the monster was, and what it was doing, it would be her.

After a moment, Ava raised her head. With Ling's help, she swam over to Sera. Neela and Becca were right behind them.

"It's not a trap," she said. "The monster's not here."

"Not here? You mean, not in the prison?" Becca said, incredulous.

"No, not by the gates," Ava replied. "It's in the prison, all right.

Deep inside. Hiding. Waiting. It knows we're here, but for some reason, it doesn't want to fight us," she said. "Not yet, at least."

Sera put her sword back in its scabbard. She turned to face her friends and said, "Why does that scare me even more?"

SIXTY-FIVE

MOURNERS PILED Regelbrott's grave high with rocks. Sera placed the last one.

Then, head bowed, she joined her voice with the others, goblin and mer, singing the soldier's dirges.

Regelbrott had died last night. The lack of food and frigid temperatures, combined with the polar fever that was working its way through the camp, had been too much for her. Her comrades had buried her with full military honors. Her grave was one of over fifty that now dotted the seafloor at the edge of the Black Fins' camp.

As the last notes of the dirge faded, another sound was heard—high, manic laughter. Sera raised her eyes. She knew what was making the sound, even before she saw them—skavveners.

They'd assembled high above the camp, on a broad ridge on Bleak Mount. Their clothing, ripped from corpses, was ragged and full of holes. Pillaged jewels dangled from their necks and earlobes. Their hair hung in their faces, dirty and lank.

"Shoot them if they come any closer," she told Garstig as she left the grave.

As she made her way back to camp, Alítheia by her side, she clapped her gloved hands together to warm them. The cold of the Southern Sea was like nothing she'd ever known. It was a predator circling for a kill.

The Black Fins had reached the Carceron a week ago and still hadn't sighted Abbadon; they'd only heard an occasional growl or echoing laughter.

They'd set up camp in a semicircle facing the Carceron but well back from its gates. Sentries had been stationed along the camp's perimeter, to watch for Astrid, or an enemy's approach. More had been posted at the prison's gate with orders to report any movement from inside.

But the monster didn't show itself.

It was eerily quiet, and there was nothing to do but watch and wait.

Dusk began to fall as Sera moved through the camp. Goblins and mer, hooded in sealskin, hunched against the cold, warmed themselves at waterfires, or gathered around the lava pond.

Thankfully, the goblins had found a seam, and had opened it wide. The Black Fins could at least warm themselves at the bubbling pool of molten rock now. Sera heard more coughing as she swam past her troops. Antoine and Gervais, two of Manon Laveau's alligators, were sneezing, even though they'd been enchanted against the cold. The swamp queen and her retinue had joined forces with Sera, too.

Even Alítheia was suffering in the Antarctic climate. Her usual quick scuttle had slowed markedly. The frigid temperatures had thickened the oil in her metal joints.

The cold, the uncertainty, the waiting . . . they had become the Black Fins' enemies, too. They frayed tempers, wore nerves thin, made Sera and her soldiers grim and tense.

Sera headed to the Carceron now. She went there several times a day to see if Abbadon had decided to show itself. As she approached the prison, she saw that she had company this evening. Ava was floating by its gates, her hands wrapped around the iron bars.

"Any sign of life?" Sera asked as she swam up to her.

Ava shook her head. "It's still in hiding. I can hear it, though, if I listen hard."

"I don't get it," Sera said, frowning. "The last time we saw it, in the Iele's caves, it broke right through the witches' protective spell and tried to kill us all. Why isn't it doing that now?"

"I think Orfeo told it to hide."

Sera's frown deepened. "Is he coming, Ava? Can you see him?"

Ava shook her head.

"What about Astrid?"

"Nothing there, either."

"Nothing at all? Are you *sure*?"

"Yes, and it doesn't make any sense," Ava said, frustration in her voice. "If Astrid got the two talismans and made it out of Shadow Manse, he'd go after her. He'd be chasing her down here. And if she *didn't* get the talismans, he'd *still* be on his way down here. Because he's no fool. He'll have found out by now that we're here with the other four talismans."

Sera nodded. "If he knows we're here, he'll know we have an army. A big one. He wouldn't come without troops of his own. He doesn't have the soldiers he thought he'd have, but there are always mercenaries to be found."

"If he was coming with an army, I'd know. All those soldiers, *mina* . . . I'd sense *something*. I'd feel all those dark hearts getting closer. Unless . . ." She hesitated, uncertainty in her voice. "Unless I *can't*. Sera, I'm scared I'm losing my ability to sense things. I mean, I sure didn't see Traho coming, back in the Spiderlair."

"That was only because you'd just escaped the Okwa Naholo. It took all you had to outsmart those things. No one would have seen Traho coming," Sera said, trying to reassure her. "Your inner sight is still sharp, Ava. When we first arrived here, you sensed that Abbadon was hiding deep inside the Carceron, didn't you?"

Ava didn't reply, but she didn't need to. Sera could see in her face that she wasn't convinced. Ava's sadness, and her self-doubt, hadn't lifted.

Ava turned her face to the gate again. Listening. Sensing.

"Why don't the gods answer, Sera? Why won't they tell us how to kill Abbadon?"

"They haven't answered *yet*," Sera said, trying to sound hopeful. "They're the gods. They tend to do things on their own schedule."

"I'm getting nothing from him now," Ava said quietly. "Not even a whisper."

"It's so weird," Sera said, peering into the murk beyond the bars. "I expected an insane monster roaring at us. I expected Orfeo, soldiers, battles, an ambush from Lucia. . . . I never expected *nothing*."

"Maybe Orfeo's trying to throw us off our guard."

"Well, he won't," Sera said resolutely. "We have sentries patrolling the camp's perimeter. He's not getting close without us knowing."

"Let's hope not," Ava said wearily.

"Get some rest. Alítheia will take you to your tent," Sera said. Her heart hurt for her despondent friend. She longed for the boisterous, colorful Ava that she knew.

Alítheia gently offered Ava one of her legs to hold. Ava took it, and the two started back to the center of camp. But after they'd gone a few yards, Ava stopped and turned around.

"Vrăja said the Six Who Ruled were strongest when they were together. She said we would be, too. Maybe you're right, Sera. Maybe the gods just haven't answered yet. Maybe they will when Astrid comes. When the talismans are reunited. When *we* are."

Ava was trying to hang on to a shred of hope. They all were.

"Maybe so, Aves," Sera said softly.

And then Ava and Alítheia disappeared into the gloom.

Sera turned back to the Carceron. She looked down at the scorched place where the Iele's waterfire used to burn, and she remembered how scared she'd been when Vrăja summoned her. Now she'd give anything to have the river witch near. Sera had talked to Kora and Lena about Abbadon. She'd talked to the trolls and the whales. No one had been able to tell her what she needed to know—how to kill it.

She heard Ava's voice in her head. *Maybe the gods just haven't answered yet.*

And then she heard something else—low, gurgling laughter. It was coming from deep inside the Carceron.

A shiver ran through her. Buttoning the collar of her sealskin coat around her neck, she headed back to her tent.

The cold stalked her as she swam, making her teeth chatter.

Tomorrow, she would double the amount of soldiers sent out to hunt. There wasn't much here, but maybe they could find the tiny translucent fish that darted along the seafloor, some mud worms, and the shrimplike amphipods. If they got enough of them, the camp's cooks could make a hot stew to warm the troops.

Finding another lava seam would help, too. She would order work crews to search for one first thing in the morning.

Sera was determined to fight the cold at every turn.

For now, it was the only enemy she *could* fight.

SIXTY-SIX

SOMETHING WAS WRONG. Sera knew it before she opened her eyes.

Before the camp's alarm sounded.

Before the shouts and commands rang out.

Before Becca, breathless, came racing into her tent.

"Sera, come quick. We've got trouble."

Dawn was just breaking. Sera had fallen asleep sitting in a chair. She was up and out of it immediately. "What is it?" she asked tersely.

"*Cadavru.* At least, that's what Vrăja called them."

"*Rotters?* Becs, a few dead goggs stumbling around are no reason to sound the alarm."

"There's an entire *army* of them, Sera. They've surrounded the camp."

Fear clutched at Sera. "Who's leading them?"

"No one, as far as we can tell. They're not advancing. They're just standing there."

"And Abbadon?"

"He suddenly woke up," Becca said grimly. "He's making noise. A *lot* of noise."

Sera quickly put her armor on, grabbed her crossbow, and followed Becca out of the tent. She swam up high in the water, then turned in a slow circle. Becca had not exaggerated. There were tens of thousands of rotters. They outnumbered her own troops. Some were skeletons, their bones stripped clean by scavengers. Others were in various stages of decay, flesh hanging off them like tattered clothing. All were armed with spears or swords. They stood perfectly still, as if waiting for orders.

"Where are the other commanders?" Sera asked.

"At the Carceron," Becca replied.

Sera sped toward the prison. Becca followed. They found Ling, Ava, Neela, Yazeed, and Garstig near the gate. Noise was emanating from within the prison—roars, laughter, shrieks.

"Abby's waking up," Yazeed said.

"Yaz, how did the rotters get here?" Sera asked. "Why didn't we see them coming?"

"They started circling just before dawn. They must've been close last night, but knew enough to stay out of the range of our scouts. We never saw them in the darkness."

"And I couldn't feel them," Ava said. "I still can't. There's nothing *there* to feel—no heart, no soul."

"Whoever sent them knew that," Ling said. "I'm sure of it."

Sera's fear grew. She fought it down. "We *know* who sent them. There's only one mage powerful enough to reanimate so many dead things. Orfeo's here," she said. "He's come for his monster."

"Why hasn't he shown himself?" Ling asked.

"I think he's about to," Yazeed said.

They all looked where he was pointing, at the seamount above. A figure, hovering by a rocky ledge, made its way down to the seafloor.

As the figure got closer, though, they all saw that it was a *she*, not a *he*.

The mermaid had blond hair, and the black-and-white tail of an orca. She wore a sleek black dress, a fitted sealskin vest, and a pearl necklace. A sword of Kobold steel hung from a scabbard at her hip. She held her head high, exuding confidence and power.

As the mermaid swam to the open patch of seafloor between the camp and the Carceron, Sera blinked, barely believing her eyes. The fear she'd felt evaporated. A feeling of triumph surged through her veins.

"Astrid *did* it! She got the talismans."

She started toward her friend, overjoyed, but a few yards away, she stopped short. Another figure was making its way down the seamount.

Sera recognized him. He'd come for her once. Through her mirror. He'd tried to kill her. He too had blond hair, and he wore it cropped close to his head. He was without sunglasses now, and she could see his eyes, as black and bottomless as the abyss. He walked instead of swam, for he was a human. Or had been once.

He joined Astrid. They smiled at each other.

"Astrid," Sera said. "Astrid . . . *no.*"

Astrid didn't reply. She threw a cold glance at Sera, then trained her gaze on the Carceron.

With a sickening jolt, Sera saw the truth: Astrid had betrayed her. She'd betrayed all of them. The things she'd said during the last convoca were all lies. She'd only said them to get the Black Fins to the Carceron with their talismans. Astrid had asked Sera how many troops she'd had and then given Orfeo that information, which was why his troops outnumbered hers.

Astrid was Orfeo's now. And Sera knew why. He had given her something no one else could: her magic, and her pride.

And now she was about to give Orfeo something in return: the talismans, her friends' lives . . . and Abbadon.

SIXTY-SEVEN

ORFEO WALKED UP TO SERA. He bowed.

"Serafina, Regina di Miromara, at last we meet in person. It's an honor," he said. "Your bravery and resourcefulness, and that of your friends, are remarkable. No one else, not even myself, has managed to find the other five talismans."

Sera did not return the bow, or the pleasantries. "You can't do this, Orfeo," she said. "You can't unleash suffering on the entire world just because you've suffered."

"Actually, I can. I vowed to get my wife back from the underworld, if it took me all of eternity. And now I will."

"Not without a fight."

Orfeo smiled. "I thought you might say that. Knowing you, you'll have prepared some brilliant military strategy, much as your mother would have. The logical choice would be for you and your fighters to head for higher waters and attack from there, knowing that my cadavru are not as strong in the water as your troops. But that would be a mistake, because *they* are," he said, pointing above him.

Sera looked up. The waters above were filled with dragons. They hovered menacingly.

"Razormouths," Neela said fearfully.

"Indeed," said Orfeo, turning to her. "I believe, Your Grace, that you're acquainted with one of them—the dragon queen herself, Hagarla. She's carrying a grudge, I'm sorry to say. She's never quite gotten over the theft of her moonstone. I've told her that it's hers the minute I'm finished with it." He smile broadened. "And that *you* are, too. But enough chatter. I want the talismans."

"You'll have to kill me for them," Sera said, raising her crossbow.

Orfeo nodded. "As you wish."

CHAPTER 67

SIXTY-EIGHT

"*A*TTACK!" ORFEO ROARED.

"Forward, brave fighters!" Sera commanded.

With rallying shouts, guttural growls, and high shrieks, the armies of the living and the dead rushed together, swords clashing against shields, spears and arrows hurtling through the water, song-spells flying.

Above them, Hagarla and her dragons dove, shrieking as they hurtled toward the fray. The humpbacks rushed in and blocked them. Sera heard Kora's war cries. She saw Lena and her catfish charge into the battle. Seaweed trolls, sand trolls, and ice trolls thundered past, swinging their giant clubs.

Sera fired her crossbow at Orfeo, but he evaded the arrow. Becca and Yazeed were battling cadavru. Ling was whirling vortexes at Astrid, who was flipping them around and throwing them back at her.

Ava, holding a dagger, tried to fight, too. She turned this way and that in the water, pointing the blade in the direction of any noise she heard.

Terrified for her, Sera grabbed her and pushed her down behind a rock. "Alítheia, protect Ava!" she shouted. The spider came pounding toward them, then crouched over the rock, swiping at any cadavru who came close.

Sera rejoined the battle in time to see Orfeo throw a vicious stilo at Neela. Neela blocked it with a water wall, then returned fire with a fragor lux. He ducked, and it exploded against the wall of the Carceron. Then he countered by whirling a silt cloud at her, to blind her, but Neela somersaulted out of the way. Waterfire followed, and then another stilo. Neela ducked and dodged, parrying his songspells, throwing her own, trying to get closer to him.

I need to help her! Sera thought frantically.

She tried to get to Neela, but every time she moved toward her friend, a rotter rushed at her, pushing her back. She used songspells and her sword to fight the creatures off, but as soon as she'd knocked one's head off with a stilo, or cut it in two with her sword, another took its place. They were everywhere.

Sera saw, with an anguished clarity, that her troops were being beaten, and not only by rotters. Ceto and his fellow whales were using all their magic to hold off the Razormouths, yet some of the dragons had broken through their line and were slaughtering Black Fins. Sera could hear death screams. The water was turning crimson.

Yazeed swam up to her. His face was covered in blood from a gash in his forehead. Ling and Becca were right behind him.

"We're getting massacred," Becca said, panting. "We've got to fall back!"

"To where?" Sera cried. The land around the Carceron was nothing but a rocky flat.

"We'll retreat to the south. There's got to be somewhere to—" Her words were cut off by a roar so terrible, they both had to cover their ears.

"Abbadon!" Becca cried fearfully. "It must've gotten out!"

"No!" Ling shouted, pointing overhead. "Look!"

Yazeed tilted his head. "No way," he said. "I do not *believe* this."

High up in the water, Guldemar—the Meerteufels' chieftain—was careening toward them at breakneck speed in a bronze chariot pulled by six gray hippokamps. He was driving the animals insanely fast, cracking a whip over their heads again and again. Rising up off the seafloor behind him like a lethal rogue wave was a nightmare come to life.

"*Gå! Förstör det onda!*" Guldemar shouted over his shoulder. *Go! Destroy this evil!*

Sera knew this nightmare. Guldemar's throne had been cast in its image. It was the stuff of legends, a mythical beast that the Meerteufel could call up in times of great peril.

Hafgufa, the kraken.

SIXTY-NINE

WITH A FURIOUS SHRIEK, Hafgufa ripped into Orfeo's army. She attacked the Razormouths first, biting heads off, gouging wounds into flesh with her yard-long claws, severing limbs with a crack of her scaly tail. Blood and gore clouded the water. Bodies sank to the seafloor.

Within minutes, she'd killed most of the dragons. After that, she turned to the cadavru. Using her tail, she churned the water into deadly vortexes and hurled them at the cadavru, then watched, her green eyes narrowed, as the vortexes ripped them apart. Skulls rolled into the silt, snapping their teeth. Bony hands scrabbled across rocks. Legs tangled themselves in thickets of seaweed, kicking uselessly.

What the vortexes missed, Hafgufa tore with her teeth. As she plowed through the army of the dead, the surviving Razormouths, led by Hagarla, made a last desperate charge. Hafgufa saw the attack coming. Pulling herself up to her full height, she lunged at the dragons, catching one in her fearsome jaws. She savaged the creature, then gave chase to the rest.

Sera, bloodied and breathless, watched as Hagarla grew smaller and smaller in the water, and then disappeared entirely. She looked for the Meerteufel chieftain, but he was nowhere to be seen. "Thank you, Guldemar," she whispered. "Wherever you are."

The dragons were routed. The rotters had been decimated. Her troops were busy destroying any that Hafgufa had missed. But Sera knew that dragons and rotters were not her most lethal enemies.

"Sera!" a voice called out. "Are you all right?"

It was Neela. She was battered and bruised, but she was alive. Ling was with her. They swam to Sera and embraced her.

"Where are the others?" Sera asked. She shouted frantically for her friends.

"Over here!" Becca yelled back. She was in the clearing between the camp and the Carceron, and she had Yazeed's arm around her neck. There was a deep gash in his tail; he could barely swim.

Sera and the others raced to them. They were joined a moment later by Alítheia and Ava.

"Thank the gods you're all alive!" Ava said.

"Where's Orfeo?" Sera asked warily, looking all around. "Where's Astrid?"

"Did we . . . did we kill them?" Becca asked.

"No," Ava said anxiously. "I can feel them. Both of them. Can you see them? They're near . . . they're—"

"Right here," Orfeo said.

Sera whirled around. He was standing by the Carceron. Astrid was next to him. They were flanked by the few dozen rotters who'd survived the carnage.

"I've had enough of these games," he said. "I want the talismans, Serafina."

Sera was exhausted and bleeding, but she raised her crossbow.

"Come and get them," she said.

Orfeo laughed scornfully. He snapped his fingers and two rotters roughly shoved someone forward—a small mermaid.

"Sera!" the little merl called out tearfully.

"No!" Sera cried as she realized who it was: Coco.

Astrid grabbed the child by her hair. She took her dagger out of its sheath. Coco whimpered in terror. She squeezed her eyes shut.

The sight completely unhinged Sera. How could Astrid *do* this? To them, to Coco?

"Who *are* you?" she shrieked at her. "That's a *child*, Astrid, a helpless child! Is your pride worth an innocent life?"

"Kill her," Orfeo commanded.

Astrid raised her knife.

"*Stop!*" Sera screamed. "Don't hurt her!" Defeated, she turned to Garstig. "Bring the strongbox," she ordered brokenly.

"A wise decision," Orfeo said, watching the goblin run for Sera's tent.

Astrid lowered her knife but kept a firm grip on Coco. The little merl was sobbing piteously. "She tricked me, Sera. She found me in my tent and told me you needed me. I'm sorry! I'm so sorry!"

A lethal rage filled Sera. Her hand went to her sword. Her fingers curled around its hilt. Before she could pull it free from its sheath, she felt someone take her arm.

"Don't," Ava whispered.

"I'll kill them," Sera vowed. "I'll kill them both."

"Shut *up*, Sera," Ava hissed, her nails digging into Sera's flesh.

Sera flinched. Ava had never spoken to her, or anyone else, like that before. She turned to look at her. Ava's expression was intense; she was trembling. Sera didn't have long to wonder at Ava's strangeness, though, for Garstig had returned with the strongbox. He looked at Sera, his eyes silently asking if there was any other way.

Sera shook her head. "Give it to him," she said.

Orfeo took it. He opened it, looked inside, then raised his eyes to Sera's. "Where's the blue diamond?"

"You have it," Sera said. "Mahdi found it for Traho, and Traho gave it to you."

"We both know that's not true," said Orfeo. "Astrid told me that the blue diamond I have is a fake. The infanta hid the real one aboard her ship, then gave it to you. Give it to *me*, please, or the little merl . . ."

Astrid raised her knife again.

Sera reached under the collar of her jacket and undid the clasp of the necklace the infanta had given her. She swam to Orfeo and handed it to him. As she did, despair descended on her. With the diamond went her last hope, and the hopes of all the waters of the world.

"Astrid, if you would be kind enough to hold this," Orfeo said, handing the strongbox to her.

Astrid sheathed her knife and released Coco. Sera reached out to Coco, but the mermaid wouldn't come to her.

She's too frightened, Sera thought. *She's paralyzed.*

Orfeo ripped the blue diamond free of its setting. He put the diamond into the box, then pulled the ruby ring out of his pocket and put that in, too. When he'd dropped his black pearl in, he looked at Astrid.

"Can you see it, child? Can you feel it?" he asked.

Astrid nodded, mesmerized. A glow was emanating from the box. Now that the talismans were together, their power was surging.

Orfeo threw his head back. "Hear me, Horok, and the denizens of the underworld!" he shouted. "I'm coming for what is mine!"

"You can't do this, Orfeo," Sera said, desperate to stop him. "The gods won't allow it."

"Then I'll destroy the gods, and the world they made," he said, staring at her with his empty black eyes. "I'll rule over a new world. A world where *I* decide who lives and dies, where *I'm* a god!"

Sera covered her face with her hands. She knew she was about to witness the destruction of everything, and everyone, she loved. And she was powerless to stop it. She'd tried, she'd fought, she'd risked everything . . . and she'd lost.

Orfeo turned to Astrid. "Come, child. We'll fit the talismans into the lock together. It's time to release Abbadon."

"Astrid, *no.* Don't let him do this," Sera begged, lowering her hands. She tried to swim to Astrid, to stop her, but Ava, who'd swum to her side, held her back again.

"Abbadon!" Orfeo shouted. "Abbadon, come!"

A terrifying shriek was heard from deep inside the Carceron. Orfeo's summons had roused the monster. It was heading for the gates. Together, Orfeo and Astrid swam to meet it. Using the hilt of a dagger that he pulled from his belt, Orfeo knocked ice off the Carceron's lock, then one by one, he and Astrid fitted the glowing talismans into it.

There was a metallic groan as the lock's tumblers turned, an echoing thunk as the bolt slid back, and then the gates swung open.

"Abbadon! Come to me!" Orfeo roared.

The monster answered with another shriek. Sera could hear it pounding through the Carceron, coming closer to them with every step.

Around her, Black Fins, both goblin and mer, backed away from the prison. Some screamed. Others ran for their tents, or hid behind rocks that littered the base of the seamount.

As Abbadon's steps grew louder, Orfeo laughed with a cruel joy. He took his black pearl out of the lock and threaded it back onto its leather string. He tied it around his neck, then removed the rest of the talismans from the lock and returned them to the strongbox.

Astrid carefully lowered the lid. The strongbox clicked shut. She smiled exultantly at Orfeo . . .

. . . and tossed the box to Coco.

SEVENTY

"**G**O, COCO! *SWIM!*" Astrid shouted as the little merl caught the strongbox.

Coco was a blur in the water. She streaked away like a marlin, over the heads of the rotters.

It took a few seconds for Sera to register what had happened.

"Ava, Astrid *didn't* betray us!" she said. "She was only pretending! Coco, too!"

Ava nodded. She was beaming. She released Sera's arm. "I knew she was on our side," she said. "I could feel it. I could see her, see the good inside her."

Orfeo, in shock, turned his empty eyes on Astrid. "What have you *done?*" he asked, menace in his voice.

"It's over, Orfeo," Astrid said. "I'm not on your side. I never was. I just pretended to be to get you—and your pearl—down here, so that my friends and I could get the Carceron open and destroy Abbadon."

"But we're *kin*, Astrid," Orfeo said, shaking his head in disbelief. "Your blood is my blood. Your magic, my magic."

"Yes, it is," Astrid said. "But my heart's my own."

As she spoke, she pulled her sword from its scabbard.

"You're a *fool*!" Orfeo spat, his face flushing with rage. "You could have had power, respect, pride—everything you ever wanted."

"I already have everything," Astrid said. "I have the love of my friends."

Orfeo turned to the Carceron. He rattled the gates. "Abbadon, this is your master calling! Come to me *now*!"

Another screech was heard, closer to the gates than before.

Astrid raised her sword. The muscles in her arms rippled with strength.

"Step away from the gate, Orfeo," she said. "You want to destroy the world? You'll have to destroy me first."

Sera joined her. Then Becca did. Ava. Ling. Neela.

"No, Orfeo," Sera said. "If you want to destroy the world, you'll have to destroy *us* first."

SEVENTY-ONE

WITH A WARRIOR'S YELL, Astrid charged, swinging her sword.

Orfeo threw up a water wall instantly, deflecting it. Her blade hit the bars of the Carceron's gate with a loud *clang*.

"Alítheia!" Sera yelled, rushing toward Orfeo.

But the spider was ahead of her. She scuttled to Ava and crouched protectively over her.

Neela, Becca, and Ling were right behind Sera, their weapons out, but before the four could even get close, Orfeo expanded his water wall, creating an impenetrable dome around himself and Astrid.

"Sorry," he said with a wink, "but this is a family affair."

"No! Orfeo, let her *go*!" Sera shouted. She dropped her crossbow and hammered her fists against the watery barrier.

"We've got to help her!" Becca shouted. She threw her shoulder into the wall. Neela fragged it. But their efforts were to no avail. The water was as solid as rock.

The four mermaids watched helplessly as Orfeo advanced on Astrid. He threw a vortex at her. The swirling water wrapped around the sword and pulled it from her hand. It thudded to the ground at his feet, raising a cloud of silt.

Without missing a beat, Astrid lifted her head and sang, casting a stilo spell. She launched the spiked water bomb at Orfeo's head.

He batted it away with a swipe of his hand. As it exploded

harmlessly against the side of the dome, he launched another vortex. Astrid tried to duck it, but it caught her and slammed her to the ground, knocking the breath out her.

She lay there, gasping for water.

"He's going to kill her," Sera said.

"Get up! Get *up*, Astrid!" Ling cried.

Becca was songcasting one spell after another, trying to break through the water wall. Ling was trying to help her, but nothing was working.

An ear-piercing roar ripped through the water then. It came from the Carceron.

"My gods," Sera said. "*Abbadon*. Orfeo unlocked the gate. It's going to get out! We need waterfire, quick!"

"I'll cast it!" said Becca. She shot to the prison.

"Ling, Neela, stay here! Keep trying to break through the water wall!" Sera said. She picked up her crossbow and sped off to catch up with Becca.

"Hurry, Becca," Sera urged. *"Hurry."*

Becca was the best waterfire caster they had. Within seconds, she was chanting the songspell. But waterfire was notoriously difficult to conjure.

As Becca continued to cast, a pair of black horns appeared behind the gates. Under them was an eyeless face, a lipless mouth.

Abbadon was as terrifying as Sera remembered. It took all her courage to stay where she was, cock her crossbow, and aim it.

"Kýrios!" the monster howled. *"Zhǔ! Dominus!"* Sera knew these were words for *master*. Abbadon was calling to Orfeo.

"Becca, watch out!" Sera shouted.

An arm, sinewy and black, streaked with red, shot out from between the bars. A hand opened. In the center of its palm was a lidless eye. More hands grasped the bars. The monster started pulling on them. The gates opened wider.

Sera fired on it. Her arrow sank into one of its arms. Abbadon snarled but kept pulling on the bars. Ice cracked. The ancient gates creaked and swung inward.

"Becca!" Sera screamed.

There was a huge *whoosh*, and then searing blue fire shot up from the ground in front of the prison, all the way to the top of the gates.

The monster shrieked. It staggered away from the bars, back into the prison.

"Stay there, Becca! Keep the flames going!"

Becca gave a quick nod, still songcasting. Sera raced back to the others and arrived at the water wall in time to see Orfeo circle Astrid.

"Did you really think you could beat me? *Me?*" he asked.

"I still do," Astrid shot back.

Fury contorted Orfeo's face. He threw a fragor lux at her. Astrid saw it coming; she rolled to one side. The stilo missed its mark, but it carved a gash into her shoulder.

"I gave you everything. *Everything!*" he snarled at her. "And this is how you repay me?"

"I'd hardly call a couple of black dresses *everything*," Astrid drawled.

Orfeo threw another vortex. This one wound around Astrid's tail, squeezing it cruelly. She arched her back, screaming in pain.

"Stop it!" Sera screamed, slapping her hands against the wall. "For gods' sake, *stop!*"

Neela was crying. Ling was still songcasting, desperate to break through the wall.

Astrid, still on the ground, tried to crawl away from her tormentor. She pulled herself through the silt with her hands, dragging her battered tail behind her. Blood was pulsing from the gash on her shoulder. Slowly, painfully, she moved to the far end of the dome, where Orfeo had stood moments ago.

But she couldn't get away from him. He came up behind her, grabbed a handful of her hair, and yanked her head back.

"Good-bye, you little fool," he hissed. "I won't make it quick. Or easy."

Then he let go of her and started to songcast.

"No . . . oh, gods, *no!*" Sera moaned, sinking down against the water wall. She started to turn away; she couldn't bear to watch what was going to happen.

Astrid's head was hanging limply. Her body was still, her tail motionless.

But her hands were scrabbling madly in the silt.

What happened next happened so fast, all Sera could do was gasp.

With a wrenching cry, Astrid launched herself off the seafloor, her sword in her hands. Whirling her powerful body around, she swung the weapon through the water.

Orfeo's eyes widened in shock. *"Noooo!"* he shouted, trying to deflect the blow.

But it was too late.

Astrid's blade bit into his neck, and sliced through it.

His head fell into the silt. His body sank through the water and came to rest near it. Blood rose in a carmine plume. The dome he'd cast caved in; its waters washed over the mermaids.

Astrid had tricked him. She was hurt, but not as badly as she'd pretended. She'd baited him, making him so angry that he forgot about her sword, which had been buried. She'd let him push her all around the dome until she could get to where it lay.

Astrid threw that sword down now. She collapsed near Orfeo's body and let out a wail that came from the depths of her soul.

SEVENTY-TWO

SERA, IN A SPELL-SHOCKED DAZE, viewed the devastation of war all around her—Orfeo's headless body; Astrid, on the ground sobbing; Yazeed, his tail bleeding badly; Ava crawling out from under Alítheia; Black Fins, some bruised and battered, others dead; the remains of thousands of rotters. Her fighters needed help, but she didn't know where to begin.

"We need to get to the wounded, Sera," Ling said. "They're our first priority."

"And Abbadon," said Neela.

Sera nodded, grateful for her capable friends. The haze receded. She snapped into action.

Some of her goblin commanders were nearby. "Garstig, Mulmig, Rök," she said, "find all the able-bodied fighters you can and have them carry the wounded to the infirmary tents."

As the three goblins hurried off, Sera glanced at the Carceron. Becca was still there, still songcasting, but it was quiet at the gates. There was no further sign of Abbadon.

Ava swam up, and Sera turned to her. "Where is it?" she asked.

"Deep inside the prison," Ava replied. "It knows Orfeo's dead. It's hiding from us."

"Orfeo's *not* dead," Astrid said, slowly rising from the silt. "I destroyed the body he used, that's all. He's still here and he's still dangerous."

She cast waterfire, high and hot, in a circle around and above Orfeo's remains. "His soul lives on. In there," she said, pointing to the black pearl, covered in blood and hanging from what was left of Orfeo's neck. "No one can touch it. He knows how to jump bodies. That's how he's endured for four thousand years."

"We should throw the body, and the pearl, into the lava pond," Ava said, shivering.

"Lava would only destroy the body," Astrid said. "The pearl is indestructible. The waterfire will keep everyone away until we figure out what to do with it."

Sera put a gentle hand on Astrid's back. Astrid turned, and the two mermaids embraced each other fiercely.

"I'm sorry," Sera whispered.

Astrid nodded, fighting to hold back tears. "It was the only way to stop him."

"But he still meant something to you."

"Yes, he did. He gave me my magic back. I'll never forget it. Or him."

When her emotion finally subsided, Astrid released Sera and hugged the others.

"Good acting job, merl," Neela said admiringly. "You had me fooled."

"Me, too," Sera admitted. "I should have known you would never go over to Orfeo's side, though. I shouldn't have doubted you."

Astrid shook her head. "I *needed* you to doubt me," she said. "The whole performance had to be convincing. If Orfeo doubted that I was on his side, I never would've gotten near the talismans."

"I could sense your intention, *mina*," Ava said. "I saw your heart. It was shining like the sun. I could feel the courage in it. Coco's, too."

"I wanted to stop you," Sera said to Astrid. "Ava's the reason I didn't. She held me back, or I might've blown the whole thing."

Ava smiled proudly.

"Coco was in on it, too?" Becca asked. She'd joined the others. Her waterfire was still burning.

"Yes," Astrid said. "Orfeo gets mer to do what he wants by threatening to hurt those they love. When the fighting started, I told him there was a child that you all cared for, and that she was probably in the camp. Orfeo told me to find her. I did. Coco knew who I was, and as soon as I told her about my plan, she was in. I tied her up and brought her to the clearing. Orfeo never suspected a thing. She's very brave."

"Where is she now?" Neela asked.

"Hiding in a sea cave just east of the camp. She told me about the cave, and I instructed her to stay there with the talismans until I came for her. After both Orfeo and Abbadon were dead."

"One down, one to go," Neela said.

All six mermaids looked at the Carceron. Becca's waterfire was burning low. In a moment, it would be out. The gate was still hanging ajar. A silence fell over them.

Sera was the first to break it. "This is it, merls. This is why Vrăja summoned us. Why we hunted for the talismans. Why we're here."

"Can we do this?" Neela asked.

"Like we have a choice?" Ling said.

"We *can* do this," Sera said decisively. *"Together."* She turned to Ava. "You thought the gods went silent on you, Ava, but they didn't. You *have* the answer you've spent your whole life searching for. You've always had it. The gods didn't take your sight just so you could survive the Okwa Naholo; they took it so you'd develop another kind of vision—the kind that lets you see deep down inside someone. If you hadn't seen inside Astrid just now, who knows what would have happened. When we get inside the Carceron, turn that vision on the monster, daughter of Nyx, and tell us what you see."

Ava nodded. A determined smile graced her lips.

Sera turned to Ling next. "Ling, Abbadon is surely the noisiest monster ever made. It howls and screams and spews rage. There must be a reason for that rage, and I think it lies not in the monster's words, but in the silences between them. You've broken through other impossible silences, daughter of Sycorax, and you can break through this one. I know you can."

"Becca," Sera said, putting her hands on her friend's shoulders, "you're the most practical, most strategic thinker of us all. Because of you, we have the right weapons loaded with the right ammo, we have warm clothing, and the right number of tents. If anyone will be able to guess the monster's next move, it will be you. Daughter of Pyrrha, help us forge our way through the Carceron."

Sera moved to Neela and took her hands. Neela's bioluminescent skin had turned sky blue. "Our shining star. Our moon and sun," she said to her best friend. "You kept me going when I'd lost everything. You keep us going now. You lift our spirits and our hopes. We're about to swim into the heart of darkness. Daughter of Navi, keep the light before us. *Please.*"

And then there was only Astrid. Sera looked into her eyes and was silent for a moment. When she finally spoke, Sera's voice was full of feeling. "You were my enemy when we first met back in the Iele's caves. Now you're my friend. We were both afraid—of each other, of ourselves. Now we've learned to make fear our ally, to listen to it. I'm listening now, Astrid, and it's telling me that the greatest mage who ever lived created Abbadon and that it's so powerful, that one of us, or all of us, might not come back out of the Carceron. But it's also telling me that we've got the daughter of Orfeo at our side. If anyone can understand his creation, it's you. And if you can understand it, you might be able to defeat it."

Sera held her hands out. Everyone else did, too. As soon as the last hands had been clasped and the circle closed, Sera felt it—a rush of power as strong and unstoppable as a tidal wave. She looked at her friends, at the brave, stubborn, hopeful mermaids beside her. She remembered Mahdi and Desiderio back home in Miromara, and her heart swelled with love.

She let her eyes linger on each of their faces. Then she took a deep breath and said, "It's time."

The six mermaids released one another's hands and swam to the gate.

Yazeed was there, his tail bandaged. Styg and Rök were with him. "Let us come with you," he said.

Sera shook her head. "No, Yaz. It started with us; it finishes with us."

Steeling herself for the biggest battle of her life, she swam inside the prison.

SEVENTY-THREE

A SCHOOL OF ICEFISH, scaleless and silvery, drifted by the six mermaids as they made their way across the open corridor behind the prison's high exterior wall.

"This was called the Death Run," Sera said, gesturing to the passage. "According to the conchs I listened to about Atlantis, there were guards with crossbows patrolling on top of the walls. If a prisoner escaped from his cell, he still had to make it across the Death Run. But no one ever did."

"I wonder if *we'll* make it across the Death Run," said Astrid.

"The cellblocks are behind that," Sera continued, pointing to the prison's inner wall "They were built like a labyrinth to confuse any escapees. Guards used a series of levers to shift the hallways and staircases every day."

"Abbadon could be anywhere in there," said Becca.

"There's a courtyard in the center of the cellblocks where the prisoners could exercise. It has a domed ceiling made of thick panels of glass set into metal frames. If I were an enraged homicidal monster, I'd try to lure us there," Sera said.

"Why?" Ava asked.

"Easier to kill us. More room," Becca said.

Sera nodded.

"So, I guess that's where we're headed," Neela said with a sigh. "Because why stop swimming straight into the jaws of death now?"

"Any idea how to get inside?" Ling asked.

"The entrance is there," Sera said, pointing at an arched doorway. "We'll have to figure out the way to the courtyard once we're inside."

The six friends all cast illuminatas as they swam through the doorway. Becca hooked arms with Ava.

"If we're going to defeat Abbadon, we have to find its weak spot," Sera said, leading the way down a dark, narrow hall. "Astrid, did Orfeo tell you anything about Abbadon while you were with him?"

"Like how to kill it?" Astrid asked, sardonically. "No. He kept me busy practicing songspells pretty much nonstop."

"While I was Lucia's prisoner—" Sera began.

"Wait . . . *what?*" Astrid said.

"I'll give you the details later, but I spent some time in Alítheia's den—"

"Miromara's big scary bronze spider?" Astrid asked. "The same who I saw clanking through the camp?"

"That's her," Sera said. "She told me that Abbadon's made of immortal souls."

"Immortal souls. As in, can't die. *Ever.* Which means there *is* no weak spot," Astrid said. She sighed. "Is it too late to change my mind about this?"

"Abbadon is *so* powerful. If only we knew where its strength comes from, we might be able to block it," Becca said.

The mermaids fell quiet as the cells loomed into view. Their doors were made of iron bars sunk deep into the stone walls. Large padlocks secured them. The illuminatas did little to dispel the gloom.

"Maybe the souls give Abbadon its power," Ava said, resuming the conversation.

"And a talisman," Ling added.

"But it doesn't have a talisman. There are only six," Neela countered. "The black pearl's still on Orfeo, and Coco has the other five."

"No, there was one more," Ling reminded them. "Orfeo had a talisman before he had the black pearl."

"The emerald!" Becca exclaimed.

"Exactly," Ling said. "When Sera and I were in Atlantis, we talked to a vitrina. She told us that Orfeo destroyed his original talisman—an emerald given to him by Eveksion, the god of healing. He ground it up and put it into the wine of the people he sacrificed to make them healthy and strong."

"But he *didn't* destroy it. He couldn't have," Becca said. "The talismans are gifts from the gods and can't be destroyed. He only changed its form."

"So, Abbadon's not only immortal, it's powered by a talisman?" Astrid said in disbelief. "We're chum, merls."

She was at the front of the group, swimming backward as she talked, when suddenly a hand shot through the bars of a cell. Fingers wrapped themselves around her neck.

Astrid's eyes widened in terror, a gasp escaped her. It felt as if those icy fingers had wrapped themselves around her heart.

"Hey, get away from her!" Neela cried.

She raced to Astrid and pried the fingers off her neck. As she was pulled clear of the cell door, Astrid could see a face pressed to the bars, framed by a mop of shaggy hair, frosted by ice. Dark eyes burned with malevolence. A vicious grin revealed a mouthful of rotten teeth.

"What *is* that thing?" she rasped, rubbing her neck.

"A ghost," Sera replied. "The Carceron was in use right up to the destruction of Atlantis. There would have been prisoners in the cells when Merrow and the others herded Abbadon inside."

"So they . . . they would've—" Ava started to say.

"Drowned," Sera finished. "When Atlantis sank."

"Wow. This just gets better and better," Astrid said.

More faces appeared at cell doors. Astrid drew her sword.

A ghost saw it and chuckled deep in his throat. "What are you going to do, mermaid? Kill me?"

"Stay clear of the cells," Sera ordered her friends. "Swim in the center of the corridor. Becs, keep a tight grip on Ava."

As the mermaids swam past cell after cell, the ghosts inside called to them, trying to get them to come close, promising them that they would soon become ghosts, too. Looking up ahead, Astrid could see that the corridor ended in a T. She was relieved when they finally reached the end of it.

"Which way, Sera?" she asked.

"To the left, I think."

"Um, nope. Not happening," Astrid said, pointing down the hall.

Three ghostly men stood there. Their chests were bare, and they wore wrap skirts of linen pleated in the front, leather belts, heavy bronze bracelets, and menacing expressions.

"Guards," Sera said. "This way," she ordered. She darted to the right, then stopped dead. Another group was blocking the way.

As Astrid tried to figure out what to do, both sets of guards walked toward the mermaids, forcing them back to the center of the T.

"We'll have to swim back the way we came," she said.

But before they could, the guards on the left grabbed hold of a massive iron lever jutting from the wall. They threw their weight on it, pulling it down.

There was a deep groaning sound, and then the heavy scrape of stone against stone. The entire prison seemed to shake. Cracks appeared in the floor, and the corridor the mermaids had just swum down rose, forcing the mermaids up with it. The guards disappeared from view. With a booming *thunk*, the moving corridor slotted into its new position, and instead of staring at a stone wall, the mermaids found themselves looking down a new passageway.

"What happened?" Ava asked.

"The guards shifted the hallway. They're driving us farther into the labyrinth," Sera explained.

Astrid peered into the murky waters ahead. There were more cells, with more ghosts inside them, but no free-roaming guards.

"We've got to be on the lookout," Becca said. "Ava, you're going in the middle. Everyone else form a circle around her."

The group made its way down the new corridor, and two more, before running into guards again. Just as before, the guards pulled a lever, but this time they lowered the corridor.

"They're herding us," Sera said. "Toward the courtyard."

"Becca was right," Ling said. "Abbadon wants to get us into an open space. So it's easier to kill us."

"And we still have no idea how to kill *it*," Sera said.

"We better come up with something fast," Neela said. She pointed ahead with her sword. A wide doorway yawned ahead of them. Light poured in from it. "There's the courtyard."

SEVENTY-FOUR

THE SIX MERMAIDS swam up to the doorway cautiously, weapons raised. When they reached it, everyone but Ava looked around, their eyes scanning the high walls, the remains of a fountain, hills of ice, but they saw nothing.

"It's got to be here," Sera whispered. "It led *us* here."

Then they heard it: a short, sharp sound, like a shot. It sounded like ice cracking. Or glass.

Astrid looked up. "Great Neria," she whispered. The others followed her gaze.

Abbadon clung to the glass ceiling with two of its hands; more were thrust out into the water, the eyes in the palms staring. Its sightless head hung down, scenting the water. Its body, the color of a shadow glazed red, was tensed and ready to spring.

"*I'm* the one who's supposed to know how to undo this thing?" Astrid said. "Then we're doomed. Because I don't have the first clue."

"We can do this, merls. Don't lose your nerve," Neela said bravely, glowing bright blue. "We can bring it to that monster."

"Ava, anything?" Sera asked.

"I'm trying," Ava said, "but it's blocking me."

"Becs—"

Becca was a stroke ahead of her. "Sera, you get out in front of it with me," she said. "Astrid, take the back. Ling, you and Neela take the sides. Ava, stay here in the doorway, and keep focusing. We need to see inside it."

At that very second, Abbadon sprang. It was so fast, the mermaids had no time to react. Its slashing claws caught Ling and sent her spinning. She hit a wall and sank to the floor with a deep gash in her right side. Blood poured out of it and her ribs showed whitely through her torn flesh.

This is how we're all going out—fast and bloody, Sera thought grimly. *Unless Ava can get a glimpse inside it. And Astrid can use what she sees to kill it.*

"Hey! Hey, lumpsucker! Over here," Astrid shouted, trying to draw the monster off Ling.

She swam close to Abbadon and jabbed it with her sword. It wheeled around instantly, and Astrid was nearly slashed herself, but the few seconds of distraction Astrid provided gave Sera time to grab Ling and get her underneath an overhang of ice.

Sera took off her jacket. "Press this against the wound," she told her, then she swam back to help the others.

They took up the positions Becca had devised and began to harry the creature with songspells.

Neela launched a frag. It hit Abbadon in the back but did little more than enrage it.

Becca tried to encircle it with waterfire, but it deftly eluded the flames and backhanded her into an ice hill. As she struggled to get up, Astrid hurled a stilo.

Her spell hit home, tearing a chunk out of the monster's shoulder. It roared and came after her. She defended herself with her sword, slicing into one of its hands. It nearly grabbed her with its other hands, but Sera threw up a water wall and blocked it.

The mermaids kept at it, battling Abbadon with everything thing they had, but only managed to inflict small injuries.

Astrid, ducking Abbadon's hands again, swam close to Sera now. "We're getting our tail fins kicked!" she shouted.

"It's going to wear us down and crush us! And then it'll get out of here! What if it breaks through the waterfire you cast over Orfeo and takes his pearl? What if Orfeo's soul jumps into Abbadon?" Sera shouted back.

Before Astrid could respond, the monster charged, forcing them to dart off in opposite directions.

Come on! Figure this out! Astrid yelled at herself, terrified by the idea of Abbadon escaping.

She was Orfeo's descendant. She was the one who'd spent time with him, who knew how he thought. But as hard as she tried, she still couldn't figure out a way to kill his monster.

Abbadon charged her again, forcing her close to the doorway and Ava. Astrid took shelter there for a moment, pausing to catch her breath.

"You okay, Ava?" she asked, turning to look at her.

Heavy silver tears were brimming in Ava's eyes.

"What's wrong?" Astrid asked, alarmed. "Are you hurt?"

Ava shook her head. "I can see them," she said in a choked voice. "I can see the souls. There are so many of them, Astrid, and they're all in terrible pain. They want to be free. For four thousand years, they've wanted to be free."

As Ava spoke, Abbadon backed Becca into an ice hill.

"No way!" Astrid shouted, streaking off.

She swung her sword with all her might, right into the monster's leg. The blade bit deeply. Abbadon roared, spun around, and lunged at her. Astrid launched herself up, somersaulted over the monster's head, and landed near the overhang where Ling was sheltering. Abbadon lunged again. Astrid shot under the overhang. The monster's hands closed on water.

Astrid leaned against the back of the ice hill, panting. She looked at Ling. Her eyes were closed. She was very pale. Blood from her wound was seeping through the makeshift bandage.

"Ling? Ling, are you all right? *Ling!*" she shouted.

Ling opened her eyes. "Astrid, if I . . . if I don't make it, sing my dirges," she rasped.

"No," Astrid said, panicking. "You'll be okay, Ling."

"Astrid, please. . . ."

"No!" Astrid shouted, anger pushing aside fear. So many mer had died because of Orfeo and his madness. She didn't want to lose one more. "I'm *not* singing your dirges, Ling! Nobody's singing *anybody's* dirges. You're going to make it. I swear to the gods you are. . . ."

Her voice trailed off. She felt as if the eye of a hurricane had just passed over her.

"Dirges," she whispered. "Oh, my gods. *Dirges.*"

How do you kill an immortal soul? Sera had asked.

"You don't," Astrid whispered aloud. "You free it. Just like Orfeo had hoped to free Alma."

"Astrid, what are you talking about?" Ling asked.

"Dirges. That's how we do this. Ling, you're a *genius!*"

"True, but what do dirges have to do—"

Astrid sheathed her sword. She swam out of the overhang. "Abbadon!" she shouted. "Hey, monster man!"

"Astrid, what are you *doing?*" Ling called after her.

"I don't know!" Astrid shouted back. "I've never done it before!"

How do you sing a dirge? she wondered desperately.

She cast her mind back to the Hall of Elders, in the Citadel, when she and Desiderio were trying to escape from Rylka. That's when she'd heard her father's dirges being sung. The songspell was a simple and beautiful old Ondalinian melody. She would borrow it, add her own lyrics, and hope that her magic was strong enough.

"Abbadon!" she shouted, swimming right toward the monster. "Abbadon, hear me!"

"Astrid, no!" Sera cried.

She started to swim toward her, but Neela stopped her. "Wait, Sera!" she said. "Listen!"

They all listened as Astrid's voice—strong and expressive—rose in the water. She'd cast a few frantic spells when she'd fought Orfeo, but this was the first time they'd really heard her sing.

Abbadon had been advancing on Becca, but as Astrid's voice grew louder, it stopped, then slowly turned toward her. It seemed spellbound by her song, and the beauty of her voice. Its hands stretched toward her. One by one, they opened. The eyes stared at Astrid, unblinking.

"Oh, gods, no. It's going to tear her in two," Becca said.

As if acting on Becca's words, Abbadon charged at Astrid, roaring.

"*No!*" Neela screamed.

Astrid's own hands were knotted into fists, but she didn't flinch. The monster stopped only yards away from her, its chest heaving. It threw its head back and roared so loudly that the mermaids had to press their hands over their ears. The entire prison shook. A section of wall behind Sera cracked and tumbled into the courtyard.

"*Dirges,*" Sera said excitedly. "She's singing the souls back to the sea."

> *The tides of life ceased long ago*
> *For those sacrificed by Orfeo.*
> *But no eternal rest for them,*
> *No rites, no graves, no requiem.*
> *Denied a place of final peace,*
> *Their grief and anger cannot cease.*
> *In endless torment they go on,*
> *Imprisoned inside Abbadon.*
> *Horok, come at our bequest,*
> *Take the stolen to their rest.*

Astrid kept singing. The monster clutched its head, then dropped to its knees. As it did, a thin crack opened up in its side. Light, pure and white, shot out of it. The water inside the courtyard started to whirl.

"Ava, what do you see?" Sera shouted.

"Souls! Thousands of them!" Ava shouted back. "They want to get out!"

Abbadon roared again. It sounded like a creature in torment.

"It's working, Astrid!" Neela shouted. "Keep it up!"

Abbadon was breaking apart. More souls were pushing their way out. Their light was swirling through the courtyard. Their energy was fearsome.

They're going to destroy the Carceron, Astrid thought. *And everyone in it.*

Another section of wall caved in. Sera grabbed Ava and Neela and swam with them into the center. Becca lifted up Ling, who was still under the overhang, and joined them. Only seconds later, the overhang split off from the rest of the ice and crashed to the ground.

"They have nowhere to go!" Neela shouted. "They want to go to the underworld, but they can't!"

"They need pearls!" Ava yelled.

"Astrid!" Neela shouted. "Use your—"

But her words were cut off when a chunk of the glass ceiling fell in, narrowly missing Astrid.

"THE PEARLS!" Neela yelled as the water cleared, frantically pointing at her neck.

Astrid didn't understand what she was trying to say. Her hand came up to her own neck. And then she felt it. *Alma's necklace!* she thought. It was made of thousands of pearls. They were small, though. Would they work?

Still singing, she unhooked the necklace and swam to Abbadon.

The monster's roars had risen to shrieks now. Its body was riven with cracks. The light pouring from them was so bright, it was blinding.

"Hurry, Astrid!" Sera urged, as another section of wall came down.

Astrid ripped the necklace apart and scattered the pearls in a circle around Abbadon.

As the mermaids all watched, rays of light swirled out of the monster and disappeared into the pearls. One by one, the freed souls found their refuge.

Abbadon took a few last breaths, then with a deep groan, toppled onto the icy courtyard floor. As Astrid and the others watched, its chest sank. The eyes in its hands became sightless and dull. Its body, nothing but a hollow shell now, crumpled.

"You did it!" Sera said, throwing her arms around Astrid.

"*We* did it," Astrid said, hugging her back. "All of us together."

Becca and Neela slapped tails. Ling, pale as a sand dollar, managed to squeeze Ava's hand.

And then the Carceron shuddered. A noise like a gunshot was heard overhead, as a crack opened in the roof's glass.

"We've got to get out of here before the whole places crashes in on us," Becca said.

"We can't leave them," Neela said, nodding at the pearls. "They need to go home. If the Carceron falls, we'll never be able to find them again."

"Ling needs a doctor," Sera said, grimacing at the blood seeping out between Ling's fingers. "Becca, can you get her back to camp?"

Becca nodded. "We'll swim through the hole in the ceiling," she said. "We don't have time to deal with the maze, or the ghosts."

"Good idea," Sera said. "Everyone else, let's move." She cast an anxious glance at the ceiling.

Sera's jacket, which Ling had pressed against her wound, was soaked with blood. Becca took off her own jacket and tied it around

Ling's torso. She looped one of Ling's arms over her neck, then swam for the ceiling.

Astrid, Neela, Ava, and Sera swooped down to the bottom of the courtyard and picked up the pearls as quickly as they could. Ava felt for them with her hands. Astrid and Sera tore fabric from their dresses and made pouches out of it. Neela and Ava used their jackets. They all had to swim for cover when another crack snaked across the ceiling, but miraculously the glass held and they were able to resume their task.

"Ava, can you sense any that we missed?" Sera asked when they were done.

Ava shook her head. "We got them all; I'm sure of it."

"Then let's go." Astrid gathered the corners of her pouch and knotted them. The others secured their pouches, too. Sera knotted Ava's for her. Taking Ava's hand, she swam toward the hole in the ceiling. Neela and Astrid followed.

The four made it through the jagged hole without any injuries and were turning toward the camp when another crack ripped through the ceiling. This one was too much for the ancient glass to bear. It imploded, lethal shards raining down over the courtyard and what was left of Orfeo's tragic creature.

"We got out just in time," Astrid said, leading the way back to camp.

The mermaids swam on in silence, then Sera said, "Will he come?"

"It depends how strong my magic was," Astrid said.

"He'll come. I know he heard you," Sera said.

Astrid nodded. "I hope so," she said. "Come on. We've got one more pearl to gather."

SEVENTY-FIVE

S ERA COULD SEE the anxious, upturned faces, mer and goblin, searching the waters over the Carceron.

Yazeed spotted them. He broke into a wide grin. "There they are!" he shouted, pointing.

Sera, Astrid, Neela, and Ava cleared the prison, then dropped down into the camp. As they placed the pouches of pearls down, their fellow fighters rushed to them.

"Did you—" Yazeed started to ask.

"We did," Neela answered.

Yazeed's whole body sagged with relief. He hugged his sister tightly. "I was so scared that you wouldn't make it."

"Really, Yaz?" Neela asked, clearly touched.

Yazeed immediately backstroked. "Well, um . . . what I meant is, I *would've* been scared. If I wasn't so tough and cool."

Neela laughed.

"Please tell me Ling's okay," Sera said, worry in her voice.

"She is," said Ling, swimming up to the group. Lena was helping her. "I'm really sore, but I'm okay." She lifted the clean shirt she was wearing. Black stitches ran in a jagged line across the bottom of her rib cage. "Twenty-two," she said. "Lena did a great job."

Lena smiled shyly, pleased by the praise. The two giant catfish behind her purred.

Kora and two of her Askari were nearby. "That will leave a beautiful scar," Kora said enviously. She turned to Sera. "The monster . . . it's really dead?"

"It is," Sera replied.

Kora threw her head back and uttered a piercing, joyous victory cry.

She took her coral armband—notched for every Razormouth she'd killed—and put it on Sera's arm. "Well done, sister Askara," she said. She touched her forehead to Sera's, then pulled her into a tight embrace.

Sera hugged Kora back, drawing strength from the fearless warrior. "Thank you," she finally said. "We couldn't have done it without you."

She released Kora. Thousands of weary, battered faces were looking at her. They'd formed a semicircle in front of the Carceron.

Sera swam before them. "Abbadon is dead!" she shouted, raising her fist high into the water.

A roiling, thunderous cheer went up from the fighters. They lifted their spears and swords, and threw their helmets into the water. The cheer carried on, long and loud, for minute after minute, until Sera raised her hands for silence.

"A great evil threatened our world!" she shouted, her voice ringing out. "Because of you, that evil is no more. Mer, goblin, sea creatures, and even the humans fought together and died together for this victory. Because of your bravery and your strength, Orfeo and Abbadon have been defeated. Because of your love for the seas and the freshwaters, their creatures have been saved from destruction. You have my gratitude, my respect, and my love. We will care for our wounded, and our dead, and then, we will care for one another. Always and forever, from this day on. Miromara, Matali, Ondalina, Atlantica, Qin, and the Freshwaters, together with our goblin allies, the troll clans, and sea creatures great and small, the Praedatori and the Wave Warriors, will never forget how greed and the hunger for power nearly destroyed our world. I promise you, on my life, that I will work with leaders from all realms to ensure peace and harmony between us. Our future, and the future of our home, depends on it."

Cheers rose once again. Fighters hugged one another, and then returned to the difficult tasks of tending the injured and collecting the bodies. As they did, Ceto Rorqual and humpbacks swam overhead. They dipped down in the water and started butting their great heads into the walls of the Carceron. The old stones creaked and groaned before giving way and crashing to the seafloor.

"It's over," Garstig said. "At last."

"Almost, but not quite," Sera said.

She turned to Ava, but Ava answered her question before Sera could ask it.

"Yes, he's coming," she said. "I can feel him."

A moment later, a majestic coelacanth, his long gray body mottled with splotches of silver, swam into the clearing. A hushed, reverent silence fell over the group. Everyone bowed his or her head.

The giant fish regarded them all, then, in a voice as ancient as time itself, said, "You summoned me, Astrid Kolfinnsdottir. Where is the soul you wish to commend?"

"We have many souls to commend, great Horok," Astrid replied. "Stolen souls who've longed for centuries to find refuge with you."

"I will receive them," Horok said.

Astrid and Neela picked up the four pouches of pearls, then swam to Horok. They placed the pouches on the seafloor before him and opened them. The pearls were glowing softly.

Horok gently took them all into his broad mouth. No matter how many disappeared into his jaws, his mouth never filled. There was room for them all.

"They're happy now," Ava whispered.

"There's one more," Astrid said.

Horok nodded. "This one has refused me for centuries, but it is finally his time to make the journey."

Astrid swam to where Orfeo's corpse lay. She put out the water-fire she'd cast and bent down to the body. Taking great care not to touch the black pearl, she took the leather string from around Orfeo's neck, then carried it to Horok. Holding one end of the string, she let the pearl slide off the other. Horok caught it as it fell, then readied himself to leave.

"Horok, wait. . . ." Astrid said.

The coelacanth stopped. He turned back to her.

"Kolfinn . . . I—I didn't have the time . . ." Astrid said, with tears in her eyes.

Sera joined her. "My mother and father . . ." she said, her voice breaking. "I never got to say good-bye. I never got to tell them—"

"They know, children," Horok said. He turned his gaze to Becca. "Abigail and Matthew know, too. Only the body dies. Love lives on."

And then, with a slow swish of his powerful tail, he swam away.

"Abigail and Matthew?" Ling asked, taking Becca's hand. "Your parents?"

Becca nodded. Ava put an arm around her. Astrid joined them, taking Becca's hand. Sera put an arm around Astrid. Neela took Sera's hand and looped her arm around Ava. They were bloodied and scarred, but the circle of their sisterhood was unbroken.

"Orfeo got what he wanted in the end," Astrid said, as they all watched Horok disappear. "He'll finally be reunited with his beloved Alma."

Sera wanted to thank her friends, to tell them what they meant to her, and how much she loved them, but her heart was so full of emotion, she couldn't speak. Instead, she took a deep breath and began to sing.

How can I tell you, mages' daughters,
My bloodbound sisters of the water,
Noble, brave, true as the seas,
Exactly what you mean to me?
Remember when it all began?
The call insistent, waves on sand
Summoned in a night's dark dream,
By one who wasn't what she seemed.
Fierce in aspect, kind of heart,
She showed us Orfeo's dark art:
A monster made of fear and rage,
Now buried in an icy cage.
She told us one would set it free,
Then made a bold, impassioned plea:
Fight this evil, save the waters,
Work together, mages' daughters.
Become as one, then save the seas?
Both seemed impossible to me.
Be brave, said she. Be smart, be swift,
But with this burden came a gift:
Five other mermaids, true and strong,
Who sometimes didn't get along.
Back in those caves, we didn't know,
How much we'd help one another grow.
We'd suffered losses, cried bitter tears.
We'd hidden hurts, and hopes, and fears.
But slowly we began to trust,
In ourselves, one another, all of us.
What doesn't kill you, leaves you broken.
Like loss and anger, grief unspoken.
But the spell of friendship, deep and real,
Can help a battered heart to heal.

Friendships forged when times are bright,
Will not withstand a sea-fret slight,
But bonds that form through strife and pain,
Will weather gales and hurricanes,
Only the gods can truly say
What happens when each goes her way,
But I know until my own life's end,
I'll call you sister, fighter, friend.
One heart, one mind, one soul are we,
My bloodbound sisters of the sea.

The last notes of Sera's sea spell rose in the water.

Clear and bright.

Perfect and true.

Shining and real.

Then gone.

SEVENTY-SIX

"**Y**OU LOOK SO BEAUTIFUL. Are you ready?"

Sera nodded. She smiled at Mahdi, so handsome in his jacket of light blue sea silk, and took his arm.

He led her through the Grand Hall and out of the palace. "Nervous?" he asked.

"About the ceremony? No. About your breathing, yes."

She'd heard a hitch in his chest. She was sure of it.

"I'm *fine*," Mahdi said. "The doctors said I could do this. Don't worry so much, Sera."

"How can I not?"

"Because I'm not in a coma anymore!" he replied, cheerfully exasperated with her.

Sera bit her lip. He tended to get frustrated if she, or anyone else, fussed over him too much. He was eager to be up and about. To resume his duties. He was getting stronger every day, but still—she worried. She couldn't help it. She'd come so close to losing him that everything scared her now. She was worried if he was pale, or flushed. If he looked tired. If he didn't eat enough. If he sneezed or coughed.

She'd come home from the Southern Sea to find him sitting up and conscious. It was the happiest day of her life. She'd hugged him and kissed him and cried tears of joy.

But he wasn't out of the kelp forest yet. He still had a long current ahead of him. His recovery had been slow and full of setbacks, but now, nine months later, he was up and about most of the day, though his doctors insisted that he rest after lunch. He would return to Matali to rule soon, when he was stronger.

They continued on their way out of the palace and into the town, with Alítheia following them—until they arrived at the *scuola superiore.*

Sera wasn't wearing a fine gown, or any sumptuous garments of state today. Instead she was dressed in plain robes of black sea silk—scholar's robes. This morning, for a few hours, she could forget that she was the regina and be just another seventeen-year-old mermaid who was about to be a proud graduate, along with the hundred-odd other students in her class.

Sera's schooling had been interrupted by an invasion of her realm, and by bloody battles against Vallerio, Orfeo, and Abbadon, but ever since she'd returned home from the Southern Sea, she'd made her studies a priority.

Mahdi swam with her to the front rows of the school's auditorium.

"I'm so proud of you, and I'll be clapping the loudest when your name's called," he said, kissing her cheek. Then he went to sit with Thalassa, Fossegrim, Desiderio, and Astrid.

Serafina found her seat between two of her classmates. The ceremony started. Music was played, speeches were given, and then the diplomas were handed out.

"Serafina di Merrovingia!" the dean called. "Summa cum laude, with Distinction in History!"

Sera swam up to the dais, shook the dean's hand, and accepted her diploma. It was written on kelp parchment and signed with squid ink. As she swam back to her seat, she hugged it to her chest.

Summa cum laude. Latin for *with highest honors.*

She'd worked her tail fins off to get good grades. In a few months, she would enter the kolegio, and begin her undergraduate degree. If all went well, she would defend her doctoral dissertation in ancient

Atlantean history in six years. She knew it wouldn't be easy to rule her realm and pursue her degree at the same time, but she'd faced harder things.

They all had.

A stab of longing pierced her heart. She wished that Neela, Ling, Becca, and Ava could be here with her today. They'd all returned to Cerulea with her to recover from their ordeal in the Southern Sea, but all of them except Astrid had gone their ways a few weeks later. Sera missed them terribly, but understood they had their own obligations.

Ling had been made an international ambassador by the Elder of Qin. She spent all her time traveling between the mer realms and addressing any disputes or conflicts between them. Her father had survived the terrible labor camp where he and Ling had been imprisoned. He'd been weak and sick when troops liberated the camp, but he'd made it home, where he was recovering. Ling's mother and brothers had been overjoyed to see him.

Becca had decided to hand in her resignation at Baudel's, and go to college to study political science. She'd applied to a school in the Lagoon, off the city of Venice. She was spending the summer there with Marco, trying to figure things out.

Astrid was living in Cerulea. Ragnar Kolfinnsson, Ondalina's admiral, and Serafina had abolished the permutavi—an ancient decree between Miromara and Ondalina that stipulated the exchange of a Miromaran royal child for an Ondalinian one. If they hadn't, Desiderio would have been required to go to Ondalina, and Astrid to Cerulea, and they never would have been allowed to be together. Astrid had chosen to come to the city because of her own free will. And because of her heart. She'd fallen in love with Des, and he with her. In another year, they'd be Promised to one another.

Ava was back in Macapá, in the Amazon River, with her parents. She'd found a job working with visually impaired children and loved it. The other mermaids had bought her a present before she'd left Cerulea—a new seeing-eye piranha named Sweetie. When they let him out of the little bamboo cage he'd arrived in, he'd promptly bitten Sera, barked at Neela and Ling, ripped a hole in Becca's skirt, and growled at Astrid. Ava adored him, though she knew she would never forget Baby.

Neela had returned home to Matali, where she had been reunited with her pet blowfish, Ooda, and had opened up the hottest clothing boutique in Matali City. It featured her own designs, plus the edgiest creations from a cadre of international designers. She was never again seen wearing pink.

Yazeed had been appointed head of the Praedatori by Duca Marco and was currently in an undisclosed location, working with his fellow fighters and the Wave Warriors to try to clean up the catastrophic garbage island in the Pacific.

Thalassa had been rescued from Shadow Manse and had returned to Cerulea. She gave Serafina songcasting lessons three times a week. Fossegrim was happily ensconced in his beloved Ostrokon, overseeing plans to repair the damage that had been inflicted upon it. Manon Laveau, together with her ghosts and her alligators, had returned to the Mississippi. She'd enjoyed her sojourn in Miromara, she'd told Sera, but it wasn't wise to leave the swamp mer unsupervised for too long.

The remaining five talismans had been safely stowed away in a specially constructed vault. Sera looked at them sometimes to make sure she never forgot what had been sacrificed in their pursuit. Determined to preside over a more open age, she had decreed that the ruins of Atlantis must be accessible to all peoples of the sea so they might learn from past mistakes and never repeat them. She was personally overseeing the construction of a learning center there, and had negotiated a peace treaty with the Opafago. Sera believed that if she didn't teach her people the truth about their past, she could not lead them into their future.

A chill ran through her as she remembered how close she'd come to not regaining her throne. If she hadn't been able to convince Alítheia not to eat her, if her Black Fins hadn't staged their attack so flawlessly . . . well, that wasn't worth thinking about.

She *had* regained her throne. The Feuerkumpel had paid for their treachery. And so had Vallerio and Portia.

Lucia had escaped the city, and seemingly, the realm. She had not been seen or heard of since the night of the Black Fins' attack on Cerulea. Sera had declared her an outlaw and had put a bounty on her head. She was optimistic that Lucia would be caught soon.

The first notes of the recessional rang out, pulling Sera out of her thoughts. She rose with the other graduates and filed out of the auditorium. Mahdi was throwing a party for all the graduates back at the palace, in the Regina's Courtyard. As Sera swam out of the school and into the current, someone raced up and threw her arms around her waist.

"Congratulations!" Coco shouted. She handed Sera the bouquet of sea roses she was carrying, and then Coco's parents congratulated Sera, too.

Sera had had every prison camp searched for them, and for Coco's sister, Ellie. To her immense relief, all three were found and the family was reunited.

The graduates and their families slowly made their way up the hill to the palace. Bells were ringing through the town. Ceruleans were crowding the current and hanging out of the windows of the houses along it, throwing kisses and sea flowers, cheering and waving and wishing them well.

Mahdi leaned over to her. "I think they love you almost as much as I do," he said.

Sera smiled and squeezed his arm. As she did, a shimmer caught her eye. It was the little shell ring he'd once carved for her. After Lucia had handed it to him as proof of Sera's death, Mahdi had kept it. He'd given it to Sera when she returned from the Southern Sea. *Mērē dila, mērī ātmā,* he'd whispered as he put the ring on her finger once more.

They would be married, she and Mahdi. Just as it had been decided years ago. One day, but not now. They both had realms to rule and much to learn. He would have to return to Matali soon, and it would be so hard to let him go. But it wouldn't be forever.

The happy procession came to a fork in the current. A statue of the former ruler and her husband stood there—Regina Isabella and Principe Bastiaan, Sera's parents.

Sera swam to it and made a deep curtsey. She missed them both profoundly and wished that they were here today, to celebrate with her. Tears threatened, but she held them back. She had lost so much. Everyone had. But she was thankful, too, for all that remained.

Love lives on, Horok had told her.

Sera swept her eyes over her people, happy and safe; she looked at her brother and her friends, and then she gazed at the merman she loved with all her heart.

"Yes," she whispered. "It does."

EPILOGUE

IN A STONE CAVE, deep under the dark waters of a wild and ancient river, the witches sang.

Hand in hand, they swam in a circle, chanting their timeless spells.

The world believed they were dead, killed by a brutal merman and his soldiers. Their names were slowly fading from memory, even from the memories of the ones who'd been summoned.

Which was exactly what they wanted. Their work needed secrecy and stealth. The fewer who knew about them, the better.

The elder sat on her throne of antlers, her black eyes bright and alert, listening to the incantas, nodding at their song. On her hands, three eyes, set in three amber rings, swiveled in their settings, wary and watchful.

If anyone, mer or human, had been close enough, they might've heard her singing with the others.

> *Daughters six, your task is done,*
> *You've defeated the monster Abbadon.*
> *He and his maker are now at rest,*
> *And so ends your dangerous quest.*
> *But the Iele's work will never cease*
> *Until all waters live in peace.*
> *Serafina now rules wisely and well,*

SEA SPELL

344

But far away, another dwells.
A soulless mermaid prowls the seas
Who once Miromara's throne did seize.
In a cave of darkness, deep and black,
She plots and plans her next attack.
Sheltered by Kharis, with Morsa's favor,
She waits till revenge is hers to savor.
Like her parents, in their time,
With wicked humans, she aligns.
Finners, trawlers, criminals all,
They listen to her siren's call,
And give her gold to grant their wish:
The whereabouts of sharks and fish.
Using slyness, wiles, and stealth,
She builds reserves of power and wealth.
Daughters six, take heed, take care
Of her maliciousness beware.
Guard against her, stalwart friends,
Help those she sells for her own ends.
Protect the creatures of the deep,
In hidden chasms, on seamounts steep.
Guard the dolphins and the whales,
Guard the ones with fins and scales.
Save the osprey, tern, and gull,
Save the harp seal from the cull.
One quest has ended, another begins,
Only time will tell who wins.
In depths below, or waters above.
Fight hard, my children, for what you love.

GLOSSARY

ABBADON an immense monster, created by Orfeo, then defeated and caged in the Antarctic waters

ABELARD Coco's sand shark

AIRFIRE flames created by humans outside of water

ALÍTHEIA a twelve-foot, venomous sea spider made out of bronze combined with drops of Merrow's blood. Bellogrim, the blacksmith god, forged her, and the sea goddess, Neria, breathed life into her to protect the throne of Miromara from any pretenders.

ALLEGRA a Miromaran farmer who is a courier of secret message conchs for Mahdi

ALMA the woman Orfeo loved; when she died, he went mad with grief

AMPLIO a songspell used to amplify sound

ANARACHNA Miromaran for *spider*

APĂ PIATRĂ an old Romanian protection songspell that raises water and hardens it into a shield

ARTEMESIA Sera's grandmother, a regina of Miromara who considered the Volnero family tainted and decreed that there would be no alliance with their bloodline

ASKARI members of Kora's personal guard in Kandina (ASKARA, sing.)

ASTRID a teenage mermaid from the realm of Ondalina; one of the six summoned by the Iele to destroy Abbadon; descendant of the mage Orfeo; Ragnar's sister and Kolfinn's daughter

ATLANTICA the mer domain in the Atlantic Ocean; Becca's home

ATLANTIS an ancient island paradise in the Mediterranean peopled with the ancestors of the mer. Six mages ruled the island wisely and well: Orfeo, Merrow, Sycorax, Navi, Pyrrha, and Nyx. When the island was destroyed, Merrow saved the Atlanteans by calling on Neria to give them fins and tails.

AVA a teenage mermaid from the Amazon River; one of the six summoned by the Iele to destroy Abbadon; descendant of the mage Nyx; she is blind but able to sense things

BABA VRĂJA the elder leader—or obârsie—of the Iele, river witches

BABY Ava's guide piranha

BACO GOGA an eel-like merman; spy for Vallerio and Portia Volnero

BECCA a teenage mermaid from the realm of Atlantica; one of the six summoned by the Iele to destroy Abbadon; descendant of the mage Pyrrha

BELLOGRIM the god of fire

BIOLUMINESCENT a sea creature that emits its own glow

BLACK FINS members of a Cerulean resistance group

BLACK PEARL Orfeo's talisman, given to him by Morsa

BLACKCLAW DRAGON one of the many types of dragons that breed in Matali and are the main source of the realm's wealth; huge and powerful and used by the military

BLOODBIND a spell in which blood from different mages is combined to form an unbreakable bond and allow them to share abilities

BLOODSONG blood drawn from one's heart that contains memories and allows them to become visible to others

BUBBLER a goblin tool for releasing just a little lava from a seam

CABALLABONG a game involving hippokamps, similar to the human game water polo

CADAVRU living human corpses, devoid of a soul (see also ROTTER)

CAMO a songspell used to change appearance

CANTA MAGUS one of the Miromaran magi, a keeper of magic (magi, pl.)

CANTA MALUS darksong, a poisonous gift to the mer from Morsa, in mockery of Neria's gifts

CARCERON the prison of Atlantis. The lock could only be opened by all six talismans. It is now located somewhere in the Southern Sea.

CERULEA the royal city in Miromara, where Serafina lived before it was attacked

CETO leader of the Clan Rorqual, humpback whales

CLIO Serafina's hippokamp

COMMODORA second-in-command to Ondalina's admiral; spymaster and in charge of the realm's military

CONCH a shell in which recorded information is stored

CONVOCA a songspell that can be used for summoning and communicating with others

COSIMA a young girl from Serafina's court; nickname: Coco

CREOLE descendants of the colonial settlers of Louisiana, especially those of French, Spanish, African, and/or Native American origin

CURRENSEA mer money; gold trocii (trocus, sing.), silver drupes, copper cowries; gold doubloons are black market currensea

DANKLING a person's deepest fears; Rorrim Drol feeds on them

DARKSONG a powerful canta malus spell that causes harm, legal to use against enemies during wartime

DEATH RIDERS Traho's soldiers, who ride on black hippokamps

DESIDERIO a merman from Miromara; a Black Fin; Serafina's older brother

DEVIL'S TAIL a protective thorn thicket that floats above Cerulea

DIRGECASTER one who sings after someone's death

DOKIMÍ Greek for *trial*; a ceremony in which the heir to the Miromaran throne has to prove that she is a true descendant of

Merrow by spilling blood for Alítheia, the sea spider. She must then songcast, make her betrothal vows, and swear to one day give the realm a daughter.

DUCA DI VENEZIA an ancient title conferred on a terragogg by Merrow, the first leader of the mer; the duca's duty is to protect the mer

EISGEISTS murderous spirits that dwell in cold water; created by Morsa, they are neither alive nor dead; they drag their victims behind them until the flesh rots away and then eat the bones

ELISABETTA a terragogg who, together with her brother, Marco, helped Becca after she was attacked by the Williwaw

ESMÉ, COUNTESS the ghost of a Creole countess; one of three ghosts who keep Manon Laveau company

EVEKSION the god of healing

FABRA the marketplace and workers' quarter of Cerulea, where the city artisans live

FEUERKUMPEL goblin miners, one of the Kolbold tribes, who channel magma from deep seams under the North Sea in order to obtain lava for lighting and heating; they allied themselves with Vallerio

FOSSEGRIM one of the Miromaran magi, the liber magus, the keeper of knowledge

FRAGOR LUX a songspell to cast a light bomb (frag, abbr.)

FRESHWATERS the mer domain that encompasses rivers, lakes, and ponds

FRYST a clan of giant ice trolls that protects Ondalina's Citadel

FYR goblin word for the underworld

GALLOWS DIRGE the final rite used to return the soul of a condemned criminal to the sea

GOLD COIN Pyrrha's talisman, with an image of Neria on it

GREAT ABYSS a deep chasm in Qin where Sycorax's talisman, a puzzle ball, was found

GRIS-GRIS a pouch of ingredients combined by a practitioner of voo-
doo in order to help its owner achieve a certain end

GULDEMAR the Meerteufel sea goblin tribe's chieftain

HAFGUFA the kraken; according to legend, Meerteufel chieftains can
call the creature forth in times of trouble

HAGARLA queen of the Razormouth dragons

HALL OF SIGHS a long corridor in Vadus, the mirror realm, whose
walls are covered in mirrors; every mirror has a corresponding
one in the terragogg world

HIPPOKAMPS creatures that are half horse, half serpent, with snake-
like eyes

HOROK the great coelacanth, Keeper of Souls, who takes the dead to
the underworld, holding each soul in a white pearl

IELE river witches

ILLUMINATA a songspell to create light

ILLUSIO a songspell to create a disguise

INFANTA Maria Theresa of Spain, whose ship was brought down by
a pirate seeking her blue diamond. She gave a fake diamond to
the pirate and the real one to Serafina.

IRON repels magic

ISABELLA Serafina's mother; the regina of Miromara before she was
assassinated by her brother, Vallerio

JEAN LAFITTE a pirate; one of three ghosts who keep Manon Laveau
company

KARGJORD a hilly, desolate barrens at the northernmost reaches of
the Meerteufel's realm; the Black Fins' headquarters and military
training ground

KEEPER OF JUSTICE represents the law in Miromara

KHARIS priestess of the death goddess Morsa

KOBOLD North Sea goblin tribes

KOLEGIO mer equivalent of college

KOLFINN Astrid and Ragnar's father and the former admiral of Ondalina; now deceased

KOLISSEO a huge open-water stone theater in Miromara that dates back to Merrow's time

KORA the mermaid ruler of the Matalin region of Kandina; leader of the Askari

LAVA GLOBE a light source, lit by magma mined and refined into white lava by the Feuerkumpel

LENA a freshwater mermaid—and owner of several catfish—who hid Serafina, Neela, and Ling from Traho

LIBER MAGUS one of the Miromaran magi, the keeper of knowledge

LING a teenage mermaid from the realm of Qin; one of the six summoned by the Iele to destroy Abbadon; descendant of the mage Sycorax; she is an omnivoxa

LUCIA VOLNERO once one of Serafina's ladies-in-waiting; now a pretender to the Miromaran throne, a member of the Volnero, a noble family as old—and nearly as powerful—as the Merrovingia

MAELSTROM a powerful whirlpool in the sea

MAHDI ruler of Matali; Promised to Serafina; cousin to Neela and Yazeed

MALIGNO a creature made out of clay and animated by blood magic

MÅNENHONNØR Ondalina's moon festival

MÅNENKAGER a cake, eaten during Månenhonnør, made of pressed krill and iced with ground mother-of-pearl, so it shines like the moon; baked with a silver drupe coin in it for good luck

MANON LAVEAU a swamp queen mermaid who lives under the Mississippi River near New Orleans

MARCO a terragogg who, together with his sister, Elisabetta, helped Becca after she was attacked by the Williwaw; he is the latest duca di Venezia, whose duty is to protect the mer

MARKUS TRAHO, CAPTAIN leader of the death riders

MATALI the mer realm in the Indian Ocean; Neela's home

MATALIN from Matali

MEERTEUFEL one of four goblin tribes

MERL Mermish equivalent of *girl*

MERMISH the common language of the sea people

MERROVINGIA descendants of Merrow

MERROW a great mage, one of the six rulers of Atlantis, and Serafina's ancestor. First ruler of the merpeople; songspell originated with her, and she decreed the Dokimí.

MIROMARA the realm Serafina comes from; an empire that spans the Mediterranean Sea, the Adriatic, Aegean, Baltic, Black, Ionian, Ligurian, and Tyrrhenean Seas, the Seas of Azov and Marmara, the Straits of Gibraltar, the Dardanelles, and the Bosphorus

MOONSTONE Navi's talisman; silvery blue and the size of an albatross's egg, with an inner glow

MORSA an ancient scavenger goddess, whose job it was to take away the bodies of the dead. She angered Neria by practicing necromancy. Neria punished her by giving her the face of death and the body of a serpent and banishing her.

NÄKKI murderous shapeshifters in the northern Atlantic; they are outlaws and arms dealers

NASHOBA a cruel Choctaw warrior in life; in death, leader of the Okwa Naholo

NAVI one of the six mages who ruled Atlantis; Neela's ancestor

NEELA a teenage mermaid from the realm of Matali; one of the six summoned by the Iele to destroy Abbadon; Serafina's best friend; Yazeed's sister; Mahdi's cousin; a descendant of the mage Navi. She is a bioluminescent.

NERIA the sea goddess

NYX one of the six mages who ruled Atlantis; Ava's ancestor

OCCULA a songspell used to see over a far distance

OKWA NAHOLO *white people of the water,* in Choctaw; spirits of murderous warriors who were cursed by the sun god to live in the swamps of the Mississippi forever; their black hearts contain memories of the crimes they committed and kill anyone who looks upon them

OLT the river in Romania where the Iele are located

OMNIVOXA (OMNI) mer who have the natural ability to speak every dialect of Mermish and communicate with sea creatures

ONDALINA the mer realm in the Arctic waters; Astrid's home

OODA Neela's pet blowfish

OPIE Marco's pet octopus

ORFEO the most powerful of the six mages who ruled Atlantis; a healer; his talisman was a green emerald; he was devastated by the death of his wife, Alma, and vowed to take on the gods to get her back; Morsa gave him a black pearl to cheat death, and he created Abbadon, a monster powerful enough to attack the underworld; Astrid's ancestor

OSTROKON the mer version of a library

PERMUTAVI a pact between Miromara and Ondalina, enacted after the War of Reykjanes Ridge, that decreed the exchange of the rulers' children

PORTIA VOLNERO mother of Lucia and a powerful duchessa of Miromara; wanted to marry Vallerio, Serafina's uncle

PRAEDATORI soldiers who defend the sea and its creatures against terragoggs; known as the Wave Warriors on land

PRAX practical magic that helps the mer survive, such as camouflage spells, echolocation spells, spells to improve speed or darken an ink cloud. Even those with little magical ability can cast them.

PROMISING an exchange of betrothal vows that, once spoken, cannot be broken until death

PUZZLE BALL Sycorax's talisman; a small, ornately carved white ball containing spheres within spheres, with the image of a phoenix on the outside

PYRRHA one of the six mages of Atlantis, a brilliant strategist; Becca's ancestor

QANIKKAAQ a giant maelstrom in the Greenland Sea where Orfeo's talisman was found

QIN the mer realm in the Pacific Ocean; Ling's home

RAGNAR the admiral of Ondalina; Astrid's older brother

RÄKÄ a goblin drink made from fermented snail slime

RAZORMOUTH DRAGON one of the many types of dragons that breed in Matali and are the main source of the realm's wealth; they are feral and murderous

RORRIM DROL lord of Vadus, the mirror realm

ROTTER an animated human corpse, devoid of a soul

RUBY RING Nyx's talisman; a large stone, with many facets, in a gold setting

RURSUS the language of Vadus, the mirror realm

RYLKA Kolfinn's commodora

SALLY WILKES a runaway slave; one of three ghosts who keep Manon Laveau company

SCAGHAUFEN capital of the Meerteufel sea goblin tribe

SCUOLA SUPERIORE mer equivalent of high school

SEEING STONE a garnet stone that, when cast with an occula spell, allows the viewer to see something/someone over a far distance

SERAFINA rightful regina of Miromara and leader of the Black Fin Resistance; one of six mermaids summoned by the Iele to destroy Abbadon; descendant of the mage Merrow

SHADOW MANSE Orfeo's palace

SICARIO Lucia's scorpion

SIREN a mermaid who sings for currensea

SIX WHO RULED the mages of Atlantis, each of whom possessed a magical talisman that enhanced their powers

SKAVVENERS sea elves that pillage battlefields and disaster sites and stalk the feeble, sick, and injured

S*KØRE TÅBER* Meerteufel goblin for *crazy fools*

S*NASK* pickled squid eyes, a goblin snack

S*OMNIO* a songspell to induce sleep

S*OPHIA* one of the best Black Fin fighters and a trusted confidante; she saved Serafina's life during the raid on Miromara's treasury

S*PIDERLAIR* a swamp named for the arachnids that hunt on its banks

S*TICKSTOFF* head of Meerteufel's military

S*TILO* a songspell that makes spikes sprout out of a water ball

S*UMMA CUM LAUDE* Latin for *with highest honors*

S*YCORAX* one of the six mages of Atlantis; Ling's ancestor

S*YLVESTRE* Serafina's pet octopus

S*YZYGY* when the sun, moon, and earth are aligned—tides are at their highest and magic is at its strongest; royal mer weddings can only take place during a syzygy

T*ALISMAN* a magical object, given by the gods, that enhances one's powers

T*AROT* a set of seventy-eight cards with pictures and symbols that is used to see what will happen in the future

T*ERRAGOGGS* (G*OGGS*) humans

T*HALASSA* the canta magus, or keeper of magic, of Miromara; addressed as Magistra

T*OTSCHLÄGER* a trusted goblin commander

T*RANSPARENSEA PEARL* a pearl that contains a songspell of invisibility; transparensea pebbles are not as strong as transparensea pearls

V*ADUS* the mirror realm

V*ALLERIO, *P*RINCIPE DEL *S*ANGUE* Miromara's high commander; Serafina's uncle, who orchestrated the invasion of Cerulea, during which Sera's mother, the regina, was assassinated; father to Lucia Volnero

V*ELO* a songspell to increase one's speed

V*ERITA* the goddess of justice

VITRINA souls of beautiful, vain humans who spent so much time
    admiring themselves in mirrors that they are now trapped inside
VORTEX a songspell used to create a whirl
WATERFIRE magical fire used to enclose or contain
WAVE WARRIORS humans who fight for the sea and its creatures
WILLIWAW a wind spirit at Cape Horn; possessor of Pyrrha's talisman
YAZEED a merman from Mitali; a Black Fin second-in-command to
    Serafina; Neela's brother and Mahdi's cousin